PRAISE FOR

"By turns gut-wrenching and exhilarating...An intimate story of love, friendship, hope, and acceptance in a disenfranchised and forgotten world...For anyone who likes a well-told story driven by intensely realistic characters."

—*Miami Herald*

"Another strong, fearless heroine with special powers... New readers will appreciate the tight focus that intensifies the depth of character and emotion."

—*Publishers Weekly*

"A postmodern fable of enormous scope and force...and a love song to the beauty and power of being different. At the novel's heart is the kind of grace Carey is known for: an illumination of the strength that lies hidden inside all of us."

—Eric Van Lustbader, *New York Times* bestselling author, on *Santa Olivia*

"A paranormal coming-of-age story...Loup [and] the secondary characters are equally well drawn."

—*RT Book Reviews*

"Carey's signature eroticism and action drive this futuristic fable and keep the pages turning."

—*Curve*

SAINTS ASTRAY

JACQUELINE CAREY

GRAND CENTRAL
PUBLISHING

NEW YORK   BOSTON

Grand Central Publishing
Hachette Book Group
237 Park Avenue
New York, NY 10017

www.HachetteBookGroup.com

Printed in the United States of America

First Edition: November 2011
10 9 8 7 6 5 4 3 2 1

Grand Central Publishing is a division of Hachette Book Group, Inc.
The Grand Central Publishing name and logo is a trademark of
Hachette Book Group, Inc.

The publisher is not responsible for websites (or their content)
that are not owned by the publisher.

Library of Congress Cataloging-in-Publication Data

Carey, Jacqueline.
Saints astray / Jacqueline Carey.—1st ed.
p. cm.
ISBN 978-0-446-57142-5
1. Women heroes—Fiction. 2. Werewolves—Fiction. 3. Vigilantes—Fiction.
4. Self-realization in women—Fiction. I. Title.
PS3603.A74S25 2011
813'.6—dc22
2011000851

For Julie, my bordertown dreamer.

SAINTS ASTRAY

ONE

The world was a very, very big place.

That was Loup's first impression as the sun rose over northern Mexico. By the time it had cleared the horizon and begun to cast strong light over the landscape, they'd been driving for an hour. Still, the road stretched before them, empty and endless.

And except for Pilar, fast asleep with her head on Loup's shoulder, everything and everyone in the world Loup had ever loved was behind her, behind the vast concrete wall that sealed off the U.S. border and sealed in a town once known as Santa Olivia, known in Loup's lifetime only as Outpost—Outpost 12.

The thought made an empty space in Loup's heart. In the light of day, the thrill of their daring escape through the excavated smugglers' tunnel had worn off. If she were capable of feeling fear, she was fairly sure she'd be feeling it now.

Pilar yawned and lifted her head. "Are we almost there?" she asked sleepily.

Behind the steering wheel, Christophe laughed. "Not even close."

Pilar's hazel eyes widened. "Seriously?"

"Oh, yes." He glanced over at the girls. "It's over a thousand kilometers to Mexico City. Over six hundred miles," he added, seeing their perplexed looks.

"Wow." Loup tried to think about what that meant and couldn't. She knew miles as units measured on a treadmill, going nowhere, not as actual distances to be traveled. It was only the third or fourth time she'd ridden in a car, and never farther than a few blocks before. "So a few more hours, huh?"

"More than a few."

"How many?"

The cousin-of-a-sort she'd only just met squinted at the convertible's speedometer. "I drive fast. We ought to be there by late afternoon."

"Shit!" Pilar said in dismay.

Christophe slid her a laughing glance. "Big world, eh?"

"Yeah, no kidding." She turned to look at the empty highway behind them. "So we're safe? No one's after us?"

"I imagine the army is tearing Santa Olivia apart searching for Loup, but no one has the slightest idea she crossed the border, and it is quite possible they do not even know *you* are missing, *bonita*. Go back to sleep," he said kindly. "Both of you, if you like. It will make the time pass faster. I don't mind. You had a long night."

"No kidding," Pilar repeated, but she closed her eyes and nestled her head back on Loup's shoulder, worn out with terror and happiness. "You okay, baby?"

"Mm-hmm."

"Okay, then."

Pilar dozed.

Christophe drove.

Hot wind whipped all around them. Loup studied her Mexican-born sort-of-cousin. Aside from the soldier who had killed her brother in the boxing ring, he was the first person Loup had ever met that was like her—not entirely human. He was the *only* one she had met who was truly like her—conceived naturally, not created in a laboratory like the father she had never known.

It had been dark when they'd escaped from Outpost. By daylight, she could see him better. He was young, not much older than her. Seventeen, eighteen at the most. Well, that made sense. He couldn't have been conceived much earlier than her. His hands were steady on the wheel. His skin was darker than hers, brown instead of caramel. He was taller, lanky. But he had the same high, rounded cheekbones, the same wide, dark eyes, wiry black hair, and sweeping lashes that she did.

"You knew my father, didn't you?" Loup asked him.

"Tío Martin? Yes, of course."

"What was he like?"

"Quiet," Christophe said, concentrating on the road. "Very intense. All of them were, the original kin. My father, too."

"Henri."

"Henri," he agreed in acknowledgment. "He was the leader, the smart one."

"He died, too?"

Christophe spared her a sympathetic glance. "They all died, Loup."

"Why?"

He sighed. "Because they burned too bright, too hard, and too fast. You know?"

"I know," Loup murmured.

After a lifetime of hiding her true nature and pretending to be something she wasn't, she'd burned bright and fast and hard in Outpost, in the town known as Santa Olivia before it was cordoned off from the rest of the world and occupied by the U.S. Army, creating a buffer zone to protect the country from a pandemic that had decimated a generation, from a threat of invasion that might or might not have been real.

The threats were gone, but the safeguards remained.

The only way to win a ticket out of Outpost was in the boxing ring, defeating one of the general's hand-picked fighters. No one ever had ever done it. Only Loup's brother had ever come close. She had dedicated her life to a single cause—redeeming her older brother's death, making it turn out right. Reliving Tom Garron's destiny. A tight canvas square hemmed by ropes. An opponent like her, like her newfound cousin.

Not quite human; strong and fast and fearless.

Truly fearless.

"How many of us are there?" she asked Christophe.

"Of us kids?" He grinned. "Only seven here, but it seems like more when we're all together. We're not so quiet. All boys, too."

"What about in America?"

"I don't know." He shook his head. "The army did a lot of genetic experiments before the program was shut down; there are maybe a hundred soldiers like that guy Johnson, maybe more. There are a lot of rumors, and no one knows the whole truth. But as far as I know, we're the only natural-born ones. And you're the only girl."

"Huh."

"Is it true you beat him in a fight? Johnson?"

"Yeah." Loup rubbed her right eyebrow. The gash had healed cleanly during her confinement, leaving a thin pink scar. "Yeah, I did."

Christophe whistled. "That must have been a hell of a fight."

"It was." She replayed the moment of victory in her memory. The crowds roaring, John Johnson climbing to his feet before she knocked him down for the third and final time. Still fearless, but surprised and rueful, knowing himself outboxed and beaten. She had trained long and hard for that fight. For one shining moment, before the soldiers put the handcuffs on her, Loup had given hope to a town that had none. "You know he killed my brother?"

He nodded. "Yes, I am sorry. Your half brother, was it not?"

"I guess. I mean, we had different fathers, but Tommy was my brother. He was the one who taught me to be careful all the time. It was an accident," Loup added. "Johnson didn't do it on purpose. It was his twin that Tommy was supposed to fight. A normal guy like Tommy, not like us. The army was afraid he'd lose. They pulled a switch and Johnson took his place in the ring." She was quiet a moment. "Tommy seemed okay at first. Afterward, he collapsed. They did try to save him at the army base." Her eyes stung, making her blink, though there were no tears. There never were. "It's just weird to think, you know? Johnson killed Tommy, then I beat him. Then he helped me escape."

"We're not like other people."

"No." A thought struck her. "Hey, Christophe? What do we call ourselves? Do we have a name for us?"

"No." He looked surprised. "We're just us."

They began to pass through towns and villages, seeing more traffic on the road. It felt strange to see so many nonmilitary cars, but the towns didn't look so different from Outpost except that all the signs were in Spanish. Christophe stopped in one town that looked much like the others, parking the convertible and turning it off.

Pilar woke with a start. "Are we there?"

"You think you slept for eight hours?" He smiled. "No, but in about ten minutes, we'll be getting on the toll highway. Best to get some breakfast before we do."

"Okay." She stretched, breasts straining against her T-shirt.

Christophe eyed her. "You're going to have seven very envious cousins," he said to Loup.

Despite everything, Loup smiled.

"Better believe it," Pilar said amiably.

They ate empanadas filled with potato and chorizo at an open-air diner. Pilar finished long before the others and watched with awe as Christophe devoured enormous quantities, fueling a metabolism as heightened and unnatural as Loup's.

"Wow. He's worse than you, baby."

He swallowed. "I am a growing boy."

"I'm just happy to have food," Loup commented.

"Aww." Pilar's voice softened. "You eat all you like. I'm not making fun. It's just kind of amazing that we're here, you know?"

"I know."

Loup had always known the army would take her into custody after the fight, once she had revealed her true nature. If it was just that they'd discovered what she was, it might not have been so bad. As Father Ramon had once observed, it wasn't illegal to be the illegitimate offspring of a genetically altered soldier.

But there was the Santa Olivia business from years earlier, when Loup and the other Santitos, the Little Saints of Santa Olivia, had administered what the Father called vigilante justice to a couple of soldiers. Although it was never proved, the orphans under the church's care had succeeded in helping Loup impersonate the town's patron saint.

It had made the general very upset...and when Loup was imprisoned, it had given the army an excuse to discover what it would take to break the will of a subject unable to feel fear, pressing her to give up her allies.

As it transpired, the question remained unanswered. Loup had confessed freely to playing Santa Olivia, knowing it was a foregone conclusion from the moment she stepped into the ring. She had refused to admit to having help.

Loup shook her head in wonder. Half a day ago, she'd been stuck in a hot, stifling cell, half-starved and deprived of sleep, resigning herself to years of wondering whether she'd get the hose and conspiracy questions or another smarmy bribe attempt.

Then her unlikely savior John Johnson had arrived, breaking her out of the cell, smuggling her off the base, and leading her through the derelict tunnel beneath the wall to find a new cousin, a new life, and the unexpected gift of Pilar's presence, reversing the hardest choice Loup had ever made, undoing the hardest sacrifice.

As grateful as Loup was for it, the thought of everything and everyone she had left behind and the promise of hope unfulfilled still made her heart ache.

She might not be able to cry, but she could still *hurt*.

"You okay?" Pilar asked.

"Yeah." She smiled at her. Pilar had left everything behind, too, and in many ways, she'd lost more than Loup. Life in Outpost wasn't easy, but it was better than a jail cell. "I'm glad to be here. And really, really glad you're here."

Pilar turned pink. "Me too."

"Okay!" Christophe said cheerfully. "Time to drive!"

The world was big and the road he called a toll highway was *huge*. Four wide lanes filled with whizzing traffic.

"Holy *crap*!" Pilar said the first time they approached a city. "Is that it?"

"No," Christophe said patiently. "We're still five hours away."

"But it's so big!"

"Mexico City is much, much bigger."

They drove and drove and drove. After countless miles of concrete unspooling like a ribbon, Pilar wore out her sense of awe and went back to napping. Loup fought against a rising tide of exhaustion and stayed awake. She was pretty sure she trusted her newfound cousin, but Tommy had conditioned her to be careful all her life, to be mindful of the dangers she should fear, but couldn't.

"She feels safe with you here," Christophe observed.

Loup raised her eyebrows. "She is."

"Yes, of course." He gave her a quick sidelong smile. "You beat Mr. John Johnson, you don't need to remind me. I guess you can . . . what do you call it? Kick my ass. No, but when we were waiting for you to come through the smugglers' tunnel, she was so scared. So scared. I never saw anyone so scared, not in real life. Only in the movies."

"Yeah." She stroked Pilar's wind-tangled hair, brown silk streaked with blond. "But she did it. You ever wonder what it's like?"

He hesitated. "Finding someone like the two of you did?"

Loup shook her head. "Being scared."

He smiled wryly. "Not really, no."

They ate cold empanadas and kept driving and reached Mexico City by late afternoon. And it was big, bigger than any city they'd passed. It went on and on, sprawling in every direction.

"Whoa," Pilar said, awake. "Does it ever end?"

"Yes, in time," Christophe said. "But the old people say it used to be you could not even drive in the city. Too crazy, too much traffic." He made a turn. "Then so many, many people died of the influenza."

"Yeah," Loup murmured, thinking of her mother's death. "We had that, too."

"Everyone did." He was quiet a moment. "The worst had passed here when I was born, but I think it must have been a very terrible time. Only now are things beginning to return to the way they were long before us."

The buildings grew taller, awesome in scale. Everything was taller and vaster than anything Loup had ever imagined. Fine and elegant, like pictures from the pages of fashion magazines worn as thin as onionskin that Pilar and Katya used to pore over for hours at the orphanage. Christophe pulled into the entrance to one of the most elegant of them all, a huge building with outflung wings and rows of arched windows.

"Are you serious?" Pilar asked, wide-eyed.

He grinned. "Oh, yes. I told you, you are guests of the Mexican government. And there is some American senator who wishes to talk to you, too. They are paying the bill for most of this. Tomorrow, I will take you shopping for suitable clothing so you may make a good impression."

"*Seriously?*"

"Yes, seriously."

Loup frowned. "Why?"

Christophe shrugged. "Does it matter?"

Before Loup could reply, a man in a crisp uniform opened the car door on Pilar's side. She looked at Loup in sudden panic. "Ohmigod. Loup, we can't go in there. I look like I crawled through a tunnel, then rode six hundred miles in a windstorm. 'Cause... I kind of did, you know?"

"Pilar..."

"I can't!"

"Pretend you are a rock star, eh?" Christophe suggested, handing his keys to another uniformed man. "A rich and famous rock star who does not have to give a damn, yes?"

"Oh." She thought about it. "Okay."

It was enough for Pilar. She got out of the car and tossed her windblown hair, then sauntered past the doorman with a considerable amount of attitude. The doorman smiled and surreptitiously checked out her ass. Loup followed, amusement fighting with bone-deep weariness and the haunting empty sensation of apprehension she couldn't feel. They waited in the lobby while Christophe talked to the woman at the registration desk. It was amazingly opulent, with rich lighting, gleaming wood, and elegant gold-hued furniture. Beyond they could glimpse marble floors and a huge, curving staircase. Everything was hushed, not even the familiar hum of a generator to break the silence.

None of it seemed real to Loup. A part of her wondered if all of this was just a dream, and she would wake to find herself in the stifling cell, waiting for the next in a series of endless interrogations.

"Look at those flowers!" Pilar whispered, nodding at a massive arrangement. "Jesus! I've read about places like this, but I didn't really believe they still existed."

Loup blinked, wavering. "Yeah."

Pilar gave her a sharp glance. "Loup, how long has it been since you slept?"

"I don't know." She shook her head. "Not much in a couple of days. Maybe three. Not much for weeks, really. I never knew what time it was in prison and they kept waking me up to ask questions or hose me down."

"You're dead on your feet." Pilar grabbed her hand. "C'mon. I'm gonna tell Christophe to hurry up, then I'm putting you to bed. And not in a fun way."

Five minutes later, all three stood in the elevator. It seemed like something out of a movie. The gleaming doors closed and there was a strange sense of moving that both Loup and Pilar found disorienting. It stopped and the doors opened onto a posh hallway.

"Here you are." Christophe led them to a room and showed them how to unlock the door with a plastic card. He carried in the satchel full of Pilar's crumpled secondhand clothes. Loup, sprung from a military jail cell, had nothing. "I'll be two doors down in Room 223. I arranged to have the bathroom stocked with extra toiletries. Anything else you need, charge to the room."

"How?" Pilar asked.

"Just put your room number on the bill and sign it." He stifled a yawn. "Call room service or the concierge. Or call me, though I will probably sleep very hard for a long time. It was a long night and day for me, too."

She examined the phone. "Push the buttons where it says to, right?"

"You've never used a phone?"

"There haven't been working phones in Outpost since before we were born," Loup said mildly. "Only for the army guys. No phones, no TV except old movies that were all shot to hell."

"Right." Christophe nodded. "I keep forgetting. We think of America as being a sophisticated place despite the troubles."

"We weren't in America," she said. "We were in Outpost."

"Not Outpost," Pilar said adamantly. "Santa Olivia."

They exchanged a glance, both of them thinking of the only home they had ever known, the home they couldn't return to.

"Santa Olivia," Loup agreed.

Christophe showed them how to use the phone. "Okay. You call me tomorrow when you're ready. No hurry."

With that, he left them.

"Okay." Pilar gave Loup a gentle nudge in the direction of the bathroom. "Go take a shower, baby. Then go to bed."

"What about you? You slept almost all the way here, Pilar. You're probably not even tired."

Pilar picked up the remote control and hit the power button. A vast screen filled with vibrant images. She pushed different buttons, changing channel after channel, and smiled. "Oh, I'll be fine."

TWO

It was late morning when Loup awoke.

The room was filled with glorious light. She wriggled, reveling in the impossibly soft sheets and the luxurious feeling of being truly, utterly rested for the first time in at least a month. At the foot of the bed, Pilar glanced over her shoulder. She was lying on her stomach perusing an array of glossy magazines, the pages as crisp and new as though no one else had ever read them, not worn by dozens of fingers over dozens of years. Her smile made the bright room brighter.

"Hey, baby."

"Hey, yourself." Loup smiled back at her, feeling her heart roll over with unexpected gladness. She sat upright, running her hands through hair tangled by sleeping on it wet. "You didn't go to bed?"

Pilar laughed. "Honey, you were out for like fifteen hours. I got up a while ago. You hungry?"

Her stomach rumbled, and she realized she smelled food. "Starving."

"I figured. It's still hot. I didn't know what you'd want, so I just ordered everything I thought you'd like."

Loup reached for the thick cotton hotel bathrobe that was nicer than any item of hand-me-down clothing she'd ever owned, and got up to explore two trays full of covered dishes. The domes covering the dishes were shiny, the silverware unscratched. The napkins were made of clean white cloth, and there was even a tiny vase with a real live flower on each tray. "Wow. This is so fancy! How'd you guess when I'd wake up?"

"I didn't." Pilar's smile turned smug. "I sent the first order back when it got cold."

Loup stared at her.

"What?" She shrugged. "I might never get to pretend I'm a rich rock star again. Who the hell knows what these government people want with us? And this place is amazing." She fanned the magazines in front of her. "I started thinking I didn't want to go shopping without knowing what was in style, you know? I mean, how would we know? So I called the concierge like Christophe said and asked him to send up some fashion magazines. Check it out. They just *did* it! Like you could ask for almost anything!"

"Wow."

"Yeah, wow."

Loup lifted one of the domes, inhaling. "You know there's no way this comes without a price, right?"

Pilar smiled wryly. "You think you need to tell Rory Salamanca's ex-girlfriend that, baby? Everything comes with a price. His was his witch of a mother, and giving up you. Until we know what this one is, we might as well enjoy it. Eat."

The food was delicious, fresh and hot, made with ingredients that tasted nothing like government rations. Loup ate her way steadily through a plate of eggs and potatoes and crispy bacon, French toast, and a plateful of fruits that she'd never tasted before, passing only on the pastry basket. When she was finished, she felt better than she had since the day of the fight. "Thanks. That was great."

"I told you I was gonna take care of you." Pilar sat cross-legged on the foot of the bed and gave her a serious look. "You're my hero, baby, but even heroes need someone to take care of them. Especially cute little heroes who don't have the sense to be afraid. And we don't have the first idea what we've gotten ourselves into here. So just promise me you'll let me, okay?"

"Okay."

"I'm serious. *Promise.*"

"I promise!"

"Good." Pilar caught a fold of Loup's bathrobe and tugged, pulling her down to kiss her. "Mmm. You taste like maple syrup."

"I thought you were in a hurry to go shopping."

"Are you kidding?" Pilar shot her an incredulous glance, then uncoiled from the bed. She crossed the room to pull the gauzy inner drapes over the window that looked out onto a vast courtyard. The brightness grew soft and muted. She came back and wound her arms around Loup's neck. "Two days ago, I thought I'd lost you, probably forever. Now I've got you and a fancy hotel room with a bed as big as a swimming pool. You think I'm gonna walk out that door without taking advantage of both?"

Loup smiled happily. "No?"

Pilar kissed her. "Damn right."

It was slow, smoldering sex, urgency tempered with luxury. The room was luxurious, the sheets were luxurious, the sheer pleasure of being together was luxurious. Loup felt the endless hours of deprivation and abuse melt away under Pilar's lips and tongue and hands.

"God, I love the way you feel," Pilar whispered against her skin, straddling her.

"When's it going to be my turn?" Loup whispered back.

"Mmm." She lifted her head. "Once you start, you'll send me through the roof, Supergirl. I wanna take my time."

She took a long, long time before playing fair.

Afterward they lay in bed and talked until the phone rang. "You go," Pilar said, lazy and sated. "I'm not sure I can walk yet. My legs are still wobbly."

"Liar," Loup said fondly, but she answered it. "Yeah, hi. Um...sort of." She raked a hand through her now extra-disheveled hair. "We kind of both need to shower." She lowered the phone. "It's Christophe. He's tired of waiting. Can we be ready in an hour?"

"I guess."

"Yeah, okay," Loup said into the phone. "Okay. See you then." She placed the receiver carefully back into the cradle, concluding her first-ever phone call, then turned to see Pilar watching her. "What?"

"Nothing." She smiled, folding her arms behind her head. "I just like looking at you. And all of this, it's like a dream. So far it's a really, really good dream. I don't wanna get out of bed."

Loup picked up a fallen magazine and held it out enticingly. "Shopping, Pilar."

"Mmm."

"What about all of those cute little bottles of shampoo and stuff in the shower? And the stall's big enough for both of us."

"Ooh." Pilar got up with alacrity. "I hadn't thought of *that*."

Christophe arrived an hour later to find them damp but dressed, Loup working her way through the previously bypassed basket of pastries, having expended a fair amount of energy. He glanced around the room with amusement, taking in the tossed bedsheets, the empty trays of food, and the scattered magazines. "You made yourselves at home. Good."

Pilar flushed. "Well, you said to."

He gave her a courtly little bow. "And I meant it. Are you ready?"

"Hell, yes."

Outside, the city seemed even larger than ever. Cars thronged the streets, not a single military vehicle in sight. Streams of pedestrians flowed along the sidewalks, not a single one of them in uniform. It felt like a different world, a world that had forgotten Santa Olivia and the Outposts on the other side of the border.

Christophe took them to a store that was only a short walk away, four stories tall and filled with an enormous, dazzling array of clothing and accessories. It was brightly lit and everything was new, new, new. In Outpost, almost everything had belonged to someone else. Loup stared, dazed by the selection. "How does anyone ever choose?"

Even Pilar was temporarily overwhelmed. She froze for a moment, awed by the array of choices confronting her, before rallying and making a beeline for the nearest rack. "Don't worry, baby. I know what looks good on you, and I read lots of magazines this morning."

It wasn't long before a pretty young saleswoman glided over to help. Between her and Pilar, with surprisingly helpful input from Christophe, they quickly amassed a large pile of clothing in a private dressing room.

"Very nice," the saleswoman said in approval when Pilar modeled her first ensemble, a narrow pencil skirt with a cute top. "Nice for business casual for a young person. You have good fashion sense." She exchanged a quick spate of Spanish with Christophe, then turned to Loup. "We need for you."

Loup eyed Pilar's skirt. "I'm not wearing something I can hardly walk in."

"Okay, no. Not for you. But nice for meeting." She rummaged through crowded hangers, handed her linen pants and a jacket, a black camisole. "Try this."

"Isn't this fun?" Pilar whispered in the changing room.

"Pilar, those look like jeans you *have*."

"No, they don't!"

"They're all faded."

"That's the style." She pointed. "Look at the stitching on the pockets. It's all different. And they don't flare as much. Anyway, they're *new*."

"I guess." Loup went out to model her outfit.

"Very nice," the saleswoman said. "With the jacket, it is business, but soft. Then take off the jacket..." She gestured at Loup, who complied. "A nice necklace and earrings, and you go out to dinner. Now you see how the pants hug the hips, very young and chic, and the nice sexy camisole makes..." She put her hands on Loup's waist, then blinked and pulled them back, startled at the feel of her not-quite-human musculature. "Um. Yes. So you are a dancer or a *gimnasta*, I think?"

Loup glanced at Christophe. "Gymnast," he clarified.

She shook her head. "Boxer."

"Oh." The saleswoman blinked. "Yes, well, because you have the toned physique, you can wear small tops like such that can look *vulgar* on someone more..." She demonstrated with her hands.

"Voluptuous," Christophe supplied. "That is the word, I think."

"Point taken," Pilar said mildly, spilling out of a low-cut shirt that was a size too small. "Christophe, can we buy just one nice dress? Like for going out dancing?"

He spread his hands. "I was told you have a line of credit here for twenty-five thousand pesos. Spend it how you like."

"How much is that in real money?"

He and the saleswoman conferred in Spanish. "Maybe twelve hundred euros, so maybe two thousand dollars. I don't know. There hasn't been much American tourism here since they closed the border. Europeans, yes. Americans, no."

"Whoa." Loup frowned. "Where's all this money coming from, anyway? I mean, I get that government people want to talk to us, but seriously. That hotel? Two thousand dollars' worth of clothes? And why is there some American senator involved? That seems kinda dangerous."

"All I know is that there are people in the American government concerned with rumors of the Outposts," Christophe said. "Friends of the same people who helped coordinate your escape on the military side of affairs."

Loup shook her head. "It doesn't add up. It's an awful lot of money to throw at a couple of runaway orphans."

Christophe shrugged. "Okay, so maybe there is one other party that wishes to talk to you. This is to make you feel welcome and interested to listen. There is no obligation."

"Yeah, sure."

"There isn't." His dark gaze was as steady and unblinking as her own. "Believe me, you are honored guests here. I would not betray a member of my family."

"Loup..."

"Okay, okay." She softened. "Go find a nice dress."

Pilar brightened. "And makeup? And maybe some earrings?"

"Sure."

The saleswoman beckoned to Pilar. "Come with me."

Half an hour later, Pilar preened in front of the mirror wearing a little black dress that managed to be sexy and elegant, subtle makeup, high heels, and big hoop earrings, her hair caught up in a rhinestone-studded clip.

"You like?" she asked Loup.

"Are you kidding? You look gorgeous."

"I do, don't I?" Pilar turned. "Okay, your turn."

She tried on the dress Pilar had picked out for her. It was orange and gauzy and looked like nothing on the hanger, but very good on Loup.

"Very nice," Pilar purred. "Not at all *vool-gar*."

Loup laughed.

"Can I get you to wear heels?"

"No."

"Yeah, I figured." Pilar handed her a pair of flat, strappy gold sandals. "Try these." She nodded in approval. "Okay. Now we can go dancing."

"Pilar, I kind of think we need to meet with these people Christophe's talking about and figure out what the fuck's going on before we go dancing." The empty space in her heart yawned wider. "We need to find out what we can do to get everyone else out of Santa Olivia, you know?"

"Yeah, you're right. I haven't forgotten, baby. It's just nice to play make-believe for a day, because thinking about what happens when it ends scares me." She wrapped her arms around Loup from behind and rested her chin on her shoulder, gazing at their combined reflections. "Hey, it's kind of fun being taller than you. Wow. Look at us. We look good together."

"Yeah, we do."

"C'mon." Pilar kissed her cheek. "I think Christophe's about dying of boredom."

They left the store laden with bags and an abundance of goodwill on the behalf of their helpful saleswoman.

"So," Loup said. "What now?"

Christophe consulted his Dataphone. "With your permission, I will confirm a meeting for eleven a.m. tomorrow."

"With who?"

"Government officials," he said guilelessly. "Ours and yours. Don't worry, they are good people."

"And this third party?"

He nodded. "They will make contact with you at the federal building."

Loup sighed. "Okay, I guess."

"Dinner?" Christophe moved his hips suggestively. Unnatural muscles shifted beneath his skin. "Dancing?"

"Dinner."

"No dancing?"

"Dancing later. I want to meet with those guys first."

He shrugged. "As you like, *prima*. You are free now. You do not need to be so cautious all the time."

Loup shrugged, too. "If you don't mind, I'd rather."

They ate at the hotel restaurant, seated at a candlelit table that looked out onto the courtyard, dressed in nice new clothes.

"Jesus." Pilar perused the menu. "I don't even know what half of this stuff is. Balsamic? Prosciutto? Are you sure this is written in English?"

"Yes." Christophe smiled. "Balsamic is a kind of vinegar, but sweet. Prosciutto is a kind of very fine ham."

She eyed him. "Why don't they just say so? How do you know all this stuff?"

His smile widened. "My mother is a manager at a hotel in Huatulco. Not so nice as this, but nice. She is hoping very much that you will come and visit us there. Would you like me to order for you?"

"Yeah, please."

He ordered a wide array of dishes: a salad of mixed greens, grilled asparagus, figs wrapped in prosciutto, saffron risotto, bouilabaisse, baked chicken with rosemary, beef tenderloin, herb-crusted salmon. They shared all the dishes, and all the dishes were delicious.

"Ohmigod." Pilar pushed her plate away. "I think I'm gonna burst."

"Dessert?" Christophe asked Loup.

"Sure."

Dessert was a crème brûlée flavored with a hint of lavender, the creamy custard and the brittle, caramelized top a revelation. "Wow." Loup licked her spoon. "I could get used to being rich."

"I'm guessing that's the idea." Pilar surreptitiously loosened the belt on her sundress.

Loup thought about I-want-to-be-your-friend Derek, who'd tried to bribe her in prison with the promise of good food and nice hotels. "Yep."

"Enjoy it," Christophe suggested. He grinned. "*I* am. So, no dancing tonight. Maybe a walk? We are very close to Chapultepec Park."

"Yeah, that sounds nice."

It was early yet, gilded light giving away to blue dusk as they strolled along the outer verges of the park. Christophe played tour guide, telling them about its attractions: museums, a zoo, an amusement park, and a genuine castle. He flirted with Pilar, who flirted happily back at him. Loup was quiet, thinking. In Outpost, such a vast, wonderful space would never have been open to civilians. Even if it had, the MPs would have been patrolling at this hour, making sure no one was breaking curfew without a permit.

"You okay, baby?" Pilar asked her.

"Yeah." She nodded. "It's just so weird, us being here. All of this. What do you think Mack's doing right this minute?"

"Mackie?" Pilar smiled. "Fixing something. You missing him?"

"All of them, yeah." Her heart contracted with a pang. "You think they know we're safe?"

"That Johnson guy said someone would get word to Father Ramon once things cooled down." Pilar squeezed her hand. "Christophe's right. It's like I said before. There's nothing we can do about it right this minute, so we might as well enjoy ourselves. But it's kind of hard to do thinking of everyone at home, huh?"

"Yeah, I guess."

Another squeeze. "I miss them, too."

Dusk turned to twilight. Christophe escorted them back to the hotel. "Did you see how everyone looked at us in the lobby?" he asked in the elevator. "They think I am the luckiest man in the city." He looked at the way Pilar was regarding Loup and laughed. "I think they are very wrong, but I do not mind them thinking it."

"Sorry." Pilar sounded unrepentant.

"I'll live."

The room was clean and immaculate; trays gone, towels replaced, magazines stacked neatly on the table. A dim light was on and music was playing. The bed was made and turned down, a pair of chocolates on the pillows. "Mmm." Pilar gazed around. "I really *could* get used to this."

"Yeah." Loup cocked her head. "Pilar, does Christophe make you feel the way I do?"

"You'd think, huh?" She gave Loup a wry look. "Given my history with guys."

"Well, yeah."

"No. It's weird, but no." Pilar shrugged. "Baby, I told you. I don't know why, but that whole cute and deadly thing just gets me. You. Everything about you. I can't even explain it, and I've given up trying to figure it out. It's just you." She put her arms around Loup's neck, her expression turning serious. "I hurt you once because I was so fucking scared of losing you. And I swear to God, Loup, I will never, ever do it again."

"Okay."

"I'm serious."

"Okay, okay!"

"Good." Pilar kissed her, slid her hands down to Loup's waist in a long, slow caress, savoring the feel of her. "Ah, you have zee toned phee-zeek. I think you are a dancer or a heem-nasta, yes?"

She shook her head, smiling. "Boxer."

"Oh, a box-air, is it?" Pilar blew softly in her ear. "I love you to pieces, my little boxer, my little Santa Olivia, my little hero. I would go to the ends of the earth to be with you. You want to see what else I bought today?"

Loup squirmed. "Uh-huh."

"Lingerie," Pilar breathed, pulling off her sundress. "Very nice, sexy, and chic for young lovers. You like?"

"Oh, yeah."

THREE

In the morning Christophe drove them to the Palacio Nacional, a massive, impressive building located in front of the biggest town square anyone could imagine.

"Wow," Pilar said, subdued. "It's really...big."

"It's okay," Christophe said cheerfully. "We are expected."

A businesslike young man met them at the door and led them to a posh meeting room where two older men were waiting.

"Welcome." The shorter of the two came forward, smiling. He greeted Christophe familiarly and shook all their hands. "I am Esteban Sandoval from the Department of Foreign Relations. We are honored to have you here."

"Thank you, sir. Loup Garron." She glanced at Pilar, who was looking overwhelmed. "And Pilar Ecchevarria."

"Hi," Pilar managed.

The other man joined them. "Let me add my welcome," he said

in a soft drawl. "Senator Timothy Ballantine from Virginia. And on behalf of my country, let me say I'm very sorry for the way you've been treated." He laid his hand on Loup's shoulder and gave it a paternal squeeze. "Oh...my!" He snatched his hand back involuntarily, looking startled. "I beg your pardon."

"It's okay," Loup said with resignation. "I'm used to it."

"I didn't expect..." He paused. "Truth be told, I didn't know what to expect. You look surprisingly—" He cleared his throat. "Well, you're both lovely young ladies."

"Thanks." Having found her voice, Pilar eyed him suspiciously. "How do we know we can trust you? How do we know you're not from some *other* part of the government that wants to get its hands on Loup?"

Senator Ballantine considered her question solemnly. "I don't suppose there's any way I can prove it to you, but I give you my word as a Southern gentleman that my intentions are honorable. I'm putting my own career at risk in this venture." He cleared his throat again. "And if you have any desire to help the townsfolk you left behind, I do strongly urge you to cooperate with us."

Loup and Pilar exchanged a glance.

Sandoval steepled his fingers. "With your permission, we would like to talk to you young ladies about your experience growing up in an Outpost. My good friend the senator is trying very hard to shed light on this subject. Naturally, I am interested in seeing this happen as part of restoring good relations between our countries. We are making progress, but progress comes slowly. It is difficult to uncover truths many wish to keep hidden. The senator is attempting to collect testimony from many American soldiers who have *served* on these bases, and others who fled when they were established decades ago. Understandably, this is a delicate undertaking. You are the first two civilians to have escaped since the occupation began, the only civilians. Your candor may prove invaluable."

"Okay," Loup agreed. Pilar hesitated, then nodded.

Prompted by questions, they talked for two solid hours, describing life in an isolated town in the no-man's-land of the cordon between the walls, where the soldiers outnumbered the townsfolk ten to one and civilians had no rights. Where generators provided the only electricity and there were no working telephones, no computer networks, no television stations. Where civilians weren't allowed to own guns or drive cars, and had to carry a permit to be out after curfew.

Where two families, the Garzas and the Salamancas, ran everything the army let them—except for the mission and clinic that Father Ramon and Sister Martha ran out of the church, aided by a shifting group of orphans nicknamed the Santitos, the Little Saints of Santa Olivia, by marauding street gangs. Where the only jobs to be had were crappy jobs working for the army one way or another, unless it was working for the Garzas or Salamancas.

Where the eccentric General Argyle held command, obsessed with boxing, and the only way to win a ticket out was to defeat one of his army champions in the ring.

"And you did this?" The senator cast a doubtful eye over Loup. "Against another GMO?"

"GMO?"

"Genetically modified organism." He colored. "I beg your pardon. Is that offensive?"

Loup shrugged. "I dunno. I forgot, Johnson told me that was the term you used. Yeah, I beat him."

"You witnessed this?" he asked Pilar.

She shook her head. "Too scared. But the whole town did. I made Mack and T.Y. tell me all about it," she added to Loup.

"Do you mind if I ask *how*?" Sandoval inquired.

"Yeah, I know, I know." Loup smiled wryly. "Big beats small. But Johnson wasn't a real good boxer. He never had to be. I spent three years doing nothing but training, trying to figure out how to beat a guy as fast as me, but bigger and stronger."

The senator consulted his notes. "And yet General Argyle took you into custody instead of giving you your freedom. Because you're a GMO, I presume?"

"Well, it was one reason..." She began explaining the Santa Olivia business.

Sandoval interrupted her. "You disguised yourself as the town's *patron saint* and assaulted members of the U.S. Army?" He looked as though he couldn't decide whether to laugh or express outrage.

"Well, yeah." She shrugged again. "Sort of. It's not like we *hurt* anyone, we just tried to teach them a lesson. I was born on Santa Olivia's day, right in the town square. The Santitos thought maybe it was a sign. And it was only to a few guys who deserved it."

"I made the dress," Pilar added. "Blue, with a white kerchief."

"Dear God," Senator Ballantine murmured. "One almost feels for the general." He looked thoughtful. "Although I suppose that's not a factor for you, Miss Garron."

"What do you mean?"

He blinked. "Given your limited emotional spectrum, I assumed..." His voice trailed off.

"Loup can *feel*," Pilar said indignantly. "Just not fear, okay? Jesus! I oughta know. Anyway, we didn't just do bad stuff. We did a good deed, too. We stole a thousand bucks from the Salamancas and gave it to a family with hungry kids."

The senator engaged in a fit of coughing.

"Yeah, well, the general didn't like that any better. He was pretty freaked out about the whole thing," Loup said matter-of-factly. "Enough to try starving me and hosing me down and asking the same stupid questions—"

"Back up." Gaining control of himself, Timothy Ballantine raised his hand. "Tell me how you were treated in custody."

While a light blinked on the recording device, she told him about the lack of food that sent her into a near-hibernatory state, the sleep deprivation. The constant heat and light, broken by the hose and the freezing interrogation room. I-want-to-be-your-friend Derek and his attempts to bribe her into revealing who had helped with the Santa Olivia conspiracy.

"He said they'd keep me there forever if I didn't," Loup said, remembering. "Because they never had a chance to try and break down someone they couldn't scare before. You think?"

"Yes." The senator looked grave. "Sadly, I do."

"Good thing I got out."

"Yes." He reached over and turned off the little recorder. "And about that, we will ask no questions."

"Okay." Loup studied his face. "So what can we do to get everyone else out of Outpost? Santa Olivia, I mean."

The two men exchanged a glance. "Exactly what you have done today by testifying, and nothing more," Senator Ballantine said firmly. "This is a serious issue of long standing, and many people are working behind the scenes to rectify it through political and diplomatic means. It's not a matter for young women playing at being vigilantes. You're safe, and we would like to keep it that way."

"Precisely," Esteban Sandoval agreed. "Leave the matter to the professionals. We worked hard and took many risks to arrange your escape. I beg you, please do not *think* of doing anything to jeopardize your freedom."

She sighed, deflated. "Is there any word of Coach Roberts or Miguel?"

"Roberts?" the senator echoed. "Miguel?"

"Garza," Loup said. "Miguel Garza. And Floyd Roberts. He trained us both. He was the general's friend. He was the only civilian allowed to carry a gun. Mig was my sparring partner. He's kind of an asshole, but he can be a good guy, too. There were supposed to be two tickets for whoever won. I gave the second one to him."

The two men exchanged another glance. The senator shook his head. "No. No word."

"Look for them," she suggested. "Especially Miguel. Coach thought he was in big trouble for training me, but he thought the general might keep his word and let Mig go north. Both of them can back up everything we said."

"I'll do that." Ballantine rose and put out his hand. "Godspeed, children."

Sandoval and Christophe exchanged words in Spanish. "Okay." Christophe nodded and turned to Loup. "The third party is a man named Magnus Lindberg from a private company called Global Security. Mr. Sandoval has done business with him on a number of occasions. He asks for half an hour of your time."

"Okay, I guess."

"What about me?" Pilar asked.

"You and I will go see the Palacio's famous murals. You know Diego Rivera?" He smiled when she shook her head. "Well, you will."

"I'd rather stay," she said.

"Mr. Lindberg wishes to speak to Loup alone," Christophe said. "His interest is only in GMOs." He held up one finger. "Half an hour of her time is the price for the fancy clothes you are wearing."

"I'll be fine," Loup said to Pilar. "Go ahead, look at the murals."

She scowled. "Okay, but don't do anything stupid."

"I won't."

The government officials took their leave with a round of farewells. Two minutes later, a tall blond man in a well-tailored suit entered the meeting room, accompanied by a striking brunette woman almost as tall as he was. He paused and gazed at Loup in appraisal. "Loup Garron?"

"Yeah."

He smiled, showing very white, even teeth. "Magnus Lindberg, Global Security. This is my assistant, Sabine."

Loup eyed them warily. They didn't look like anyone else she'd ever met. She wished Pilar was there. "Hi."

"Please, sit." Magnus took a seat. Sabine took a position standing behind him. Loup sat opposite him. "You have an unusual name, Loup. Did you know it's French for 'wolf'?"

"Yeah, I know."

"Ah, I think perhaps you're weary of talking. Very well, I'll be brief." He smiled again. "Global Security is an international company that provides security for very, very important clients."

"Is this the secret agent bodyguard thing again?" she asked. "That guy Derek mentioned something about it when I was in prison."

"Perhaps." He nodded. "In our business, there is a tremendous amount of competition. Once it was enough to have a retired policeman. Then it was soldiers, and not just any soldiers, but special forces, like your Navy SEALS. And then it was Mossad agents, and the craze for thugs... Do you remember the craze for thugs, Sabine?"

Sabine nodded curtly.

"A nightmare." Magnus shuddered. "But celebrities crave novelty.

They must have the newest and best thing, the most dangerous thing, the most exotic thing." He flashed another smile. "And the one thing *no* private firm offers today is a genetically modified bodyguard. I've been on the lookout for someone like you."

"So you're, like, offering me a job?"

Sabine's lip curled.

"A very, very lucrative job," he said smoothly. "I've no doubt that the government here would do the same. Your cousin Christophe has an arrangement and seems content with it. But we can offer so much more. Government wages are meager. Our clients would pay hundreds of thousands of euros for the only GMO in the business. And, of course, we could help insulate you from the danger to which you've already been exposed."

Loup frowned. "What danger?"

Magnus Lindberg showed his white teeth in yet another smile. "You've collaborated with insurrectionist forces in the United States government, Loup."

"Insurrectionist?"

Sabine winced.

"Rebels, let us say," Magnus suggested. "Men like Senator Ballantine who would upset the status quo. He's an honorable enough fellow, but if his efforts were to be compromised..." He shuddered again. "Well, I fear you would be vulnerable. After all, you're on record now, and you were born on the far side of the U.S. border. All good intentions aside, given their role in extricating you from a military prison, the Mexican authorities would be hard-pressed to refuse an extradition request."

"So I could be taken into custody again," Loup said slowly.

He waved a dismissive hand. "If you came to work for Global Security, it would be *exceedingly* unlikely. Most of your work would be in Europe or Asia. You would be safer there. We enjoy a different relationship with the United States, and a different attitude toward human rights. Including the rights of GMOs, even though your existence is largely a matter of informed speculation."

"Except it wouldn't be if you were advertising me, right? Everyone would know."

"Have you ever heard the phrase 'hide in plain sight'"? Magnus inquired. Loup shook her head. "It's a classic technique. Of course, it would be necessary to obtain false papers for you in order to conceal your origins, but that, too, is something Global Security is prepared to offer. We have certain...connections...in that arena."

"Papers?" Loup asked.

"A passport," he clarified. "I trust you've nothing of the kind?"

"No."

"Without one, you're essentially trapped here," Magnus observed. "I fear you'll never leave Mexico. Even if the Mexican authorities were to offer you citizenship, you wouldn't be allowed into the United States given the delicate state of relations. Only the highest-ranking Mexican diplomats are permitted into the States. But Global Security is prepared to offer you the world." He paused to let his words sink in, then cleared his throat. "Of course, there would be a brief training period to teach you additional skills and, ah, polish up the rough edges, but you'd be well provided for. As you've seen, we like to treat our people well."

"Yeah, thanks." Loup cocked her head. "What about Pilar?"

"Pilar?"

Sabine murmured something in a foreign language.

"Ah, yes." He nodded. "I understand GMOs have a genetic predisposition to forming strong attachments. Miss Ecchevarria would be welcome to accompany you. When you're not on a job, of course. I assure you, the fees you would command would more than suffice to cover your living expenses."

Loup shook her head. "No, hiring her."

Magnus blinked. "I wasn't aware that the young lady had any particular skills of interest to us."

"She's good at spending other people's money," Sabine muttered in accented English.

"Yeah, well, you gave it to us. Anyway, important people need people to do stuff like that, don't they?" Loup asked pragmatically. "Maybe I'd make a great secret agent bodyguard in a lot of ways, but in case you hadn't noticed, it might not be the brightest idea in the world to put someone who can't feel fear in charge of keeping other people safe. Pilar and I make a good team. And I promised to let her take care of me."

He blinked again, thoughtfully.

Sabine scoffed.

Loup eyed her. "So what are *her* skills of interest?" she asked Magnus.

The woman stiffened in affront. "I speak five languages fluently," she said in an acid tone. "And I hold a seventh-rank black belt in tae kwon do. I could put you on the ground in three seconds ten different ways."

Loup laughed.

"Permission to demonstrate, sir?" Sabine inquired.

"Go ahead." He nodded. "I'm curious."

Sabine flowed forward and executed a low, sweeping hook kick that was meant to yank the chair out from under Loup and send her tumbling to the floor. The empty chair clattered across the room. Loup, three steps away, regarded her mildly.

"Lady, if you want to spar, I'll need gloves and you'll need gear," she said. "I'm out of practice and I don't want to hurt you by accident. Otherwise, you're just gonna have to chase me around the table all day."

"Amazing," Magnus murmured. "I've never seen anyone move so fast."

"What'd you think you were trying to hire?" Loup continued to keep an eye on the tall woman.

"You." For the first time, his smile seemed genuine. "It's impressive, that's all." He waved a hand. "Sabine, stand down for God's sake. So. Will you consider our offer?"

"Only if you'll hire Pilar, too. And only if she wants to do it."

"I'll consider it." Magnus nodded, half to himself. "You know, it's not an unworkable idea. A personal assistant and the world's only genetically modified bodyguard, all wrapped up in one attractive package." He took a slim cell phone out of his breast pocket. "Here. I'll call you with our response to your proposal. I assume you'll be wanting to visit your…family, I suppose…in Huatulco?"

"Yeah." Loup came back to accept the cell phone. "I'd like that, anyway."

"Very good. My personal number is programmed in the phone if you have any questions." He pursed his lips. "It would be a terrible thing if your family were to be exposed by extension, wouldn't it? I understand the U.S. Army is very possessive of their…special…DNA strains. But take your time, consider."

"Okay."

She shook Magnus' hand. Sabine didn't offer hers. The business-like young man who'd escorted them to the room appeared to take Loup to meet with Christophe and Pilar. She found them still gazing at the vivid, detailed murals.

"Wow."

"Hey, baby." Pilar turned around, eyes shining. "Aren't these amazing? It's like the whole history of Mexico from way back." She pointed at the image of a massive stepped pyramid. "Christophe says these are still there, and we can visit them and everything. So what's up?"

"Job offer. Secret agent bodyguard. Lots of money. And he kind of tried to threaten me. But I think maybe he had a point, too."

Pilar looked worried. "You didn't say yes, did you?"

"Whaddya think?" Loup smiled at her. "I told them I'd think about it. That I wouldn't do it unless they hired you, too. And you wanted to."

"Oh." She looked relieved. "Good."

Loup looked at Christophe. "You knew, didn't you?"

"Yes." He gave her an apologetic glance. "I agreed not to say anything before they had their chance." His stomach growled. "Maybe we can talk about it over lunch?"

"Sure."

FOUR

So they asked you, too?" Loup asked, curious.

"Yes." Christophe methodically heaped spoonful after spoonful of fragrant, steaming paella onto his plate. "I am the oldest of us here, the only one who is eighteen. My father, he was the first to arrive. He met my mother quickly, like your father did."

"Why'd you say no?" Pilar asked him.

He made a face. "Global Security, they found out about the original kin years ago through contacts at the government. They asked them, too. It sounds nice, yes, but Tío Jean and Tío Daniel, they knew men, ordinary men, who took such jobs after the army. Good money, but stupid stuff, like sitting the babies."

"Huh?"

"Babysitting."

"Yes." Christophe nodded. "Babysitting for famous people. More trouble than it is worth."

"Did he threaten you, too?" Loup asked.

He shrugged. "A little, perhaps. But I was born in this country. It is different for me and my brothers. I did not take the threat seriously."

"The original kin weren't born here."

"No. But they were not born in the United States, either. They were born in Haiti. And if anyone has a claim to their DNA, it is the Chinese scientists who developed it there." Christophe grinned. "Anyway, I do not think he would have dared to threaten *them*. They were…imposing."

"Mmm." Pilar rested her chin in her hand. "So if we did this we'd be, like, traveling around the world with celebrities and rich people?"

"Pretty much," Loup agreed.

"That's not so bad."

"Nope."

"You won't like it so much," Christophe warned them. "Very annoying. Also, I do not like this business with the false passports. It gives them a hold over you."

"Yeah, well." Loup shrugged. "If it's illegal, it gives us a hold over them, too, right?"

"I suppose."

"Anyway, who doesn't?" Pilar said in a practical tone. "Those guys we talked to today do. They've got us on record."

Loup glanced at her. "So are we thinking about it?"

"Maybe," Pilar said. "*If* they want me, too. And I'm, um, not exactly sure I'd make a good secret agent bodyguard."

"Not as a bodyguard." Loup shook her head. "More like an assistant. You'd shop for famous people and stuff."

"Oh, I could do that, for sure. Jesus!" Pilar looked dismayed. "Loup, we don't even know who's famous anymore. I mean, everything we know is from shit that's over thirty years old. How are we gonna know?"

"Money," Christophe said complacently, shoveling saffron-tinted rice into his mouth. He chewed and swallowed, wiped his lips with a napkin. "If they have the money to pay for you, they will be rich and famous. Do you care?"

"No," Loup said.

Pilar flushed. "Yeah, kinda. I need more magazines."

Christophe laughed.

Her flush deepened. "I know you think it's silly. But you know what? In Outpost, that was one of the only ways there was to see what the rest of the world was like—or what it used to be like, anyway. That the stories that my dad told me before he died were true. It's how I learn, okay?"

"It's not silly," Loup said. "It's better than watching *The Sound of Music* for the billionth time. I haven't ever seen a movie made since I was born."

Christophe looked mildly chastened. "Okay, so we will go to the movies and start your education. Then we will go buy some of those stupid magazines girls on the beach are always reading. Okay?"

"Definitely."

They went to see an action film starring a smart-talking Australian guy that Christophe assured them was one of the hottest stars of the day. Loup marveled at the immense scale of the screen, the clarity of the picture, the booming surround sound, the fact that such things still existed in the vast outside world. Pilar clutched her arm and let out a squeak every time someone got shot or a car blew up, which happened a lot. Afterward they went to a newsstand that stocked international magazines, where Pilar selected half a dozen.

"You really think you might wanna do this?" Loup asked her.

"Yeah, maybe." She flipped through the pages. "I don't know. That

Magnus guy sounds kinda shady, but at least he wasn't telling us to just stay out of the way and keep our mouths shut. And I know that's not your style, baby." She glanced at Loup. "I know, it's weird. I never had any ambition 'cause I figured I'd never have a chance to go anywhere or do anything. All I wanted was...well, you know."

"A cute rich boy."

"I gave up the cute rich boy for you, baby," Pilar reminded her. "And anyway, it's all different now. This, all of this." She gestured at the bustling streets. "That store, those paintings today...it makes me want to see the world, you know?"

"Yeah." Loup smiled. "I do."

"And I want to go dancing," she added. "I really, really want to go dancing. Please, can we go dancing tonight?"

"Okay, okay."

"Did you not have dancing in Santa Olivia?" Christophe asked.

"Only sort of," Loup said. "There was always music and dancing on Santa Olivia's Day. Otherwise, the Salamancas ran a couple of nightclubs that had dancing, but they were for the soldiers. If a girl went, it meant she was for hire."

"And *no*, I never went," Pilar said adamantly. "Well, except for that time you guys used me as bait to get the guy who raped Katya." She shivered. "Soldiers kinda scare me."

"I was not going to ask," Christophe said mildly. "And you are most definitely not the best prospect for a bodyguard. What kind of dancing do you like? Disco? Rock? Salsa? Merengue? Reggae?"

She blinked. "I dunno."

"Then you have to let me teach you to salsa." He grinned and executed a few steps, arms extended, hips shimmying. "You will love it. Very sensual, very fun."

"Okay."

"But first—"

"I can guess." Pilar eyed him. "More food."

"Well, yes."

They returned to the hotel and charged another massive meal to Global Security's account. Afterward, Christophe took them to a dance club with live music.

"Ohmigod." Pilar gazed at the dance floor filled with swirling, twirling couples snaking around one another. "Christophe, that looks really *hard*."

"Not so hard." He took one of her hands, put the other on his shoulder. "Here is the basic step. So...so...so, and back. I lead and you follow." He pointed at Loup. "You next, *prima*."

She studied the dancers. "Okay."

By the time Christophe led Pilar back, flushed and exhilarated, Loup had a good sense of it.

"Yes!" Christophe laughed with delight, spinning her. "You see."

"Yep."

"No fair," Pilar complained. "You're...you."

Loup glanced over her shoulder. "Pilar, I think you have a line forming."

She looked at the trio of men waiting to ask her to dance. "Oh, good."

In the late hours of the night or the small hours of the morning, Christophe approached the band with a generous tip. He beckoned to Loup, smiling. "I always wanted to do this. Fast, fast, fast. You think you can keep up?"

She frowned. "Is it safe?"

He gave her a perplexed look. "Yes, of course. Why would it not be?"

It was hard to abandon a lifetime of caution. "Yeah, okay, I guess so. If you don't get too fancy."

"No, no."

The music played fast.

Faster.

Faster.

The musicians sweated under the stage lights, stepping up the time, playing faster and faster. The beat doubled, then tripled. On the dance floor, couples dropped out, one by one, staring at them in amazement and whispering. Christophe's feet moved in a blur. Loup followed him effortlessly, matching his pace.

"Woo!" He flung up his arms when the song ended with a flourish, then offered Loup his courtly bow. There was a smattering of stunned applause. "Thank you."

Her eyes sparkled. "It was fun."

"Yes."

"It was fucking amazing." Pilar extricated herself from a would-be suitor and wound her arms around Loup's neck. The music started again, slower and more sensual. She wriggled her hips. "Think you can lead as well as you follow, Supergirl?"

"I can try."

They danced together.

"Ohh-kay." Christophe intervened. "Time for the hotel, I think."

The hotel was quiet, the lobby empty. Pilar glanced around and sighed. "I'm gonna miss this place. Christophe, are there dance clubs like that in Hucatulco?"

"Huatulco. Yes, a couple." He held the elevator door for them. "It's a small place, nothing like a city. Lovely beaches. Tourists, but not so many, not like other places."

"Lots of fish," Loup said, remembering.

"Yes."

Pilar yawned. "And I could probably get a job there, right? If this secret agent bodyguard assistant thing doesn't work out?"

"Bartending? Oh, yes."

"Pilar's a good bartender," Loup offered.

Christophe eyed her. "I am not sure that matters."

"I am, though." She stifled another yawn. "But I guess we'll just have to wait and see if those Global guys want you bad enough to take me, too, huh?"

"Yep," Loup said. "We'll see."

FIVE

Two *days*!" Pilar's eyes widened. "That's a long drive."

"It's a big country," Christophe said affably, sitting at the breakfast table with a heaped plate in front of him. "You're lucky I know it so well."

"How do you?" Loup asked, curious.

"I'm the wanderer in the family." He shoveled eggs into his mouth. "I had a little money from my father, from the fishing business I told you about. When I was sixteen, I went to explore."

"Cool."

He swallowed and grinned. "Yes. I only stopped to help come rescue you when the government contacted me and said they would pay good money. Our lost little cousin." He twined his fingers and flexed his hands. "I worked with some soldiers. We took shifts, one or two at a time. We had to be very careful, very quiet. I spent more time working in the tunnel than anyone."

"Thanks," Loup said.

"Of course." He turned serious. "I'm glad you're coming, *prima*. Everyone has been wanting to meet Martin's daughter for so long." His grin returned. "Now everyone will want to make the band play fast and dance with you!"

"So, no girlfriends, huh?" Pilar asked him.

"Me, no." Christophe shook his head. "Out of the seven of us, only Alejandro has found someone. Paco and the twins are too young. For the rest..." He shrugged. "You know it's difficult for us?"

Her voice softened. "Yeah, I know."

"Not *so* difficult," he said. "Maybe one in a hundred, two hundred pretty girls I meet feels..." He nodded at Loup. "The way you do about her. Very sexy. But I have not stayed with anyone long enough to fall in love. It happens fast with us, you know?"

"Ooh, a playboy."

"I am a young man, okay?"

"It's actually really nice," Loup offered. "Being in love, I mean."

Pilar smiled at her. "Thanks, baby."

She smiled back. "Well, it is."

Christophe shrugged, unabashed. "Yes, well, so is being a playboy, if you like. So I am the lone wolf. I like it for now."

"Christophe?" Loup cocked her head. "Are we *actually* part wolf or what?"

"I don't know." He slathered a piece of toast with butter. "The government did tests on the original kin. DNA analysis. If you want to know, you can find out." He took a big bite of toast, chewed and swallowed. "I never wanted to know."

"Why?" Pilar asked.

"Me, I don't care." He pointed at her. "But you? Okay, maybe you think Loup is a little bit wolf, a little bit leopard. That, you like. What if it's not? What if it's a little bit chimpanzee?" He shrugged a third time. "Better not to know."

"Chimpanzee."

"It is possible."

Pilar studied Loup. "Nah. Too cute."

"So think what you—"

The cell phone that Magnus Lindberg had given Loup rang. "Oh, hey." She fished it out of the front pocket of her jeans. "Christophe, how the fuck do I answer this thing?"

He showed her. "Push here."

"Hello? Yeah, it's me." She listened. "Yeah? Okay, well, what does that mean?" She listened some more. "I dunno. We'll talk about it. Yeah, we're leaving today. Okay. I'll call you."

"Here." Christophe pointed at the button to end the call.

"So?" Pilar asked, anxious.

Loup folded the phone. "Well, they're kind of willing to go for it. Only you'd have to go through the same training as me and pass. That guy Magnus said they wouldn't market you as a bodyguard, but they wouldn't send you out without the basic skills."

"Like what?"

"Self-defense, surveillance, and stuff. Like army training, I guess."

"Huh." Pilar looked dubious. "I don't know if I'd make it through something like that."

"Pilar, if you can go dancing for four hours, you can make it through some dumb training. You can do anything if you *want* it. You just have to decide whether or not you do."

"Mmm."

"Well, we don't have to decide today," Loup said pragmatically. "So let's drive down to Huatulco. We'll meet all my cousins and see if we like it there and want to stay for a while. If we do, you can get a job bartending, and I'll...I dunno. Do something."

"Construction," Christophe suggested. "There are many buildings in need of repair after so long. My mother's brother has a company. Alejandro works for him. I think he would hire you even though you have no experience. He likes us because we are fast and strong, and we have no fear of heights, and very good balance."

Pilar shuddered. "Sitting the babies sounds a lot safer."

They checked out of the hotel after breakfast and began the long drive. Christophe made the time pass by telling them stories about his aunts and uncles and cousins and growing up in Huatulco, doing things to terrorize the tourists like jumping from the roof-tops into swimming pools. Loup listened wistfully, thinking how very different it was from her childhood, always having to hide what she was.

"You okay, honey?" Pilar asked.

"Yeah." She nodded. "I was just thinking about Tommy. I remember when he told me that I might not live that long, and I figured out if it was true, it meant my father was probably already dead." She smiled a little. "Tommy said maybe there were other kids like me. A bunch of little *loup-garous* running around Mexico. Turns out it was true, huh?"

Pilar stroked her hair. "Such a good guy, your big brother."

"*Loup-garous?*" Christophe asked.

"Werewolves," Loup said. "I guess that's what they call them in Haiti. My father asked my mother to name me after them."

He smiled. "Loup Garron. I see. He had a sense of humor, Tío Martin."

"Yeah?"

He nodded. "They weren't *always* serious. The children, we could make them laugh. It made them happy to see us wild and free. Loup, do you know about meditating?"

"Huh?"

"Meditating," Christophe said patiently. "To take time every day to slow down your body. Even ten minutes helps."

"No. Why?"

"To extend our life spans." He concentrated on the road. "They figured it out in the United States with fancy machines and things."

"Biofeedback," Loup said, remembering something I-want-to-be-your-friend Derek had said.

"Yes." He nodded again. "Too late for the original kin, but us, it can help. You don't need fancy machines, only to slow down for a little while every day. I will show you."

"And *I'll* make sure you do it." Pilar yanked a lock of Loup's hair.

"Ow!"

"I wanna keep you around, baby."

Christophe smiled. "I think maybe your Santitos were as bad as a pack of *loup-garous*, *prima*."

They drove for hours and hours, then turned off the big toll highway onto a smaller road that wound into mountains. Unlike the big highways, this one wasn't well maintained. Up and up and up, dodging potholes, until they reached the highest peaks.

"Holy shit!" Pilar's nails dug into Loup's arm. "Look at it!"

"The ocean," Christophe said softly.

Far, far below them it stretched out forever, a shining expanse of water with no end, reaching to the horizon and beyond, gleaming gold in the late-afternoon sunlight. It held all the promise of infinity, and it was beautiful.

"Wow," Loup murmured. "I hope Mig got to see it. He really wanted to see the ocean."

Pilar shook her head. "You and Miguel Garza."

"Not like *that*."

"*He* wanted to."

"Only when he was drunk," Loup said. "And *I* didn't. He turned out to be a pretty good guy in the end, okay?"

"Yeah, he did," Pilar admitted.

"Anyway." Christophe pointed to a building with the word *hotel* painted on its roof, slowing the car as they approached. "This is a good place. We will stay here tonight. Tomorrow, we will finish the drive."

It was a simple, rustic place, but the view was amazing and the rooms had porches overlooking the gorge. After they were settled, Christophe joined Loup on her porch. "Okay." He sat cross-legged opposite her, hands loose on his knees. "Close your eyes if you like.

Sit without moving, and think of slow things. I like to think of trees growing, big trees, so slow you cannot see it. Or maybe a mountain wearing down to sand."

"Okay."

"Breathe slow and deep. Think slow thoughts. Think of your body growing slower and slower, almost stopping. Every cell, stopping for a moment. Resting. Still."

It was a peaceful feeling. Christophe's voice fell silent.

Loup sat, motionless.

Still.

"Jesus!" Pilar said. "It's like watching a couple of statues."

"You are not helping, *bonita*."

"I get the idea." Loup opened her eyes. "So that's it? Slow?"

"Yes." Christophe nodded. "But you must do it every day. I do it in the morning before anything else."

"Okay."

"I'll be quiet," Pilar promised.

They ate at the little hotel's restaurant where all the tables and chairs were painted bright colors. Christophe flirted with their waitress, who spoke no English and giggled uncontrollably at the amount of food he and Loup ate.

"One in a hundred?" Pilar guessed.

"No." He shook his head. A hint of melancholy shadowed his face. "Just a nice girl. She would not like it so much if she touched me."

"Oh. Sorry." Pilar glanced at Loup. "I remember what that was like for you, baby."

"It still is with most people," Loup said. "Sorry, Christophe. It's pretty awful, I know."

The shadow passed. "I told you, I'll live."

Afterward they watched the sun set over the ocean. Pilar let out a sigh as the last curve of the orange disc vanished beneath the distant horizon. "Wow. I never thought I'd see anything like that."

"No," Loup agreed.

When the dusk deepened to blue, they retreated to their rooms.

"Mmm." Pilar, lying on the bed in her new sexy lingerie, smiled.

"Baby, you make me shiver inside when you look at me that way." She beckoned. "C'mere."

Loup slid into bed beside her, kissed her.

"Jesus." Pilar shuddered against her. "Hey, Loup?"

"Yeah?"

"Do you really think I could do it?" Her hazel eyes searched Loup's face. "That secret agent bodyguard training thing?"

She blinked, surprised. "Of course."

"I like me with you," Pilar said softly. She ran her fingers through Loup's unruly hair, traced the line of her full lips. "A lot. I like who I am. No one else ever believed in me that way before."

Loup gazed at her. "They should have."

"Yeah, but you *do*."

"Yep." She kissed her again. "A lot."

SIX

They arrived in Huatulco by midafternoon.

The place was actually a collection of small towns, all very close together. "You will stay in Santa Cruz, at my mother's hotel," Christophe informed them. "She insists. And tonight there will be a party."

"Ohmigod!" Pilar caught her breath when they entered the town. "It's so *cute*!"

He smiled. "Yes."

The hotel was located beside the small marina. Christophe parked the car and glanced toward the water. "Come. We will see if Raimundo and Nacio's boat is here. Fishing," he explained to Loup. "They used their money to buy out the rest of us."

They walked down the docks under the hot sun. Palm fronds waved languidly. Small boats bobbed on the water. Pilar looked dazed. "Jesus!" she murmured. "It really is like being in a movie."

"Yeah, kinda," Loup agreed.

"Hey!" Christophe grinned and pointed to a boat with a couple of figures lounging under the awning. He cupped his mouth and shouted something in Spanish. One of the figures shouted back, then both bounded over with exuberant, inhuman speed.

"Whoa!" Pilar exclaimed.

Loup fought the urge to tell them to slow down.

Both were young men, brown-skinned and shirtless, lithe with dense muscle. They fell on Christophe like eager puppies, hugging him with rough affection, then turned swiftly to Loup, pouring out questions in Spanish.

"Um . . . *Ingles, por favor?*" Loup tried out one of the phrases Christophe had taught them.

"*Despacio,*" Christophe said, laughing. "Slow down! Okay. This is Nacio." He nodded at the taller of the two. "And Raimundo."

"*Hola, prima.*" Nacio shook her hand, grinning widely.

The other hugged her. "Hey, Lupita!"

"This is Pilar," Christophe said. "*Su novia.*"

The cousins looked at Pilar and gave slow, identical blinks, pondering the information. "Good job, *prima,*" Raimundo said to Loup. "So, you want to go fishing?"

"Uh . . . maybe later?"

"*Idiotas,*" Christophe said to his cousins with affection. "You and your fish. No, we are going to meet my mother. We will see you tonight, okay?"

"Okay!" They went back to the boat, laughing and scuffling and tussling.

"They're very . . . lively," Pilar observed.

"Yes."

Christophe led them to the hotel, where his mother, Marcela, met them in the lobby. She was a tall, elegant woman with kind, intelligent eyes. She gazed at Loup for a long, long time, then embraced her, pressing her cheek against Loup's.

"Welcome, *mija,*" she said in a gentle voice. "We are so very, very glad to have you here."

No one had hugged her like that since her mother died, with such tenderness and none of the slight flinch of withdrawal that most people felt. Loup's throat tightened. "Thank you, ma'am."

"Ma'am!" Marcela laughed. "No, no. You can call me Tía Marcela." She turned to Pilar. "And you too. Pilar, yes? Christophe spoke of you on the telephone." She smiled. "Welcome."

"Thank you."

"Come." She beckoned. "I have a very nice room for you, and you will stay as long as you wish. Christophe, be a nice boy and bring their suitcases."

"*Sí, Mami.*"

The room was clean and bright and airy, looking out at the sparkling water of the little marina.

"Wow." Pilar gazed around. "This is so nice. You're so...*nice!*"

"I do this in memory of Martin," Marcela murmured. "It was his great sorrow that he never knew his child. That she grew up in a place where she could not be free. And you, *bonita*, do not have such an easy path, either. It is wonderful and maddening loving one of *them*, but it is not easy." She glanced at Christophe and smiled wryly. "Though it is easier than being a mother to one of them. So. Enjoy."

Christophe eyed the bed. "Trust me, *Mami*, they will."

"Bad boy!" she scolded him. "So, Christophe will fetch you in a couple of hours for the party. If you need anything, call the front desk. Ask for Ana Maria if she does not answer; she speaks good English."

"Okay," Loup agreed. "*Gracias*, Tía Marcela."

"Martin's daughter." Her gaze lingered on Loup. "He would have been so proud. So very, very proud."

They left.

Pilar looked apprehensive. "God, she's so nice. It makes me feel kinda guilty. I don't think she'd be so nice to me if she knew what I'd done. How bad I hurt you when I left you for Rory."

Loup sat on the bed. "I do. I think she'd understand it better than anyone. Didn't you hear her? She said it wasn't easy loving one of us. And she *did* lose Tío Henri. I bet there were times she thought about giving up."

"Maybe." Pilar was quiet a moment. "I still wish I hadn't done it."

She glanced up. "I know. I know you do. But you're here now, and that's all that matters." Her voice softened. "I know I can't understand it the way normal people do, but believe me, I know what you did to get here was pretty damn terrifying. You gave up everything! I won't ever forget it."

"Thanks." Pilar's expression eased. "It's not, you know."

"Huh?"

"Hard." She smiled ruefully. "Loving you. I mean, it's kind of scary, yeah, but otherwise it's pretty spectacularly easy."

Loup smiled back at her. "I think the scary part was what she meant."

"Yeah," Pilar agreed. "But I can live with it. Thinking of losing you again..." She shuddered. "*That's* scarier."

Two hours later, Christophe came to collect them. He regarded the disheveled bedspread without comment. "You ready, *bonitas*?"

"Almost!" Loup called from the bathroom.

"Look up," Pilar suggested, wielding a mascara brush.

"Ow."

"Sorry." She dabbed at the outer corner of Loup's left eye with a tissue. "There. Perfect. You can do it yourself next time."

"I could have done it myself this time," Loup observed.

Pilar surveyed her handiwork. "Yeah, but I do a better job, and you're meeting your whole family for the first time." She tapped Loup lightly on the nose. "Just so you know, *normal* people would be nervous. Excited, but nervous."

"Oh. Are you?"

"Yeah," she admitted. "But at least we look nice."

"You both look very lovely," Christophe commented. "Shall we go?"

The party was held on a hotel garden terrace strung with lights and festive paper decorations. Most of the guests had already arrived, and they let out a heartfelt cheer when Christophe entered with Loup and Pilar on his arms. It was an odd assortment: Marcela and five other women of middle years, all beaming, and seven boys and young men ranging in age and size from a pair of identical twins who looked to be about eight to Christophe, the oldest. The boys descended on Loup in a swarm, chattering at her in a mixture of Spanish and English.

"Back, back!" Christophe swatted at them, laughing. "Easy!"

They ignored him or cuffed him back, roughhousing with the careless ease of long practice. Although they varied in height and hue, all of them had the same familiar wide, dark eyes and uncanny sense of physical presence.

Not a one of them made the slightest attempt to hide what they were. It evoked the sensation of nothingness where uneasiness should be, and made her feel strangely alone in the midst of the throng.

"Okay, okay." Christophe began naming them, pointing at the twins. "Marcel and Daniel, and this one we call Paco. Raimundo and Nacio from the boat, and this is Alejandro. Oh, and the shy girl hiding behind the palm tree is his sweetheart, Amaya."

"Venga, venga!" The twins dragged Loup away to meet their mother, who pressed Loup's hands between hers and spoke warmly to her in Spanish. Paco, a couple years older, tugged at a fold of her dress and clamored to go next.

"It is a little overwhelming, I think." Marcela joined them.

"A little, yeah." Loup glanced over her shoulder and saw Pilar held captive to the crowded attention of Nacio and Raimundo, looking half-delighted and half-alarmed.

"Don't worry." Marcela followed her gaze. "They're all good-hearted boys, and they know to be respectful. They are excited, though." She smiled sadly. "And they no longer have fathers to help them behave."

"Yeah, I know," Loup said softly. "I'm sorry."

"Of course." She put a hand on her shoulder. "Come, meet the others."

The women were gentler, easier. By the end of the evening, Loup had them sorted out. Dolores, the twins' mother, sold embroidered clothing in the market. Paco's mother, Cruz, was a hairdresser and the most talkative of the lot. Alejandro and Nacio's mothers both worked for one of the big hotels in the next town, and Raimundo's mother, Consuelo, worked for an agency specializing in rental properties.

All of them shared a shadow of loss and sorrow, as well as an exasperated sense of sisterhood born of the difficulties of raising boisterous, fearless boys. And all of them welcomed Loup with the utmost warmth.

It made her feel good, but it made her feel bad, too. It made her miss home.

Hotel staff began to circulate with platters of hors d'oeuvres. The boys surrounded them. Pilar escaped and made her way to Loup's side.

"Holy shit!" she murmured. "They're a little wild."

"You okay?"

"Yeah." Pilar smiled. "So far Nacio's promised to teach me to swim, fish, and scuba dive, and I think one of the little ones, Paco, said he was gonna marry me when he grew up." She ruffled Loup's hair. "You having a nice time, baby?"

"Yeah." She nodded. "It's a lot to take in, but yeah."

"I'm glad."

They ate and mingled. Alejandro brought over his shy, pretty girl-friend and introduced her. She gazed at them with awe, as though they'd come from someplace exotic, and kept a tight grip on Alejandro's hand. He was sixteen or seventeen, and less excitable than the rest of his cousins.

"Know why?" Pilar whispered in Loup's ear. She shook her head. " 'Cause he's the only one getting laid a lot."

She laughed. "Pilar!"

"What? I bet it's true."

Then there was more food, dinner served at a long table. Platter after platter of food, served by amused, indulgent hotel staff, vanishing at incredible rates into the mouths of seven not-quite-human boys and young men. The sun set in the west, making the lights illuminating the terrace twinkle brightly.

"Hey!" Christophe called down the table when most of the plates had been scraped clean. "We're going to have music and dancing, but they want to hear your story, *prima*. About the big fight and escaping."

"Okay, but you can't go around telling other people," she warned them. "Remember, it's still supposed to be a secret."

Christophe looked offended. "Yes, of course. Everyone understands."

Loup told it with myriad interruptions for translation. The women listened with horrified fascination, and the boys with gleeful excitement and a multitude of questions, all wanting to know how she'd beaten a bigger, stronger opponent.

"Enough!" Marcela shuddered when Loup described letting Miguel Garza hit her with buckshot-weighted gloves to get used to the sensation. "Don't translate that, *mijo*," she said to Christophe. "You'll only give them ideas."

"*Sí, Mami.*"

She clapped her hands. "Anyway, time for music!"

A three-piece band that had been quietly setting up began to play. Everyone danced without reservation, trading partners freely, even shy Amaya taking turns with the younger boys. From time to time, someone would call out for the band to play fast, fast, fast and the band would oblige for a time. Everyone would drop out but whatever delighted cousin was dancing with Loup.

"Fun," Pilar commented when the band took a break. She was flushed and her eyes were sparkling.

Loup smiled. "Yeah."

"Hey, Lupita!" Raimundo approached her. He put up his fists. "Show me, huh?"

She shook her head. "Not here."

"Aw, c'mon!" He shuffled his feet and essayed a couple of lightning-swift jabs at her. She slipped them without thinking. He beckoned. "Just a little."

"It's a party. I'm wearing a *dress*, Raimundo."

"C'mon!" He flashed an engaging grin, then turned like a shot and grabbed a startled Pilar, slinging her effortlessly over his shoulder and holding her in place with one arm. "I give her back when you show me!"

On the far side of him, Pilar let out a stifled squeak. "Put me down, you asshole!"

"When she shows me!"

Consuelo stormed over, railing at her son in Spanish. He defended himself in the same language, sounding aggrieved, heedless of Pilar dangling over his shoulder, heels kicking. Loup watched them uncertainly, not wanting to do anything that would result in Pilar being dropped on her head.

"Show him," Christophe suggested behind Loup.

"You serious?"

He nodded. "Hard."

She glanced at his mother. Marcela nodded, resigned. "Sometimes it is the only way."

"Okay!" Loup called. "Put her the fuck down, Raimundo. I'll do it." He obliged, beaming. "You okay?" she asked Pilar.

"Yeah." She adjusted her dress, disgruntled. "Mostly."

Loup beckoned to Raimundo. He came at her, swinging happily. She ducked and slipped his first two punches, caught and deflected another, then feinted and took him down with a combination—two quick shots to the body, then a right hook that clouted his left ear and knocked him off his feet.

"Ow, ow, ow!" He rolled on the terrace, clutching his ear.

The other cousins yelled and hooted, laughing at him. Their mothers exchanged glances and shook their heads.

Pilar kissed Loup's cheek. "Thanks, baby."

She shook out her stinging right hand. "Sure."

Raimundo got to his feet, still clutching his swollen ear. "Good job, *prima*."

"He meant it to be nice in a way," Christophe informed her. "Our fathers, they let us be a little crazy with one another. He meant it to show you are one of us, Loup." He frowned at Raimundo and said something to him in Spanish. "But not with others, eh? Only us. Leave Pilar alone."

"*Perdóname*," Raimundo said to Pilar. "Please?"

She folded her arms beneath her breasts. "Maybe."

Loup eyed her cleavage. "Pilar, that's not helping."

"Too bad."

The band, prompted by Marcela, resumed playing a lively tune. "Please?" Raimundo repeated to Pilar. "I will not do it again, I promise."

She sniffed. "Okay."

The evening ended happily, in part because the incident was nothing unusual for most of the clan, and in part because Pilar was too good-natured to hold a grudge. Before the night was out, she'd danced with Raimundo and forgiven him.

"You're good for the boys," Tía Marcela said to Loup.

"Yeah?"

"Yes." She smiled. "You show them they have limits, that there are things they cannot do, when so many things come so easy to them. You have worked hard for things. You will stay for a while, I hope?"

Loup glanced at Pilar, who nodded. "For a while, yeah."

"Good."

In the bedroom, with a breeze blowing through the open window, they lolled between crisp, clean sheets.

"You think you would have been like them, baby?" Pilar asked dreamily, stroking Loup's body with her fingertips. "If you hadn't grown up where you did, having to hide what you are? Kinda wild, kinda crazy?"

Loup shook her head. "I dunno. I like them, but it's hard to get used to."

"I'm glad you didn't. I like you how you are." Pilar regarded her. "And if you hadn't, I'd never have known you. Is that wrong?"

"No."

"Hey, Loup?"

"Uh-huh?"

"Could you do what Raimundo did? Throw me over your shoulder?"

"Yeah, sure." Loup propped herself on one elbow. "You *liked* it?"

"No!" Pilar said indignantly. "But, um...it might be kind of fun if *you* did it. And then you could ravage me."

"Ravish."

"That, too."

Loup smiled. "Okay."

"Oh, good." Pilar wriggled happily. "But not tonight, okay? I'm kinda worn out."

"Yeah, they're kind of exhausting." She yawned. "Even for me."

"Baby, you just got out of prison a few days ago. Give yourself a break." Pilar twirled a lock of her hair around one finger and tugged it gently. "You think you might want to stay here?"

"I dunno. But I'm glad we're here."

"Me too."

SEVEN

The days that followed were idyllic.

It was hard to get used to that, too.

The weather was glorious, hot and sunny. On the first day, Christophe appointed himself their tour guide. He took them to the bank where Loup signed papers for an account held in her name. It was only a little over thirteen thousand pesos, but it was enough to live on for a while, especially since they were Tía Marcela's guests for now.

Afterward he took them to the market and assisted with the purchase of bikinis and towels, sunglasses and sunblock.

They walked to the beach, a curving slice of white sand with a backdrop of palm trees. The ocean was shallow here, a pale turquoise. Dozens of people were lying in the sun.

"So, um...that's all you do?" Loup asked. "Lie there?"

"Pretty much," Christophe agreed. "Or swim." He nodded at a net. "Sometimes there are volleyball games. When I was younger, the others and I would play and make all the tourists stare."

"And no one cares?"

"No." He shook his head. "I have told you, it's not illegal to be what we are. Only in America they say you're government property. All the hotels and restaurants, they know about us, so there is always someone to explain." He grinned. "Sometimes tourists come just to see us. One in a hundred, you know?"

"I hadn't thought about *that*," Pilar said in alarm. She narrowed her eyes at a tall, suntanned blond woman sauntering toward the water. "Jesus, what about her, Loup? Do you think she's prettier than me?"

"No," she said honestly.

Christophe eyed Pilar. "I don't think you have a whole lot to worry about, *bonita*. Anyway, we are very constant in love."

"*You* aren't."

He smiled. "I told you, I've managed to avoid it. I move too fast for love to catch me. Put on sunblock, okay? A lot of sunblock. The sun is strong here."

They slathered on lotion, stretched their towels, and lay in the sun. For the first ten minutes, Loup thought it felt great. The bright warmth beating down sank deep into her, making her feel loose and lazy.

In the next ten minutes, she got bored. "Can I have one of those?" she asked Pilar, who was perusing one of her celebrity magazines.

"Sure, baby."

Ten minutes later she was still bored. "How can you read this stuff? It's all about movies and music and TV shows we've never seen."

"It's homework." Pilar lowered her sunglasses and peered at her. "We need to know this stuff if we decide to be secret agent body-guards."

"No, we don't. It's only because you want to know who's famous."

"Oh, fine."

"The agency will have files on their clients," Christophe said drowsily, arms behind his head. "They will have all the information you could ever wish to know, including how rich and famous they are, whether they are vegetarians, and what kind of prostitutes they like."

"Oh." Pilar shrugged. "Well, I still like to know."

Loup got to her feet, impelled by restlessness. "I'm gonna go see if I can figure out how to swim."

"Don't drown!" Christophe called after her. "We don't float so well because our muscles weigh more than normal."

"Shit!" Pilar jumped up.

"She'll be fine."

She shot him a look. "Yeah, well, I'm not taking any chances."

Christophe laughed and rose to follow her.

By the time he'd given them both their first swimming lesson, two figures came pelting across the sand at an inhuman speed, a trail of startled glances in their wake. Nacio and Raimundo plunged into the ocean, sending up geysers of water. They double-teamed their older cousin, dunking him and holding him underwater for a long time.

"Hey," Loup said mildly. "Am I gonna have to hit someone again?"

They let Christophe up. A flailing, splashing, shouting scuffle ensued, clearing an area around them. Nacio broke away from the scuffle and approached the girls. "I promised!" he said to Pilar. "*I* teach you to swim. Why do you not wait?"

She blinked. "I thought you had some fishing thing today."

He consulted in Spanish with Christophe, who left off wrestling with Raimundo and came over rubbing a knot on the back of his head. "They canceled it to be with you."

"This language thing sucks," Pilar muttered. "Um...Christophe? Do these guys get that I'm not available?" She pointed at Loup. "That we're together?"

"Yes." He grinned. "But they are hoping you will change your mind. They have not spent several days on the road with you two. Also, you are a terrible flirt."

Pilar flushed and gave Loup a guilty look.

"Well, you are," Loup said unapologetically.

"You're lucky you're their cousin," she commented.

"True," Christophe agreed, contemplating Loup. "You do look very good wet, *prima*. Wet is very sexy for you." He turned to Raimundo, who was addressing him in Spanish, listened, and laughed. "*Sí.* You want to do something fun? We did this as children, our fathers did it to us. Everyone does, but no one else throws so high and so far. We would laugh and laugh, and all the tourists would stare."

"What?" Pilar asked, suspicious.

"We'll show you," he said. "It's better with children or girls, though. We can't do each other so well. Too heavy." Christophe cupped his hands together below the water. Raimundo put one foot in his cupped hands, his hands on his cousin's shoulders. Christophe heaved and sent him soaring overhead. He managed half a somersault before splashing into the sea.

In the background, tourists squealed and pointed.

"Fun," Loup observed.

"Yes. Very fun." Nacio grinned and beckoned to her. "You let me?"

"Sure." Setting aside the voice of caution Tommy had drilled into her, she put her foot in his cupped hands, rested her hands on his shoulders. It felt strange, familiar and unfamiliar all at once. They came from different backgrounds, but they had a physicality in common. Nacio sent her soaring upward in one swift, powerful surge, confident of her impeccable balance. The blue sky rotated around her; the aquamarine sea splashed and geysered.

"Whoa!" Loup dashed the water out of her eyes. "Very fun!"

Nacio beckoned to Pilar. "Now you."

She backed away a few paces toward Loup. "Y'know, I really just want to lie on the beach and read my magazines."

"Just once," he entreated her.

"Pilar, you don't have to let anyone throw you," Loup said. "Go read your magazines. I won't drown, I promise."

"Okay." Pilar reached out and grabbed Loup's bikini top, yanked her close, and kissed her with considerable thoroughness. "Get it?" she asked the cousins, who were watching open-mouthed. "Yeah, I flirt. It doesn't mean anything. I left my whole life behind and followed a total stranger into the world's scariest tunnel because I wanted to be with Loup. I'm not changing my mind. Okay?"

They understood enough to nod.

"Good." She glanced at Loup. "What?"

"Nothing." Loup flashed a grin at her. "I like when you get all feisty. But the next time you stick your tongue halfway down my throat, you're *so* getting ravished."

"Mmm." Pilar blew her a kiss and turned for the shore.

All four of them watched her go. Christophe muttered something under his breath. "*Prima*, in a tiny desert town, how did you manage to find *that* one?"

"Her aunt made the orphanage take her." Loup smiled at the memory of Pilar's aunt dragging her up the walk. "She said her body was the Devil's playground."

"Yes." He shook himself. "Would you like me to throw you?"

"Okay."

They splashed and played until a curious family of tourists came over to talk to them. Loup watched their two young boys shriek with unfettered delight as her cousins tossed them high, high into the air. It didn't seem possible that the same sun that shone on the sparkling water and the happy tourists shone on the cracked, dusty streets of Outpost. The thought made her heart ache all over again.

"It's so different here," she said to Christophe. She turned and pointed to the coastline. "Hey, I've seen people running along there. Can anyone do it?"

"Yes, of course," he said, surprised. "As much as you like. If you go far enough, there are other bays that are still natural and undeveloped. Very nice."

"And I can just...run? As fast as I want?"

"Of course."

"Wow." She shook her head in amazement. "The only time I got to do that at home was on the treadmill in the garage. And it used to break all the time, and Mack would have to fix it."

"*Pobrecita*. It was an awful place."

Loup shrugged. "Yeah, but it was home. Is it time for lunch?"

He grinned. "Definitely."

They ate right there beside the beach under a thatched palapa, bare feet in the sand; fish and shrimp and lobster grilled fresh to order, hot with spices, washed down with cold beer.

"Holy shit," Pilar said fervently. "I know I keep saying it, but I didn't know people could live like this."

"I catch and cook for you," Nacio offered. "Even better."

She eyed him. "Maybe."

"I know, I know!" He put up his hands. "Both of you, okay?"

"Okay."

"You were very convincing," Christophe assured her. "Also, if we could be afraid, I think they would be a little bit scared of our small cousin with the very big punch." He tousled Loup's wet hair with easy affection. "We are not *entirely* stupid."

"Good."

They spent the rest of the day idling at the beach and went out together at night, too, to a small nightclub near the hotel with a DJ and dancing. No salsa; only pop music, bright and sprightly.

"Hey!" On the dance floor, Pilar lit up. "Baby, I know this song."

"You do?"

"Uh-huh." She looked smug. "It's called 'Hate to Be Your Next Ex-Boyfriend.' Some English band called Kate. Very famous. Bad boys that the little girls love. I read about them."

Loup laughed. "Kate?"

"It's something from a play. Shakespeare or something. Remember Anna made us read that one about the guy and his bitchy wife?"

She glanced over Loup's shoulder. "Ooh, look. Christophe found one."

"One what?"

"One in a hundred. What a fuckin' playboy!"

Loup turned to watch Christophe dancing with a dazed-looking young woman who couldn't seem to stop stroking his chest. "I don't know. I don't think it makes him as happy as he pretends. I think he's lonely. I guess it doesn't work for every one in a hundred like it did for us."

"*She's* happy, anyway. Do I look at you that way?" Pilar asked, drawing a finger down Loup's throat. "Like someone hit me over the head?"

"Yeah, sometimes."

"Oh, well."

"Yeah, but I look at you back the same way."

"True." Pilar kissed her very deliberately.

"Umm…"

"Not enough?" She kissed her again. "Better?"

"You *so* asked for this." Loup stooped and caught Pilar around the knees, slung her over her shoulder.

"Not here!" Pilar laughed helplessly. "Loup! I'm serious! I can't breathe!" She gasped as Loup set her upright, ignoring a knot of startled, staring dancers. "You've gotta wait till we're alone, baby."

"*You* didn't."

Pilar smiled. "Still gonna ravage me?"

"Yep."

EIGHT

One sunlit day poured into another.

They dined at each of the cousins' homes, enjoying home-cooked meals and noisy hospitality. Pilar found a kindred spirit and shopping companion in Paco's mother, Cruz. They spent hours browsing the shops in the marketplace and gossiping while Loup ran alone on the beach, reveling in her speed and freedom.

It helped keep the empty feeling at bay.

But she thought about home because it was home and she couldn't help it, and she thought about the government officials warning her not to try anything foolish, which only made her frustrated and angry.

She thought about Magnus Lindberg's offer and the freedom he promised. She thought about his warnings, too.

At Nacio and Raimundo's insistence, they went fishing. To the boys' disappointment, Loup hadn't inherited their passion for it, and Pilar was fairly hopeless. A snorkeling excursion proved more successful, and Nacio began teaching them to scuba dive.

Christophe had a brief, torrid affair with the girl from the nightclub, which ended when her family went home to Guatemala, taking their heartbroken daughter with them. He was quiet and withdrawn for several days.

After deciding which were her favorite bars in town, Pilar asked about bartending jobs. The second place gave her a tryout and offered to hire her on the spot.

"She *is* pretty good," Christophe said in surprise, watching her mix, shake, and pour with deft accuracy.

"She likes it," Loup said. "All the flirting."

Pilar promised to give them an answer by the end of the month. Loup spent a day working beside Alejandro on a construction job at a fancy hotel being restored in one of the nearby towns. She liked her quietest cousin, and the rough camaraderie of the workers reminded her of the guys training at the gym.

"What about the work?" Pilar asked.

She shrugged. "It's okay, I guess."

"If you could do anything in the world, what would you want to do?"

"Box," Loup said ruefully. "But there's not really anyone for me to fight."

"What about the bodyguard thing?"

"I dunno." She wrapped her arms around her knees. "I'm thinking about it. I don't exactly trust that Lindberg guy, and I don't know how I feel about being…what did he call it? A novelty. And I like it here. I like getting to know my family. But that thing Lindberg said about me maybe putting *them* in danger if the truth gets out…what if it's true?"

"Christophe was pretty sure he was bluffing," Pilar observed.

"Maybe," Loup said. "Or maybe not. But the thing is, we *want* the truth to come out, right? That's the only way the Outposts will ever get opened." She glanced at Pilar. "Anyway, it just doesn't feel right that everyone we know is stuck back in Santa Olivia while we're lying around on a beach, eating fresh fish, and going dancing. I feel like I should be doing something more, you know?"

Pilar smiled at her. "Yes, my little hero."

"But I'm not exactly sure how becoming a celebrity bodyguard changes anything," Loup admitted. "Other than getting us fake passports."

"Oh, you'd probably save some famous person's life in an amazing way, and become this big star, everyone's hero. And then your story would be all over the place, and everyone would hear about Outpost, and the American government would have to admit everything."

Loup laughed. "Yeah, sure."

"Well, maybe. Anyway, we'd make a lot of money. We could come back here to visit whenever we wanted." Pilar kissed her cheek. "We don't have to decide today. Let's just enjoy the rest of the month, okay?"

"Okay."

More sunlit days. The towns were small enough that they became known by the locals. Everyone knew about the cousins, a source of pride and occasional dismay. They accepted Loup with ease, and Pilar was Pilar. Within days, she knew half the locals in town. When Loup ran along the beach, men in boats waved to her. When Pilar wandered through the marketplace, shopkeepers called out to her and offered her bargains.

"Just think how much everyone would love you if they knew your story," Pilar said toward the end of the month while they were having breakfast at the hotel.

"It's your story, too."

"You're the hero of Santa Olivia. I'm just the sexy sidekick. Ooh." She nudged Loup's foot under the table. "There's your boyfriend."

Loup glanced up to see a young waiter who seemed to have a crush on her. He blushed and ducked away. "Don't make fun of him."

"I'm not!" Pilar said. "I feel bad for him. You want me to read his mind? I know exactly what he's thinking."

"You can read minds now?"

"His." Her voice softened. "I know what it's like to be a one in a hundred. He *looks* at you, baby. He sees the little ways you're different, more *there*. The way watching you move is like listening to music. The more he looks, the more he can't stop himself from looking. He thinks about the way you knocked down Raimundo, how you don't look like you oughta be able to do what you do. It makes him crazy, and he wonders if there's something wrong with him. He wonders why he can't stop thinking about you. And he thinks you're one of the most beautiful things he's seen, like some beautiful animal no one's named yet." She glanced at Loup's expression and continued. "He thinks about touching you, wonders what it would feel like. If it would be like petting a tiger. But don't let him." She shook her head. "If he stroked your arm, he'd wonder what it would be like to feel you against him. If you hugged him, he'd wonder what it would be like if you were naked, skin to skin. If he kissed you, he'd wonder what it would be like to have your mouth on...okay, I'm gonna shut up before I have to drag you back to the room."

"Whoa." Loup blinked.

"You ever wonder why the way I feel about you scared the shit out of me for so long?" Pilar smiled wryly, resting her chin on her hand. "It's like that. Seeing him, seeing that girl Christophe picked up, it makes me remember."

"Is it different now?"

"Worse," she said. "You think the curiosity will kill you, but *knowing* is worse. Because it's everything you imagined and more."

"You were, too. Way more."

Pilar narrowed her eyes. "Were?"

"Are!"

"You thought about me the same way?"

"Yeah." Loup cocked her head. "I'm not saying it's exactly the same. I guess we can't ever know. But the way I felt when you'd touch me..." She shivered. "I'd get dizzy. I still do. No matter what he says, I think that's what Christophe's looking for. And I never felt that with anyone else. Plus, you're probably the sexiest sidekick in the universe."

Pilar tossed her napkin on the table. "Oh, we're so going back to the room."

"Uh-huh."

A month's worth of sunlit days dwindled. On the day before Pilar had promised to give her answer about the bartending job, Loup went for a long, long run along the shoreline. She ran long enough and hard enough to tire herself, far enough to leave civilization behind. When she got tired, she stopped and sat in the sands of an untouched bay, gazing at the green waters. Usually, she practiced meditating when she'd run that far, sitting motionless and thinking slow thoughts.

Today, she just thought.

Thought about the family that had embraced her in Huatulco— the rambunctious cousins, the kind, loving aunts. Thought about Magnus Lindberg's not-so-veiled threats that they could be in danger if the American investigation was exposed.

Thought about the family she'd left behind in Outpost; Santa Olivia, forgotten Santa Olvidada.

Mack and T.Y.; clever Jaime and Jane, denied the education they deserved. All the Santitos. Brave Father Ramon, tireless Sister Martha, gentle Anna.

Her mother and brother, buried there.

Miguel Garza, fate unknown.

She sighed, resting her forehead against her knees.

Birds wheeled overhead.

Loup made a decision and rose. She ran the long miles back to Santa Cruz, her bare feet splashing in the water and sending up silvery spray that hung in her wake.

She found Pilar reading magazines beside the hotel pool. "Hey."

Pilar glanced up. "Hey, yourself. What's up?"

Loup sat on the chaise beside her. "You look like a movie star in those sunglasses. Pilar, do you still want to see the world?"

"Yeah, I do." She put down her magazine. "You wanna do it, don't you? The bodyguard thing?"

"Yeah." Loup nodded. "I do. If there's a chance we're putting my cousins in danger here, I'd rather not stay. Maybe we'll learn something useful. At least it will take my mind off everything else."

"And you really, truly think I can get through this training thing?"

"Really and truly. I'll be there with you every step of the way. I'll help you."

"Okay." Pilar gave her a dazzling smile. "Let's do it."

They found Tía Marcela in her office and told her their decision. She looked at the two of them in their bikinis and shook her head, smiling a little sadly. "May God help the world of international security. I hoped that you would decide to stay, but I understand. It's a big offer, and you've both had so little." She hugged them, kissing them on both cheeks. "You know you will always have a home here, yes?"

"*Sí, Tía,*" Loup said, eyes stinging a bit. "Thank you for everything."

In the room, they pored over the cell phone, figuring out how to call the number programmed in it under Magnus Lindberg's name.

"It's ringing." Loup pressed it to her ear. "Oh! Mr. Lindberg, hi. It's Loup Garron. Yeah, Pilar and I decided to take your offer." She listened. "Okay, that's good. We'll be here. Yeah, it's the marina hotel. Okay, bye."

"What's up?" Pilar asked.

"He said it will take a few days to get the passports," she said. "With fake names and everything just in case we're on some international watch list. I guess we're gonna be Canadian."

"Ooh, do we get to pick our own names?"

"No."

"Too bad."

"Yeah," Loup agreed. "He's flying back to Mexico City. He said with any luck, he and Sabine will come pick us up by the end of the week."

"Who's Sabine?"

"I didn't tell you about her? His assistant."

"Is she pretty?" Pilar asked.

"I guess." Loup considered. "Kind of a bitch, though. She seemed really pissed at me for some reason."

"You?" She looked surprised. "Why? You never do anything to make anyone mad at you, baby."

"Pilar, you were mad at me for a whole *year*! You wouldn't even talk to me!"

"That was different." Pilar folded her arms. "You were gonna get yourself killed or taken into custody fighting that Johnson guy. And you decided to do it *right* after I kissed you for the first time."

"You told me to pretend it never happened!"

"I had issues," she admitted. "Anyway, I got over it, didn't I?"

"Yeah." Loup smiled. "Pretty spectacularly. Anyway, I don't know what this Sabine's problem is, but they'll be here in five or six days. Lindberg said he'd call when he knew for sure."

"Okay." Pilar paused. "How pretty?"

"Pilar!"

She laughed and kissed her. "I was just kidding that time."

NINE

You're going to hate it," Christophe predicted.

Loup shrugged. "Then we'll quit."

"I still do not like this business with the illegal passports," he said. "If they wish, they could turn you in at any time."

"At least it's a passport," she said. "No one else was offering one."

"I suppose." He didn't sound convinced. "Give me your phone, eh? I will put in all the family's phone numbers, but also Mr. Sandoval and some allies in America like Mr. Ballantine and Mr. Johnson. If you get in any trouble, start calling, okay?"

"Okay."

"I'm going to miss you, *prima*." He glanced at Pilar and smiled. "Both of you. You definitely make life interesting."

The last days were an endless farewell party. They went to all their favorite places, ate and drank and danced. On a day when the sea was calm, Nacio took them on a scuba-diving excursion that they weren't technically qualified for since he wasn't a licensed instructor. They marveled at the coral reefs, the jewel-toned fish, the startling moray eels, and the ability to linger in a translucent, underwater world.

"Wow!" In the boat, Pilar wrung salt water out of her hair. "Thank you, Nacio." She kissed his cheek. "That was amazing."

He beamed. "You do very good. Except for the eel."

"They're pretty scary."

"See?" Loup said. "You *can* do anything, Pilar. Did you ever imagine you'd do something like this?"

"Are you kidding?" She laughed. "Did *you*?"

"No." Loup looked around at the sparkling sea. "Seriously? No."

"Me either." Pilar smiled. "But I get what you mean. Thanks, baby."

"Sure." She eyed her. "You also look really, really hot in a wet suit."

"Yeah?"

"Yes," Nacio agreed. "Do not hit me, *prima*."

"I won't."

On the morning of the fourth day, Magnus Lindberg called and left a message on Loup's phone that he and Sabine would arrive to retrieve them the following day. The hotel was booked with other functions, but Tía Marcela exerted her considerable organizational skills and arranged for a last farewell party at one of the beachside restaurants.

They convened in the late afternoon. The sun still hovered well above the horizon, warming the sand. The cousins laughed and played and chased one another, delighting the watching tourists. In the water, the twins and Paco begged to be thrown.

"*Ahora, ahora!*" Daniel demanded, clambering up Loup's body, agile and strong as a monkey. "*Tú, prima!*"

"Me? Now?" She caught his narrow foot in her hands.

"*Sí!*"

"Okay!" She sent him flying.

He chortled in midair, somersaulted, and landed in a compact splash.

"You okay?" Loup called. "*Estas bien?*"

"*Claro!*" Daniel surfaced, fearless.

Under the palapa, the twins' mother, Dolores, spoke to Loup in earnest Spanish. She looked helplessly at Marcela, understanding only one word in ten.

"It is as I said," Marcela said, her gaze warm and soft. "You are good with the boys, *mija*. You are more like their fathers than any of them, our wild boys. You have a care where they do not. You have faced limitations and they have not. She wishes you would stay. *I* wish you would stay."

The part of Loup that missed her mother longed to say yes, but the restlessness and the empty feeling inside her wouldn't allow it. "I'm sorry. I can't."

"I know." Her aunt pressed a gentle kiss on her brow. "But you will come back and visit, yes?"

"Yeah, of course. As long as it's safe."

The sun sank below the horizon, gilding the waters. The restaurant staff lit torches that flung dancing shadows over the pitted sand. There was food, an abundance of food. Afterward the cousins burned off more of their restless energy by racing one another to the shoreline and back. Loup stood a little distance away, watching them.

"Sorry to leave, baby?" Pilar wrapped her arms around her from behind.

"Not exactly. I just never thought I would if I found them, you know?"

Pilar kissed her ear. "We can call it off."

"No, I wanna try this. I do. At least it's *something*. I can't stand doing nothing."

"Okay." Her arms tightened. "Funny. You're all the family I have in the world now."

Loup turned. "You know I love you, right?" she asked, serious. "You know I'd never leave you?"

After a moment, Pilar nodded.

"Good."

The evening ended with a surprise cake, singing, and many lingering farewells, but at last they dispersed into the night.

"I'm gonna miss it here," Pilar said in the hotel room, gazing out the window at the moonlit harbor below. "I hope we can come back soon. Although you might have to knock Raimundo down again. He squeezed my ass when he hugged me."

"Hmm." Loup, lying on the bed, glanced at her. "You do have a pretty spectacular ass."

"You're not very chivalrous."

"I'll knock him down if he does it again." She smiled. "Tired?"

Pilar gave her a smoldering look. "Nope."

At noon the next day, a black limousine pulled into the hotel's parking lot. Magnus Lindberg strode into the lobby, Sabine gliding behind him.

"How very good to see you again!" he said to Loup when the front desk summoned her. He shook her hand. "I'm so pleased you decided to accept our offer."

"Thanks."

"And Ms. Ecchevarria." He flashed a smile at Pilar, who was rendered unaccustomedly tongue-tied by his polish and professionalism, and shook her hand. "We're so very delighted to have you too."

Behind him, Sabine gave a slight cough.

"Sabine." Lindberg gave her a look. "Perhaps you would be good enough to see about a table for four? We can discuss the future over lunch."

She strode off in the direction of the hotel restaurant.

"Jesus," Pilar muttered.

"Told you," Loup said.

Over lunch, he distributed their new passports to them. Pilar cracked hers open to see what her new name was.

"Pilar Mendez. Hey, I got to keep my first name!"

"It's not so unusual as to attract attention," Magnus Lindberg said to her. "Yours, on the other hand, Loup..."

She opened it. "Guadalupe Herrera?"

He shrugged. "Lupe is a common nickname. Close enough?"

"Yeah, sure." She closed it. "So what happens next?"

"After lunch, we will drive to the airport. We have reservations for a five o'clock flight to Aberdeen."

"Aberdeen?"

Sabine curled her lip.

Lindberg ignored her. "It's in Scotland. We have a facility north of there where the two of you will undergo an intensive four-month course of training."

"Scotland, huh?"

"You know, baby," Pilar offered. "Kilts and bagpipes."

"Oh, right."

"Yes," Lindberg agreed smoothly. "Though I fear you will see little of either. You will learn hand-to-hand combat skills, marksmanship, surveillance and threat assessment, containment and damage control, evasive maneuvers...ah, do either of you know how to drive a car?"

They shook their heads.

"That, too." He nodded at Sabine. "Sabine here is a highly skilled driver. She has competed in a number of amateur European touring cups."

She looked smug.

"During your training program, all your needs will be provided for," Lindberg continued. "If you graduate successfully, each of you will receive a ten thousand euro signing bonus. Subsequent to graduation, your wages will be dependent on commission." He glanced at their puzzled expressions. "The money you earn will depend on how high a fee we're able to command for your services, dependent on the difficulty and duration of the job in question." He steepled his fingers and smiled. "I expect to be able to command very, very high fees for you, Loup."

"But we work as a team, right?"

He sighed. "At your insistence, yes."

"What happens if we don't make it through the training?" Pilar asked.

"Ah." Lindberg looked grave. "I fear we cannot hire you. However, we are not ungenerous. We will gladly pay your airfare back to

Huatulco or your destination of choice." He hesitated, tapping his fork on the edge of his plate. "Pilar, if you find yourself unsuited for this line of work, I would hope you would not stand in Loup's way. This is a great opportunity for her."

"It's a great opportunity for *you*," she retorted. "C'mon! You're dying to get your hands on her. How much of our fee do *you* pocket?"

It startled a genuine smile from him. "It's negotiable, depending on demand."

She folded her arms. "So when the time comes, we'll negotiate. Okay, I might not be cut out to be the best secret agent bodyguard in the world, but I care about Loup and you don't. And I don't think you exactly get that whole can't-feel-fear thing. So yeah, that makes me fuckin' *suited* for this job."

"She's right," Loup agreed.

Sabine made a strangled sound. "You are not going to be a *secret agent*," she said in accented but fluent frustration. "We are bodyguards. Nothing more. We provide executive protection to an exclusive clientele. And *you*, not even that."

"Okay, assistant. Whatever."

"I dunno." Loup flicked the edge of her new passport. "Fake identities and forged documents? Seems pretty secret agenty to me."

"They're not forged," Magnus Lindberg observed. "Illegitimate, but not forged. I had to call in a number of markers for this favor. We are taking a considerable chance on you. And yes, it is because I believe it will be very lucrative for all of us. Are you still willing to take a chance on us?"

Loup looked at Pilar.

She hesitated, then nodded.

"Yeah," Loup said. "We'll do it."

"Excellent." Lindberg beckoned to their blushing waiter, who tripped over his feet several times and stammered in Spanish before accepting the proffered credit card. "My God! What ails that boy?"

Pilar smiled sidelong at Loup. "You do, baby."

"You know," Sabine said to her in a silken, poisonous tone, "you still have to make it through the training. It is very, very difficult."

"She will," Loup said mildly.

Magnus Lindberg dabbed his lips with a napkin. "I am hoping that is the case. But we will see, will we not?"

"Yeah, we will."

TEN

The limousine took them to the airport.

"Wow." Pilar gazed at the thatched buildings. "Airports in the movies are a lot bigger."

"Most are," Magnus Lindberg assured her. "We will change planes twice, once in Mexico City and once in Paris."

"How come Paris?" Loup asked. "Isn't that in France? I thought we were going to Scotland."

"Yes," he said patiently. "But there is no direct flight. Because flight departure times vary, sometimes the quickest route is not always the shortest."

"Huh."

Sabine muttered something in a foreign language.

"They will learn," Lindberg said to her in a reproving tone. "It's not their fault they grew up in isolation."

An hour and a half later, they were on the plane. Loup listened to the turbo engines whine to life, feeling the subtle vibration.

Beside her, Pilar shivered. "Exactly what keeps a plane from falling out of the sky, anyway?"

"I dunno. Jaime could tell us if he was here." Loup took Pilar's hand. "Scared?"

"Uh-huh." Pilar clutched hard. "But I don't want *her* to know."

Across the aisle, Lindberg leaned forward. "It's all right," he said kindly. "Taking off and landing are the worst parts. I don't care for it myself. But these planes have an excellent safety record."

She closed her eyes as the plane began to taxi. "Good."

Loup watched the runway rush by outside the window, faster and faster, then fall away as the plane angled into the sky. The plane climbed, banking slightly. It felt strange to leave behind a whole world she had only just found in exchange for an even bigger one. She hoped it was a good decision, one that her brother would approve of. "It's okay. We're up. Look, you can see the bays."

Pilar opened her eyes and leaned across her. "Wow!"

"Feel better?"

"Yeah." She smiled and kissed Loup. "Thanks, baby."

On the far side of the other aisle, Sabine muttered.

"It's not unprofessional if they're not on a job, Sabine," Lindberg said with irritation. "Now be quiet and let me read the paper."

They landed uneventfully in Mexico City and transferred to the international terminal. Loup gazed around in awe at the number of shops and people, the moving conveyor walks, the multitude of large television screens.

"Do you have to gawk like a peasant?" Sabine snapped at her.

"What do you care?"

"It's embarrassing!"

"Why?"

"Loup doesn't do embarrassment," Pilar informed Sabine. "She'd have to be afraid of what other people think, you know?"

Sabine flushed with anger at the implied insult.

"Interesting," Lindberg observed. "That hadn't occurred to me. I see we do have a lot to learn about this condition of fearlessness."

They waited for their next flight in a special lounge for premiere passengers.

"Hey, Magnus?" Pilar said, and then flushed involuntarily. "Can we call you that or are we supposed to call you Mr. Lindberg?"

He looked up from his paper and smiled at her. "In a business setting, we always use the formal address. But in a casual environment, yes, you may call me Magnus. What is it?"

"Is it a long flight?"

"About twelve hours."

"Can I go buy some magazines? I've read all of mine."

"Certainly." He nodded. "Sabine, will you escort her to the bookstore?"

"I'll go," Loup offered. "I'm bored, too."

"I would prefer that Sabine escort you," Lindberg said diplomatically. "Until you are both somewhat less...naive...in the ways of the greater world, I think it is best you have a guide."

Pilar sighed. "Fine."

Sabine led them to the nearest bookstore, stalking through the airport. She waited, watching contemptuously as Pilar picked out a handful of entertainment magazines and Loup browsed the English language section.

"What'd you buy, baby?" Pilar asked Loup outside the store.

She showed her. "It's a travel book all about Europe. I figured I could start learning about the places we'll go."

"That's a great idea!"

Sabine rolled her eyes.

"What?" Loup regarded her. "Jesus, lady! Seriously, what'd I do to piss you off?"

"Do you really want to know?" Her mouth tightened. "You were *born*. I am very good at what I do. One of the best. I worked very, very hard to become one of the best in this business. I spent years perfecting my skills. And you!" She shook her head in disgust. "I stand to be bested by an ignorant, inarticulate little guttersnipe who owes all her gifts to an accident of birth."

"Okay," Loup said. "I kinda get that. But I can't exactly help it, you know? And it doesn't take away from everything you've done."

"Plus, it's *so* not true!" Pilar added indignantly. "Loup trained really, really hard for three years to beat that Johnson guy! It's not like she was born a boxer."

"*You*." Sabine's voice was tight. "I do not even wish to speak of *you*. Your presence here offends my every sensibility. The day you fail out of training will be one of the happiest days of my life."

"Gee, thanks."

"You don't know," Loup said. "Pilar hasn't had any training yet. She might turn out to be really good at this. I mean, you didn't start out as a ninth-level expert in Haikwondo, did you?"

A muscle twitched below her right eye. "*Tae* kwon do."

"Whatever."

"I thought that kung fu stuff was supposed to make you all wise and peaceful and shit. Guess not, huh?" Pilar let out a squeak and ducked behind Loup when Sabine took a step forward, glaring at her.

"For God's sake, she's *hiding* behind you!" Sabine jabbed her forefinger at Loup.

Loup batted her hand away, her arm moving in an inhuman blur. "Yeah, well, do you blame her?"

People streamed around them, giving them a wide berth. Sabine wrestled herself under control. "Come," she said curtly, striding back toward the lounge.

"What a bitch!" Pilar whispered.

"Yeah," Loup agreed. "Hey, what's a guttersnipe?"

"I dunno." She smiled at her. "But I guess I like 'em."

They boarded the plane an hour later, sitting in first class. Outside the windows, night was falling. Hushed flight attendants glided up and down the aisles, murmuring offers of beverages.

"Hey, Magnus," Pilar called. "Is it okay if we say yes?"

"Of course." Across the aisle, he rested his head, eyes closed. Beside him, Sabine lowered a black satin sleep mask, determinedly blocking out their presence. "Order whatever you like. It's one of the privileges of traveling first class."

"Ooh, cool!" She ordered two of their best tequilas, neat.

"Pilar's a really good bartender," Loup informed him. Behind her mask, Sabine snorted. "She is!"

"Oh?" Magnus Lindberg opened his eyes briefly. "Actually, that's also a skill that could come in rather handy. We do provide discreet security for social events from time to time."

The plane taxied and turned, began to pick up speed. Engines whined.

Pilar grabbed Loup's hand. "Tell me when we're up."

"Okay." She watched the ground fall away, the lights of the city sprawling beneath them. "You can look now."

"Wow," she breathed. "Big world, huh?"

"Very," Loup agreed.

"Hey." Pilar touched the rim of her glass to hers. "This is the good stuff we used to keep on hand for Rosa Salamanca at the bar. Remember? We snuck some on your birthday when everyone else was at the festival."

Loup sipped. Liquid gold. "Yeah," she said softly. "You said I felt like it tasted. Expensive."

"Uh-huh." Pilar kissed her languidly, tasting of smooth, smoky tequila. "You do."

"Please do not attempt to join the mile-high club while I am present," Magnus Lindberg said without opening his eyes. "I fear Sabine might expire of outrage."

"Mile-high club?"

"Forget I spoke." He cracked one eye open at Pilar. "I do not mean to give you ideas."

"Okay, fine."

The plane soared on into the darkness. They finished their drinks. The murmuring flight attendants circulated, taking away the empty glasses, offering blankets. Pilar snuggled into hers, making her chair recline and resting her head on Loup's shoulder.

"Wake me up if the plane crashes, okay?"

Loup kissed the top of her head. "It won't."

ELEVEN

It was early evening when they arrived in Aberdeen.

"I don't get it," Pilar said, puzzled. "Shouldn't it only be, like, noon?"

"We're in a different time zone," Magnus said. "Back in Huatulco, it's noon. But here, it's almost six o'clock."

"How can it be different times in different places?" she asked.

Sabine gritted her teeth. "Oh, for God's sake!"

"I can't help it if I don't know this stuff!"

"Sabine, will you attempt for five minutes to imagine you spent your entire life in a small town under military occupation without access to a proper education?" he said in exasperation, and then to Pilar, "It's because the earth is very large and rotates on its axis. That's what causes day and night, you see? Whether or not where you are is facing the sun, or turning its face away."

"Oh, okay." Pilar smiled at him. "You're a good teacher, Magnus."

He smiled back at her. "Thank you."

They drove into the delightful Scottish countryside—Sabine at the wheel, Loup and Pilar in the backseat, gazing out the windows in awe. The drive took them to a big stone manor house sitting in front of an oak forest.

"Wow, that's practically a castle!" Loup said.

Magnus laughed. "Hardly. Perhaps you will have a chance to see a real castle. There are several very fine ones in the area. But I think you will find this quite comfortable."

A tall, very fit young man came out to greet them.

"This is Ben Rogers," Magnus introduced him. "For the next six weeks, he'll be one of your trainers. His job is to ensure you're able to complete the basic fitness course in the allotted time limit. If you succeed, you'll move on to the next phase of your training."

"Fitness course?" Pilar asked.

"Five-K run and the obstacle course," Ben Rogers said in a curt tone. Planting his hands on his hips, he looked them both up and down. "You the geemo?" he asked Loup.

"Geemo?"

"GMO."

"Yeah, I guess."

Magnus tapped his chin in thought. "We're going to have to find a better marketing term," he murmured to himself.

Ben Rogers turned his gaze on Pilar. "That must make you the excess baggage."

She colored. "That's not very nice."

He shrugged. "I take my job seriously. Don't expect me to be happy to be saddled with some flighty bird that makes it harder for no good reason."

Loup scowled.

"You insisted on this," Magnus reminded them. "Mr. Rogers will do his best whether he likes it or not. I expect you to do the same."

Pilar sighed.

Inside the manor, Magnus introduced them to a pleasant-looking woman named Adelaide. "You might say she is our chatelaine," he said, laughing at his own joke. Neither of the girls got it. "Ah... manager. If you need anything, you may ask Adelaide. She'll show you to your rooms." He paused. "Do you prefer one or two rooms?"

"Do you want your own room, baby?" Pilar asked.

"Oh, for God's sake!" Sabine said in disgust. "She's not a child. Why do you insist on calling her that all the time?"

"I dunno." She blinked. "I guess I just like to. Loup doesn't mind, do you?"

"No," Loup said. "I don't even notice most of the time."

"It's just an endearment, Sabine," Magnus said wearily.

"It's inane!"

"I don't particularly care." He glanced at Pilar. "Though I would prefer you don't do it on the job. So. One room?" They nodded. "Very good." He consulted his watch. "All right, we'll be off. Rest assured that you're in very capable hands here."

"You're not staying?" Loup asked.

"No." Magnus smiled. "I have business to attend to. But I'll be receiving reports and checking on your progress. I wish you both the best of luck. We're very eager to have you on our team."

Sabine muttered darkly.

"Jesus." Pilar eyed her. "Does the way that I fucking *breathe* annoy you?"

"No." Sabine gave her a poisonous smile. "Just the fact that you do."

"Nice."

After they left, Adelaide led the girls to a bedroom on the second floor, Ben Rogers following with their luggage. The room was warm and cozy, overlooking the back of the grounds.

"It's cute, anyway." Pilar peered out the window and turned pale. "Holy shit! What's that?"

"Obstacle course," Rogers said with cheerful malice.

Loup joined Pilar. Between the forest and the manor was a long line of ladders, walls, pits, bars, and ropes, all looming in the twilight. "Huh."

"You'll be spending a *lot* of time on it," he predicted.

"Oh, give the poor things time to catch their breath," Adelaide scolded him. "Girls, breakfast's at seven, lunch at noon, and dinner at six. The kitchen's kept plates warm for you tonight. Anyone hungry?"

"Me," Loup said. "I usually am."

"Do you, ah, have any special dietary needs?" she asked. She clarified at Loup's blank look, "Do you eat regular food, dear? Forgive me, I should have inquired about it earlier."

"Yeah," Loup said wearily. "Regular food. Just a lot of it."

She beckoned. "Come along, then. We'll get you fixed right up. You can stow your things later."

"I'll see you tomorrow after lunch," Rogers said. "Back of the manor, one o'clock sharp. Addie'll see you've got togs."

"Togs?"

"Clothing, dear," Adelaide said.

"So we get to sleep in tomorrow?" Pilar asked hopefully.

Rogers laughed. "Hardly! You'll be meeting with Clive bright and early. He likes 'em all nice and jet-lagged. Part of the technique."

"Technique?"

"You'll see."

"Mr. Clive will be expecting you at eight o'clock tomorrow morning in the gymnasium," Adelaide confirmed. "Just you set your alarm clock. Now come along and have a nibble."

They ate warmed-over roast beef and potatoes in the kitchen.

"Loup?" Pilar asked in a tentative voice. "How far is five...K?"

"I don't know," she said, filling a heaping forkful. "I only ever ran in miles."

Pilar toyed with the food on her plate, looking worried. "Loup, I'm not sure I can do this. What if we made a mistake?"

"Then we'll leave," Loup said promptly. "But, Pilar, you haven't even *tried* yet."

She sighed. "I know. I'm just beginning to think this was a bad idea. And I don't know if we even *can* leave. Magnus said he'd buy me a ticket to Huatulco or wherever, but he never said anything about you."

"You're just tired."

"You know what's weird?" Pilar glanced out the windows. "I'm not. I'm wide-awake. It's dark out and I'm not even tired."

Loup smiled. "That's not exactly a bad thing, Pilar."

She brightened. "Ooh, true."

In the morning it was a different story. The old-fashioned telephone in their bedroom rang and rang, insistent. Pilar murmured and grumbled in her disrupted sleep, shoving Loup. "You go, baby. Please?"

"Okay, okay!" Loup stumbled out of bed. "Yeah, hi. Yeah, you're right. We forgot to set it. Okay. Thanks, Adelaide."

"What?" Pilar gave her a bleary glance.

"Breakfast." Loup yawned. "Gymnasium."

"Now?"

"Yeah, now."

They put on the clothing Adelaide had provided for them: black track pants and matching jackets with the Global Security logo on the breast, black tank tops with a larger version of the logo. They'd been provided with seven identical outfits. Loup eyed Pilar, who was putting her hair in a ponytail.

"What?"

"Nothing. I never saw you wear anything like that before."

"Do I look stupid?"

"Pilar, you'd look good wearing a plastic bag."

She yawned and sat on the bed to tie her shoes. "You do. You look like a cute little corporate ninja. With a serious case of sex hair," she added. "You might want to run a comb through that mess, baby."

"Oh, fuck."

Pilar rubbed her eyes. "What time do you think it is in Huatulco?"

Loup, working on her hair, glanced at the clock. "About one thirty in the morning."

"This is gonna suck."

"Uh-huh."

Still half-asleep, they stumbled downstairs to the kitchen and forced down black coffee, scrambled eggs, and sausage.

"Wow," Pilar said. "You're not even hungry!"

"I'm not even *awake*!"

"All right, dears!" Adelaide appeared in the doorway, bright and cheerful. "Mr. Clive's waiting for you in the gymnasium. Step lively!"

She led them briskly through the manor to a huge room that looked like it might have been a banquet hall once. Now it was filled with gleaming exercise equipment, weight benches, and punching bags. A short, compact man with a bald head was awaiting them on an empty mat, and there were a handful of other people using the equipment—Ben Rogers and several other youngish men.

"Here they are, Mr. Clive!" Adelaide said cheerily.

"Huh." He folded his muscular arms over his chest and regarded the sleepy-eyed pair. "Which one of you...?" His gaze settled on Loup. "You, right? You don't look like so much. And you're shorter than I expected."

She stifled a yawn. "Sorry, sir. Can't help my height. And I'm not at my best today."

"That's plain." His voice hardened. "Do you expect me to cut you some kind of slack because you're *special*?"

"No."

"Do you think I'm being mean, hauling you out of your nice cushy beds at this hour?" he pressed her. "Mean and nasty?"

"Honestly?" Loup said, ignoring Pilar's nervous attempt to hush her. "A little, yeah."

Clive thumped a fist into his palm and fixed them both with a glare. "Listen, girlies. In this business, you don't get to choose when trouble comes. Could be in the wee hours of the night when you've been on your feet all day, you're feeling rotten and fagged, and you just want to go home. Unnerstand?"

"Yeah, I think so."

"I can teach you." He pointed at Loup. "Word is you've done a bit of boxing, eh? That's good. I'm not gonna teach you a whole lot of that nancy-pants martial art shit. Half that shit goes clear outta your head in a real scuffle. Just a handful of straightforward moves. Most important, I'll teach you to *use* 'em. First, I wanna see how you think on your feet." He lifted a whistle that hung on a cord around his neck to his lips and gave a short blast.

Everyone else in the room converged on them.

"Fuck!" Loup felt a pair of strong arms wrap around her from behind, pinning her arms—and then an involuntary start of surprise in her attacker's body. She wrenched free and spun, driving a quick jab into Ben Rogers' belly. He flew backward, mouth gaping. Her other attacker turned white and took a step away from her.

"Hold it!" one of the others called. He had one arm around Pilar's throat and her left arm twisted behind her back. "We'll hurt her!"

"The fuck you will!" She grabbed Mr. Clive from behind before he could move and locked her left forearm over his throat, pressing hard. "Let her go or I swear I'll break his fucking neck!"

He raised one hand in acquiescence.

Pilar's attacker released her. "It's just an exercise, doll!"

"Oh, my!" Clive gasped, bending over. He coughed. "Oh, my, my, my! What *are* you like at your best, sunshine?"

"Faster," Loup said curtly. "And better at pulling my punches." She glanced down at Ben Rogers. "Sorry."

Struggling to regain his wind, he didn't answer.

"So that's what has Magnus all in a twit." Clive straightened, eyes bright. "You're a natural, you are. Not just a fighter. Did you see?" he asked Rogers, who was slowly climbing to his feet, his breathing raspy. "Didn't even flinch at their bluff. She went straight for the highest-value target in the room and controlled the situation on her own terms."

"I saw." He sounded disgruntled.

"Oh, my." Clive beamed. "Magnus is going to be very pleased with his investment."

"Half of it, anyway," Pilar muttered, rubbing her arm.

"You didn't do too badly, sunshine," he said to her. "From what I saw before your girlfriend here went all Tasmanian Devil on us, you stomped his foot and elbowed his ribs. That's not bad tactics. If you knew how to throw a nice sharp elbow strike, you might have broken his hold." He smiled. "And if you'd been wearing a nice pointy high heel, he'd be hopping."

"Oh." She looked somewhat mollified.

"I like to see what's instinctive to you. That's what we'll build on, because that's always gonna be your first, well, instinct in a fight." Clive nodded at Loup. "You, I imagine you're always gonna lead with your fists. But no reason you can't add to your arsenal, and I can teach you a few holds that'll immobilize an attacker without threatening to crush his windpipe. Celebrity clientele don't like dead bodies, you hear?"

"Yes, sir."

"All right!" He clapped his hands. "Let's get to work." He demonstrated a couple of kicks to Loup. "Straight kick and a roundhouse. All you ever need. And it ain't about how high you go. That looks good in competition, but there are no fuckin' Queensberry rules out in the real world." He beckoned to Ben Rogers, who came over and obligingly aimed a high roundhouse kick at Clive's bald, shiny head. Clive caught his foot and mimed aiming a jab at Rogers' balls. "Get it?"

"Got it." Loup nodded. "I was in some street fights before I started boxing."

"Better and better! You too?" he asked Pilar.

She shook her head. "Nope."

"Ah, well." Clive considered them. "Taz, you wanna go work the bags and practice those kicks? I get the feeling you're gonna be a fast learner, and I gotta lotta work to bring sunshine here up to speed."

"Yeah, sure," Loup agreed.

"I thought you said I did okay," Pilar protested.

"You did." He laid a hand on her shoulder. "But, honey, you're starting at ground zero, and your little friend here's in a league of her own. Okay?"

"Okay."

For almost three hours, Clive drilled Pilar relentlessly while Loup worked the bags happily on her own, creating a steady percussive cacophony that echoed through the gymnasium. From time to time, Clive called over with words of advice. "Pivot on the roundhouse, darlin'! Power comes from the waist, just like a good punch."

"Ohmigod," Pilar groaned when they finally broke for the day. "I swear to God, this is gonna kill me."

Loup stroked her sweat-damp hair. "You did great."

"You did," Clive assured her. "This ain't easy, sunshine. This is boot camp."

"Ugh."

Lunch was served in the sunroom, where there were several small tables. They learned that other than Ben Rogers, their attackers were volunteers from a gym in a nearby village where Clive taught self-defense when he wasn't training recruits for Global Security.

"They're good lads," he told them. "Ooh, stovies!"

Loup blinked. "Huh?"

"Stovied tatties." Clive rubbed his hands together as one of the kitchen staff set a plate of mushy fried potatoes dotted with bits of beef, peas, and carrots before him. "One of me favorites."

"Leftovers." Pilar poked listlessly at hers.

"The best kind," he affirmed. "Don't get shirty, sunshine. And eat up. You've got Mr. Rogers yet to go!"

They took their leave of Clive after lunch and met Ben Rogers behind the manor at one o'clock sharp.

"Right, then." He eyed Loup warily. "Here's the story. By the end of six weeks, you've got to be able to do a five-K run and complete the obstacle course inside of an hour. Let's have a little run, shall we? And then we'll walk the course."

He led them on a run through the oak forest along clearly marked trails. Loup matched her pace to his and jogged effortlessly, enjoying the scenery and the minor challenges offered by the varying terrain.

Pilar struggled.

"C'mon, damnit!" Rogers urged her. "You've walked long enough, now move your arse! That's it, just a little farther. C'mon, c'mon... See? There's the manor, almost there... See? Here we are."

"Aw, fuck!" She gazed at the first obstacle in dismay.

"Hand over hand." He swung on the monkey bars, demonstrating. "See? Easy as pie!"

Pilar tried and dropped. "Ow!"

"You can do it," Loup said softly, hoisting her.

"Shut up."

Pilar fell on the monkey bars and fell off the balance beam. She did well enough on the over-and-unders, the belly crawl, and the trip-wire dodge. She scrambled up and down the net rope, complaining. She scaled the vertical ladder, then shuddered at the drop and climbed down manually, where Loup dropped to execute a neat four-point landing. She failed to hurdle the pit. The sloping assault wall at the end kicked her ass.

It was hard.

Very hard.

"Jesus." Pilar lay on the bed afterward, arms folded over her face. "I don't think I can move."

"Did you get hurt out there?" Loup asked.

"No. I don't know. I can't feel my body." She unfolded her arms with an effort. "Loup, whatever you do, *don't* tell me you know I can do it. Not right now. I know you believe in me and I love you to pieces for it, but right now I'm also trying real hard not to hate you a little bit for having this be so fucking easy. And I'm not real proud of thinking like Sabine."

"Not even close." Loup stretched out beside her. "Pilar, we don't have to do this. You could be on a plane to Huatulco tomorrow. I'll figure out something."

"Huatulco." Pilar sighed. "No, we're doing it. *I'm* doing it. If for no other reason than to prove that fucking bitch wrong."

"You can. You will."

"Shut up."

TWELVE

"Ohmigod." Pilar groaned and burrowed into the blankets when the alarm went off. "I can't do it."

"Pilar..."

"Don't say it."

"Zee day you fail out of training vill be von of zee hoppiest days of my life," Loup intoned.

"Shit," Pilar muttered. She pushed herself upright. "Ow, ow! Fuck! I hurt *everywhere*. Muscles I didn't even know I *had* hurt."

At breakfast, Adelaide eyed Pilar without comment and set a couple of aspirin tablets beside her juice. In the gym, Clive chuckled. "You're moving like you're a hundred years old, sunshine."

Pilar glared at him. "Yeah, thanks."

"Just wait," he said cheerfully. "The second day's the worst."

She groaned.

He taught Loup a series of simple elbow and knee strikes and set her to work on the bag. "That's it. Just keep practicing."

"Can I try some combinations?" she asked.

"Not yet." Clive shook his head. "Get the basics down first." He watched her assault the heavy bag. "You've got good discipline, Taz. Is that a geemo thing? Are all of them like you?" He scratched one ear. "Mr. Lindberg's been on the lookout for ages, but you're the first one I ever met."

"I don't know." She thought of her wild, rambunctious cousins in Huatulco. "No, I don't think so."

"What in the world made you decide to take up boxing?"

"Guy killed my brother in the ring." She concentrated on driving her knee into the bag like a steady, blurred piston. "Guy was a—a GMO, like me. I wanted to fight him."

"Did you win?"

"Uh-huh."

He patted her back. "Good girl."

For the rest of the morning, Clive concentrated on working one-on-one with Pilar. That afternoon, Rogers led them on another run. He skipped the obstacle course in favor of setting up a regimen of strength training.

"We're going to build up your upper-body strength," he told Pilar with grim determination. "You're going to get over that goddamn wall or die trying."

"Don't remind me."

The second day *was* worse than the first. By the time their afternoon training session ended, Pilar could barely move. She hobbled back to their room and collapsed on the bed.

Loup winced. "Want me to give you a back rub?"

"No." Pilar closed her eyes. "I don't want anyone touching me. Not even you. I don't want my *clothes* touching me."

"Hot bath? It'll help."

"Yeah, okay."

She emerged from the bath moving marginally less stiffly and sat gingerly on the bed. "You're not even sore, are you?"

Loup shrugged in apology.

Pilar sighed. "Baby...don't take this wrong. I know how hard you've worked. But right now we're trying to do the same thing and it's kinda killing me. And I know you want to help, but you can't. You're the opposite of helping."

"I'm sorry," she offered.

"I know, I know. It's not your fault." Pilar was silent a moment. "Loup, I'm scared, okay? I don't like it here. Addie's nice and Clive's okay, but no one really wants me here. And I *don't* know if I can do it."

"We don't have to—"

"I know, I know!" Pilar interrupted her. "But the thing is, it's perfect for you, isn't it? It's exactly the kind of thing you were born to do."

Loup didn't answer.

"Magnus was right," Pilar said. "I don't want to hold you back. Maybe it was stupid to think we could work as a team."

"I don't want to do it without you," Loup said steadily. "Pilar, you're the only person in the world outside of Santa Olivia that I'm absolutely, positively sure I trust with my whole heart. And I need that. You and Tommy, Father Ramon and Sister Martha, all the Santitos, you taught me that much. You don't have to be a secret agent bodyguard. All you have to do is get through this training."

Pilar gave her a reluctant glance. "What happens if I really *can't*, Loup? I don't want you to give it up for me."

"Not your choice." Loup shook her head. "Anyway, you asked me to give up the fight, and I didn't. I owe you one."

"Yeah, but that was different. I'd be keeping you from something good, not something that would get you thrown into prison. And I think...I think I'd have a hard time living with myself if I did that to you." Pilar stared at the ceiling, coming to a decision. "Okay. I'll keep trying. But I think I kinda need to pretend you don't exist for a while if I'm gonna get through this." She yawned. "That asshole Rogers says I oughta see a big difference in a couple of weeks."

Loup blinked, confused. "So...you want to pretend I don't exist for a couple of weeks?"

"Okay, that's not exactly right, but kind of. Just to keep myself from feeling all jealous and inadequate like that fucking Sabine." She gave Loup a pleading look. "I know it sounds weird, but I think it'll help."

"Okay," Loup agreed without really getting it. "I'll talk to Addie about getting a room of my own until then."

"No, don't do that. I still want you here."

"Pilar, you're not making any sense!"

"I know." She flopped backward onto the bed. "Just humor me, okay?"

"I guess."

For the next two weeks, they lived in an odd coexistence. In the gym and on the trail, Pilar ignored Loup altogether, concentrating on her trainers' instructions. The rest of the time, she only mostly ignored her.

It hurt, an unfortunate reminder of the year that had followed Tommy's death, a year in which Pilar had refused to talk to her, a year of grief, confusion, and bewilderment in which Loup hadn't understood that Pilar's rejection was born of a fear of losing her.

At least this time, she understood, and understood that if Pilar failed at this, it would change things between them. That thought evoked a sensation of nothingness that told her it was an outcome to fear.

"Are the two of you not speaking?" Adelaide asked Loup after the third silent meal she and Pilar spent together. "You seemed so very fond!"

"No, we're okay, I think. She's pretending I don't exist for a while."

"Whatever for?"

"Because this is really hard for her and she doesn't want to be jealous of me."

"Hmm." Adelaide looked doubtful. "That *almost* makes sense."

"But not quite, right?"

"Well." She laid a hand on Loup's shoulder, then withdrew it. "If it gets her through it, I suppose it does."

By the end of the first week, Clive let Loup throw whatever combinations she wanted on the heavy bag. She experimented, mixing punches and kicks with elbow and knee strikes. He gave her a lesson on how to fall and taught her a few basic throws, then let her practice with Ben Rogers while he focused on working with Pilar.

"Ah, shite!" Rogers grunted as he hit the mat. "Not so hard."

"Sorry. I'm learning."

He sat up and rubbed the small of his back. "Clive oughta be working with you. No one takes a fall like Clive."

"He's working with Pilar."

"Yeah, what's the story there? We're supposed to go all out busting our bollocks to get your sweetheart through this, and you're not even talking?"

"She's concentrating," Loup informed him.

"She's trying hard, that's for sure," he admitted grudgingly.

Pilar did better on her second attempt at the obstacle course. She made it almost all the way across the monkey bars and didn't fall off the balance beam, but she chickened out on the drop and failed to clear the pit, though not by much. It was the steep assault wall at the end that was the worst.

"You'll get it," Rogers assured her. "You've got five weeks to go."

"Ow," Loup said that night in their room when Pilar undressed. She had serious bruises blossoming on both shins. "Poor you!"

"It's the fucking pit," Pilar said briefly. "I hit the edge."

It was hard to resist the urge to encourage her. "Pilar, if you can handle falling into the pit, you can handle the ladder drop."

"I didn't fall into the pit on purpose." Pilar shot a glare her way. "And don't talk to me. Not yet."

"Okay, okay." Loup picked up her travel book and started reading.

On the second week, Clive eased up on the ferocity of his training and began interspersing their sessions with lectures.

"Bear in mind that everything I'm teaching you is a last resort, girlies," he said to them. "You've got to know it and be prepared to use it, but your business is to protect the client. You want to learn to spot trouble and head it off in advance. If you can't, your first move is to extract the client. Get 'em the fuck out of there. If you can't do *that*, try to control the situation. Keep a cool head, keep it from escalating. Understand?"

They nodded.

"Nine times out of ten, you can talk someone out of whatever piece of dumbwittery they're contemplating. But that tenth time..." He raised a finger. "You've got to be prepared. And no half measures. What you start, you finish."

"What about, like, assassins and stuff?" Loup asked.

Clive smiled a little. "You're not likely to be guarding heads of state, sweetheart. Or at least not as part of a team specializing in counterterrorism. You're a novelty act—for show, for bragging rights."

"Oh." She looked disappointed.

"Don't worry. If you get through this first six weeks, I'll still teach you the basics of threat assessment. Just don't think you're going to be running around shouting 'He's got a gun!' and tackling bad guys. More likely you'll be fending off some puffed-up pop star's groupies or attending a meeting with some Japanese corporate mogul who wants to show the world he can afford to hire the one and only."

"Sitting the babies," Loup murmured.

The corners of Pilar's mouth twitched.

"What's that?" Clive asked. "Oh, babysitting. Too right."

The routine—and Pilar's silence toward Loup—continued mostly unbroken for another week. Clive decided Pilar had made enough progress to spend some time working the bag on her own, and spent some time with Loup on throws and locks and what he called comealong grips.

"How's your hand strength?" he asked, sticking out his own. "Give me a good squeeze."

She squeezed.

"Ow! Mind me bones." He shook out his hand. "See, then, you can pull this off. Simplest thing in the world." He grabbed her right wrist and bent her thumb backward. "Most people'll come along nice and quiet rather than suffer a dislocated thumb. Separates us from the animals, you know." He let her go and looked thoughtfully at her. "I know I said no nancy-pants shit, but there's a fellow not far from here teaches jujitsu and knows all about nerve points. Most folks don't have the touch for it, but you might."

"Okay," she agreed.

At the end of the second week, Pilar made her third attempt on the obstacle course. She made it across the monkey bars with a good deal of difficulty, did the ladder drop with a good deal of trepidation, and cleared the pit.

Not the wall.

"I just don't have anything left by the time I get there," she said to Rogers.

"You will." He rubbed her shoulders. "Keep working that upper body."

On the following Sunday, they were actually given an afternoon of free time. Loup went for a long run by herself, bypassing the forest to explore the countryside. Afterward she wandered into the gym, and found Pilar doing pull-ups. She stood for a moment, watching her.

"Hey," Pilar gasped, unexpectedly acknowledging her. "You're *so* totally checking me out."

"Maybe." Loup smiled. "Look at you, all *muy macha*."

She dropped. "I can only do six or seven. But that's six or seven more than I could do two weeks ago." She thrust out her bare arm, tensing her muscles. "Look. You can see the difference."

"Pretty impressive," Loup agreed.

"Do you like me better this way?"

"Better? No. I like you every way."

"Good." Pilar sighed. "Because if I get through this, I swear to God, I'm never working out this hard again in my life."

"Does this mean I exist again?"

"Yeah, I guess." She smiled wryly. "I don't know for sure if I'll pass, but at least I don't think it's gonna kill me anymore. Anyway, I miss you."

Loup shook her head. "Pilar..."

"I know, I know. Shut up. It worked for me." Pilar grabbed her hand. "Hey, let me try and throw you."

On the mat, she executed a fairly decent hip throw. Loup ignored all of Clive's instructions on falling and caught Pilar around the waist at the last minute, bringing her down atop her and cushioning her fall.

"Oof!" Pilar caught her breath. "No fair, baby." She kissed Loup's throat. "But I'm not exactly complaining."

"Oh, you don't get off that easy." Loup rolled her over. She pinned Pilar's lower body with her legs, bracing herself on her arms above her. "Two weeks!"

"I told you why!" Pilar wound her arms around Loup's neck, trying in vain to tug her head down. "Don't be mean."

"I'm not." Loup relented and kissed her.

"Mmm." Pilar got her legs free and scissored them around Loup's waist, trying to roll her. Loup let her, enjoying Pilar's pleasure in her newfound strength. Her hands slid under Loup's tank top as she kissed her. "Now *I* have *you*."

"Inneresting technique," a voice above them offered.

Pilar scrambled to her feet, flushing. "We were just...umm..."

"I can *see* what you were doing, sunshine," Clive said mildly. "All made up, are we?"

"Are we?" Loup asked Pilar.

She smiled sidelong at her. "Yeah."

Clive cleared his throat. "Well, it's very commendable to find you both in the gymnasium during your free time, but if all you're planning on practicing is snogging and groping, I suggest you take it elsewhere."

"Okay." Pilar pulled Loup to her feet and began leading her toward the door.

"I didn't mean this very second!" he called after them.

"Too late!" Loup called over her shoulder.

It was a blissful relief to have things back to normal between them, but it didn't fix everything. By the end of five weeks, Pilar could complete a 5K run and do the whole obstacle course—even the wall.

She just couldn't do it in under an hour.

"More cardio," Rogers advised her. "You've got to push yourself, sweetheart."

"I *am*!"

"Push harder."

They got a break from the hand-to-hand training in the final week when Clive taught them marksmanship.

"We provide discreet security," he said. "When you carry, you're gonna carry concealed." He slid a small pistol from a side pocket holster. "This here's what we call a Baby Glock. It's a nine-millimeter subcompact semiautomatic pistol, and before you get your hands anywhere near it, you're getting a long talk on gun safety."

It was a long talk, indeed.

"Is it loaded?" Pilar asked when he finished, eyeing it fearfully.

He shook his head. "Not yet."

After further demonstrations, he led them to the firing range, taught them the correct stance and grip and how to align the sight and pull the trigger. He had them dry-fire the pistol until he was satisfied, then showed them how to load it and check the chamber, drilling them over and over.

"Right." He pushed a button, and a paper target with the outline of a man slid forward. "Here goes."

The pistol cracked three times in succession, spitting out casings. Pilar jumped and put her hands over her ears. Three neat holes appeared around the edges of the figure's marked heart. Clive pushed the button again and removed the target, summoned a new one.

"Give it a go, Taz," he said, handing the pistol to Loup.

She aligned the sight and squeezed the trigger. The pistol kicked in her hand. A hole appeared in the target.

"Nicked his spleen," Clive observed. "Try again."

She fired it three more times, getting closer to the heart.

"Not bad. It takes practice." His Dataphone rang. He fished it out and glanced at it. "I've got to take this. Sit tight until I finish. No unsupervised gunplay." They nodded, and he answered his phone, walking a distance away. "Yes, Mr. Lindberg."

"Ooh, Magnus." Pilar nudged Loup. "Go eavesdrop, baby. You've got really sharp ears."

"Okay," Loup agreed.

She drifted closer toward Clive, pretending to examine the target mechanism.

"Yessir, absolutely," he was saying. "Not a problem in the world. If I had ten of Loup, I could invade a small country." Pause. "To be honest, I've not made up me mind." His voice was troubled. "She's a nice girl and she's trying hard. If she were just some bird taking a self-defense class, I'd pass her with flying colors, but the caliber you want for this line of work?" He shook his head. "I'm not sure." He listened. "That's Rogers' lookout. She might make it, she might not. My call, that's purely on defense skills." He listened some more. "We'll see. Maybe she'll surprise me."

Loup sidled back.

"Well?" Pilar asked.

She shook her head, the lie making her heart ache a little. "Nothing."

"All right, then." Clive came striding back. "You ready, sunshine? Your turn."

Pilar handled the loaded gun gingerly.

"It's not gonna bite and it's not gonna go off by itself," he said. "Widen your stance a touch. Flexed elbows, locked wrists. There you go."

She lined up the sight and pulled the trigger. The pistol fired and a hole appeared in the target, slightly off center in the heart. She blinked. "Ohmigod. Did I do that?"

"Jaysus!" Clive breathed. "Can you do it again?"

She fired three more times, holding the pistol with increased confidence with every shot. All but one of the shots pierced the target's heart, and the one that missed, missed by only inches. "Holy shit!"

"Holy shit, indeed." He called up the target, unhooked it, and presented it to her with a bow. "Nice shooting, sunshine. Who'd of thought it, eh?"

Pilar accepted it, dazed—but not so dazed that she didn't remember to keep the pistol safely pointed at the ground. "No kidding."

Loup smiled happily. "Surprise!"

Clive narrowed his eyes at her. "Little pitchers have big ears, methinks."

"Huh?"

"Hey, Clive?" Pilar folded her target. "Is Sabine a good shot?"

"That one?" He scratched his head. "Just missed qualifying for the Moscow Olympics. I forget which event. It might have been the fifty-meter rifle. Why?"

Pilar sighed. "No reason."

THIRTEEN

B en Rogers clicked off his stopwatch. "Sixty-one minutes, seventeen seconds."

Pilar dropped to the ground, gasping for breath. *"Fuck!"*

"How bad do you want it?"

She glared up at him. "After all this? Bad!"

He shrugged. "Tomorrow's the day. What can I tell you, sweetheart? I've done all I can for you. Run faster."

At dinner Pilar was downcast, picking at her fish.

"You've gotta eat," Loup said. "You're gonna need the energy. Forget the fish, eat your fries. Floyd always said carbs were best."

She shook her head. "Doesn't matter," she said in a defeated, weary tone. "I've tried and tried. I can't do it, Loup. I can't crack an hour. I'm sorry, I really am. And they don't call them fries here, baby. They call them chips."

"Whatever. Pilar, let me pace you tomorrow."

"Huh?"

"On the run," Loup said patiently. "Rogers is right; you need to run faster. You're holding back because you're still scared of the obstacle course."

Pilar scowled. "No offense, baby, but what do you know about being scared?"

"A lot in some ways, because I have to work harder to figure it out. Not just for me, for other people, too. You're scared. But you don't have to be." She slid one hand up Pilar's arm, squeezed her bicep gently. "You're *muy macha* now, *sí*? You're not gonna fall off the monkey bars, and you *can* make it over the wall, even if you're tired."

A faint ray of hope dawned on Pilar's face. "You really think it would work?"

She nodded. "I can keep time in my head really good. All those years of running on that stupid fucking treadmill in the stupid fucking garage. I won't go fast, only exactly as fast as you need to go to finish under an hour. All you've gotta do is keep up with me."

"Promise?"

"I promise." Loup smiled. "We can do this."

Pilar smiled back at her. "Okay." She took a deep breath. "I'm picturing the look on that bitch Sabine's face when she hears I passed."

"Hold that thought," Loup advised her.

The following day, Clive was there to observe the trial. Loup told him her idea.

"Yeah, go ahead," he said. "But when you hit the obstacle course, I want you out in front, girlie. I don't want any reason to remotely *suspect* you've done something like give her a boost over the wall."

"I wouldn't!" she protested.

"You might if we'd thought of it," Pilar said pragmatically.

"Ready?" Rogers held up the stopwatch. They nodded. "Go!"

They took off running down the wooded trail. Loup let Pilar settle into her pace, then increased it marginally, marking time in her head and holding on to hope. They ran and ran, sneakered feet thudding softly on the dirt trail. "Keep up," Loup warned when Pilar lagged slightly. "I'm cutting it real close like I promised."

Pilar nodded, not sparing breath to speak.

They ran.

"Okay," Loup said, seeing the end of the trail approaching. "When we reach the lawn, I'm gonna pull ahead. You're good. Just hit the course as hard as you can, just like in training."

Another breathless nod.

On open ground, Loup went ahead of Pilar. She gauged her pace carefully—enough for Clive to see distance between them, not so much that it intimidated Pilar. She swung along the monkey bars, raced lightly along the balance beam, vaulted and ducked through the over-and-unders. Wriggled agilely under the belly crawl netting and danced through the trip wires. Scrambled up and down the rope netting and completed the ladder drop with fearless aplomb. Hurdled the pit, scaled the assault wall, and crossed the finish line. Rogers glanced at his stopwatch and gave her a brief nod.

All of them watched Pilar.

"C'mon," Rogers muttered over his breath, looking from her to the watch. "C'mon, c'mon, c'mon!"

She cleared the wall and ran the last few yards. He clicked the watch. She doubled over, gasping, hands braced on her knees. "Well?"

He was beaming. "Fifty-nine minutes, forty-six seconds."

She straightened. "Are you *serious*?"

"Too fucking right!"

"Ohmigod!" Pilar flung her arms around him.

"You did it, sunshine!" Clive shouted, grinning. She hugged him, too, kissing his cheek. "Way to go!"

"You." Pilar turned to Loup, grabbed her face, and kissed her. "Thanks, baby."

"Yeah." Loup grinned. "You were awesome."

Clive had his phone out. "Yessir, it's me, Mr. Lindberg. Yessir, just this minute. Uh-huh. With fourteen seconds to spare. Yessir, I'm passing her on the strength of her marksmanship. We're both passing her." He listened, smiling. "I will, sir. Bye now." He ended the call. "Mr. Lindberg sends his congratulations to both of you."

Dinner that night was a celebration. Clive, Rogers, and Adelaide all joined them for dinner and the table was adorned with a lush bouquet of peach-hued roses and an oversized ice bucket with an extra-large bottle of champagne in it. There was a note of congratulations tied around the neck of the bottle.

"A magnum from Magnus," Clive declared. "Right magnanimous! Shall I do the honors?"

"Sure," Loup agreed.

He popped the cork and poured out five glasses. Pale gold champagne fizzed softly in the tall flutes. "Savor it," he advised them. "Mr. Lindberg only sends the best."

"Did he sound surprised?" Pilar asked.

"Yeah." Clive smiled. "And rather tickled in the bargain."

"I think he kinda likes you, Pilar." Loup sipped her champagne. It was crisp and creamy all at once, tiny bubbles making her tongue tingle. "Wow. This is nothing like the stuff we had at Diego and Maria's wedding. You remember?" Pilar made a noncommittal sound. "You do. That's when I asked you why you weren't talking to me."

"Do you make a habit of it, dear?" Adelaide inquired.

"No!" Pilar said in exasperation. "I just...you had to be there, okay?" She blew out her breath. "You really think Magnus likes me?" she asked Loup.

"Uh-huh." She took another sip. "He loosens up around you."

"Mr. Lindberg expressed the opinion that he found you quite unintentionally charming," Clive confirmed, holding up his glass and studying the rising bubbles. "And he very much wishes to retain Loup's services. He's looking forward to exploring ways of employing you creatively as a team." He lowered his glass and tapped his temple with one finger. "Mind, you've got ten more weeks of training in which we'll be cramming your wee noggins with all sorts of knowledge. You're not out of the woods yet, girlies."

"Oh, give 'em a break, Clive!" Rogers said in a surprisingly good-natured tone. "They've earned the right to celebrate."

Pilar glanced at Loup. "Speaking of celebrating..."

"Oh, we will."

Later that night, with the luxury of a morning of free time to follow, they celebrated for a long, long time—until Pilar, breathless and writhing, her fingers tangled in Loup's hair, begged her to stop. "Fuck! I'm serious, baby! Stop, you've gotta stop. I can't take any more; you're gonna give me a heart attack."

Loup slithered up the length of her body. "Good thing you're in such awesome shape, huh?"

"No shit." Pilar closed her eyes, smiling. "And no fair. Give me a minute to catch my breath."

"Not tonight." She trailed her fingertips along the soft, taut skin of Pilar's inner thigh, higher and higher. "You're the one who worked your ass off. This is *your* celebration."

Pilar's eyes flew open. "You're not gonna—" Her back arched, one hand scrabbling at the bedclothes. "Oh, *shit!*"

By the time Loup was finished with her, she was beyond arguing.

"Jesus," she murmured, running her fingers idly through Loup's hair. "I don't know whether I love or hate the fact that you can do that to me without even trying."

"Oh, I was trying," Loup assured her.

"You know what I mean."

"Well, then I'm gonna go with love it."

Pilar laughed, then stretched, slow and languorous, shivering with lingering pleasure. "Yeah, me too."

"All those years," Loup said softly. "All those years, I never knew what it could be like to be with someone like this. I tried, but it never felt right, you know? Not for me, not for anyone else, no matter how much I wanted it to. Not even Mack, and he tried harder than anyone. It just made me feel lonely. And all those years, I kept thinking about you." She drew a line from the hollow of Pilar's throat to her navel. "It's still…awesome. Not just in that epic sex way, though yeah, that, too. But like the way Father Ramon used the word when he talked about God."

"I'm not sure Father Ramon believed in God, baby," Pilar said gently. "He wasn't really a priest, remember? He just put on the robes."

"No, I know. But he gave people what they needed. Awe. Hope."

"Yeah." She rolled onto her side, regarding Loup. "So did you, Santa Olivia. That town went fucking *wild* after your fight. I can't even imagine what it was like after you disappeared."

"*We* disappeared," Loup reminded her.

Pilar cupped her cheek. "Baby, you left behind an empty cell with a basket and a boxing robe in Santa Olivia's colors, and one big fucking mystery. I left behind one pissed-off Rory Salamanca. It's not the same thing."

Loup made a face. "Rory, yeah."

"Oh, hush." Pilar kissed her. "You know perfectly well why I left you, and perfectly well that I'll never do it again." She studied Loup's face. "We're going back someday, aren't we? After we make enough money doing this secret agent bodyguard shit. You're gonna do something stupid and heroic."

"Probably," Loup admitted. "I can't stand thinking about every-one we left behind."

"I figured." Pilar rolled onto her back, folding her arms beneath her head. "Do you actually have a plan?"

Loup shook her head. "Jaime and Jane were the ones who were good at making plans. I haven't figured it out yet."

"I'll try to make sure it's not *too* stupid." She blew out her breath. "Whatever it is, I'm just glad we're in it together."

"Me too." Loup hesitated. "Do you still hate it here?"

Pilar thought for a moment. "No, I guess not," she said. "I've done things I never thought I could. It's a good feeling. And I guess…I'm kinda curious to see what else I can do. It might turn out we need some of this stuff, you know?"

"Yep."

She freed one hand, tracing a line up Loup's spine. "So, *awe*, huh?"

Loup nodded, serious.

Pilar smiled. "Maybe you could show me just one more time."

She did.

FOURTEEN

Their education began in earnest the following day.

"All righty," Clive said. "Say you've been hired to escort a famous actress on a press junket for her new movie. It's, erm…let's say it's about an ass-kicking heroine, so her people wanted to hire the biggest badass girlie they could find as a nice PR stunt." He pointed at Loup. "What do you need to know?"

"Um…how to be a badass?"

He snorted. "Beyond that part, Taz."

She shrugged. "Where I'm supposed to be and what I'm supposed to do, I guess."

"It's a start," Clive allowed. "Everything starts with the itinerary.

Say you're picking her up at the airport. Over the course of two days, you're escorting her to the hotel, to a press conference, a couple of one-on-one interviews, a photo op, and a movie premiere. What do you need to know?"

"Where everything is?"

Another snort. "At a bare minimum." He walked them through the initial preparations involved in a job of that nature—ascertaining locations, routes, and travel times and alternate routes in case of trouble. "Not that you'll be driving," he added. "That's become a specialized job unto itself. But say you're being chased by a horde of paparazzi. You might need to use the driver's car as a decoy and nip into a cab. You've got to know the best route to get Missy Movie Star to her next engagement."

"How?" Pilar asked.

"Homework and preparation, sunshine," Clive said. "You'll have access to Global's databases and navigational services, but we expect you to do the research ahead of time and commit it to memory, too. You've got to be able to think on the fly."

He went on at length about the various issues involved. Communicating with hotel and on-site security. Working with a celebrity's handlers. Venue surveillance. Memorizing discreet side entrances and exits. Detecting paparazzi stakeouts.

"Celebs are all different," he said. "Some avoid the press like the plague; some are pure media whores. Find out up front and deal accordingly."

"What about the shopping?" Pilar asked.

"Huh?" Clive rubbed his bald pate.

"Personal assistant stuff."

"Oh, right." He smiled wryly. "I'm gonna turn you over to Addie for that, sunshine. She spent years working for Mr. Lindberg in that capacity before he appointed her to manage the facility here."

"Is Addie a bodyguard, too?" Loup asked. Clive shook his head. "Okay, if Sabine's such a hotshot bodyguard, how come *she's* working as Magnus' assistant now?"

"Mr. Lindberg travels in, ah, unstable parts of the world on occasion," he said. "Comes with the territory—more and more as the world begins to recover from the effects of the pandemic. And it was Sabine's choice, not that it's any of your business. The lady can pick and choose her contracts. She chose to work with Magnus."

"Ooh!" Pilar said with delight. "She's totally got a crush on him. No wonder she's so jealous of you, baby."

"I don't think so," Loup said. "I'm not the one he found charming."

"Unintentionally charming," Pilar reminded her. "I'm not exactly sure that's a compliment."

Clive cleared his throat. "A little focus, girlies!"

He bombarded them with a further onslaught of information, jumping from evasive tactics to polite but firm methods of dealing with an aggressive press, to cultural dos and don'ts, like never showing the bottoms of your shoes in Japan. He informed them that they'd be learning basic CPR. He regaled them with the importance of always carrying a couple hundred euros' worth of cash in order to be able to pay out the myriad tips and bribes that kept the machinery greased. When he saw their eyes begin to glaze, he stopped.

"Enough, eh?" He grinned. "I'm rambling, I know bloody well I'm rambling. Don't worry, you'll learn it bit by bit. But right now you're all full of yourselves after completing basic, and I like to impress on new recruits that there's a hell of a lot more to this job than laying someone out on a mat. Got it?"

"Very much got it, sir," Loup agreed.

"Good girl." Clive fetched a pair of bound manuals with the Global Security logo on the cover. "These here are your bibles," he said reverently. "Learn 'em. Study 'em. Everything I'm telling you and more is in these."

Pilar flipped hers open, studying a diagram of a limousine blocked at an intersection. "Is there going to be a test?"

"You bet your ass, sunshine." He relented a bit. "Don't worry, you'll have real-time experience, too."

Loup brightened. "Like what?"

"Oh, opportunities to shadow some of our operatives on the job. Get your feet wet, as it were." Clive smiled smugly. "And if you're good girls and do your homework and keep up your training, I might just have a treat in store for you sooner than you think."

"What?"

"You'll see."

They spent the next two weeks immersed in learning the minutiae of good bodyguarding skills, while keeping up on their self-defense training and marksmanship, and for Pilar, additional sessions with Adelaide on the art of anticipating a client's every need and providing immaculate personal assistance. It was mentally exhausting in a way that basic hadn't been.

"Damn, you're a good shot, Pilar," Loup commented after a day on the range, lying crosswise on the bed, disinclined to study.

"Yeah, go figure." Pilar pored over the manual. "Okay, here's one. What's the best floor in a high-rise hotel?"

"Penthouse?"

"Nope." She swatted her lightly on the shoulder. "Fifth, sixth, or seventh. High enough to avoid the risk of thrown objects from street level, but lower risk in the event of a fire. You've gotta know this stuff, Loup."

"Yeah, yeah."

"You do!" Pilar swatted her again. "I know, I know. Magnus wants you so bad, they're gonna pass you no matter what. But it's about keeping *you* safe, too, baby."

"Okay." Loup hauled herself upright. "Give me another."

"Hmm." She studied the manual. "When approaching a doorway, do you proceed in advance or defer to the client and hold the door?"

"Defer?"

Pilar shook her head. "Proceed in order to assess threats."

"Well, that's not exactly keeping *me* safe, is it?"

"No." Pilar frowned. "But I think it's kind of a balance, you know? It's not like this is the safest job in the world. But if you learn to follow the rules, it keeps everyone safer. Okay?"

Loup reached for her manual. "Okay, okay! I'll study harder."

At the end of two weeks, Clive was sufficiently impressed that he allowed them their treat. "Kate's coming to town," he said, smug. "To Aberdeen. And I know the bloke in charge of their security. We've worked together, he and I. He's willing to do me a favor or two."

"Kate?" Loup asked, bewildered.

Pilar let out a squeal. "The *band*?"

"Too right." Clive nodded. "And a right bunch of prats they are. Still, you'll get a good look at real-time security in action." He tossed out a pair of security badges. "Get ready for a field day tomorrow, eh?"

The following day, they drove into the city. The Aberdeen Music Hall was swarming with technicians and crew members rigging lights and sound equipment. Clive walked them through the procedures that would take place that night.

"You'll spend a bit of time shadowing the fellows working the doors," he said. "They're the ones making sure nothing gets in that shouldn't. No knapsacks, none of those oversized purses that can hide God knows what. No bottles o' booze smuggled in baggy pants. It's dull work, but crucial. This is a small venue for those lads, and if things go to pot, it gets ugly fast. Old building, lousy fire exits."

"There and there?" Pilar pointed.

Clive smiled. "Good girl. Now, your biggest worry's gonna be groupies." He nodded at the area in front of the stage. "Six hours from now, this is going to be a seething mass of teenage flesh. Security's onstage to make sure no one rushes it, yeah, but also to make sure no one gets trampled."

He led them backstage and introduced them to a sturdily built man named Bill Jones, with a crooked nose and bristling gray hair. Bill eyed them dubiously.

"Sure they're not just fans, Clive?"

"Well, I'm not sure this one *isn't*." He put his hand on Pilar's shoulder. "But they're my trainees, sure enough."

"Awfully young."

"They've lived through a fair bit. Plus..." He grinned. "Give the man a nice, firm handshake, Loup."

She did.

"Bollocks!" Bill's eyes widened. "So it's true? A real live geemo?"

"Sure enough," Clive agreed.

"Right, then." He showed them where to stand backstage so that they'd be out of the way, yet have a view of the security team's work onstage. "Keep 'em out of trouble, Clive."

"I will."

Since they had time to spare, Clive led them on a walking tour of the city, along cobbled streets, past magnificent gray granite buildings and gorgeous flower gardens. He chuckled at the way Loup craned her neck and gazed all around, but without malice.

"Nice little city, eh?"

"Yeah."

They ate an early dinner at one of his favorite pubs in town, one that served stovied tatties. Clive ordered a half pint of lager.

"Mind, I'm only having a wee bit o' beer because we're not really on the job and nothing goes better with stovies," he said in warning. "Never, never, never drink on the job. You've got to have a clear head and keep your wits about you."

"You're telling me those security guys with the band never drink?" Pilar asked skeptically.

"Not the good ones." He fixed her with a stern look. "You find yourself at three in the morning with a pop star foaming at the mouth from a heroin overdose, you damn sure want to be sober, girlie."

"Ew."

"Too right."

They returned to the venue. There was a long line out front, almost all kids in their teens and twenties, with a marked preponderance of girls and young women. Clive led them around to the back entrance, where they were admitted after showing their badges.

"Here." A strapping guard shoved T-shirts at them. Like his, they had SECURITY printed in large letters on the front and back. "Hard to spot a badge in all that mess. Don't want anyone getting confused and thinking a couple fangirls snuck backstage."

"Do they do that?" Loup asked.

"Every chance they get."

After they'd donned their T-shirts, Clive escorted them to the front entrance and assigned each of them a security guard to shadow. For the better part of an hour, they hovered and observed as the guards confiscated backpacks and liquor bottles, examined purses, and patted down suspiciously baggy outfits.

"You're right," Loup said when Clive came to fetch them. "That's pretty goddamned dull."

"Eh?" He took a wax plug out of his ear. "Sorry. Can't abide the shrieking."

"Dull! It's dull."

"Dull's part of the business, girlie. Best you learn it now."

Backstage, they took up their posts, doing their best to stay out of the way of the sound and lighting technicians and security guards and dozens of other people hurrying around, swearing at equipment or muttering into earpieces. Beyond the stage, the hall filled to capacity and more.

"Kinda exciting, huh?" Pilar squeezed Loup's hand.

"Kinda, yeah." She squeezed back. "I think we're supposed to be acting professional."

"Oh, right." Pilar let go.

The crowd was calm enough during the opening act, a young soloist who played guitar and sat on a stool crooning love ballads. He played to tepid applause and finished his set in twenty minutes.

The crowd began chanting.

"Kate, Kate, Kate!"

"Ohmigod!" Pilar clutched Loup's arm, forgetting to be professional. "Here they come!"

She watched three skinny young men in T-shirts and jeans slouch past them. "Yep."

Massive shrieking ensued.

Onstage the members of Kate were transformed, bouncing and energized as they launched into their opening number. Loup ignored the band and watched the crowd surge forward, watched the vigilant response of the guards.

"Think we'll get to meet the band?" Pilar shouted in her ear over the noise.

She shrugged. "Dunno."

For a while, the concert was uneventful. Then there was a roiling in the crowded pit. One of the guards jumped into the fray, shoving and elbowing. He emerged with the slight, unconscious figure of a girl in his arms. He passed her off to one of the other guards, then hopped back onstage.

The second guard caught Loup's eye and beckoned with a nod as he passed with his burden. She followed him.

"You're one of Clive's girls, yeah?" he asked, laying the fan on a cot backstage.

"Yeah."

"Got a fainter. It happens." He popped the prongs of an oxygen tube into the girl's nostrils with the expertise of long practice. Her eyelids fluttered. He glanced at his watch. "She doesn't come around in a minute's time, fetch Bill. She comes around, keep a sharp eye on her. We get a lot of fakers." He pointed at the security doors toward the rear of the space. "Don't let her get back there."

"Okay," Loup agreed.

The girl came around. "Who're you?" she asked, narrowing eyes ringed with heavy black liner.

"Security," Loup said mildly. "You feeling okay?"

"Yeah." She sat up and plucked out the oxygen tube. "Yeah, thanks. I'll just be going back to my friends now, right?"

"Sure, I guess. Let me check." Not sure how to proceed, Loup glanced around for Bill or anyone else on the real security team. "Hey!"

The groupie was on her feet and sidling toward the back door.

Loup hauled her back toward the cot. "Oh, no. Sit here and wait."

"Okay, okay!" She pouted. "I'll sit right here."

"Fine." Two steps later, Loup glanced backward and spotted her making a beeline for the doors. "Fuck!" She put a come-along grip on the girl, who responded by whimpering and falling to her knees. "Oh, c'mon! I just need to find someone to tell me what to do with you."

"Don't hurt me!" the girl wailed. "You don't understand! I love them!"

"I'm not gonna fucking hurt you!" she said in disgust, pointing. "Sit. Wait."

The girl sat demurely on the cot for the time it took for Loup to turn her back, then bolted for the door.

"Ohh-kay." Loup scooped her up, tossed her over her shoulder, and held her in place while she searched, ignoring the girl's kicking and flailing. "Bill! Hey, Bill! Clive! Anyone?"

Onstage, the band played, heedless.

"I'm gonna spew down your back, I swear!" the girl gasped.

"Go right ahead." She found Bill muttering into his earpiece. "Sir? Excuse me, sir. What should I do with her?"

He stared for a second, then cracked a huge grin. "Fainter?"

"More of a faker, I think." Loup shifted her struggling burden, adjusting her grip. "Keeps making a run for the back door."

"Just put her back in the crowd." Bill pointed toward the stage. "Be...no, you know what?" His grin widened. "Don't be discreet."

"Okay."

The groupie yelled and thrashed. "Hey, baby," Pilar called in amusement as Loup passed her. "Where you going with that? Hope you're not planning to ravage her."

She turned, quick enough that the groupie made an *urping* sound. "More like drop her on her head. No, Bill told me to put her back."

"Ooh, you're going onstage?"

"Yep."

"Cool."

Onstage, the amplifiers created a wall of sound Loup could feel on her skin. She crossed the stage to the left of the band, heading in the general direction from which the girl had come. A few people in the audience pointed and stared. Behind her, the drummer faltered. The security guards turned around to look and began cracking up with laughter. The groupie kicked and squirmed. At the edge of the stage, Loup shaded her eyes against the glaring lights with her free hand and scanned the packed audience.

A gaggle of heavily made-up young teenage girls a few feet away waved frantically. Loup pointed to her burden with an inquiring look. They nodded and began to make room, jostling the crowd around them.

"Up you go," she said, her voice inaudible beneath the music and crowd noise. She swung the girl upright, catching her under her arms.

The groupie spat in her face.

"Oh, *yuck*." Loup eyed the dangling girl with disgust, half forgetting that she was still holding her off the ground. The girl stared back at her with a mix of defiance and terror. "Okay. Professional. Down you go."

She lowered the girl effortlessly to her waiting friends, then turned, wiping her face on the sleeve of her T-shirt before heading backstage. The security guards gave her beaming smiles and a thumbs-up salute. The lead singer and the bass player were carrying on as though nothing odd had occurred, but the drummer stared open-mouthed as Loup passed, still playing off the beat.

"Now *that* was *muy macha*," Pilar commented.

"That was disgusting." Loup wiped her face again. "She spat on me."

"Gross!"

"Yeah. So much for the glamorous life of a secret agent bodyguard."

FIFTEEN

Clive was pleased, although he wouldn't let them backstage to meet the band after the concert.

"No offense, sunshine, but I don't quite trust you not to act like a gobsmacked fan," he said to Pilar. "I don't mean to punish you for being a perfectly normal young lady, but if you're gonna be in this business, you've got to act professional. You made a reasonably good first impression tonight, and I don't want to spoil it. Understand?"

"I guess."

"And you!" He grinned at Loup. "You did a lovely job of setting the rumor mill in motion, darlin'."

"I was just doing what I was told."

"Yeah, and how!" Clive chuckled. "Mr. Lindberg will be tickled."

Even with the spitting, it had been an exciting break in their routine, but afterward, it was back to training and studies. The week that followed contained a crash course in basic electronic technology when he discovered that neither of them had more than the most rudimentary of skills.

"We didn't have computers that could talk to one another," Loup explained. "Just old ones that broke all the time. If it hadn't been for Jaime, we wouldn't have had any at all."

"Jaime would love this," Pilar murmured.

"Yeah." They exchanged a glance.

They learned quickly, and a week after the concert, Clive took the step of presenting them both with their own fully equipped Dataphones. "Have a care with those," he advised them. "That's a valuable piece of equipment."

Loup examined hers. "What's it do?"

"In a word? Everything."

They practiced using the GPS system to plot routes between hypothetical destinations. Clive gave them Global's limited-access password and they practiced accessing the database to obtain blueprints of hotels and public venues and perform risk-assessment analyses using software programs augmented by common sense. They practiced using the voice-activated software to make phone calls. They practiced mundane skills like making airline reservations. They snapped photos of each other.

"You took one of me sleeping?" Loup asked, flipping through Pilar's.

"Mm-hmm." She looked over her shoulder. "Look how cute you are! You look so innocent and harmless. Like a little cherub with messy hair."

"I like the ones I took of you better."

"In the lingerie?" Pilar smiled and ran a finger around the curve of Loup's ear. "Don't let Clive see them."

She shivered. "I won't."

They learned to drive, which proved to be an adventure.

For that, Clive took them to a professional driving school. They sat through the lectures and practiced on the simulator. Pilar managed tolerably well in and out of the classroom, but it was on the actual course that Loup struggled, unable to find the balance between her own fast reflexes and the unfamiliar velocity of a moving vehicle.

"Jaysus!" The instructor, a capable woman named Sally, grabbed a safety strap as Loup veered too sharply around an obstacle. "Slow down!"

She braked—too hard, too fast. They both lurched forward. "Sorry!"

"Right." Sally caught her breath. "You're overreacting, love."

"Yeah, I know," Loup said. "I'm having a hard time getting the feel of it, you know? I'm used to being in my own body. This is different."

The instructor blinked. "Well...yes."

"Never mind. I'll get it."

It took about twenty hours of driving time with Sally the instructor sitting white-knuckled beside her, but eventually Loup established a rapport with the physics of driving. Once she did, she got good, fast. When the course of instruction ended, she and Pilar took their official road tests and passed.

"Check us out," Pilar said with satisfaction, gazing at her brand-new international driver's license. "We are becoming women of many skills."

"Well, Guadalupe Herrera and Pilar Mendez are."

"Close enough."

Driving lessons were followed by a two-day seminar in first aid and CPR. They treated and resuscitated sophisticated dummies.

"Oops." Pilar, administering chest compressions, winced as the buzzer indicating she'd broken a rib went off. She watched Loup's technique. "How come you're not breaking any bones, Supergirl?"

"Dunno. I've had more practice being careful with other people's bodies, I guess."

"Mmm. True."

After they received their CPR certification, Clive split up their training, sending Pilar to work with Adelaide to learn more practical personal assistant skills, while he brought in the jujitsu instructor he'd mentioned earlier to teach Loup about pressure points. He was a quiet, unassuming man named Dominick, and he smiled with genuine pleasure when Loup shook his hand.

"Oh, my yes!" he said to Clive. "If she's got the knack, I can work with her."

Dominick demonstrated a few harmless pressure points to Loup—points on the wrist that weakened an opponent's grip when pressed.

"Wow." She felt her hand grow numb. "Cool."

"Others cause severe pain, even unconsciousness." He put his knuckle in the hollow below the hinge of her jaw, pressing lightly. "Here. A sharp blow can knock out an opponent, but even merely grinding produces severe pain."

"Show me."

Dominick hesitated, glancing at Clive.

"Go ahead," he said. "Taz can take it."

He ground his knuckle hard into her flesh, angling toward the center of her head. "Whoa!" Loup blinked at the resulting pain, stars shooting across her vision. She ignored it and concentrated on memorizing the exact spot, angle, and amount of pressure. "Okay, I think I got it."

Dominick removed his hand, uncertain. "You felt it?"

"Well, it hurt like hell, yeah."

"I thought perhaps your physiognomy made a difference. There's usually a more, ah, pronounced reaction."

"It's just pain. And I didn't think I was supposed to fight back," Loup said, glancing at Clive. "Was I?"

"No, no." He was grinning. "You did exactly right, darlin'. You're me golden girl. Can you do it?" He thrust out his pugnacious chin, tapped the spot below his jaw. "Show me."

She did.

"Gah!" Clive jerked away. "She's got the touch, sure enough." He looked at Loup with pride. "That's the finest in American engineering at work, Dom, me lad. They may be paranoid, belligerent bastards, but they do good work."

"Actually, it's Chinese," Loup offered. "And I wasn't engineered. Just born."

"Huh?" He peered at her. "You don't look Chinese."

"No, I know. My father was from Haiti. That's where the Chinese did the experiments, because it was a really poor country and they could get away with anything. The Americans took over the facility when my father was just a kid."

Clive scratched his head. "I'll be damned. I never knew that."

"Yeah," Loup agreed. "There's a lot people don't know."

He looked thoughtful. "Too right, that. You're nothing like I'd have expected a geemo to be."

"How's that?" Loup asked.

Clive pursed his lips. "I can't say, exactly. But not so...normal. You're a lot like a regular girl, Taz." He eyed her. "Except in all the ways you ain't."

She worked with Dominick for a few more days, learning a variety of pressure points—how to exploit them and the dangers of doing so. When they were finished, he bowed from the waist, smiling. "Thank you. It has been an unexpected privilege to teach such an unusual pupil."

Loup returned an exact copy of his bow. "Thanks, sir."

That night, lying in bed, she told Pilar about it.

"It reminded me of Floyd," Loup said. "Coach Roberts. He said something like that once. When I was deciding for sure to go through with the fight."

"I remember," Pilar said softly.

Loup shook her head. "No, it was after you left me so that I *could* decide. The day I actually did. I just wish I knew what happened to him. He risked everything to train me, you know?"

"Yeah." She propped herself on one elbow. " 'Cause it was the right thing to do, and he fucking well knew it. But we'll find out, baby. We will."

"You think?"

"Uh-huh." Pilar leaned over and kissed her. "I do."

The following day Clive summoned both of them together. He was all smiles.

"I've got another field trip for you, girlies."

Pilar brightened. "Is it another band?"

"No, but I think *you're* gonna like this one." He pointed at her. "It's Fashion Week in London and some high-and-mighty Italian designer who doesn't usually deign to leave the Continent is showing. Seems there's an issue with his usual security detail."

"Fashion designers need security?" Loup asked.

"This one thinks he does. Vincenzo Picco." Clive lowered his voice. "Word is he comes from a Mafia family."

"Like in the movies?" Pilar asked.

"It's just a rumor. But at any rate, he's a right paranoid bloke, and he always travels with a four-man detail. If this snafu doesn't get untangled in the next two days, Global's going to provide security." He pointed at Loup. "You'll be on his detail. You'll be junior to the others and do whatever they tell you."

"Okay."

"What about me?" Pilar asked.

"You'll assist his assistant." Clive smiled wryly. "Poor thing's going to have her hands full, and she doesn't know the first thing about London."

"Neither do I."

"Right." He nodded. "I suggest you start learning. Might want to access the Italian language module, too. I'm not sure how much English these folks speak." He looked serious. "If this comes through, this is going to be your first real test out in the field. So don't slack on this one, girlies. Make me proud."

They nodded.

"Hey, Clive?" Pilar said. "We probably need some new clothes, right? I mean, escorting a big designer and all."

He smiled and tossed a credit card at her. "As a matter of fact, you will. Hang on to this. If the deal's on, in two days you're going shopping."

"Ooh, yay!"

SIXTEEN

Operation Designer was a go.

Clive accompanied them to London on the train. "I'll introduce you to the head of the security team," he said to them. "And you can contact me at need. Other than that, you're gonna be on your own, understand? I'm not gonna hold your hands."

"Yes, sir."

"*Sì, signore,*" Pilar added.

He smiled a little. "Wish this hadn't come up before we got to deportment and elocution."

"Huh?"

"Proper manners and speech." He adjusted his tie. "You might not think it, but I can put on a posh act when I need to. Just...try to act like well-bred young ladies, eh?"

"Certainly, sir!" Loup sat ramrod straight.

"Oh, go on!" He laughed. "Be yourselves, but mind your manners. Be polite and professional. Remember you're representing Global Security."

"What happens if we screw up?" Pilar asked.

"Depends on how bad of a cock-up it is," Clive said cheerfully. "You're bound to slip up here and there. But if we end up with an unhappy client..." He made a throat-slitting gesture. "Could end your career before it starts, sunshine."

"Oh." She turned on her Dataphone. "Think maybe I'll study that dossier on this Vincenzo guy some more. Um...Mr. Picco, that is."

"Good girl," he said in approval.

Loup put in her earpiece and listened to Italian lessons, watching the Scottish countryside pass outside her window.

They arrived in London at dusk and took a cab to the hotel, a luxurious place overlooking a green park.

"All righty," Clive said after they checked in. "The rest of the team's already here. We're on our own until we pick up the client at Heathrow tomorrow morning. Let's meet for dinner in the Grill Room in an hour and you can meet the others."

"Okay," Loup agreed.

"Yes sir, sir!"

"Enough!" he said to Pilar. "You're not in the army, sunshine."

In the hotel room, Pilar explored the amenities while Loup unpacked. "Oh, cute!" She showed Loup a miniature sewing kit. "Hey, you gonna wear one of those new white dress shirts tomorrow, baby?"

"Yeah, Clive said to. White shirt, black pants. Why?"

"I'd like to take the seams in a little." Pilar pulled a white button-down shirt out of the closet and examined it. "It's a cute cut, but it's not tailored quite *perfectly* for zee toned phee-zeek."

Loup smiled. "I like when you get all domestic."

"For you and you alone. Remember the boxing robe?" She put the shirt back and tossed the sewing kit in her purse. "Probably take too long to do by hand. Maybe I'll try it when we get back. Addie's got a sewing machine."

"Okay." Loup's smile turned wistful. "I loved that robe. I wish I hadn't had to leave it behind."

"That's okay." Pilar kissed her cheek. "All part of the mystery, Santa Olivia. It's probably in a shrine somewhere. *I* wish I'd had the nerve to watch the fight. Watch you walk out wearing that robe in front of all of Outpost, then kick that guy's ass." She paused. "You know, it's funny. I think if it were happening today, I would. And I don't think I ever would have left you in the first place, even knowing I was gonna lose you. I think I would have stayed no matter how much it hurt."

"You were always stronger than you thought, Pilar."

"Maybe. I think a lot of it's being with you." She shook her head. "Anyway, enough being all serious."

"You started it!"

"I know, I know."

In an hour's time, they found their way to the restaurant, where Clive was waiting with three tall, good-looking youngish men in suits and ties. Their gazes flicked back and forth between the two girls as Clive made introductions, settling on Loup.

"So you're the geemo," said the leader, Henry Kensington. He shook her hand with a slight flinch. "Welcome to the team."

"Thanks. It's not official yet."

"Sounds like it's just a matter of time." His tone was neutral.

Throughout the dinner, Henry quizzed them intensively about the itinerary, his demeanor easing only when he was satisfied that both of them had memorized it fairly well. But it wasn't until Loup ordered a second entree that he left off talking shop.

"Working the expense account, eh?" he said without malice.

"No." She took a bite of salmon. "Not on purpose, anyway. They serve small portions here."

"Taz here eats like a horse," Clive informed him. "It's her metabolism."

"Taz?"

He grinned. "Old-time cartoon. One of the classics. Tasmanian Devil. You never saw it?" He mimed a whirlwind with one hand. "You've gotta see the girl in action. Though, ah, I hope it's not necessary."

"Can't imagine it would be," one of the other bodyguards said laconically. "Not over a goddamn fashion designer."

"Don't get careless," Henry warned him, eyeing Loup with curiosity. "I don't suppose you'd like to offer a demonstration?"

She glanced around the restaurant with its gilded fixtures and elegant diners, silverware clinking softly and the murmur of conversation. "Here? Um, no."

"No, of course not." He smiled ruefully. "Right, then. We'll meet in the lobby at eight o'clock sharp."

After dinner, they returned to the room.

Loup flung herself on the bed with a sigh. "Why do they always want a demonstration?"

Pilar picked up the remote and turned on the TV. "Because they do. They're curious, that's all. Does it bother you?"

"A little, I guess." She watched the channels flip past. "I mean, I know, I get it. I just get a little tired of it, you know? It's been going on since I was ten years old and C.C. tried to punch me in the face to see if it was true."

"C.C. did? Our C.C.?"

"Uh-huh."

"What'd you do?"

"Knocked the wind out of him," Loup said absently. "Quickest way to shut people—hey." She shot upright. "Pilar, go back, go back!"

"Where?"

She snatched the remote from her and flipped back to an international news channel. "Holy shit!"

"Oh my God." Pilar stared at the screen. "It's Miguel fucking Garza!"

They both stared, riveted.

Miguel was being interviewed in an undisclosed location by Senator Timothy Ballantine from Virginia. The camera cut back and forth
between the two men. The senator was statesmanlike and grave,
asking probing questions about Outpost 12, the town once known
as Santa Olivia, Texas. Miguel Garza answered every question with
blunt gravitas, his broad face filling the screen, his answers excoriat-
ing the American government.

"Holy *shit*!" Loup leaped to her feet. "Go, Mig!"

"He got out," Pilar said, dazed. "He actually got out, and that senator guy found him like you told him to! And he's...he's..."

"He's being a fuckin' hero," Loup said softly, splaying her fingers
and touching the television screen. "Aw, Mig! I told you so."

The coverage cut away.

"Shit," Pilar murmured.

"It's happening." Loup whirled, eyes shining. "Things are moving,
changing. And we made it happen!"

"*You* did, baby."

"You and me, we're a *we*."

"Shit," Pilar repeated, taking the remote back and flipping channels in the hope of finding more coverage. "God, I want to know
more!"

They searched in vain for almost an hour before Loup yawned
and suggested they give up. "We can check the news feeds tomorrow.
Right now, I think we'd better get some sleep. Big day tomorrow."

"Okay."

In bed, Pilar curled against her back, warm and soft.

"Hey, Loup?"

"Hmm?"

"You don't have a thing for Miguel, do you?"

"No!"

"You sure?"

Loup made an exasperated sound and rolled over. "Of course I'm
sure! I *like* Miguel, yeah. I know he's crude and a bully and an asshole sometimes, but he's a decent guy under it all." She was quiet a
moment. "He didn't help train me just to get a ticket north. In the
end, I think he would have done it anyway. Like you said Floyd did,

because it was the right thing to do. And he didn't have any reason to feel guilty about Tommy's death like Floyd did." She touched Pilar's cheek. "When Tommy died, it left a big hole in my heart."

"I know," Pilar whispered.

"Yeah, well, in his own grouchy, pervy way, Miguel helped fill it. Okay? I lost the best big brother in the world. Mig's the big brother I never wanted, but kinda can't help caring a lot about anyway. The only person I have a *thing* for is you."

"Okay, okay! I was just asking."

"Good."

"The *only* person?" Pilar asked after a moment.

"Since I was fourteen years old," Loup said drowsily. "Now go to sleep, okay?"

"Okay."

SEVENTEEN

Vincenzo Picco arrived with an entourage, several rolling cargo crates of couture, and an outsized attitude.

They saw him from a distance as he swept into the baggage claim area—a tall, slender man with a flamboyant mane of gray hair, yellow-tinted sunglasses, and an immaculately tailored suit.

"Do you suppose—" Pilar began.

"Uh-huh."

He spotted the sign that one of the other bodyguards was holding and swooped down upon them, trailing a handful of scurrying assistants.

"Mr. Picco?" Henry stepped forward. "Global Security. Welcome to London."

Vincenzo Picco looked from one strapping bodyguard to another, then looked down his nose at Loup and sniffed. He snapped his fingers. A young woman hurried to his side. He uttered a rapid spate of Italian.

"Vincenzo Picco would like to know why his detail is not matched in appearance and height," she said in harried English. "Vincenzo Picco very much likes symmetry."

"Ahh…" Henry blinked. "Apologies to Mr. Picco." He put one hand on Loup's shoulder, then withdrew it. "Perhaps Mr. Picco would be interested to know that Ms. Herrera is the world's only optimally engineered bodyguard."

She translated.

Vincenzo Picco stooped, peering through his tinted glasses at Loup. He poked her sternum experimentally with one long finger; poked harder when she didn't budge, but Loup merely raised her brows at him. He spoke to his assistant.

"Vincenzo Picco is intrigued," she said, turning to Pilar. "Who are you and why are you here?"

"Pilar…Mendez. I'm just here to assist you, ma'am."

The assistant sniffed. "Alessandra."

"Alessandra."

Another exchange.

"Vincenzo Picco approves of your dress," Alessandra said grudgingly. "Now you must all retrieve the wardrobe."

They waited at the carousel where Vincenzo Picco pointed imperiously at crate after crate.

"You *so* got the best clothes out of this deal," Loup whispered.

Pilar glanced down at her 1940s-inspired wraparound dress with little polka dots. "I know. I totally did."

The entourage and bodyguards rescued the last crate of couture.

"Ready, sir?" Henry asked.

Vincenzo Picco clapped his hands twice with authority, then let out an alarmed cry at the sight of a careening, giggling toddler carrying an open, sloshing cup of soda bearing down on him, his mother in hot pursuit.

"Whoa!" Loup darted around the client, lightning quick. "Whoa, whoa, whoa, little man!" She snatched up the boy in one arm, securing the cup in her free hand. She bounced the delighted toddler on her left hip before setting him on his feet. "Here you go, lady," she said, handing over the unspilled drink. "Sorry about that."

The mother gawked.

A lot of people gawked.

Vincenzo Picco brushed off the sleeves of his suit and inclined his head, issuing a soft utterance in Italian.

"Vincenzo Picco is impressed," his assistant offered.

Loup eyed her. "Does he talk about himself that way or is that just you?"

She tilted her head in an effort to look down her nose. "That is not your concern."

"Whatever. Ma'am."

They escorted the designer out of the airport, falling into a neat four-square formation while members of his entourage pushed the rolling crates. When it came to loading the crates into the cargo van, Loup helped, hoisting them effortlessly.

"Jesus," Henry Kensington murmured. "What you did back there with the kid...you know what kills me?"

"No."

He nodded at her crisp white shirt. "You didn't even spill a drop."

Loup shrugged. "I'm pretty dexterous."

"In oh, so many ways," Pilar added absently, studying the news feed on her Dataphone.

Henry Kensington blushed. "Ah...right."

The designer insisted on going directly to the venue, an elegant space that had once been an art gallery. There was a showdown with the Fashion Week security people, who refused to admit them without passes. Vincenzo Picco harangued his assistant in Italian. Alessandra translated his harangues into voluminous English. Many phone calls were made. Photographers snapped pictures of it all. Loup took her cue from Henry and the other guards and simply held her position, alert and attentive.

In the end, they were admitted. The cargo trunks were rolled into the secondary gallery space that served as the backstage. The entourage fanned out and began unpacking the clothing and hanging it on racks while Vincenzo Picco strode up and down, examining items and giving curt orders.

"Um...what do we do now?" Loup asked Henry.

"Stand around and look stern. Stay out of everyone's way." He sti-fled a yawn. "Truth is, we're probably just window dressing on a job like this. PR stunt. But on the other hand, you can see why someone might want to kill the bloke, eh?"

"Yeah, kinda."

"You! Assistant!" Alessandra beckoned imperiously to Pilar. "I have a job for you."

"Yes, ma'am!"

She pointed to a gleaming espresso machine that had emerged from one of the crates. "Watch." She demonstrated. "One level scoop. No more, no less. Use only bottled water." Frothing brown espresso hissed into a delicate white cup. "When Vincenzo Picco shouts, '*Caffè!*' you will make one immediately and bring it to him. Understand?"

Pilar sighed. "Yes, ma'am."

"Good."

They stood around for hours while the designer and his entourage engaged in a flurry of activity, steaming and primping his collection. Or at least Loup and the other guards did; Pilar dragged a folding chair over to her coffee station and sat, reading the news online in between cries of "*Caffè!*"

"So what's up?" Loup asked eventually, deciding she could stand and look stern next to Pilar as well as anywhere.

She made a face. "Not as much as we'd hoped. That guy Ballantine, he's trying to get Congress to hold hearings, but he can't force them. And the administration's made it a big huge crime for members of the military to talk about it. National security."

"That's bullshit. They're just afraid their big huge lie's gonna get out."

"Yeah, I know." Pilar looked up. "It's crazy, you know? People there really think Mexico tried to invade America?"

"We did, too," Loup reminded her.

"*You* didn't. Anyway, it's not like any of us had access to real news." She gestured with her Dataphone. "They do!"

"I think the whole world went kinda crazy for a while."

"True." Pilar looked thoughtful. "If this is all coming out in the open, I wonder if Ballantine showed anyone the interview we did."

"Maybe," Loup said. "If he did, that means Magnus was right."

Pilar paled. "And maybe it's a good thing we're here, and not in Mexico, huh?"

"With fake passports and everything," Loup agreed in a low voice. "Do you ever get the feeling Magnus knows more than—" She glanced over at a sudden commotion. "Oops. I gotta go be a bodyguard."

Vincenzo Picco was flinging plastic cups of fruit-flavored sherbet to the floor while members of his entourage dove to protect the clothing from splatters. He massaged his throat, complaining to a defensive Alessandra in voluble Italian.

"Hey, Alessandra," Pilar called from behind Loup, having abandoned her coffee station. "Did he say something about gelato?"

"Yes!" she said irritably.

"There's an Italian gelateria about five blocks from here."

Loup glanced at her. "There is? How'd you know that?"

"*I* did my homework, baby." Pilar poked her. "See, this is the kind of stuff Addie taught me to do. It was in the dossier. Lemon gelato. It's like ice cream, only Italian. It soothes his throat."

Alessandra conferred with a mollified Vincenzo Picco. "Yes, please. But he would like the fast one to go. As fast as possible."

"Me?" Loup blinked. "Okay, but it'll attract attention."

The corners of Vincenzo Picco's mouth twitched upward.

"He wants to attract attention," Pilar whispered in Loup's ear. "And he so totally speaks English."

"Mm-hmm. Give me the directions."

She ran the five blocks at a quick jog, dodging startled pedestrians, overshot the unobtrusive gelateria, and backtracked, finding it. By the time the lemon gelato she ordered was ready, there was a small knot of onlookers awaiting her on the sidewalk.

"Excuse me—" a man began.

"Can't talk." Loup shook her head. "Got a big, important designer waiting for his fancy ice cream. Vincenzo Picco, you know? Very important."

"Erm…"

She took off at a run and made it back to the venue before the gelato had even begun to soften. The designer received it with a courtly bow. After the first spoonful, he smiled and spoke to Alessandra.

"Vincenzo Picco is pleased." She turned to Pilar. "Is it, um, possible that you might know of a reputable sushi restaurant nearby? Vincenzo Picco wishes to have lunch catered so everyone may keep working without pause."

Pilar smiled happily. "*Sì, signorina!*"

After a day of standing around interspersed with errand-running, they got the designer and his entourage ensconced in the hotel. Mercifully, he elected to dine alone in his room. "Vincenzo Picco desires privacy the night before a big show," Alessandra informed them. "He will expect you in the morning."

"Of course," Henry Kensington agreed.

In their hotel room, Pilar flopped down on the bed. "Ohmigod. My feet are totally killing me."

"That's what you get for wearing sexy little pumps that are a little too tight." Loup pried them off. She sat cross-legged on the bed and rubbed Pilar's feet. "I told you not to buy them. You could have waited to shop in London."

"Mmm. I know. But they were perfect with the dress."

"Vincenzo Picco approves of your dress," Loup intoned.

"Hey! That's actually a pretty big deal."

"I know, I know." Loup squeezed her foot. "You were great today. Everyone was impressed."

"I made coffee."

"You did a lot more than make coffee, Pilar."

"You think?"

"Uh-huh." She dropped Pilar's foot and slithered up her body, bracing herself. "And not a single screwup. We just have to get through the big show tomorrow."

Pilar kissed her. "We can do that, right?"

"Right."

Backstage at the venue the following day was pandemonium. In addition to Vincenzo Picco's entourage, there was a small army of dressers and stylists provided by the event organizers to assist, plus members of the media and assorted celebrities and fashionistas. Pilar was back on coffee duty, while Loup and the security detail were expected to restrict access to the designer. In between granting interviews and schmoozing with luminaries, the designer ranted and raved about tardy models.

At last the models began trickling in, and were immediately set upon by the army of stylists. Vincenzo Picco ordered everyone not involved with the show to clear the backstage area.

"Pardon me, sir." Loup took hold of a recalcitrant photographer's elbow. "Time to go. Mr. Picco's orders."

"Just one more...hey!" He gave her a startled look as he found himself being steered firmly and inexorably toward the exit.

"Okay. Bye-bye, now."

After that came more standing around while everyone else worked frantically. There was a flurry of gossip surrounding the belated entry of one of the show's top models, who ignored it to drift her way elegantly toward the stylists' tables.

"Elise, you're *late*!" a stylist snapped.

"Not for me, love," she said complacently, blowing a kiss toward a scowling Vincenzo Picco. She caught sight of Loup and smiled. "Look at you! Are you supposed to be a bodyguard?"

"Yes, ma'am."

"That's just the cutest thing! Was it Vincenzo's idea?"

"Um...no. I'm with Global Security."

"That's perfectly adorable." The model gave her a one-armed hug and kissed her cheek, then looked startled. "Oh!"

"It's not a gimmick, Elise," someone called. "She's a GMO."

One of the other models glanced up from beneath a cloud of hair spray. "Honest to God?"

"Yeah, it's true."

Elise stroked Loup's arm, then snatched her hand away. "It's so odd! You feel like...I don't know what."

"I want to see!"

"Me too!"

Loup blinked, unsure how to respond to being surrounded by a sudden crowd of tall, curious models, touching her with the impersonal lack of self-consciousness of women used to being handled intimately by relative strangers.

"Ooh! It *is* odd!"

"Ever work with big snakes?" one model asked another, shivering a little. "I did a shoot with a Burmese python once. It's sort of like that but completely different."

"*Basta!*" Vincenzo Picco came roaring down on them, scattering the models. He railed in Italian until they sat obediently in their chairs.

"Sorry, sir," Loup murmured.

His expression softened. He spoke to a breathless Alessandra, arriving on his heels.

"Vincenzo Picco says it's not your fault. You may wait with your friend and bring *caffè* for him when he calls. Things will move very quickly now."

"Okay."

At the coffee station, Pilar eyed her. "You know, baby, I wouldn't have wasted time worrying about Miguel Garza if I'd known you were gonna get petted by a bunch of models today."

"Yeah, well, *petted* is about right. I think they thought that's what I am. A pet."

"Clive warned us you were just gonna be a novelty act," Pilar said with sympathy. "I'm afraid there's gonna be a lot more of that, baby."

"I guess. Pilar, do I feel like a big snake?"

She smiled. "No, but you can sure as hell move like one when you feel like it."

"*Caffè!*"

Despite the chaos, the show began almost on time. Pop music boomed in the main gallery as model after model sauntered onto the catwalk wearing whimsical creations. Backstage, frantic dressers rushed them through wardrobe changes. Quarrels broke out between members of Vincenzo Picco's entourage and the hired assistants.

"Shit!" Loup watched a model in towering heels and a postmodern bridal gown begin to topple when someone stepped on her gown's long tulle train. She hurried over and steadied the model as the train gave way with a pronounced rip. One of the Italians working on another girl shouted at the model's dresser, who stormed off in a huff. The model glanced back at the ruined train and burst into tears.

"Hey, hey, don't cry!" Pilar said in alarm. "You'll ruin your makeup. Don't worry, we'll find someone to…" She glanced around and saw absolutely no one free to help. "Oh, fuck it. Loup, grab my purse."

She was already on her way.

"Okay, hang on." Pilar knelt and whipped out the hotel sewing kit. "I'm just gonna do a running stitch, but it'll hold and it won't even show that much with the netting. Okay, honey?"

The model sniffled. "Uh-huh."

"Loup, get her a tissue."

"Yes, ma'am!"

"There." Pilar finished as the casting coordinator beckoned frantically. "Go, go!"

They watched her go.

"Nice work, super-assistant," Loup offered.

Pilar let out a sigh of relief. "Think I'd rather be a secret agent bodyguard. It's less stressful."

EIGHTEEN

Vincenzo Picco was very pleased.

The show was hailed as a raving success and celebrated at a raging after-party where the champagne and compliments flowed freely.

Pilar, off the clock, sipped champagne and watched the fashion people mingle. "Damn, baby. I wish you didn't have to work. That's no fair."

"That's the job," Loup said pragmatically. "You get to dress up, look fabulous, and drink champagne, while I stand around looking like a waiter at a fancy restaurant."

"It's not *that* bad." Pilar adjusted the lay of Loup's collar, opening it wider. "You need a necklace. Something that would draw attention right here." She traced a circle around the hollow of Loup's throat.

"Mmm. Henry's giving us a no-no look."

"What? I'm not working!"

"Yeah, but I am."

"Okay, okay."

Sometime after midnight, the model from the bridal train near-disaster wandered over and delivered a heartfelt, drunken speech of thanks to Pilar, kissing her effusively on both cheeks. "You saved my life!" she slurred. "I thought you were a dresser. I didn't know you were with the security people."

"Well, kinda."

"C'mon! You've got to meet everyone." She tugged her hand, then took Loup's. "You too. Everyone wants to."

"I can't." Loup nodded at Vincenzo Picco a few feet away. "I'm working."

"Ah, go on! He's just a big old drama queen."

Loup shook her head. "Doesn't matter. Pilar, you go."

"You sure, baby?"

"Uh-huh."

She watched Pilar meet and mingle with the happy, drunken throng, looking very much at home. It was after two o'clock when the party finally wound down and they escorted Vincenzo Picco and his entourage back to the hotel. He made a formal speech in Italian in the lobby, offering a courtly bow to all of them.

"Vincenzo Picco thanks you for your service," Alessandra translated, sounding tired. "Especially you," she added to Pilar. "He heard that you saved the postmodern bridal extravaganza."

Pilar flushed. "Thanks."

Alessandra smiled unexpectedly. "You did a good job, eh? We'll see you in the morning."

In the hotel room, Loup ransacked the courtesy bar, tearing open a bag of nuts.

"Aw, baby! You didn't get enough to eat today, did you?"

"Nope."

"Remind me to pick up some snacks," Pilar said sleepily. "That way I can keep something on hand for you. Hey, Loup? Those models—"

"No."

"No, what?"

"No, I don't think any of them were prettier than you." Loup poured the last of the nuts into her mouth, chewed, and swallowed. "And no, I don't think any of them were Christophe's one in a hundred. And no, even if they were, I wouldn't care, because you're the sexiest sidekick in the universe, and you worry about whether or not I have enough to eat, and I really, really, love you. Does that cover it?"

Pilar gave her a sheepish look. "Well, yeah."

"Good."

In the morning they escorted Vincenzo Picco, his entourage, and his collection back to the airport. He thanked them again and shook Henry's hand, pressing folded bills into it. They watched him pass through security, then stride away toward his terminal, surrounded by his people, gray mane flowing.

"Nice work, team." Henry doled out a one-hundred-euro note to each of them. "Nice tip, too."

"Wow!" Pilar gazed at hers. "We get to keep this?"

"Of course." He smiled at her. "You earned it."

Back at the hotel they had a late lunch and debriefed with Clive, who beamed with pride over Henry's report.

"So not a single cock-up, eh?" he asked.

"Honestly, no. The client was very pleased with their performance."

"Vincenzo Picco was pleased," Loup agreed.

"Mind your manners, girlie," Clive said, but he was grinning. "You know what this means?"

They shook their heads.

"We've got a few more lessons to cover, but based on your performance so far, you two are pretty damn close to being made full-fledged members of the Global Security team."

"Yay!" Pilar said happily.

After lunch they said their farewells to Henry and the security team and prepared to take an overnight train back to Aberdeen. Pilar ducked out to shop while Loup packed their things, returning with a stylish patent leather tote bag filled with energy bars and bags of mixed nuts and several glossy magazines.

"See?" She showed Loup. "Okay, the magazines are for me, but the snacks are for you. I'll make sure I always have some with me. So if you ever get hungry on the job, just let me know." She smiled. "Maybe a badass secret agent bodyguard can't carry around a purse full of snacks, but *I* can."

Loup hugged her. "Thanks, Pilar."

"Just trying to take care of you, baby."

They boarded the train in the evening, Pilar exclaiming over the tiny sleeper cabin.

"Right cozy, eh?" Clive said. "Thought about booking you a cabin with two berths, but I reckoned you'd end up sharing a bunk no matter what."

"It's perfect."

"Good. Get yourselves settled and we'll meet in the lounge car for a bite."

Loup unpacked a few necessary toiletries while Pilar checked the news feeds. "Anything new?"

"Nah. Same stories, no updates." She glanced up. "Although a couple of them referred to Miguel Garza as ruggedly handsome."

Loup laughed. "That'll go straight to his head."

They joined Clive in the lounge car, where he'd already ordered a bottle of red wine. "Cheers to you, girls," he said, pouring for them and hoisting his glass. "You made me right proud today. Well done."

"Thanks, sir."

"Thanks," Pilar echoed softly. "We couldn't of done it without you. Well, *I* couldn't. You and Addie."

He sipped his wine and smacked his lips. "Just doing our jobs. Here's to your first satisfied client. May he be the first of many!"

They ate dinner in the lounge car, lulled by the train's steady rhythm and the warm red drapes around the windows framing the dark, invisible countryside. After dinner, Clive insisted on ordering a celebratory nightcap.

"Speyside single malt," he said. "Best in the world."

"Mmm." Pilar tried hers and eyed Loup thoughtfully. "Tastes expensive."

"I *so* know what you're thinking," Loup said.

"Mm-hmm."

"Dial it down a notch, sunshine," Clive advised her. "When you get your smolder on, I worry about innocent bystanders bursting into flame. Not to mention meself."

"Sorry, sir." Pilar tried to look penitent and non-smoldering.

"Ah, get out!" He laughed. "Young love and all. Finish your drinks, go back to your cabin. You've earned the right to celebrate."

"Okay!"

In their cabin, Pilar rummaged in her things while Loup washed up in the tiny sink. "Hey, baby, c'mere. Close your eyes."

"Why?"

"Just do it. Please?"

"Okay, okay!" Loup closed her eyes and felt something thin and cool settle around her throat, Pilar's hands fidgeting at the nape of her neck.

"Okay, you can look."

She went to look in the mirror and saw a finely linked gold chain, five glittering stones nestled in a subtle V formation beneath the hollow of her throat, winking brightly against her caramel skin and adding a point of interest to the plain white shirt she still wore. Loup touched the necklace with wondering fingers. "You bought this for me?"

"Uh-huh. They're not real diamonds or anything," Pilar added apologetically. "All I had was my tip money."

"I don't care. I love it."

"C'mere." Pilar tugged her over to sit on the single berth. "Loup... look. I don't ever mean to get all weird and jealous." She smiled wryly. "I never told you, but when we were first together, it freaked me out a little that you didn't get jealous when I flirted with other people. All the guys I ever dated did. I thought it meant you didn't care."

"No! It's just—"

"Oh, hush." She pressed a finger against Loup's lips, silencing her. "I figured it out, okay? It took me a while, but I did. You knew it didn't mean anything. You don't get jealous because you're not insecure, and you don't get insecure because you can't. I can and I do. But that's just stupid, right?"

"It's not stupid."

"Yeah, it is." Pilar kissed her, soft and lingering. "Because I know you, baby. And I trust you. Like you said, with all my heart." She pulled back, serious. "Things are different out here, you know? In Outpost, you had to hide what you were. Here, you don't. And I love it. It makes me really happy. I love seeing you be yourself. But it also means that instead of a handful of people trying to keep your secret, there's a ton of people totally intrigued by you. You're you. You're a one-and-only. I'm just trying to adjust, okay?"

Loup nodded. "Okay."

"So this isn't just a present for you." She stroked the necklace. "It's to help remind me how much I *do* trust you, and…I dunno. Lots of things." She glanced at Loup. "Okay, it's still just a cheap necklace. You don't have to go all big and shiny-eyed on me."

"Can't help it." Loup smiled. "I really do love it. And, Pilar, I don't care about the flirting because it's part of who you are."

Pilar made a face.

"It is!" Loup took her hand, twined their fingers together. "Remember when I used to stop by to pick you up at the bar when your shift ended? I always tried to come in without you noticing, and I'd watch you flirt with all your regulars. You were always having fun, but I liked it because whenever you'd notice I was there, no matter what you were doing, you'd smile at me like I was the best part of your day."

"Well, you were."

"Were?"

"Were and are." Pilar wrapped her arms around Loup's neck and kissed her. "And you damn well know it, so don't tease me, Santa Olivia." She let her go and began undoing the buttons of her shirt. "Know what else would make this outfit more interesting?"

"Ummm…no?"

Her hands glided over Loup's breasts. "A nice, lacy black bra."

Loup shivered. "Really?"

"Mm-hmm." Pilar traced lazy circles. "So you could just see the faintest shadow through the fabric. And all day long I could think about taking it off you."

"Okay," Loup agreed, a little breathless.

"But right *now*..." Pilar slid the unbuttoned shirt from Loup's shoulders. "I really want to see how you look wearing nothing but that necklace, baby."

A moment later, Loup asked, "Well?"

She got a very long, very smoldering look in reply. "Pilar Ecchevarria approves."

NINETEEN

Back in Aberdeen, their lessons finished with more security drills, business protocol, deportment, and elocution.

The latter were painful.

"This is Ms. Coxcombe," Clive said, introducing a slender, gray-haired woman with a regal bearing.

Pilar suppressed a giggle. Ms. Coxcombe arched one perfectly plucked eyebrow, and Pilar sobered. "Sorry, ma'am."

"Indeed," was the frosty reply.

She drilled them relentlessly for an entire day on how to shake hands, how to handle introductions, how to stand, and how to sit. She corrected their grammar and ruthlessly rooted out profanity and an endless string of *yeahs*, *dunnos*, and *gonnas*.

"So?" Clive said at the end of the day. "Is there hope?"

Ms. Coxcombe pursed her lips. "We have a good deal of work to do."

"My colleague and I are entirely committed to pursuing this venture," Loup said in a formal tone. "We are grateful for your generous..." She searched for a word.

"Tutelage," Pilar supplied helpfully. "Ma'am."

Clive chuckled, then cleared his throat.

"Indeed." Ms. Coxcombe inclined her head, looking rather like she was biting the inside of her cheek in an effort to hide a glint of amusement. "I'll return on the morrow, shall I? We'll address formal dining etiquette."

"Okay," Loup agreed cheerfully. "I like anything to do with food."

Ms. Coxcombe raised one finger.

"Very good, then." Loup amended her words. "I shall anticipate tomorrow's lesson with pleasure, as I...um..."

"Revel in indulging in the culinary arts!" Pilar finished triumphantly.

"Yeah, exactly!"

Their new tutor sighed. "Ladies."

"We're trying!" Pilar protested.

"Indeed." She laid a hand on Pilar's shoulder, her expression softening. "Don't try quite so hard, child. I'm not trying to change who you are. I'm just trying to give you a veneer of polish."

"Ok—" Pilar caught herself. "Thank you."

Ms. Coxcombe smiled. "Well done. Simple and gracious. Remember, you'll never go amiss with simple and gracious."

Over the following week, they learned the intricacies of fish forks and finger bowls and received a crash course in arts and culture, all the while suffering the indignity of constant corrections to their speech.

"Manet," Loup said, identifying a painting on-screen. "No, Monet. Do we really have to know this stuff? I don't get what it has to do with being a bodyguard."

A raised finger.

She sighed. "Sorry. Um...I don't understand the connection between Impressionist paintings and security work."

"Depending on your clients, you may find yourselves moving in elite circles," Ms. Coxcombe said mildly. "In a situation that calls for discretion, you very well may be called on to make polite conversation. It helps a great deal to have something to talk about. Two days ago, you hadn't the faintest idea what an Impressionist artist was. Today, you can identify a number of them by name. Doesn't that make you feel good?"

"It's a lot to learn, that's all."

"I kinda like the art part," Pilar offered, then winced. "No kinda, no kinda! Got it. I enjoy learning about art."

"Well done."

At the end of a week, Ms. Coxcombe administered their final test. She took them into the city to attend a fundraising dinner for the Aberdeen Art Gallery & Museum, where she was a member of the board. She introduced them as the daughter and friend of a dear friend from Canada, traveling on a scholarship.

"Very good!" a jovial man said to Loup. "What are you studying?"

"Ahh...the Impressionists?"

He launched into a lengthy dissertation on Monet's haystack series, in which Loup discovered that the easiest way to make polite conversation was to look interested, nod frequently, and make inquiring noises.

They got through the dinner without any incidents or mishaps. Pilar struggled with the European-style handling of the fork and knife Ms. Coxcombe insisted they learn, but managed to charm her dinner companions. Loup wielded her utensils adroitly, did a lot of listening and nodding, invented details about her fictitious home in Canada, and managed not to stare longingly at her dinner companions' unfinished portions.

"Well?" Pilar said anxiously afterward. "Did we do okay?"

That got her the cautionary raised finger.

"Sorry! I'm nervous. Did we, um, manage not to embarrass you?"

"You did." Ms. Coxcombe inclined her head. "Well done."

In the morning, they came yawning down to the sunroom for breakfast to find a beaming Clive and a smiling Adelaide awaiting them.

"Hey," Pilar said sleepily. "What's on the schedule for today?"

"Not a blessed thing, sunshine," Clive said.

"Huh?"

He tapped his watch, his grin widening. "Do you pay no attention to the date, girlie? That's it. You're done."

"Seriously?" Loup asked, brightening.

Adelaide cleared her throat. "Mr. Lindberg, sir?"

Magnus Lindberg strode into the room with a white, toothy smile, Sabine gliding in his wake, carrying a briefcase. "Congratulations, ladies. You've passed the training phase, the both of you." He made a subtle gesture to Sabine, who laid the briefcase on one of the tables and opened it, expressionless. He whipped out a pair of contracts. "As promised. It's Global's standard three-year contract. You'll receive a ten thousand euro bonus just for signing."

Loup eyed him. "Three years? That's a long time."

"It's standard," he assured her.

"Yeah, well, *I'm* not."

Pilar scanned the text. "You're only offering us a fifteen percent commission on the fees you get for us? That's bullshit." She tapped her Dataphone. "I've looked into this kind of thing."

"We have a lot invested in you," Magnus said smoothly. "And as you'll note, it increases by five percent every year."

"Don't sign," she advised Loup.

"I'm not."

Sabine made an impatient sound.

"Oh, please!" Pilar said to her. "I bet *you* never sold yourself cheap." She folded her arms. "One year. Twenty-five percent, with an increase negotiable at the time of renewal."

"That's ridiculous. We'll barely recoup our investment in a year."

"Well, you won't recoup any of it if we don't sign."

Magnus raised his brows. "The pair of you barely have more than the clothes on your backs. You'd walk away from a ten thousand euro bonus?"

"There's always bartending," Pilar said philosophically. "Hey, Loup! You could totally get a job as a bouncer. We could work together."

"True."

"We really do not have time for this," Sabine said through gritted teeth.

"Why not?" Loup cocked her head. "Something's going on, isn't it?"

Magnus and Sabine exchanged a glance. "We have a client with an unusual dilemma and a tight deadline," he admitted. "She's a relative of Vincenzo Picco's and he recommended our services to her. *Your* services in particular," he added to Pilar.

"Mine?" She looked startled.

Sabine looked disgusted.

"Indeed." Magnus steepled his fingers. "If I agree to amend the contracts, can the two of you be ready to travel in an hour's time?"

Loup glanced at Pilar, who nodded. "Yes, sir."

"Very good." He noted and initialed the changes on the contracts, then handed over the pen, watching as both of them signed. "And a second set for your own records. Sabine, stop glaring. You'll be working with them on this job; you might as well start getting used to the idea."

"She will?" Pilar looked up in dismay. "You didn't mention that before we signed."

Magnus smiled. "No, I didn't, did I?"

TWENTY

An hour later, they bade hurried farewells to Clive and Addie.

"Thanks so much," Pilar said, hugging both of them. "I know it was really hard getting me through this. I'll do my best to make you proud."

"You already have, dear," Adelaide said cheerfully.

"You take care of yourselves," Clive added.

And then they were off to the airport, Sabine at the wheel.

"So, um, where are we going?" Loup asked from the backseat.

"Palermo, Sicily." Magnus rested his head on the headrest. "All the information's on the database in a file labeled Picco Wedding."

"Shit!" Pilar turned on her Dataphone. "I mean, oh, dear. I've only got a plane ride to learn all about Palermo, Sicily?"

"No, no." Magnus glanced back with a smile. "If the client approves, you won't be an assistant on this job, Pilar."

Her eyes widened. "I'll be a bodyguard?"

Sabine snorted.

"You'll be a wedding guest," Magnus clarified. "And hopefully, an irresistible distraction. Read the dossier and I'll let the client explain."

They read in silence for a while.

"Feuding families?" Pilar whispered to Loup. "I bet this is so totally a Mafia thing. Wasn't that where those guys in that movie were from? Sicily?"

"Yep."

"Hey, Magnus? Do we do a lot of work for the Mafia?"

"We work with many wealthy clients. Some have more...interesting...connections than others," he said without looking back. "I will ask you to keep any speculations to yourselves. In fact, I demand it."

"Okay, okay!"

From the airport in Aberdeen, they flew through Amsterdam and Rome and arrived in Palermo in the early evening. The air was warm and balmy, the foliage lush and green.

"Nice." Loup breathed deeply while Sabine negotiated with a taxi driver in fluent Italian. "Are we near the ocean? It smells like it."

"It's a port city, yes. Once, you would have smelled nothing but car exhaust, but the population is much smaller than it was. Although, in fact, I cannot say I smell the ocean." Magnus gave her a curious look. "Are your senses keener than those of ordinary humans?"

She shrugged. "I dunno. *Don't* know, I mean. I've always had good hearing. I never thought about whether or not I could smell better than other people."

"Interesting."

"Little animal," Sabine muttered under her breath, opening the door to the taxi.

In the cab, Pilar leaned over and growled softly in Loup's ear, making her squirm and giggle. "What?" she said in defensive response to Sabine's glare. "We're not *on* the job yet, are we? And you're the one called her a little animal."

"You are insufferable."

Pilar smiled sweetly at her. "Vincenzo Picco begs to differ."

"Vincenzo Picco is a flamboyant idiot."

"I kinda liked him," Loup offered. "I mean, he yelled a lot, but he thanked us and gave us a nice tip."

"No kinda, baby," Pilar reminded her.

"Right. I rather liked him."

"Dear God," Magnus murmured. "If we do not get this job, I fear I may slit my throat. Sabine, not a word."

She glowered.

The taxi deposited them at an opulent old hotel overlooking the harbor, surrounded by palm trees.

"Very good," Magnus said once they'd checked in. "Perhaps we should meet..." He glanced at Sabine's face. "Ah, perhaps not. I'll leave you on your own for supper, shall I? We'll meet in the lobby in the morning. Say, ten thirty? We have an eleven o'clock meeting with the client." He beckoned to Sabine. "Their credit cards?"

She handed them over grudgingly.

"These are for job-related expenses." He gave them each a card with the Global logo. "Meals and the like. And these..." He handed over two more. "These are for your personal accounts. Your bonus money."

"Ten thousand euros," Pilar breathed.

"*Now* you care," Magnus said wryly.

"Well, yeah." She smiled at Loup, tracing the glinting line of gold that circled her throat. "Guess I should've waited to buy you a necklace, baby."

"No." Loup shook her head. "This one's special."

Magnus cleared his throat. "So. On the morrow?"

"We'll be there."

After stashing their suitcases in the hotel room, they ventured out into the city, standing in line to gain admission to a small bistro on a narrow street at Pilar's insistence.

"Holy shit!" Loup spooned up mouthful after mouthful of fresh pappardelle with shrimp and mushrooms. "This is *so good*. How'd you find this place?"

She looked smug. "Research. I know what Magnus said, but I figured I could use the practice."

"You're so good at it!"

"I'm not bad, huh?"

Loup's spoon scraped an empty bowl. She looked at it sadly. "Think I could order another one?"

"Why not?"

Afterward, they wandered the city for a while, marveling at the illuminated nightscape of medieval cathedrals and ancient theaters.

"Just think." Pilar took Loup's hand. "Four months ago, Magnus wouldn't let us go to the airport bookstore without a babysitter. Now we're walking around a strange city at night, all on our own, with accounts worth ten thousand euros."

"Yeah, I wouldn't advertise that last part, Pilar."

"You're right, that was dumb. Sorry." She squeezed her hand. "I have to remember to be smart about danger. That's my job, right? But it's easy to forget when I'm with you, because I *do* feel so safe." She smiled. "My little animal."

Loup laughed and growled deep in her throat; it was low, feral, and menacing, and nothing like Pilar's sexy, teasing growl earlier.

"Jesus!" Pilar stared at her open-mouthed. "Do it again."

She did.

"That made all the hair on my arms stand up." Pilar showed her. "Baby, sometimes I forget how much deadly your cute is hiding. Did you know you could do that?"

"No," Loup said thoughtfully. "It never occurred to me."

"Is it weird that it kinda turned me on?" Pilar shook her head. "Don't answer that. It's weird. Swear to God, I think there's something wrong with me."

"Sorry."

"Oh, don't worry. It's nothing I'd want fixed." She glanced around. "I'm just trying to figure out the quickest way back to the hotel."

In the morning, they met with the prospective client.

Fiorella Picco received them in an elegant, spacious office of the headquarters of the family import and export business. Like her kinsman, she was tall with an imperious demeanor. Unlike the designer, she spoke—or admitted to speaking—fluent English. She paced back and forth behind her gleaming desk, outlining her dilemma. Her fiancé, Domenico, sat quietly in a chair, content to let her run the show. A bodyguard in a tailored suit stood nearby, arms folded.

"This quarrel." She paced, gesticulating. "My brother, his brother. They will ruin the wedding. I know it. I know it. They cannot be in a room together without coming to blows. They ruined our engagement party. They will ruin the wedding reception."

Magnus crossed his legs, smoothing the immaculate crease of his trousers. "I take it their attendance is a given?"

She gave him an incredulous look. "They are family!"

"Of course." He inclined his head. "And your own security...?"

"Oh, no. No, no, no!" She shook her head vigorously. "It will not suffice. Both sides will have their people there. What one begins, the other...what is the word?" She snapped her fingers. "Escalates."

"Our engagement party became a brawl," Domenico confirmed. "Bones were broken."

"Guns?" Magnus inquired.

"Drawn, but not fired."

Pilar swallowed visibly.

"So you see why we require a neutral party to keep the peace," Fiorella Picco said. "I will *not* have my wedding ruined. Vincenzo's idea has promise." Her gaze settled on Pilar. "I see what he meant. Stand up. How old are you?"

"Eighteen," Pilar said, standing. "Nineteen next month."

"Such a baby!" Fiorella patted her cheek, then eyed her critically. "You could pass for younger in less professional clothes. Shall we say seventeen?"

"Excuse me?"

"My brother, Pasquale, he is very..." She snapped her fingers. "Lecherous. Very lecherous. He likes young women, very young women, pretty ones with..." She hoisted her own breasts. "With a lot to show. So. Vincenzo said you were vivacious. You think you could distract my lecherous brother for a few hours?"

"Yeah, sure, I suppose."

Another pat on the cheek. "Good girl. If he is thinking with his prick, he is not thinking with his fists."

"What about Gustavo?" Domenico inquired.

"Loup can handle your brother," Magnus assured him. "You see, that's the beauty of her services. No man in his right mind wishes to court public humiliation at the hands of a young woman half his size."

They looked skeptical.

"Allow me to demonstrate." He rose. "Permit me the use of your man?" They nodded. "Very good. You, sir." He pointed to the bodyguard. "Try to get past Loup to reach me. Loup, don't let him."

"Yes, sir." She put herself between them.

The bodyguard shook his head and grinned, then attempted to brush past Loup. She shifted to block him, placing one hand on his chest and holding him at bay. He tried to wrench her arm away, glanced down in surprise when it didn't budge. She took his hand in a come-along grip, grabbed his other elbow, and steered him gently backward. He went, stumbling, a comical look on his face.

"Luciano!" Fiorella uttered a string of Italian.

"No, *signorina!*" he said helplessly. "No pretending!"

Domenico gave a low whistle. "So it is true."

"Absolutely." Magnus offered a courtly bow. "Lupe Herrera is the world's only optimally engineered bodyguard."

"Actually, I wasn't—" Loup began.

He gave her a look. "Quite a team, aren't they?"

"Indeed." Fiorella looked perturbed. "Though explaining their presence—"

"Ah." Magnus raised one finger. "That's where Sabine plays a role. As it happens, you both attended the same boarding school in Lausanne a mere two years apart. You shall claim to be her dear girlhood friend who happens to be traveling with young visitors in tow."

Sabine's lip curled.

"He totally stole that idea from Ms. Coxcombe," Pilar whispered to Loup.

"I know," she whispered back.

Magnus gave them both a look. "And Sabine has a great deal of experience. She is a highly skilled, highly trained bodyguard with years of work in the field. Her presence would ensure an unparalleled level of competence and professionalism. I assure you, we can promise you a peaceable wedding and reception."

The Italian couple conferred in Italian.

"Mr. Lindberg." Fiorella Picco put out her hand. "I believe we have a deal."

He smiled toothily. "Excellent!"

Back at the hotel, Pilar collapsed in disgust. "Jesus fucking Christ! You mean to tell me I spent four months busting my ass and frying my brain to become a secret agent bodyguard personal assistant, and the first time I get hired for real, it's for my *tits*?"

Loup eyed her. "Yep."

"Some things never change."

"It's just one job." Loup stroked her arm. "And Vincenzo Picco would never have recommended you if you hadn't done such an awesome job."

"You think?"

"I know." Loup went to answer a knock at the door. She blinked in surprise at Sabine. "Umm...hi."

"I am to take you shopping," Sabine said without preamble. "You require clothing suitable for a wedding and we have only two days to prepare."

"I can shop without your help," Pilar called in reply. "As you noticed."

Gritted teeth. "Mr. Lindberg insists. We are to practice being civil to one another and rehearse our cover story."

"Fine."

They shared a cab to a shopping district filled with expensive boutiques, where Pilar combed through racks of clothing, holding up dresses against her body.

"Too vulgar," Sabine opined.

"It's got to be a little bit *vool-gar*," Pilar said absently. "Not enough to offend anyone, not inappropriate or anything, just enough for the guy to notice. Men don't go for subtle."

"Now you are an expert on men?" Sabine asked with a pointed glance at Loup.

"Courtesy of my torrid past." Pilar fished out a long, slinky red dress and thrust it at Sabine. "This would look really good on you. Not for the wedding, but you should try it on."

Sabine shoved the dress back at her. "I do not wear red. And you are too young to have a torrid past."

"I started early."

"She did," Loup agreed.

"And you *should* wear red," Pilar added. "You've got the coloring to carry it off." She looked at Sabine's suspicious face. "What? I'm trying to bond with you through the universal female language of clothing, okay? Just try the damn dress on."

She did, grumbling.

The dress looked fabulous.

"See?" Pilar said with satisfaction. "I bet Magnus' eyes would pop out of his head if he saw you right now."

Sabine narrowed her eyes. "Why do you say that?"

She busied herself with another clothing rack. "No reason. Loup, are you finding anything? Okay, try this one."

"It will not be a good length for her."

Pilar considered the dress. "You know, you're right. Thanks."

Sabine offered a slightly less poisonous smile than usual. "We are not *bonding*, you and I. But I am not willing to be outdone by you in a game of civility."

"Works for me," Loup said.

After finding dresses, they moved on to shoes.

"No." Loup shook her head, rejecting Sabine's suggestion of a high-heeled pump to match the champagne-colored shantung silk sheath dress she'd bought. "No heels."

"It's a wedding!" The look of disgust returned. "You will be required to wear formal attire at formal occasions in this job."

"They mess with my center of balance. I don't like it."

"Oh, for God's sake!"

"It's okay, baby," Pilar said. "We'll find something that will work."

Sabine sniffed. "I'm surprised you're siding with her on this."

"Yeah, well, Loup's got an amazing sense of balance." Pilar examined a sleek, pointed mule in pale beige. "I think for her to have something mess with it's kinda like someone with perfect pitch having to listen to a tone-deaf singer. Let me see that dress, baby. Yeah, this would work." She showed Loup the low kitten heel. "Think you could manage?"

"Yeah. Thanks, Pilar."

She smiled at her. "I like shopping for you. Does this meet with your approval?" she asked Sabine.

"It's fine."

"Good," Pilar said cheerfully. "And I'll make up for it by getting a pair of nice, high fuck-me heels."

"Oh, for God's sake!"

"What? I'm just doing my job. I'm a nymphet-for-hire on this one, right?"

"She has a point," Loup added.

"It's just..." Sabine sighed. "Never mind."

They rehearsed their cover story over a late lunch. It was indeed very much like what Ms. Coxcombe had conceived, only with additional details.

"I need to do more research on being Canadian," Pilar mused. "Why did Magnus pick Canada, anyway?"

"Your accents say North America," Sabine said pragmatically. "And you are Canadian because when it came time to acquire passports, those were the relevant connections Mr. Lindberg possessed. Also, no one in their right mind would believe I was traveling with two young American acquaintances. Your country sank into an abyss of paranoia and isolationism from which it has yet to emerge."

"That reminds me, have you checked the news feeds today?" Loup asked Pilar.

"No, I'll do it when we get back."

Sabine blinked. "News feeds?"

"Yeah." Loup nodded. "I mean, yes. The Outpost thing's been in the news. Our friend Miguel Garza, he got out."

"*You* got him out," Pilar reminded her. "You won the ticket for him."

"Yeah, well, he must have done some pretty impressive bullshitting for them to let him go, and then he managed to give them the slip. Anyway, he did an interview with this senator who's trying to get Congress to hold hearings. The guy who interviewed us in Mexico, Senator Ballantine. And I guess they've got Mig stashed away in secret someplace. We're waiting to see what happens."

Sabine was quiet a moment. "I see. I haven't followed much news out of the United States."

"We don't *all* suck, you know." Loup sighed. "I still wish I knew what happened to Coach Roberts. I told Senator Ballantine to look for him, too, but there hasn't been any mention in the news. And he was gonna be in more trouble than anyone for training me."

"Your boxing coach?"

"Yeah. I mean, yes. He wasn't an Outposter. He was a real U.S. citizen and everything."

"Why don't you contact the senator and ask if he knows anything?" Sabine suggested. "He's a public official; his office number and email address will be on his website."

Pilar looked at Loup. "We're idiots."

"*I'm* an idiot," Loup said. "Christophe gave me his private number. It's on that cell phone Magnus gave me."

"Yeah, well, I'm the one bragging about being a good researcher." Pilar smacked her forehead. "Addie would be ashamed of me."

"You've had a lot happening," Sabine said with unexpected gentleness. "Call when you get back to the hotel. I hope you learn something."

"I will," Loup said. "Thank you, Sabine."

"You're welcome."

"Hey, we're getting pretty good at this civil stuff," Pilar observed.

Sabine's mouth twitched in the faintest hint of a nonpoisonous smile. "Do not become too accustomed to it."

TWENTY-ONE

At the hotel, Loup called Senator Ballantine.

"Hi, sir. This is Loup Garron. From the Santa Olivia Outpost? Yeah, fine, thank you. Pilar and I, we've been following the news about Miguel and the hearings. I was wondering if you knew anything about Coach Roberts." She listened. "Yeah, that's too bad. I'm sorry. I'm still really glad to hear it."

Pilar made an inquiring face.

Loup shook her head at her. "About Miguel, does he have a phone number? Could I talk to him?" She listened, wincing. "Uh-huh. I understand. Well, what about us? I'd be willing..." There was a long pause. "No, I understand. Are we in any danger *now*? Or my cousins?" She listened. "Okay, and if you can arrange it, that would be nice. Is there anything else you can tell me? Any idea what's happening in Outpost?" She nodded. "Thank you. I appreciate it. Okay, bye."

"Well?" Pilar said anxiously.

"He found Coach Roberts and he's okay," Loup said with relief. "He's left Outpost for a retirement community in Florida."

"That's nice, baby, but what was that bit about us being in danger?"

"We're not," Loup assured her. "Not as long as we stay out of the country. I guess there's been some kind of undercover investigation, and the Mexican authorities reported that we disappeared after the debriefing."

"So Magnus was right," Pilar said. "The interview *did* get out."

Loup nodded. "Only to some secret commission, but yeah. Anyway, Coach Roberts refused to let them interview him or talk about it at all. Says it's a matter of national security."

"The army got to him."

"Yeah, I know. But I can't entirely blame him. He's an old guy, you know? He did a really brave thing in training me. Maybe that was all he had left in him. I think he just wants to live out the rest of his life in peace."

"What about Miguel?"

Loup grinned. "Mig's being a huge pain in the ass and they're having a hard time keeping him in protective custody. He wants to go party. They're afraid he'll get disappeared if they let him go, and they need a live body to testify if they ever get hearings."

Pilar gave her a suspicious look. "You told him you'd do it, didn't you?"

"Well...yeah. Pilar, don't be mad. I'd *have* to if it was the only way. But he said no, they've got Miguel and at least he's not a GMO who's considered government property and escaped from a military prison and has a bunch of charges against him."

"I'm not mad, baby. I know you want to fix things, but we have to be smart about it. Don't go volunteering for stuff like that unless we've talked about it, okay?"

"Okay."

"Promise?"

"Yes! I promise."

"Good." Pilar gave an exasperated sigh. "I mean, Jesus! If they want live bodies, they've gotta know where to find them. We left behind a whole town full of 'em, and I don't think Santa Olivia's the only Outpost."

"They're trying, but the army and the administration aren't budging. No access, and no one's talking. That's all he could tell me. He's gonna try to set up a supervised phone call with Mig," Loup added. "They don't trust him not to try and arrange to give them the slip."

"Your big hero," Pilar observed.

She laughed. "He's still Miguel fucking Garza, you know?"

"Yeah. I'm glad your coach is okay, baby."

"Me too."

They left the following morning for the village of Taormina, Sabine driving an expensive rental car. The town's narrow streets retained a charming medieval feel, but its origins were far older. At Magnus' request, Sabine took them to see one of its most famous sights, a view overlooking an ancient Greek amphitheater with the sea and Mount Etna in the background. Through the bright autumn air, the distant snowcapped volcano issued plumes of steam.

"Ohmigod." Pilar stared. "Is that *real*?"

"I feel like I did the first time we saw the ocean," Loup said softly. "It's just so big and so beautiful, you know?"

Pilar caught her hand without thinking. "I know."

Magnus smiled. "I must admit, there's a certain pleasure in seeing the world through such unspoiled eyes. Don't you agree, Sabine?"

She made a noncommittal noise.

"But you *are* here on a job," he reminded them. "No holding hands."

"Sorry!" Pilar let go.

They dined together in relative civility that night in a restaurant with a garden terrace. Sabine confirmed that they had both studied their dossiers thoroughly and walked them through the plan.

"The wedding itself is not a concern," she said. "No one will profane the sanctity of the church. It is afterward, at the reception at the villa, once the wine begins to flow." She pointed at Pilar. "When dinner is served, you will be seated at a table beside Pasquale Picco. There will be no other women of interest at the table. Your job is to charm, flatter, and monopolize him. Understood?"

"*Sì, signorina.*"

"Do not attempt to speak Italian. Your accent is abominable." Sabine turned to Loup. "I will be seated at a table with Gustavo Vittori. I will manage him throughout the dinner. It is once the formal events have ended that there is the most likelihood of a contretemps."

"Contretemps?" Loup inquired.

"Trouble," she said briefly. "He becomes belligerent as he drinks. You and I, we will watch Gustavo. I have experience in these matters. If I sense he is about to make a move, I will signal you." Her lip curled. "And *you* will move to intercept and defuse him."

"Sure," Loup agreed. "I can do that."

"It's not that you're not more than capable," Magnus said soothingly to Sabine. "It's just that should the need arise, it's my hope that Loup will make such an unexpected impression that it will stun him into compliance."

She ground her teeth. "I understand that, sir."

"Of course you do."

"It's your height," Pilar supplied helpfully. "You're very, um... statuesque, right? If I were a guy, I wouldn't be surprised that you could kick my ass. I mean, you've got that whole killer ice queen dominatrix vibe going on."

A familiar muscle twitched below Sabine's right eye.

"What?" Pilar protested. "It works for you. It does."

"Surprise is a virtue," Magnus interceded, hoisting his wineglass. "Let us hope that tomorrow holds none not of our planning."

They clinked glasses.

"What are *you* going to be doing, Magnus?" Loup asked. "Ah... Mr. Lindberg?"

He contemplated the depths of his wineglass. "Praying."

The wedding took place at four o'clock on the following day. Pilar spent most of the afternoon fussing with her hair.

"Guys like it down, they do, I know they do. All guys have a long hair fetish. But it looks like shit with this dress. Shit! I'm not sure. I'm out of practice. What do you think, baby?"

Loup glanced up from her travel book. "Up, but with swirlies."

"Swirlies?"

She gestured. "Hanging down."

"Like this?" Pilar coiled a few loose tendrils around her fingers, then let them dangle.

"Perfect. Why are you so nervous? All you have to do is flirt with this guy. You could do that in your sleep, Pilar."

"I don't know." She sat on the edge of the bed. "It's always been fun. The only time it wasn't was with Rory Salamanca, and I don't feel good about that. I hurt you, and I wasn't exactly fair to him, either."

"I know." Loup kissed her cheek. "But this is totally different. You'll be using your awesome flirting superpowers for good instead of evil."

Pilar smiled reluctantly. "You think?"

"Yep."

"Do I look okay?"

"Model for me," Loup said. She watched Pilar stand and turn on high heels. Her dress had a bold floral pattern and a plunging neckline, and it clung to her shapely ass like a lover. "You look more than okay. You look hotter than fucking hell. And you're not wearing any underwear, are you?"

"No. Okay, quit looking at me that way. I'm gonna get all turned on and distracted." Pilar smiled again, more relaxed. "And you look really pretty, too. Like an ice cream caramel sundae."

"Huh?" Loup glanced down at herself.

"Cool and sweet and lickable. Okay, I'm shutting up now."

The wedding took place in a Renaissance cathedral. It was formal and interminable and involved a great deal of kneeling while the priest droned on in Italian. Loup looked around at the wedding guests, trying to identify their targets from the backs of their heads. She spotted Vincenzo Picco's distinctive gray mane. She studied the pink marble columns, carved at the top to look like fish scales.

She thought about the church at home and wondered what Father Ramon and all the Santitos were doing. She wished there was a way to tell them that the world was changing, that things might not always be as they had been, and that Miguel Garza might turn out to be a hero after all.

At last it ended. When they went through the receiving line, Fiorella greeted Sabine like a long-lost friend, hugging her and kissing her on both cheeks. She exclaimed over Loup and Pilar, and made a point of introducing them all to the wedding party.

"How delightful!" Pasquale Picco kissed Pilar's hand, lingering long enough to peer down her cleavage. "I hope to see you at the reception, *signorina*."

She giggled. "You Italian men are so charming!"

He smiled at her. "Some more than others, I hope."

On the groom's side of the wedding party, Gustavo Vittori glowered briefly, replacing the expression with a smooth mask of courtesy to greet the next guest.

The reception was at a country villa twenty minutes outside of town. They drove in a long convoy of cars, Sabine at the wheel.

"Well, you definitely made the right first impression," Loup offered.

Pilar shuddered. "Ick."

"At least he's better looking than the photos in his dossier. Hey, do you have anything to eat? I'm starving."

"Yeah, but he's one of those guys who look at you in a way that makes your skin crawl." Pilar fished in her decorative little purse and handed Loup a small bag of mixed nuts. "Sorry. That's all I could fit."

"Oh, for God's sake!" Sabine said irritably. "There will be food at the reception."

"Yeah, and I don't want to have to wolf it down like I've been on a deserted island, okay? I'm trying to be discreet."

Sabine's lips thinned. "Fine. Just try not to gawk at the villa."

"Yes, ma'am!"

The villa was gorgeous, the reception impossibly luxurious. The guests mingled on the expansive pool terrace while servers in white tuxedo shirts and crisp black pants circulated with trays of champagne flutes and hors d'oeuvres. When Pasquale Picco arrived, he made a beeline for Pilar.

"You must let me show you the grounds, *signorina*," he said smoothly, taking her arm.

She went with him, rolling her eyes when he wasn't looking.

"Vincenzo Picco called that one right, huh?" Loup said to Sabine.

"So it appears," she said absently, glancing around. "Gustavo is the one I worry about. Did you see his expression in the cathedral?"

"The one where he looked ready to explode?"

"Yes." Sabine gave her a serious look. "Keep a sharp eye on him, Loup. If you have to make a move without my signal, do it. Tonight, I will not begrudge you your speed. Our reputation is at stake." She paused. "Also, Magnus agreed to certain terms. We will not get paid if we cannot avert violence."

"Okay. You might not want to mention that to Pilar. She's already a little nervous."

The newlyweds arrived. There were innumerable champagne toasts. Pasquale returned to offer one, temporarily freeing Pilar.

"You okay?" Loup whispered to her.

"Mildly groped, but otherwise, yes. You?"

"Yeah." She nodded at an increasingly florid-faced Gustavo Vittori. "Just trying to keep an eye on him."

They were ushered in to dinner without incident. Loup, seated at a table without anyone she knew, watched Pilar flirt shamelessly with Pasquale, while at yet another table, Sabine made an attempt to engage the glowering Gustavo.

"So, Canada, eh?" A young man seated to her right smiled at her. "What is it like there?"

"Cold. Lots of wolves."

He blinked. "Wolves?"

"I'm kidding." She returned his smile. "Joking. You know joking, right?"

"Of course," he said. "Maybe you will dance with me later, Canada?"

Her smile turned rueful, knowing the odds were good he wouldn't like it if she did. It made her miss the easy camaraderie of her cousins. "Maybe."

There were more toasts after dinner. Vincenzo Picco gave a lengthy one. He caught Loup's gaze toward the end and closed one eye in a deliberate wink. She smiled despite herself. The bride and bridegroom glowed, joyous and happy.

And then it was back to the terrace, now adorned with hanging lanterns, for more champagne and dancing. The pool shimmered with wavering blue-green light. A string quartet in formal attire played.

The bride and groom danced alone to the first song.

Then others danced.

Pasquale held Pilar close, whispering in her ear. She giggled obligingly.

Gustavo's shoulders hunched and twitched. He conferred with a handful of men around him, then moved toward the dance floor.

"Loup—" Sabine began.

"On my way!" She threaded her way quickly and deftly through the wedding guests and intercepted Gustavo Vittori, blocking his way. "Hi."

He stared at her. "*Che cosa?*"

She slid her right hand up his left arm and pressed hard on a point on his inner elbow with her thumb, smiling sweetly at him. "You speak English, right? Well, I'm this wedding's guardian fucking angel. And you're not going to make any trouble, are you, *signore*? Because if you are, I'm going to have to press hard enough to do permanent damage to the nerve center and you'll never use this hand again. It's already numb, isn't it?"

Gustavo glowered.

Sabine arrived, gliding behind Loup. "I believe your car is waiting, *signore*," she said, smooth and diplomatic. "You would be well advised to say your farewells and leave."

He hesitated, still glowering.

"If it's any consolation, your new brother-in-law is *so* not getting laid tonight," Loup added with another sweet smile, maintaining pressure. "This wedding has more than one guardian angel."

The corners of his mouth twitched upward. "Truly?"

"Absolutely."

It was enough to make him relent. He gathered his men, said his farewells, and left peaceably.

"That was brilliant!" Fiorella effused. "I don't know what you said to make him leave quietly, but I like it very much." She gave Loup a hug and kissed her on both cheeks, then drew back, startled. "Oh!"

"I know, I know," she said, resigned. "I feel weird. Sorry."

The bride wore an odd expression. "That is not the word I would use."

"Ohh-kay." Loup took a quick step backward. "Hey, where's Pilar?"

They looked around the terrace. There was no sign of Pilar or Pasquale.

"Ah...try the conservatory," Fiorella said, still looking somewhat flustered. "It is on the ground floor past the great hall, a room with a large piano. Pasquale plays very well, and it is his favorite pretext for getting young women alone."

"Thank you."

They entered the villa and looked for the conservatory.

"Exactly what did you do to our client back there?" Sabine inquired.

"I'm not sure, but I think I just weirded out her wedding night." Loup cocked her head. "I hear a piano. This way."

"Very well. Let me handle this."

They arrived in time to see Pasquale finish with a flourish, then lunge for Pilar and pull her onto his lap, hands wandering busily.

"Hey!" she protested.

Sabine strode into the room. "Little trollop!" she scolded. "This has gone on long enough. I promised your mother I would ensure your good behavior on this trip. I'm so sorry, *signore*, I know she has been bothering you all evening."

He stood, dislodging Pilar. "No, no! Not at all."

"You are too kind." She switched to Italian, uttering profuse apologies and ignoring his passionate disclaimers. Behind his back, Pilar made a face and adjusted her dress. "Come," Sabine said sternly. "You will stay at my side for the rest of the evening. No more bothering Mr. Picco."

"But—" he said desperately.

"No, no." Sabine shook her head. "I insist."

Back on the terrace, they watched the elegant wedding guests dance. Pasquale Picco reemerged. After casting a few yearning glances Pilar's way, he began trolling the other young female guests for a second choice.

"You *so* enjoyed bitching me out," Pilar said to Sabine.

She gave a little smile. "Yes, well, it allowed me to extricate you without arousing his suspicion. Gustavo went peacefully once he saw the humor in the situation, but Pasquale may be rather irked to find he's been played for a fool."

The remainder of the night passed without incident. Guests began to leave. Pasquale Picco, failing in his quest, drank himself into a stupor and passed out on a chaise longue. Preparing to retire, the newlyweds made the rounds and thanked their guests.

"Excellent work," Domenico Vittori murmured, pressing a tip discreetly into Sabine's hand. "We are very pleased. Are we not, *caro*?" he added to Fiorella.

She blinked. "Oh, yes. Very pleased."

The valet went to fetch the rental car. They waited on the edge of the big circular driveway.

"Why was Fiorella acting so weird?" Pilar asked. "We *did* do a good job."

"She hugged me," Loup said. "I think she liked it."

"No!" She whirled around, staring back at the villa. "One of Christophe's one in a hundred?"

"Maybe."

Pilar stifled a giggle. "Shit! I mean, oh dear. That's so going to mess with her wedding night."

Sabine gave them both a look. "You presume a great deal."

"Nope." Pilar shook her head. "Trust me, if she liked the way Loup felt, she's going to be thinking about it for days. Days and days," she said dreamily. "And wondering what the hell is wrong with her." She gave herself another shake. "Remember that waiter in Huatulco who couldn't stop staring at Loup? Christophe says only one in maybe a hundred people feel that way, but when they do, look out."

Sabine gazed at the sky, her lips moving silently.

Pilar sighed. "What?"

"Nothing. I am thanking God that I am one of the other ninety-nine."

TWENTY-TWO

Incidence of one in a hundredism notwithstanding, Magnus deemed the job a success.

"We did the job we were hired to do," he said philosophically at the breakfast table. "I take it Loup did nothing to provoke this response?"

"No," Sabine admitted grudgingly.

He shrugged. "So? As an attractive woman, surely you've dealt with similar situations. Only without the, ah, genetically engineered aspect."

Loup looked up from her omelet. "Why do you keep saying that? I mean, I don't care, but it's not true. I wasn't engineered."

"It sounds better than GMO or genetically modified, which *is* technically correct. Whether or not you were conceived naturally, your genes are modified by science. And it certainly sounds better than half-breed genetic mutant."

"True."

"So what happens now?" Pilar asked. "I mean, now that the job's done. Do we go back to Aberdeen?"

Magnus smiled at her. "You're quite at liberty, my dear. Until I arrange another job for you, you're free to go where you will. Travel the world or pick a place to live. All I ask is that you make yourselves available for work within twenty-four hours' notice at all times."

"Anywhere?" Loup said. "We can go anywhere?"

"Certainly."

"You trust us?" Pilar asked, skeptical. "I mean, what if we decide to take our bonuses and disappear?"

"Ah." He folded his hands. "I wouldn't recommend it. Not traveling on illegitimate passports."

"Oh, great. Christophe was right, you *are* gonna blackmail us."

"Not at all." Magnus looked complacent. "We have an instance of perfectly balanced trust here. If you fulfill the terms of your contract, which I will remind you are extremely generous, you stand to become young women of certain means within a year's time. But if you violate our trust, we *will* violate yours."

"I guess that's fair," Loup admitted.

"Indeed." He checked his watch. "Sabine and I will be returning to Palermo today and taking a late flight to Geneva. You're welcome to ride to the city with us. If you would prefer to stay in Taormina, Global will cover today's expenses and another night's stay at the hotel. After that, you're on your own."

"Let's stay, baby," Pilar said without hesitation. "We've got to figure out where we want to go. Anyway, it's nice here."

"Okay."

They said their goodbyes in the hotel lobby. Magnus shook both their hands.

"You did good work," he said, formal and serious. "I'm very pleased. And I suspect I'll have more work for you in short order. The Picco family is very well connected."

"Whatever our next job is, can it please not involve me getting felt up by some skeevy Mafia guy?" Pilar said hopefully.

"I promise. That was an…unusual…situation."

Back in the hotel room, Loup fanned the pages of her travel book. "Got any ideas?" she asked Pilar.

"Paris," she said promptly. "I want to go to Paris."

"Why didn't you say so?" Loup blinked. "We could have ridden with…oh, yeah. I get your point."

"Mm-hmm." Pilar wrapped her arms around Loup from behind,

nuzzling her neck. "I get that she finds me *een-sufferable*. But I get tired of being reminded. Holy shit, you feel good, baby."

Loup squirmed.

"Paris," Pilar whispered in her ear. "City of lovers."

"Do we have to wait until Paris?"

"God, no!"

Later in the day, Pilar made their travel arrangements on her Dataphone. "Okay. We're booked. Flights, hotels, and everything. We'll take the bus to Palermo tomorrow and fly out the next morning." She frowned. "The bus part's cheap. The rest is pretty expensive. Money goes fast, huh?"

"We'll make more," Loup assured her. Somewhere in the room, her cell phone rang. "Oh, crap! Where did I put that thing? I've gotta figure out how to forward calls to my Dataphone." She scrambled and found it. "Hello? Yeah, good afternoon, Senator. Oh, right. Morning to you." Her face brightened. "Now? Sure. Now's a great time." She lowered the phone. "He's putting Miguel on."

"Whoopee," Pilar said, but without malice.

"Hey, Mig!" Loup said, delighted. "Yeah, we're fine. Both of us. Huh? No, Sicily. We're going to Paris tomorrow." She made a face and held the phone away from her ear for a moment, letting him bellow. "Okay, okay! I get it. It sucks. But just think about how much it means to everyone at home!"

"He's pissed?"

Loup nodded. "Mig, c'mon. Would you really feel that much better about it if I was stuck in a jail cell getting starved, hosed down, and interrogated?" She paused. "Yeah, they did." Another pause. Her voice softened. "Okay, I will. You too. Don't do anything stupid. This is a really awesome thing you're doing. Okay, bye."

"Sounds like your grouchy surrogate brother wasn't so glad to hear from you," Pilar commented.

"Yeah." Loup smiled ruefully. "I think in his own way, he was. But he's bored out of his skull and utterly disgusted that we're running around Europe while he's stuck in protective custody. He never wanted to be a hero, you know?"

"You are a strange and wonderful influence, my little wolf-girl." Pilar gave her a light kiss. "Time to get you something to eat?"

"Yes, please."

Two days later, they were in Paris.

Their hotel was located in the Latin Quarter. It wasn't as luxurious as the places they'd been staying when Global Security was paying, but it was charming and comfortable, and the staff was remarkably friendly.

"Is this your first visit?" the young man at the reception desk asked, having determined they didn't speak French.

"Yes." Pilar smiled at him. "Pretty much everything's a first time for us."

He returned her smile, plucked a rose from the arrangement on the counter, and handed it to her. "Welcome to Paris." He lowered his voice. "Do not buy pastries at the hotel café. There is an excellent bakery across the street. Try the *pain au chocolat*, you will like it."

They did.

"Ohmigod." Pilar's eyes almost rolled back in her head. "This is one of the best things I've ever eaten."

Loup eyed her, grinning.

"What?"

"It's fun to see you crazy over food for a change."

"Try it."

She took a bite. Layers of flaky pastry melted in her mouth, giving way to a firm center of dark, rich chocolate. "Holy shit!"

"Told you."

They explored the city, going first across the bridge to Notre Dame Cathedral on its little river island, located only blocks from their hotel.

"Wow." Loup stood for a long time just gazing at the facade. "Sorry."

"I don't care." Pilar squeezed her arm. "Gawk all you like, baby. It doesn't bother me one bit."

Inside, they wandered. Loup regarded the figure of the Our Lady of Paris, thinking about Our Lady of the Sorrows in the church at home, her cheeks stained with rusty, faded tears. She paid to light a votive candle in honor of Father Ramon, Sister Martha, Anna, and all the Santitos. In honor of her mother and brother, and even Miguel Garza.

"God has turned his face away," Pilar murmured. "That's what the old priest said before we were born, isn't it? The one before Father Ramon. God has turned his face away."

"Yeah. Just before he hung himself from the bell tower."

"Do you think it's true? About God, I mean?"

"I don't know. Seems like we fucked up pretty bad when everyone got sick. But most of the world seems to have recovered okay. Just not us."

"Loup..." Pilar searched her face. "I *don't* believe it. I mean, I don't know if I believe in God or whatever. But I believe there are good people in the world. Really good, like Father Ramon and Sister Martha. And I believe that *you* are a goddamned fucking miracle. If there is a God, no fucking way he'd turn his face away from you. And if there isn't..." She shrugged. "You're enough of a miracle for me, Santa Olivia."

Her heart felt too big for her chest. "Pilar..."

"Oh, hush! We're in one of the world's most famous churches. I'm being contemplative. C'mon, we haven't even seen the gargoyles yet."

They climbed the winding towers and went to see the gargoyles.

"Whoa!" Pilar gasped at the view of the city.

Loup leaned over the parapet. "Awesome."

Pilar hooked her fingers in the waistband of Loup's jeans, dragging her backward. "You make me nervous, baby."

"Sorry."

She studied the nearest gargoyle. "They look sort of...nice, don't they? I thought they'd be all ferocious, but they look kind of calm." She nudged Loup. "They're like you, only inside out. And they're kind of like bodyguards, too, right? You think maybe people knew somehow way back when?"

"I dunno." Loup smiled. "I like you being all mystical and thoughtful, but before you get too carried away, I've got two words for you."

"Hmm?"

"Nacio and Raimundo."

Pilar laughed. "Yeah, okay. But you *are* different. And those guys, maybe they will be too when they grow up a little more. I mean different in a different way, not the way they already are. You know?"

"I'm not sure."

"That's okay." Pilar smiled at her. "*I* do."

On their third day in Paris, Magnus called.

"Hi, Mr. Lindberg," Loup said. "Uh-huh. Paris." She listened. "Okay, the Beau Rivage. We'll call you when we get in."

"What's up?" Pilar asked.

Loup gave a crisp military salute perfected by virtue of growing up in an occupied town. "We're to report to headquarters immediately."

"Geneva?"

"Yep. Magnus says he's got another request for our services. Well, mine, this time. There's a room reserved for us at the Beau Rivage hotel."

"Okay." Pilar flipped on her Dataphone. "There's an eight forty a.m. train that will get us there by noon. Sound good?"

"Sure."

"This is a business expense, right?" She pulled out her Global credit card. "We're *so* going first class."

The following morning, they traveled through the spectacular French Alps and arrived in Geneva. At the hotel, Loup called and reported to Magnus.

"Okay," she said. "Three o'clock. See you then." She ended the call. "He's sending a car for us. They'll pick us up outside the hotel. Magnus will brief us, then we'll meet with the client afterward."

"At least it gives us time for lunch." Pilar inspected her hair in the mirror, smoothing a few errant strands. "Did he say anything about the job?"

Loup shook her head. "No."

"I guess we'll find out."

They ate at one of the hotel's restaurants before being picked up by an unsmiling driver who took them to Global Security's headquarters. Unlike much of the surrounding architecture, it was a newer building, sleek and modern. Inside, an unsmiling receptionist scanned their passports before issuing security passes.

"Clip them to your clothing," she said crisply with barely a trace of an accent. "Be sure they are visible at all times." She pressed an intercom and said something in a different language.

A moment later, Sabine came to fetch them. "Good. Come with me."

"Nice to see you again so soon, too," Pilar remarked.

Sabine raised one finger, looking serious. "No joking or bickering today. This is not the time for bad blood."

She escorted them to a conference room where Magnus was waiting, along with Henry Kensington, who'd led the security team at Fashion Week.

"Here is the situation," Magnus said without preamble. "We are providing security for an event hosted by Mr. Hugh Danielson. A birthday party for his daughter's thirteenth birthday."

Loup blinked. "This is all about some kid's birthday party?"

"Please do not be frivolous. Mr. Danielson is the chairman of the British-Swiss Chamber of Commerce. It is an organization that has achieved certain prominence in financial circles in the last decade. Recently, it has been targeted by a group of radical economic populists. They call themselves One World. *I* call them terrorists." His jaw tightened. "Their goal is to call attention to financial inequity in the world by highlighting the decadence of the very wealthy. They use violence to achieve their means. Two days ago, they issued a death threat against Mr. Danielson's daughter."

"Damn," Pilar murmured.

"Yes." Magnus nodded. "The party as scheduled is very lavish. They warn that if it is not canceled, it will end in tragedy."

"He won't cancel?" Loup asked.

"No." He shook his head. "Mr. Danielson refuses to succumb to blackmail. He is a widower, a proud and stubborn man who dotes on his daughter. He will not cancel."

"Is the threat credible?" she asked.

"Good question." Magnus gave Loup a look of harried approval. "Yes. Yes, it is. One World has been responsible for a number of deaths. Eighteen months ago, they succeeded in blowing up a limousine carrying the former sultan of Dubai. But this is the first time they have targeted a child." He steepled his fingers. "Loup, this choice is yours. Mr. Danielson received word of your existence through, ah, certain channels. He inquired about your services, thinking you could provide an extra layer of protection. Global Security has committed to this job, but I have not committed *you*. You're young and inexperienced. If you wish to pass, I will call off the meeting and extend our regrets."

"Yeah, but I'm good." Loup looked at Pilar. "What do you think?"

Pilar sighed. "Oh, hell. It's a kid, you know?"

"Uh-huh."

"So you wish to be considered for the job?" Magnus asked, clarifying.

"Yeah," Loup said thoughtfully. "I kind of get what the One World people are saying, you know? The world could be a lot more fair than it is, and that sucks. A lot of rich and powerful people suck. But killing them for it is wrong. Especially kids."

He breathed a sigh of relief. "If the client concurs, your sole duty will be to guard his daughter throughout the duration of this party. He'll want a demonstration. Are you prepared to do a standard disarmament drill with Mr. Kensington here?"

Loup glanced at Henry. "Sure."

"What about me?" Pilar asked. "I'm not letting Loup do this alone."

"It, ah, might be better if you did."

She folded her arms. "You hired us as a team."

"All right, all right!" Magnus put up his hands. "Clive insists you're a decent marksman. You can be auxiliary backup. Do you really have experience tending a bar?"

"Yeah, for two years."

"Fine."

The client arrived ten minutes later, ushered into the conference room by Sabine. Hugh Danielson was a fleshy, middle-aged British man with stubborn lines etched around his mouth. "'Lo, Magnus. Which one's the GMO?" he asked, glancing around the table.

Loup stood up. "I am, sir."

The lines deepened. "You don't look like much."

Magnus snapped his fingers. "Henry?"

Henry rose, drawing his pistol. Loup crossed the room in a blurred flash, deflecting his weapon hand downward. She feinted a punch at his face, pulling it at the last second. When he flinched, she threw him neatly over her hip, plucking the pistol out of his hand as he soared. "Sorry!" She winced as he hit the conference room floor hard. "You okay?"

"Yeah," he grunted.

Hugh Danielson stared.

Loup checked the pistol to confirm it was unloaded, then set it carefully on the table. "If that was for real, I would have just taken him out. I wouldn't have pulled my punch. But I hope you get the idea, sir."

He stared some more, then turned to Magnus. "I want her."

"You understand it will cost?" Magnus turned smooth and obsequious. "Lupe Herrera *is* the only one of her kind."

"I don't care," Danielson said bluntly. "I want her."

Magnus smiled. "Then you shall have her."

TWENTY-THREE

Loup stared at the scripted itinerary for the party. "You're joking."

"Wish I were," Henry Kensington said laconically.

"A *pirate attack*?"

"Not just any old pirate attack, baby," Pilar said, scanning the details. "Danielson's hired Diarmuid McDermott to reprise his role as the dashing pirate captain Mick O'Malley."

"Who?"

"His daughter Rose's favorite actor," Henry offered. "Young Irish bloke did a big swashbuckler film last year. Word is he's got serious gambling debts, bad enough to make him willing to take on a gig like this. The rest of the outfit's a production company specializing in major spectacles. But it's a bloody security nightmare, and the sea battle's the worst of it."

"And the kid's gotta be on the ship, huh?"

"Oh, yes." He looked weary. "In order for the dashing Mick O'Malley to board her and lose his heart to the fair English Rose, declaring her his pirate queen."

"Jesus," Loup muttered. "They really oughta cancel."

"Quite," he agreed. "But they won't. We'll meet with the clients and the event coordinator tomorrow. Since the threat was issued, we've been negotiating to determine how many of the crew will be actors, and how many members of the security team. I want you on that ship, Loup."

"And me, right?" Pilar added.

"Actually, yes." Henry sighed. "I'd love to staff the entire enterprise with our people. But I can't guarantee it. They insist on having a certain number of professional actors supplied by the company to provide authenticity of experience. We're running background checks on all of them."

Loup read more of the script. "Pyrotechnics, huh? Nothing like a few fake explosions to make things more complicated."

He winced. "Don't remind me."

They met the client, his daughter, and the event coordinator the following day at the Danielsons' elegant townhouse. The event coordinator was a thin, steely-eyed woman named Jeanne Blondet.

The daughter Rose was a pubescent nightmare.

She took one look at Loup and Pilar and declared, "I don't want them, Papa! I don't want them on my ship, and I don't want them at my party!"

"Hush, pet," Hugh Danielson soothed her. "I promised you the best of everything, didn't I? Wait until you see what Ms. Herrera can do." He shot Loup an urgent look. "*Do* something, won't you?"

"Yes, sir." Loup looked at the girl's narrow, suspicious face and decided it would be best to be nonthreatening. She plucked a polished apple from a gleaming silver bowl and tossed it across the salon in a high arc, then flashed across the room to snatch it out of the air when it had scarce cleared its apex. She returned in a shot, bowed, and presented the apple. "Here you go, my lady."

"I don't want it."

"Okay." Loup placed the apple carefully back in the bowl. "But that's what I can do, you see? If there are bad guys out to get you, I can protect you faster and better than anyone in the world."

Rose sniffed. "I'm not a *child*. Don't talk to me like one!"

"You're right. I'm sorry."

Father and daughter engaged in a silent contest of wills. "Oh, all right!" Rose relented. "She can be on the ship, and she can come with me to the pirate ship. But she can't be a girl. She has to be a boy."

"How about your faithful cabin boy?" Jeanne Blondet, recovering from her astonishment at Loup's demonstration, opened a portfolio and whipped out a sketch of a slight figure in a striped shirt, ragged breeches, and a stocking cap. "That's a character I'm willing to recast." She sent an uncertain smile in Loup's direction. "I think she would be quite charming as the faithful cabin boy following his little mistress into adventure."

"I don't *want* her to be charming!"

"She means it would make the picture *you* make all the more charming," Danielson said smoothly. "Isn't that right?"

"Don't patronize me, Papa!"

"I don't know," Loup said in a dubious tone, examining the sketch. "I'm not crazy about that hat."

"It's gonna look pretty silly on you, baby," Pilar agreed.

"You *will* wear the hat!" Rose said in a flash of temper. "All day and all night. If you're going to attend me, I want you to be my faithful cabin boy for the whole party and never leave my side!"

Loup hesitated, feigning reluctance.

"Our client has made a request, Ms. Herrera," Henry Kensington said in a stern voice.

"All right, all right! I'll be your faithful cabin boy."

"Good." Rose was mollified. "But I don't want *her* there." She pointed at Pilar. "She's not anything special, is she, Papa?"

"She's a trained bodyguard, pet. They work as a team. I've already agreed."

"Did you agree she could be on the ship?"

"No," he said. "I agreed that she could tend bar. Sweetheart, it's not a bad idea to have security people no one would ever suspect. Ms. Mendez certainly fits that description."

The girl narrowed her eyes. "So as long as nothing happens, she'd just be another servant?"

"Ah..." He paused. "That's exactly right."

"Fine."

They hashed out a few further details of the arrangements, and Jeanne Blondet gave Loup an address to report to later in the day to have the cabin boy's costume altered to fit her.

"Yikes!" In the back of their sedan, Pilar shuddered. "That child's a piece of work."

"She's a handful and a half," Henry agreed from the front. "Don't suppose it's all her fault, but still." He glanced back at them. "Nice work, by the way. That bit about the hat. It brought her right around. A little of the old reverse psychology, eh?"

"Yep," Loup agreed. "If that means what I think it means."

"It does."

"I don't like not being on the ship," Pilar fretted. "That's the most dangerous part, right?"

"We're taking every precaution and then some," Henry assured her.

"Still." She eyed Loup. "If anything happens to you on that stupid fucking ship, I'll never forgive you."

"It won't."

"Promise?"

"Promise." Loup glanced out the window. "Hey, Henry. I thought we were going back to the hotel?"

He shook his head. "Headquarters, first. We're going to visit the armory and get the both of you outfitted and legal. HQ's been working on the permits; they ought to have come through. Clive trained the two of you on the Glock 26, yeah? The Baby Glock?"

Pilar brightened. "We get to carry on this job?"

He gave her a look. "I told you. We're taking *every* precaution. Pray you don't need to use it."

"I will."

The production company was nothing but efficient. Within

twenty-four hours of Loup's fitting, the costume arrived. She tried it on in the hotel room at Pilar's insistence and stood before her barefoot in ragged black pants, a black-and-white striped shirt, a cropped vest that concealed a tailored shoulder holster, and a red stocking cap.

"Well?" Loup asked.

Pilar giggled. "You look somewhere between ridiculous and adorable. Which pretty much adds up to charming, baby."

"Mmm." Loup caught her around the waist, dropping her voice an octave. "Think we can rewrite the script so the faithful cabin boy ends up with the hot bartender?"

"Is the door locked?"

"Mm-hmm."

"God, yes."

Afterward they lounged in bed, both studying their dossiers and memorizing the details of the elaborate itinerary and guest list.

"I kinda feel sorry for the kid," Pilar said. "You notice there aren't a lot of other kids on the list? I mean, she's a spoiled brat and all, but thirteen's a tough age. I bet she doesn't have a lot of friends."

"No wonder."

"I'm just saying it's tough. And losing her mom, too."

"Yeah." Loup glanced up. "We were thirteen when we met. We'd both lost our parents."

"True." Pilar toyed with the tassel on the end of Loup's cap, which was the only item of clothing Loup was wearing. "But we didn't have anyone to spoil us. And if there was one good thing about growing up in the orphanage, it's that we learned that people have to take care of one another—the way Father Ramon and Sister Martha took care of everyone, and the Santitos took care of each other." She smiled. "You know, I thought you were younger at first."

"Oh, yeah?"

"Mm-hmm. You were just this cute, wiry kid with intense eyes. I didn't believe C.C. when he told me about you and swore me to secrecy. I thought he was just spouting some wild bullshit."

Loup smiled. "Sometimes it was hard to tell with C.C."

"No kidding. Then I saw you and T.Y. messing around in the courtyard one day. He was trying to hit you with a tennis ball, and you were zipping around like crazy, laughing your head off. But I still thought of you as a kid."

"A kid with a hot older brother," Loup reminded her. "You had a crush on Tommy, remember?"

"Everyone did." Pilar tickled Loup's nose with the tassel. "And it's not my fault I was an early bloomer. When you did a year or so later...God, I can't believe I didn't notice now. Not until the day of my aunt's funeral, when my uncle tried to drag me back home with him. You stopped him, remember?"

"Vividly."

"I hugged you." She abandoned the tassel to run her hand along the sleek curve of Loup's back. "I was just so glad you'd made him let me go, you know?" She shook her head. "Except I didn't want to stop, and nothing's ever been the same since."

Loup laughed. "Pilar, does this conversation still have anything to do with our bratty client? Because you're *so* getting your smolder on."

"Umm...no?" Pilar raised her eyebrows. "You okay with that?"

"Yep!"

TWENTY-FOUR

The party took place at a château on the shore of Lake Geneva.

The sea battle took place *on* Lake Geneva. A mixed crew of actors and security team members boarded a scaled-down model of an eighteenth-century brig at the jetty. The sailors looked jaunty and the officers looked impressive in their velvet doublets trimmed with gold braid and tricorn hats, an effect only slightly marred by the radio earpieces several of them wore.

Waiting to board, Rose Danielson shivered with anticipation. She wore an elaborate period gown and her cheeks were flushed with pleasure.

"It will be such an exciting voyage, don't you think, Tip?" she said to Loup, standing beside her in her cabin boy's costume.

"Huh?" Loup blinked.

The girl's nostrils flared. "You're to say 'yes, mistress,' or 'yes, mum'!"

"Yes, mum," Loup said obligingly. "Sorry. I didn't know I was Tip."

"Tip is a perfectly good name for a cabin boy, don't you think?"

"Yes, mum."

The captain, who was an actor, escorted Rose aboard the ship personally, giving her his arm and behaving unctuously. Her flush deepened. Loup padded obediently behind her diminutive mistress, alert and attentive. Henry Kensington, the first mate, gave her a subtle nod.

Once they were aboard, the captain gave the order to hoist sails. Up went the sails, while a discreet motor purred into life.

"Forward go we to seek our fortunes in the new world!" the captain shouted.

On the shore, a crowd of partygoers in period attire shouted, "Huzzah!"

Rose leaned over the railing, waving a kerchief. "Goodbye, Papa! Goodbye! Don't weep for me, Papa!"

He blew her a dozen kisses, looking profoundly worried.

"Idiot," Loup murmured under her breath.

The girl gave her a sharp glance. "What's that you say, Tip?"

She returned a look of wide-eyed innocence. "Nothing, mum."

They chugged toward the center of the lake. The actors fawned over Rose, making a show of being attentive toward her. She blushed and giggled, reveling in the attention. Loup stuck close to her side, scanning the crew intently.

Right on schedule, the scaled-down pirate galleon glided into view, bearing swiftly down upon them.

"It's Mick O'Malley!" the captain cried. "Man the starboard guns!"

There was a booming sound and a puff of smoke. The pirate galleon tacked, then essayed a smoky boom of its own.

Rose squealed.

Pyrotechnic effects on the brig's rigging sizzled and guttered, failing to ignite. Members of the crew glanced at one another.

"We're hit!" the captain called, ignoring evidence to the contrary. "It's every man for himself!"

Actors began diving overboard.

"I pray you, kind Tip, don't leave me." Rose clutched Loup's arm. "I fear the pirate captain's cruel intentions."

"No, mum."

The girl eyed her. "You feel...odd. I don't care for it."

"Good."

Amid a bit of staged swordplay, Diarmuid McDermott vaulted aboard the ship in character as Mick O'Malley. He was a handsome young man with a thick shock of fair hair and vivid green eyes. He tilted his head back and issued a full-throated laugh, breaking it off at the sight of Rose. "But what is this?" he asked, wondering. "Is it a woman or a child? So young, and yet so valiant! I profess myself quite overcome."

Rose blushed violently. "Good sir..."

"No, no!" He sank to his knees, pressing her hand between his. "You are exquisite. You are beyond compare. This life does not suffice to sustain you. You must come with me and be my pirate queen. And I shall issue my personal amnesty for all your crew!"

"All—all right," she stammered. "Come, Tip!"

"Yes, mum."

Loup watched the costumed movie star help her client navigate the tricky crossing to the pirate ship, then vaulted over effortlessly, landing on her bare feet.

The dashing pirate captain eyed her. "Oh, my. You're something else, aren't you?"

"Nope." She adjusted her red stocking cap. "Security, that's all."

"Rightio."

After a bit of byplay in which the pirates hailed Rose as their pirate queen, the pirate ship sailed to the jetty. The brig ostensibly limped behind it, having retrieved several drenched actors. The crowd greeted their arrival with cheers. Hugh Danielson swept his daughter into his arms as she disembarked, then shook Diarmuid McDermott's hand and thanked him for bringing her back safely.

"They made a botch of it, Papa," Rose said in a more subdued tone than she might have used if her movie idol hadn't been present. "The fire and smoke didn't go. It was terribly disappointing. You'll have someone dismissed for this, won't you?"

"Absolutely, pet."

Henry Kensington's voice crackled in Loup's ear. "Land team, are we secure for arrival?"

"Affirmative," came the reply.

"Sea team, four square and perimeter," Henry said. "Loup, stay close to the target."

She touched the transmit button. "Affirmative."

Rose pouted. "Whoever are you talking to, Tip?"

"Ah...First Mate Kensington, mum."

"Well, I don't care for it!"

Loup gave her a look, warning her not to push it.

Inside the château, they adjourned to the great hall on the second floor. It was a splendid space with vast windows and a high, vaulted rococo ceiling. Even in daylight, the spectacular crystal chandelier blazed. Henry Kensington relaxed visibly, feeling better about his team's security now that they weren't on open water and exposed. Waitstaff in contemporary black-and-white garb struggled to circulate through the throng.

"They're too slow!" Rose complained. "Tip, fetch champagne for Captain O'Malley and myself."

"You sure, mum?"

"Papa said I might have two glasses. I would like the first one *now*."

Loup threaded her way through the crowd to Pilar's station at the far end of the hall, cutting to the head of the line. "Sorry," she apologized. "It's for the birthday girl. I need two glasses of champagne, Pilar."

"Everything go okay out there?" Pilar asked, relieved to see her.

"More or less. The fireworks fizzled." Loup wrinkled her nose. "Still smells like smoke, though."

"To you, maybe." Pilar handed her two champagne flutes. "Back to your mistress, cabin boy."

"Aye, aye."

By the time she returned, Rose and McDermott had already been served. "Never mind." He quaffed his first glass while well-wishers greeted his pirate queen, then surreptitiously downed the two that Loup had brought. "I could use something with a wee bit more bite." He glanced longingly in the direction of Pilar's station. "Tell her ladyship I'll be right back."

"Okay."

Several minutes later, Rose noticed his absence and glanced around to spot him leaning on the counter of the bar, flirting with Pilar. "I *knew* I didn't want her here!" She stamped her foot. "Tip, fetch him back!"

"Don't want to leave you unattended, mum." Loup pushed the transmit button. "Pilar, please send the nice pirate captain away."

A few members of the security team hid smiles. Diarmuid McDermott returned with a glass of whiskey, weaving very slightly.

"Forgive me, my English Rose," he said smoothly. "I do but wish to toast to your beauty!" He hoisted his glass and drank.

She lifted her chin. "You're *not* what I expected."

He lowered his glass and gave her a rakish grin. "Do you not read the tabloids, love?"

While servers circled the tables, pouring ice water in preparation for the early dinner, a band in Regency attire began to play. McDermott handed his glass to Loup and bowed to Rose. "Let me make it up to you on the dance floor, my lady."

Loup shifted to get a better angle, watching them dance. Other couples joined them. The flush returned to Rose's cheeks—but then, it was unseasonably warm and growing warmer in the crowded hall.

And she still smelled smoke.

She sniffed her clothing, then the clothing of a startled actor in pirate costume. There was a lingering trace of smoke and a cordite-like smell from the botched special effects. Not the same smell. Loup moved closer to the balcony, where a handful of guests were smoking cigars. It wasn't that, either.

"Henry," she said into her earpiece. "Can you come here a second?"

He made his way to her. "What is it?"

"I smell smoke."

"Probably just from the special effects." He lowered his voice, conspiratorial. "We arranged for them to flub the big one for safety's sake. Dear Papa was in on it."

She shook her head. "It's not. Trust me, I can tell the difference. If it were my call, I think we should evacuate."

Henry looked around the crowded hall. "I'll check it out. We vetted this place pretty thoroughly."

Five minutes later, the fire broke out.

It started as a charred spot on the eastern wall, spreading rapidly and bursting into open flame that quickly began to devour antique wallpaper and hanging draperies. At the first scream of "Fire!" a stampede ensued, turning swiftly to a deadly, crushing pandemonium as guests unwittingly blocked the doors.

"Shit!" Loup plowed her way against the tide of people. She passed the fleeing Diarmuid McDermott and grabbed a terrified Rose, dragging her in the opposite direction. The girl kicked and screamed. "You can't go that way! People are getting trampled!"

"I don't want to die in the fire!"

"You won't!" She jerked her chin at Pilar, half-frozen behind her bar station, trying to summon her while hauling Rose to the farthest western corner and yanking open a window. "Stick your head out the window, okay? Breathe the fresh air."

"Loup!" Henry's voice came over her earpiece, tight and strained, barely audible over the screaming. "Do you have the target in a safe place?"

"Yeah!" she shouted back.

"Do *not* attempt to exit right now. Hold your position until my word. Do you copy?"

"Copy. Don't worry. I can get her out safe."

"I wouldn't count on it," a man's voice said, calm and menacing.

Loup squinted through the thickening smoke to see a figure holding a gun emerge—an actor in a striped sailor's shirt. She shifted instinctively to block Rose, who let out a terrified squeak and hid behind her.

"Move away from the girl." The sailor gestured with his gun. "This isn't your fight."

"Fuck you." She stared at the round black bore and felt the distant, empty feeling inside her where fear should be, coupled with rising anger. The sailor stopped at a wary distance, but well within shooting range. Loup calculated and realized that even with her speed, she couldn't get to him before he got off a shot—at least not without exposing her client. She made a quick move for the holster concealed under her vest.

Fast as she was, she wasn't faster than a speeding bullet.

The sailor fired over her head, then aimed at her chest. The gunshot set off more screaming in the background. Henry was shouting in her earpiece. The sailor raised his voice. "Step away from the girl!"

Loup sighed, the empty feeling growing. She really, really didn't want to get shot and killed trying to protect a thirteen-year-old spoiled brat, but she couldn't abandon her, either. She hoped Pilar would understand and forgive her one day. "I can't."

The sailor's finger began to tighten on the trigger.

"Drop your fucking gun!" Pilar stepped out of the coiling smoke and took a shooter's stance beside Loup. Her voice was shaking, but the gun was steady.

The sailor's gun didn't budge, either. "Drop yours or I shoot her."

She hesitated.

"Rose," Loup murmured, sidling closer. "Get behind Pilar. Pilar, get ready to shoot the fucker."

"Baby, don't—"

"Just do it!"

The instant Rose obeyed and took cover behind Pilar, Loup darted off at an angle with inhuman speed. Out of the corner of her eye, she saw the gun in the sailor's hand move instinctively to track her, and launched into a diving roll.

There were two gunshots. Neither one hit her. She came up in a spinning crouch, unharmed, pistol drawn.

The sailor blinked at her, wavering on his feet. There was a bloodstain spreading on his upper right arm and he couldn't get his hand to raise the gun.

"I'm sorry!" Pilar said behind her, tears in her voice. "I choked. I couldn't shoot to kill."

"You did great." Loup rose and holstered her pistol. "Perfect, even. If he lives through this, they're gonna want to question him." She plucked the gun from his nerveless hand, ejected the cartridge, and checked the chamber, then tossed both out the window.

"You—" he began.

"Shut up." For the first time in her life, she hit an ordinary human being with all her strength, throwing a right hook that shattered bones in his jaw and took him down like a sack of potatoes. "Okay." The smoke was getting thick enough to sear her throat. "He's going out the window, and so are we."

"It's too high!" Rose wailed.

Loup hoisted the limp sailor and dangled him out the window. "For him, maybe." She let the body fall with a sickening thud. "But better broken bones than burning to death. Now you, you're going to be safe as can be, because I'm going to catch you. I'm going to catch both of you."

Pilar looked at the two-story drop, then at her, worried. "Loup, it's awfully far."

"I can do it. Can you lower Rose like I did the killer sailor?"

"Yeah, I think so." She nodded, eyes bright with tears. "*Muy macha, sí?*"

"*Sí.*" Loup kissed her cheek, then climbed over the windowsill, mindful of the limp figure below. She hung from her hands, then let herself drop.

It was a long drop.

The manicured lawn rushed up to meet her. She landed in a perfect four-point stance, absorbing and dispersing the impact. Even so, it jarred her entire body. It took her a few seconds to collect herself; then she rose on numb feet, shaking out her numb hands. She dragged the unconscious sailor's body out of the way.

"Okay!" she shouted.

Rose panicked when Pilar lowered her by her wrists, flailing in the air.

"I'm losing my grip!" Pilar struggled, leaning too far out the window. "Fuck! She's gonna pull me over!"

"*Rose!*" The word came out half shout, half growl. "Cut it out! Remember the apple? I *will* fucking catch you!"

The girl stopped flailing.

"Now!"

Pilar let her go.

Loup caught her deftly and set her feet gently on the ground.

"You...you hurt my sides." Rose sniffled, more bewildered and terrified than hurt.

"I'm sorry, sweetheart. I tried to be as careful as I could." Loup turned back to the window. "Ready?"

Pilar, white-faced, didn't answer, only climbed out the window and let herself hang from the sill, arms trembling.

"Okay!" Loup called.

She let go.

Loup caught her around the waist, staggering a little under the greater impact, then setting her down. "You okay?"

"Yeah." Pilar turned breathlessly in her arms. "Thanks, baby." She pulled herself together and knelt in front of Rose. "How about you, honey? Are you all right?"

"Bruised ribs, maybe," Loup said. "I did my best."

"Does this hurt?" Pilar pressed lightly. "Here?"

"No." The girl's eyes were wide, pupils dilated. "It doesn't... it doesn't hurt, really. I was just frightened." She burst into tears. "Where's...where's my papa? Is he in there?"

Loup glanced up at the window, seeing flames. She reached for the transmit button on her earpiece and realized she'd lost it along with her cap when she dove to avoid the killer's bullet. "Pilar, is your radio working?"

"I'll check." She held the sobbing Rose with one arm, pressing her earpiece with her free hand. "Henry? Anyone? What's the status? We've got Rose out here, she's safe."

They couldn't hear anything but shouting and noise. Pilar's gaze met Loup's.

"I'll go," Loup said. "Let's get to a safe distance." She took the unconscious man under the arms and dragged him some twenty yards across the lawn. Pilar followed, carrying the thirteen-year-old Rose with some effort. The crying girl clung to her, disdainful young lady turned scared child. They could hear sirens as fire engines and medical vehicles began to arrive. "Okay, good. Get Rose over to the ambulances and have her checked out. You too. And tell them about this guy." She nodded at the sailor. One of his legs was bent at an unnatural angle, and his gunshot arm was bleeding. "He's not going anywhere."

"Okay. Be *careful*, Loup!"

"I will."

She raced around to the front of the château. A handful of guests had escaped unharmed and were milling on the front terrace in confusion. Loup cut through them and plunged back into the château.

The scene on the great marble staircase that led to the second story was a nightmare. The fire and the worst of the smoke were upstairs, but the second and third waves of people attempting to escape had overtaken the first, trampling them. The staircase was clogged with partygoers, those on top trying to clamber desperately over those on the bottom. The sound of the cries from those trapped below was pitiful.

"Fuck!" Loup grabbed the nearest body and hoisted, putting him down and whipping around to prevent someone else from taking his place. "Calm the fuck down, people!" she shouted, helping a battered woman to her feet.

They didn't.

Swearing and hoisting, she worked to clear the stairs. Within minutes, firefighters arrived and began to assist. One caught Loup's arm and said something in German, pointing toward the door.

Another shook his head and said something else in an awestruck tone.

She kept working.

"Lupe!" Hugh Danielson, freed by a firefighter, staggered over to her. He was limping and had a welt rising on one cheek. He looked at her with the expression of a man not daring to hope. "Rose?"

"She's fine, sir." Loup glanced at the staircase. The firefighters were beginning to restore order and clear a path. "Come with me."

She led him over to the ambulances, where they found Rose and Pilar, the former still clinging to the latter's hand.

"Papa!" She launched herself at him. He knelt and held her close, whispering against her hair, then held her away from him and examined her.

"The medic says she's fine," Pilar offered.

"She doesn't have a scratch." He looked up, bewildered. "How? I thought you were trapped toward the rear of the hall. And there were…" He swallowed. "Gunshots."

"Where's the guy?" Loup asked Pilar.

She pointed to a figure on a stretcher, a policeman standing guard. "Over there."

"That's your shooter, sir," Loup said to Danielson. "He shot at me and missed, and Pilar shot him in the arm. I knocked him out and threw him out the window, then we went out the window after him. Looks like they've got him in custody now."

He blinked slowly, glancing back at the château. Smoke was pouring out the second-story windows, vying with thick streams of water now that the fire engines were in place. "You…jumped?"

"Loup jumped," Pilar clarified. "She caught us."

He blinked again. "And you…shot that man?"

"Yeah. Yes." She shivered. "I did."

"Oh. Thank you."

"You're—" Pilar startled and touched her earpiece. "Henry? Are you okay? Yeah, fine. Rose is fine. Loup, too. She lost her radio. We're over by the ambulances with Mr. Danielson. Okay." She nodded at Hugh Danielson. "You should get checked out by the medics, sir."

"Right." He limped away, dazed, his daughter clutching his hand.

"Shit." Loup leaned against the side of an ambulance, feeling the bone-jarring ache of her hard landing and the strain of exertion in every fiber of her body, her throat and lungs smoke-scoured. She regarded the contained chaos of the ongoing rescue mission. "You think after all this they'll figure it was worthwhile going through with it?"

"I hope to God not."

"Me too."

"Loup…"

"I know, I know." She rolled her aching shoulders. "It was stupid and dangerous. But it was the only way I could think of to distract him and give you a clean shot without endangering the kid. It was dumb, but it worked. Okay?"

"Okay. I don't want to argue. Not today." Pilar kissed her, soft and lingering. "Stupid fucking little hero," she added, tears in her eyes.

Loup smiled at her. "Yeah, well. You too, huh?"

"I guess."

"Believe me, you are."

TWENTY-FIVE

There was an investigation and lengthy debriefing in the aftermath of the Danielson affair.

Thanks to heroic efforts all around, there were no fatalities, but there were multiple injuries, many of them serious. The worst was a woman with a crushed rib cage and collapsed lungs, who was still in grave condition.

And, of course, their client had nearly been assassinated.

"This was a disaster of epic proportion," Magnus said, curt and icy. "How did it happen?"

"Intelligence failure and human error, sir," Henry Kensington said steadily, his right arm in a sling. "I take full responsibility."

"Tell me."

"According to their specs, Château Legaspe's wiring was thoroughly modernized and brought up to code seven years ago. The specs were provided by the company they contracted to perform the update, and we had no reason to question them." He looked ill. "But according to the arson investigator, the majority of the old wiring was never actually replaced. The work that was done was largely cosmetic. They were bilked. The place has been a firetrap for years."

Magnus stared. "You're telling me the fire was a *coincidence*?"

"Basically, yes."

"What about the assassin?"

"He's not talking, but we're fairly certain he meant to make his attempt on the ship during the pyrotechnics and get away underwater. He might have succeeded if we hadn't gotten Dear Papa to agree to botching the effects. The police found an emergency oxygen cylinder in his pocket. It would have bought him fifteen minutes' time, enough to get to a waiting boat."

"That could have been intended to prevent smoke inhalation."

Henry shook his head. "It's a model designed specifically for underwater emergencies. It's not fire-safe."

"And how the *hell* did he get on that ship?"

He took a deep breath. "Ah...it appears he incapacitated one of the actors earlier in the day and took his place using a forged ID."

"And no one noticed?"

"No." Henry looked more ill. "We checked IDs, but we didn't cross-reference them against the original photos in the dossier. Due to the last-minute changes, the other performers simply assumed he was part of the security team."

"I see." Magnus was quiet for a moment. No one in the conference room made a sound. "Henceforth, all venues will be inspected by a qualified electrical engineer contracted by Global Security. All identity checks will include visual cross-referencing." He waved one hand. "You are dismissed."

Several dozen men and women rose and hurried gratefully for the door.

"Ms. Herrera!" Magnus called. "I'd like you and Ms. Mendez to stay."

Pilar glanced at Loup, who shrugged.

"I expect you've some idea what this is about," he said to them when everyone had left, save for Sabine standing sentinel behind him.

"Is it because I didn't shoot to kill?" Pilar winced. "I choked, I know."

"No, no."

"Is it the swearing?" Loup asked. "I'm sorry, I didn't mean to swear at the kid. Oh, and the other guests. I just forgot in the heat of the moment, you know?"

"No one mentioned the swearing." Magnus looked bemused. "No. Loup, Pilar...against all odds, your performances were the only bright spot in this godforsaken catastrophe." His mouth twisted. "It's the only reason Hugh Danielson isn't suing us yet." He beckoned to Sabine, who laid a briefcase on the table and opened it. "He wishes to buy out your contracts and assign you as full-time bodyguards to his daughter."

Loup looked at the offer. "Whoa! For a million bucks?"

"Euros, yes. Under the terms of your contract, you'd each receive a hundred and twenty-five thousand euros to serve out the remaining eleven months. After that, you'd be free to renegotiate on your own terms."

"And *you'd* make a nice profit," Pilar commented.

"A profit, yes." Magnus steepled his fingers. "Not as hearty as one might suppose after factoring in months of private training, signing bonuses, generous business expenses, and the political markers called in to get your passports. I will be honest. I am only entertaining this offer because Global failed a client. But the choice is yours."

"What happens if we pass?" Loup asked. "Do you get sued?"

He hesitated. "It's possible. But that isn't your concern. We failed to perform due diligence." He shrugged. "If Danielson sues us, we will sue Château Legaspe for providing false data and endangering hundreds of people."

"I told you to make him sign a waiver," Sabine muttered.

Magnus glanced up. "Yes, you did."

"That idiocy with the pirate ship."

"Duly acknowledged, Sabine." He looked back at them. "Well? Hugh Danielson is a very, very wealthy man. When it came time to renegotiate, I suspect you'd do very well."

"What do you think?" Pilar asked Loup.

Loup studied the offer again, then set it down. "I think I'm really glad we saved the kid. And I think they're so glad, they're forgetting that she couldn't stand you and didn't care too much for me before it happened. I'm pretty sure she'd drive us crazy once things got back to normal. And I'm not sure I want to work for a guy so whipped by his kid that he wouldn't cancel a stupid party over a fucking *death threat.*" She winced. "Sorry."

Sabine's mouth twitched. "You can take the snipe out of the gutter, but you can't take the gutter out of the snipe," she murmured. "However, I concur with the sentiment."

"Are you actually saying you don't want us to go?" Pilar asked, eyeing her suspiciously.

"I didn't say that."

"You kinda did," Loup said. "Okay. We'll stay."

Magnus smiled. "I'm very pleased."

"So what's next?" Pilar asked. "For us, I mean."

"For now, you're at leisure. The same terms apply. Be available at a day's notice. We've a bit of a mess on our hands, so it may be a couple of weeks before you hear from me." He paused. "I want you to know that you both did an exemplary job. Loup, I know your capabilities make you . . . different, but I would never have thrust you into that situation, inexperienced as you are, if I'd thought it would come down to your being the last line of defense. You more than rose to the occasion. And, Pilar . . ."

"I know. I was just supposed to be tending bar."

"Mr. Lindberg is in a bit of shock," Sabine said dryly. "You kept your head. You got the job done. We do not call that *choking.*"

Pilar flushed. "Thanks."

"You are welcome."

"You're being serious, right?"

"Yes. Do not ruin the moment."

"Okay."

Back at the Hotel Beau Rivage, they relaxed after the debriefing, rehashing the events of the catastrophic party for the hundredth time since its occurrence.

"So the fire was a *coincidence,*" Pilar marveled. "That's crazy, isn't it?"

"Yeah." Loup, her head in Pilar's lap, yawned until her jaw cracked. "Sorry. I'm still tired. Guess it's not that crazy when you think about it. Faulty old wiring. They had every fucking light in that place blazing."

Pilar massaged Loup's temples with her fingertips, making little circles. "How many people do you think you saved, baby?"

"Hmm?"

"How many? On the stairway?"

"Oh, I dunno. The firemen got there pretty quick."

"I bet a dozen." Pilar leaned over to kiss her upside down. "That guy, the killer sailor...Loup, it scared the shit out of me. I'm not sure I could have done what I did if it hadn't been *you* he was aiming at."

"You did it, though. Sabine's right. You got the job done. That's all that matters."

"The way you stared him down..." Pilar shivered. "He had a gun on you, he fucking fired it over your head, and you just looked pissed. Loup, what's it like? Not being scared at a time like that?"

"It's like nothing," Loup said honestly. "It's an empty feeling. Like there's some part of me that knows something's missing. It's not bad, exactly. It's just...nothing."

"It scares me."

"I know." Loup caught her hand and kissed it. "But I can't help what I am, Pilar."

"I love what you are." Pilar smoothed her unruly hair. "I'm just being honest. I guess near-death experiences do that to me."

"Kind of like big cathedrals make you all philosophical?" Loup asked fondly. "Hey, we should think about where we want to go next. Do you want to go back to Paris?"

"You know where I'd go if I could go anywhere?"

"Where?"

"Home," Pilar said wistfully. "Even if it was just for a day."

Loup craned her neck to look up at her. "Are you sorry you left?"

"No!" She tweaked a lock of her hair. "God, no. Don't ever think that, baby. The best thing I ever did in my life is walk away from my life to climb into that stupid fucking tunnel. It's been, what? Six months? And I've seen and done things I never could have imagined. And you..." Pilar shook her head. "You. I'd give everything up all over again to be with you. It's just..." She sighed. "I miss them."

"So do I," Loup said softly.

Pilar smiled. "Can you imagine the look on T.Y.'s face if he heard what I did the other day? He never thought I was good enough for you."

"That's not true."

"Oh, it's *so* true." She tweaked her hair again. "I know what the Santitos thought. It's okay, I gave them reasons to. I thought it, too. But I did kind of save your life, didn't I?"

"No." Loup levered herself upright with a lithe twist, turning on the bed to face Pilar, her face grave. "You *totally* saved my life. And the kid's, too."

"You didn't give me a whole lot of choice, baby."

"I knew you could do it."

"You and your fucking trust and expectations." Pilar twined her arms around Loup's neck. "It's enough to make me feel sorry for Miguel Garza. I'm not a hero, okay? I'm just here because I love you."

Loup smiled.

"Oh, shut up." Pilar kissed her, grateful to have her alive and whole. She laughed when Loup kissed her back ardently. "I thought you were tired."

"Suddenly less so." She cocked her head. "We could try it, you know. Santa Olivia. The tunnel's still there."

"No," Pilar said after a brief pause. "Jesus! I can't believe I even considered it. No," she said again, more firmly. "We've got an obligation to Global, and it's stupid to take that kind of risk now. I bet the army filled in that tunnel again, too. And even if they didn't, they're still looking for you. If we got caught, they'd make sure you never got away again. Let's see how this business with Miguel and the hearings plays out. I lost you once and I really, really don't want to lose you again."

"It was just a thought."

"Well, quit thinking it."

"Okay, okay!" She looked thoughtfully at Pilar. "What about visiting Huatulco?"

"You think it's safe for us to go to Mexico?"

Loup shrugged. "Not for us, but for Guadalupe Herrera and Pilar Mendez, maybe. We can ask Christophe, he'll know. I know it's not home, but there are people who care about us there. And I think that's a big part of what we're missing, huh? I mean, we'll be okay as long as we've got each other, but it's nice to feel part of something bigger, too."

"Yeah." Pilar thought about it and gave her a dazzling smile. "I'd like that."

"Good."

Her arms tightened around Loup's neck. "So not *too* tired, huh?"

"Not anymore."

TWENTY-SIX

"Yes, yes," Christophe assured them on the phone. "There were inquiries, but it is over now, and the Americans did not find out about our family in Huatulco. It is safe for you to visit." He paused. "But maybe not to run *so* fast on the beach and make the tourists gossip anymore. Gossip travels, you know?"

Tía Marcela's warm embrace made the entire trip worthwhile. "My lovely girls!" she exclaimed. "I'm so very glad you came."

"*Gracias*, Tía." Loup smiled.

"Look at you." She held first Loup, then Pilar at arm's length. "You've been working as bodyguards? Truly?"

"Loup, mostly," Pilar said. "Me, only sort of. But we caught a bad guy and everything."

"Well." Marcela gave them both another hug and kiss. "I can see there will be stories. Come, I have your same room waiting for you."

"Okay." Loup pulled out her credit card. "But we can pay this time."

"No." She raised a stern finger. "You are here visiting as family. I will not hear of it."

"But—"

"Absolutely not."

"All right. Thank you."

Everything was as they had left it—the charming room overlooking the little marina, the palm trees, the bobbing fishing boats. They wandered into town and through the marketplace and saw the same shops, the same bars and restaurants. Even the weather seemed unchanged—warm and sunny, the aquamarine sea lapping the white-sand beach. They had lunch beneath the thatched palapa, eating spiced grilled fish and drinking cold beer.

It wasn't the same, though.

"It all seems different, doesn't it?" Pilar asked. "I wish it was the way it was before. I hate that you have to pretend again."

"Yeah, me too."

She rested her chin on her hand and gazed out at the sunbathers. "It changes everything, doesn't it? Because nothing else has changed."

"We have." Loup switched their plates and began finishing Pilar's fish. "Think about it. Other than a couple days in Mexico City, this was pretty much the only place we'd ever been other than Outpost in our entire lives."

"Snipes fresh out of the gutter," Pilar mused.

Loup laughed. "Pretty much, yeah."

"Do I seem all that different?"

"In some ways." Loup studied her. "You know a lot more, that's for sure. We both do. You're more...I don't know. Sophisticated?"

"You think?"

"Yeah." Loup nodded. "More confident and worldly. Do I seem different?"

"Nah." Pilar gave her a fond smile. "Not really, no. But you didn't exactly need confidence. You were always my fearless little hero with the very big appetite, and I don't think anything in the world could change that. There's nothing about you I'd change." She reached across the table and caressed Loup's cheek. "I had a lot farther to go, baby."

"No, you didn't."

Pilar shook her head. "You and your ridiculously unconditional love. Oh, don't give me that big, shiny-eyed look." She touched the necklace nestled in the hollow of Loup's throat. "It makes me get all choked up."

"Is that so bad?" Loup asked honestly.

"No." She thought about it. "No, I guess it's not."

There was an impromptu party that night on the hotel terrace. Most of the aunts and cousins were in attendance.

"*Prima!*" Raimundo said, exultant. He hugged Loup, then Pilar, lingering over the latter. "*Bonita!* I am so happy you are here!"

Nacio elbowed him out of the way. "Yes, so am I. Very happy."

"Careful," Loup said cheerfully. "Pilar shot a man."

They exchanged glances. "*Es verdad?*" Raimundo asked, disbelieving. "You did this thing? You?"

"*Verdad, sí,*" Pilar agreed. "I shot a man."

"*Prima.*" Young Alejandro touched Loup's arm. "Did you know that you are a little bit famous?" A flush of pride darkened his cheeks. "Amaya has learned it."

Loup blinked. "Huh?"

He nodded adoringly to his shy girlfriend. "Show them."

She opened up a thin netbook computer. Her fingers danced over the keyboard, clicking links. "*Mira.*"

They looked.

Pilar laughed. "That's the concert in Aberdeen, baby. The spitter."

"Oh, right." Loup watched badly lit footage of the band Kate in concert and saw herself stride onstage, the teenage fan slung over her shoulder. She saw herself approach the edge of the stage, shading her eyes against the spotlights' glare, then dangle and lower the spitting girl. "Yuck. I remember."

Amaya said something soft in Spanish.

"Kate's fans, they are all curious," Alejandro said with pride. "They call you Mystery Girl. But we have not told anyone anything to put you in danger. Still, they come, hoping to see you again. More and more, all the time. Amaya read about it in the fan feeds."

"Huh."

Pilar eyed Loup. "Job offer?"

"Nah. They'd have contacted us by now, don't you think?"

Alejandro conferred with Amaya in Spanish. "No one knows who you are." He smiled. "*What* you are."

"Sure, they do," Loup said. "At least their head of security does. What was the guy's name, Pilar? Clive's friend?"

"Jones," Pilar said absently, watching Amaya replay the footage. "Bill Jones. But why's he gonna tell them? He's got his own business; he's not gonna want to cut guys on his payroll." She fished out her Dataphone. "Amaya, can you send me that link?" She mimed an exchange. "I'll send it to Magnus in the morning. Maybe it's a lead worth following."

"You're such a groupie," Loup said, amused.

"Hey." Pilar gave her a look. "We had a job that actually *was* baby-sitting and nearly got killed. And I liked Vincenzo Picco, but I'm not crazy about the whole Mafia wedding connection. Right now, spitting fans are looking pretty good."

"Okay, okay."

"Can we hear about the shooting and almost getting killed now?" Nacio asked hopefully.

"Sure."

A week later, they heard from Magnus.

It was in the late afternoon of another idyllic day. Loup went for one of her long runs along the shoreline while Pilar lounged in the sun and read her magazines. She slowed to a reluctant jog as she neared the beach, watching a tall, well-built tourist flirt with Pilar, then picked her way across the sand.

Pilar brightened. "Hey, baby!"

"Hey, yourself."

"This is your friend?" the tourist inquired. He pointed. "Perhaps she would like to meet *my* friend, and we could all be friends together."

"I don't think so." Pilar smiled sweetly at him. "She's my girl-friend."

He flushed. "You said—"

"You asked if I had a boyfriend, and I said no. It's not my fault you made the wrong assumption."

He went away, grumbling good-naturedly.

Loup dropped onto the sand. "One day you're gonna do that to the wrong guy, and he's gonna haul off and belt you."

"Well, you'll just have to belt him back."

"How come I have to do the belting when you're the one doing the flirting?"

"Because you're so very good at it, baby. Anyway, it's good for them. It reminds them not to make assumptions." Pilar eyed her. "How far did you run? You've got this trickle of sweat running down your throat that's driving me a little crazy."

"Pretty far. I had to go a long way to get out of sight. You know, there are some cute places for sale along the bays."

Pilar blinked. "You want to buy a house?"

"Not the way things are now, but maybe someday. If I didn't have to pretend anymore." Loup rolled onto her stomach and propped her head on her hands. "I mean, we're always going to want to come back, right? And we have to have someplace to call home in between jobs." She paused. "And no, I'm *not* giving up on Santa Olivia. But I kind of think whatever happens, it's never going to be home in the same way."

"No, I know." She gave her a wondering look. "You and me with a house?"

Loup smiled. "People live in houses, Pilar. You played house with Rory Salamanca for a year."

"Oh, hush." She brushed caked sand off Loup's arm. "That's exactly what it was, too. His horrible mother took care of everything. This just seems so grown-up."

"I'm just thinking."

"This thinking, I like. Do you really think it would be totally safe someday? That you wouldn't have to pretend anymore?"

"I don't know," Loup said honestly. "But God, I hope so."

Pilar glanced around. "I do like it here. I like it a lot. It feels good, you know?"

"Yeah."

"And I like that you have family here." Her voice softened. "They'd love for you to be more than just a visitor."

"You too."

"A house." Pilar cocked her head. "Could we get one of those cute little motor scooters, too?"

"Yeah, sure." Loup laughed. "And you can ride it to the market with your shopping bag over the handles and your big movie-star sunglasses and look all cool and sexy, okay?"

Pilar smiled happily. "Okay!"

They went back to the hotel to shower and get ready for dinner.

"Hey!" Pilar waved her Dataphone as Loup emerged from the bathroom wrapped in a towel. "News."

"Miguel?"

She made a face. "Not Miguel, no. Magnus. He followed up on the Kate lead. Turns out I was right. The band's been dying to find you. They fired that Jones guy for stonewalling them."

"No kidding?"

"Nope." Pilar looked smug. "So Global's in negotiation to take over their contract. And they want us as part of the deal. Well, you—but enough that they'll take me, too. Magnus is trying to set up an interview for next week."

Loup toweled her hair. "You want this one, don't you?"

"Yeah, I do. Do you hate the idea?"

"Only the spitting."

"It's not about that." Pilar shook her head. "I read a bunch of stuff on the fan feeds. It's about Kate having this, whaddya call it? This mystique. About having the coolest security guard in the business. That's you, baby."

"Big money?" Loup asked.

"Uh-huh." Pilar tugged experimentally on the edge of her towel. "*House* money, maybe." She glanced upward, her face soft and vulnerable. "You're serious? Serious, serious? You and me and a house?"

"Pilar." Loup straddled her lap, heedless of her falling towel. She cupped Pilar's face in her hands, gazing intently into her hazel eyes. "I love you, okay? When the fuck have I ever *not* been serious with you?"

"Umm...never?"

She kissed her. "That's exactly right."

TWENTY-SEVEN

A week later, they were in London.

The interview took place in the band's hotel suite. On the flight to London, Pilar prepared for it by alternately reading celebrity tabloids, fan feeds, and Global's official dossier. Loup prepared for it by listening to Pilar.

"Ooh, check it out. Charlie's got a thing for schoolgirls. There's a piece in the dossier about how they hushed up a story in Japan about him visiting a place where all the hookers dress like schoolgirls."

"Ew. Which one's Charlie again?"

"The bass player." Pilar studied his photo. "He looks really sweet. You'd never know he was a pervert."

"Nice. You think their fans would care?"

"I think their fans would put on schoolgirl costumes if they knew." Pilar glanced over. "Why are you looking at me like that?"

"Just wondering if you're getting ideas."

"Loup!"

She laughed. "Well, you're acting pretty fangirly."

"Okay, okay." Pilar rolled her eyes. "I'm excited, that's all. Anyway, you don't have anything to worry about. There's you and not-you, and believe me, after you, not-you just isn't the same."

"That almost made sense."

"Oh, you know what I mean." She turned serious. "Loup, don't tease me about cheating on you, okay? Because I still feel like shit about it. I can still picture the look on your face the day you found out about Rory and it makes me sick to my stomach."

"I'm sorry," Loup said softly. "I do understand why you did it, you know. And it wasn't all your fault. I drove you to it."

"I know." Pilar raked a restless hand through her hair. "But it was a shitty, cowardly thing to do. I felt sick about it then, and I still do." She smiled wryly. "I actually threw up the first time I slept with Rory."

"Seriously?"

"Yeah. Not *on* him or anything," she added hastily. "Afterward in the bathroom. He never knew."

"I'm sorry," Loup repeated. "I didn't mean to be mean."

"You weren't." Pilar glanced at the screen of her Dataphone. "I'm acting like an idiot. I deserve to be teased. But I'm asking you not to, okay?"

"Okay. I won't, I promise."

"Thanks, baby."

Magnus and Sabine met them in London. Over dinner, Magnus filled them in on the details of the arrangement.

"There's good news and bad news," he said philosophically. "The bad news is that they've had a change of heart and rehired Bill Jones' outfit. They're leaving in ten days for a monthlong tour of Australia and Japan, and Jones' team already has the details down. I suspect firing him was all a ploy. The good news is that they still want you on the tour."

"How bad?" Loup asked.

Magnus smiled smoothly. "Quite badly. They didn't blink at two hundred thousand plus expenses."

"Not bad." Loup attempted to calculate in her head. "So our cut would be—"

"Twenty-five thousand apiece," Sabine said impatiently.

"Not bad for a month's work," Pilar said. "Hey, Magnus? This is all a big PR stunt, right?"

"Fair to say, yes."

"These guys are really popular. What *does* happen if it gets out there? More than it already is, enough that people other than Kate's fans start asking questions? I mean, the U.S. government still wants Loup back. What happens if they figure out that Lupe Herrera is Loup Garron?"

"Ah." He steepled his fingers. "A very good question. As it happens, I asked Sabine to look into the matter some time ago. Loup may recall, we spoke about the matter during our first meeting."

"You're safe," Sabine said briefly to Loup. "As long as you stay out of America."

"You're sure?"

"Yes. Although there is a considerable amount of uncertainty regarding the existence of GMOs, the American policy is known and loathed throughout the world on sheer principle. You could claim asylum anywhere. There is no country in this hemisphere that would honor an extradition request." Sabine gave a tight smile. "And for that reason, the U.S. government would not make such a request."

"Bet it could make things...interesting...though," Loup said thoughtfully. "If the story got out there."

Magnus shrugged. "That's always been a possibility."

Loup glanced at Pilar. "What do you think?"

"It's the kind of job we came here to do, baby." She smiled. "As long as you're safe, I'm for it. And maybe *interesting* will turn out to be a good thing."

"I want you to be on good behavior tomorrow," Magnus interjected. "*Professional* behavior. This deal is not yet concluded. The band wants you, yes. Their manager, Geordie Davies, is less sanguine about the merit of this affair." He gave them a stern look. "Do not give him a reason to turn us down."

Loup saluted. "Aye, sir."

"Dear God." He dabbed his lips with a napkin, hiding a reluctant smile. "Please do not do that, either."

"No, sir!"

"Insufferable," Sabine murmured to herself, more mildly than usual.

They reconvened in the afternoon of the following day. At the band's hotel, Magnus called up to the suite and spoke to the manager. When they reached the suite, a skinny, bleary-eyed young man in a ratty T-shirt answered Magnus' crisp knock on the door. His gaze roamed over them, settling on Loup and brightening.

"Oh, hey. Hey!" He turned. "It's Mystery Girl!"

"No shit," a slightly-less-bleary young man replied. "They just called, you gormless idiot."

"I was in the loo." He wiped his hands on faded jeans. "Come on in."

"Mr. Lindberg!" An older man in the background busily cleared the coffee table of empty beer cans, of which there were dozens. "Please, do come in. I apologize for the mess." He plucked a pair of panties from the couch. "Lads, is there someone around to claim these?"

"In Charlie's bedroom," the less bleary one said.

"Legal age?"

He shrugged. "Hope so."

Sabine looked at Magnus, a muscle twitching under her right eye.

"Ah, Mr. Davies, I assume?" he said to the older man. "Shall we return at a later time?"

"No, no." Davies looked sour. "There's no guarantee matters will improve. Randall, will you please wake Charlie and oust his guest?"

He nodded and shambled away.

"Lead singer," Pilar whispered to Loup. "Randall Wilkes."

"I'm Donny," the one who'd answered the door said helpfully. "Donny Fairbrook."

"The drummer, right?"

"Yeah." He grinned. "That was awesome, what you did onstage. Can't wait to see you do it again."

In fairly short order, a scantily clad young woman was evicted and a third skinny young man joined them, tousle-haired and yawning.

"Sorry," he apologized, scratching his belly. "Late night." He smiled sleepily at Loup and Pilar. "Hey, Mystery Girl and Mystery Girl's friend!"

"Right." Magnus dusted some dubious-looking crumbs off a chair and sat, crossing his legs with debonair aplomb. "Shall we get down to business, gentlemen? Mr. Davies, I understand you have some concerns. Did you read the testimonials I sent you?"

"We have testimonials?" Pilar asked.

"You do indeed," he said. "Hugh Danielson provided a particularly glowing one, despite his disappointment over your declining his generous offer."

"I read 'em," Geordie Davies said. "They're still a couple of teenaged girls." He gestured at the members of the band. "Can you not see why this is potentially a very bad idea?"

Magnus folded his hands. "I assure you, the young women are very professional."

Sabine coughed.

"Aw, c'mon, Geordie." Randall Wilkes pushed his long, floppy bangs out of his eyes. "It's all just for show anyway. And the fans want it." He pointed at Loup. "She's shifting our demographic, eh? We're starting to pull in more thrill seekers along with the teeny-boppers. An older, harder-edge crowd. That's what we want, eh? An audience we can grow?"

He eyed Loup. "She's a genuine GMO?"

"An optimally engineered human being," Magnus agreed. "The only one of her particular kind."

"If you're so perfect, why didn't they make more of you?" Donny asked Loup, his face puzzled.

"It's just a term." She cocked her head and gambled. "I wasn't made in a laboratory. My father was. I'm a half-breed genetic mutant."

"Fucking hell!" he breathed. "You serious?"

"Yes."

"We gotta have her." Donny gave Geordie a pleading look. "C'mon, man! That's just too fucking cool."

"Are you one, too?" Charlie asked Pilar.

"No. But Loup and I work together."

"Why?"

"Because we're a good team," she said. "And it's in our contract."

"Okay." He gave her a sweet, sleepy smile. "No matter, eh? The more the merrier."

"I'm still not convinced the entire thing wasn't a trick in the first place," Geordie Davies said dubiously. "Thought the Yanks had 'em all under lock and key, if they even exist at all. Can we not have a demonstration?"

Magnus raised his brows at Loup.

She sighed. "What would you like me to do, Mr. Davies?"

"I don't know. Convince me."

Loup stood and eyed the manager. He was sitting in a high-backed chair. She moved behind him, stooped, and grabbed the back legs of the chair and levered it into the air. He let out an undignified squeak and clutched the chair arms.

The band roared with laughter.

"Convinced?" she asked the back of the chair.

"Yes! Yes, please!"

She lowered him carefully. "Okay, then."

"Geordie, man," Randall said. "C'mon. We've gotta do this. Nobody else has anything like it. It's free PR everywhere we go."

He chewed his thumbnail. "It's not *free*, lad. But I suppose it might be worth the risk." He sighed. "All right. Against my better judgment, we'll try it. After all, what's the worst that could happen?"

The drummer whooped.

Magnus smiled. "I'm sure you'll be very pleased."

TWENTY-EIGHT

The band was playing a couple of small gigs in London, honing their chops for the tour. They wanted Loup and Pilar to start right away. In the end, Magnus negotiated an additional fee of fifty thousand for the extra ten days.

"Five thousand quid a day." The lead singer, Randall, smiled through his floppy bangs at Pilar. "What kind of special benefits does that get us?"

"Not that kind, sorry."

He gave her the yearning look that made his fans swoon. "We'll see."

Loup rolled her eyes.

"Right." Magnus placed the signed contracts in his briefcase and handed it to Sabine. "We'll be on our way, shall we? We've a lot of work to do yet at headquarters."

"You're leaving us here?" Pilar asked in mild alarm.

He looked amused. "You're on their payroll now, Ms. Mendez. And I imagine you've got a lot of details to arrange, starting with transferring hotels and coordinating with Mr. Jones on the itinerary. That's your end of this bargain, is it not?"

"Yes, sir."

"No need to get a room," the bass player said helpfully. "Plenty of space here in the suite."

Pilar glanced at Geordie Davies. "Do you have a block of rooms reserved for security?"

"We do." He picked up a phone. "I'll call down to the front desk and authorize you."

Two hours later, they'd said their farewells to Magnus and Sabine, checked out of their old hotel and into the band's hotel, which was hipper and trendier.

"Weird lighting." Pilar flipped on a light switch and glanced around at the subterranean glow. "Their place was so trashed, I didn't even notice. And what's with all the pillows?"

"I don't know." Loup reclined against several of the dozen geometrically shaped pillows adorning the bed, folding her arms behind her head. "So are you happy we got the job?"

"Yeah, I guess."

"Not sure?"

"No, I am." Pilar flopped down beside her. "They're just sort of younger and hornier than I expected. And smellier."

Loup laughed. "Yeah, I noticed."

"Are you happy?"

"Sure." She ran a few strands of Pilar's hair through her fingers. "I'm happy if you're happy."

Pilar leaned over to kiss her. "I could make you happier."

"Mmm. Okay."

Ten minutes later there was a knock at the door that grew to a steady, insistent pounding. "Oy! Mystery Girls! C'mon!"

"Okay, okay!" Loup called, buttoning her undone shirt. "Jesus!"

It was Donny Fairbrook with a silver bucket of ice. "C'mon!" he said impatiently. "We finally got rid of Geordie and we've got loads of champers. Time to celebrate, right?" He looked past her at Pilar sitting on the rumpled bed, sliding her shoes on and trying unsuccessfully to look demure. His eyes narrowed. "What were you up to, eh?"

"Unpacking," Loup said.

He looked at her disheveled hair, then back at Pilar. "Nah. Nah. Oh, hell, no! Tell me it ain't so."

"Sorry." Pilar gave up on demure. "I talked to Mr. Jones. I didn't think we were on duty until tomorrow."

"You aren't," Donny said mournfully. "We just wanted to celebrate, see? I got the extra ice myself and everything."

"We can celebrate," Loup said, feeling sorry for him.

"Yeah, it's just..." He sighed. "Never mind." He brushed the sleeve of Loup's white shirt with his free hand. "You don't have to dress all bodyguard formal, you know. It's rock and roll, eh?" His gaze lingered on her throat. "Pretty necklace, though. It looks nice on you."

"Um...thanks."

"Ohmigod," Pilar said. "I know that look."

Loup winced. "So do I."

He tore his gaze away. "Huh?"

"Welcome to the one-in-a-hundred club," Pilar said with resignation.

They celebrated anyway. The other two band members took the news better when Donny blurted it out.

"Oh, yeah? You're into each other?" Randall nodded, bangs flopping. "That's cool, that's cool. Sorry, man," he added to Donny.

"So you all knew about this?" Pilar asked.

They exchanged glances. Charlie grinned. "That Donny had a thing for Mystery Girl? Yeah, of course."

Donny sighed. "Ah, fuck me." He swigged from a champagne bottle. "Don't tell Geordie. He thinks it was all about the fans and PR."

"Okay," Loup said gently. "I hope that part works out."

"Oh, it will." He gave her another mournful look. "We even came up with an idea for a set of special security togs for you. It's gonna look hot as hell onstage."

"Hey, do you ever dress up for each other?" Charlie asked cheerfully. "Y'know, play a scene?"

"No," Loup said. "No schoolgirl shit, okay?"

Pilar eyed her. "Well..."

"Pilar!"

"I'm just saying I could see it," she said, unrepentant. "Remember the cabin boy outfit? You'd look pretty damn cute in a schoolgirl costume, baby."

Donny groaned and put his head in his hands.

"We are *so* being unprofessional," Loup said.

"Yeah, well." Pilar shrugged. "We're not on duty and we just found out half the reason we got this job is because the drummer has a mad crush on you. I'm not exactly feeling real professional at the moment."

"Yeah, but—"

"Oh, please don't." Randall gave Loup one of his yearning looks through his bangs. "We're handled and managed within an inch of our lives, and all I ever wanted is to be an artist, you know? It's so hard when no one's real. You two, you seem really real. I wish you wouldn't change. It's nice, you know?"

"I guess."

"It is." Charlie draped himself over Pilar. "Can I watch?" he asked hopefully. "If you talk her into the schoolgirl costume?"

She shoved him. "No."

"Ow!" He fell onto his ass and giggled. "What are you, some kind of secret agent bodyguard?"

"Yep."

He lay on his back and sighed, making a languid motion with one hand. "We need girls. More girls. Girls who aren't into girls."

"No, we don't," Randall said laconically. "You get us in enough trouble as it is, Charlie. Give it a rest for a day." He tossed his bangs out of his eyes. "Are we cool, girls?"

"Yeah, we're fine." Loup glanced at Pilar. "Does this feel weirdly familiar?"

"Yeah." She smiled. "It's a little like hanging out with the Santitos."

Donny lifted his head. "Is that a band?"

"No." Loup smiled wistfully. "Just the kids at the orphanage where we grew up. Well, mostly grew up. Kids in the street gangs used to tease us, call us the Santitos, the Little Saints of Santa Olivia."

"You grew up in an orphanage?"

"Pretty much." She shrugged. "My mom died when I was ten. I

never knew my father. Only that he deserted from the army and he was different."

Charlie sat up and poured more champagne into Pilar's glass. "What about you?"

"Lost my mom when I was little." She sipped. "My dad when I was nine. My aunt and uncle took me in for a while, then they pawned me off on the church."

"In Canada, right?" Randall asked.

Loup and Pilar exchanged a glance.

"No," Pilar said. "You know, I'm really tired of lying about this, and we're gonna be spending a lot of time together. We're from America, not Canada. A little town in Texas, near the border. Ever watch the news? It was one of the Outposts."

Two of them shook their heads, but Randall nodded. "Yeah, yeah. I watch late at night when I can't sleep. I seen that bit. But I thought no one ever got out except that one big guy they interviewed."

"Miguel Garza," Loup said.

"You know him?"

"Sure. We used to box together. He was my sparring partner."

He whistled. "Holy shit! You two, you have a *story*, eh?"

"Loup has a story," Pilar said. "I'm just the sexy sidekick."

Randall pushed back his bangs and grinned. "That's for fucking sure."

"Hey, man." Donny looked sidelong at him. "What are you thinkin', huh?"

"I dunno. Might be material for a song." He considered. "Maybe an album. Paranoia and the military industrial complex versus the will of the individual. Something dark, edgy, you know?"

"Epic?"

"Yeah, maybe epic."

"We could make a statement."

"A statement, yeah."

They regarded the girls. "Tell us more," Randall said. "I wanna hear the whole story. How'd you get out?"

Loup's stomach growled. "Okay. But I need food."

They ordered room service and more champagne, consuming

copious amounts of both and adding to the clutter and disarray in the suite while Loup and Pilar told their story, climaxing in Loup's epic boxing match against the genetically modified John Johnson and her subsequent imprisonment by the U.S. Army, and ending with their separate escapes through the smugglers' tunnel.

"Damn." Donny gazed at Loup with helpless fascination. "So they totally tortured you, eh? That's bollocks!"

"I don't know if it was torture, exactly. It's not like they were yanking out my fingernails or anything."

Pilar passed over her unfinished plate of steak au poivre and pommes frites without being asked. "Baby, it was *so* torture. They tried starving you!"

"Yeah. That sucked."

Randall ran a hand through his hair, tossing his bangs with an absentminded flick of his head. "Damn," he said. "Damn. I'm gonna have to think about this for a while."

"We should probably go. You guys have a gig tomorrow." Pilar glanced around the room. "I'll call room service to have them pick up all this stuff. Do you want me to put the trays in the hallway?"

"Oh, leave it." Charlie waved a half-empty champagne bottle. "They'll get it in the morning."

"Are you kidding?" she said with asperity. "It's *disgusting* in here. And you guys…" She wrinkled her nose. "You could really use showers."

"It's our manly essence!" he protested. "It's natural."

"No," Loup said. "You kind of stink. I get that you want to be all dark and edgy, but dirty and smelly isn't cutting it."

Randall laughed.

"What?" Pilar picked up the phone. "You wanted real, you're getting real."

"It's cool. I like it."

They hauled the room service trays and half a dozen empty champagne bottles into the hallway before saying good night and beating a retreat.

"Poor Donny," Pilar whispered in the hotel room, fiddling with Loup's collar. "You're not…?"

"No!"

"You sure?"

"Uh-huh." Loup slid her hands around Pilar's waist, then lower, pulling her hard against her, kissing her with commendable thoroughness. "Want me to show you how very, very sure I am?"

"Yeah." Pilar smiled, breathless and happy. "You know, I hate being interrupted, but I *love* unfinished business."

"Mm-hmm."

TWENTY-NINE

Their first official gig with the band was an unpublicized concert at a small, popular, and exceedingly dingy venue in Camden Town, a bohemian section of the city. Geordie Davies sighed with deep misgivings when they arrived.

"Are you boys *sure* about this?"

"Yeah." Randall tossed his bangs and smiled sweetly. "C'mon, man! We'll play the big stadiums for the screaming teens all next month. Let us try out some of the harder-edged stuff I'm working on for a real music crowd." He slid a sideways glance at Loup and Pilar. "I've got a lot of new ideas coming."

"Fine. It's your noggin on the line."

Bill Jones and his security team were already there. He greeted Loup without animosity. "Clive's supergirl. No hard feelings, eh?"

"No, sir."

"You'll take stage left." He handed her a radio earpiece. "Any trouble on the floor, call for club backup. Your job is to stay onstage and cover the band."

"Yes, sir."

"What about me?" Pilar inquired.

"Ah. Clive's other girl." Bill Jones shrugged. "Do whatever the band hired you to do. I'm not putting you on the front line."

Loup eyed an impressive array of bottles. "You could be the back-stage bartender."

"Perfect." Jones clapped Pilar's shoulder. "Keep the lads happy and keep them from getting shitfaced, eh?"

"I'll try."

The crowd that night was an inhospitable mix of raucous, hard-drinking music lovers and underage girls who'd snuck in to see Kate. The former cheered the opening act, which was loud and fast and thrashing. The latter called for Kate between every song.

"Good set," Donny offered as the opening act slouched offstage.

The lead singer, clad in black leather and heavy eyeliner, spat casually at his feet in passing.

"Hey!" Loup tapped his arm. "That's not very polite."

He looked at his bandmates and grinned, then hawked up another gob of spittle.

Loup intercepted it and smeared it on his narrow chest in one blurred motion, shaking off her hand in disgust. "Jesus! I'm serious. What's with all the spitting?"

He gaped. "What the hell are you?"

"The future face of humanity," Randall offered, drifting amiably over. "Fearless, noble, and free."

"The fuck?"

His head bobbed to imaginary music. "I'm working on it."

Kate took the stage. Half the crowd squealed; the other half booed. Loup took her position onstage in the left wing. The band launched into a song they'd never recorded, something new and half-finished, with a low, snaking bass line and driving percussion. Randall sang and played guitar, his airy vocals offset by the wailing chords he plucked.

It went well for a while. The underage fans fell silent in confusion, while the regulars deigned to listen. It wasn't until the end of their set that the mood turned ugly, when they played one of their sprightly pop hits in acknowledgment of the fans.

"Oy!" A big man shoved his way toward the stage. "Don't play that shite here!"

They kept playing.

"Wankers!" He hurled a half-empty beer bottle.

Loup caught it in midair, pressing her earpiece. "Security! Bald guy in a plaid sleeveless shirt."

He began attempting to climb onstage. "Little fuckin' bitch!"

"Oh, shut up." Loup delivered a quick, sharp tap to the hollow behind the hinge of his jaw. He fell down writhing. She scanned the crowd. One of the big guy's friends had a frightened young Kate fan pinned against the stage and was grinding against her, humping and laughing. "Hey, you!" She squatted at the edge of the stage and reached for the front of his shirt, hauling him off his feet with one hand. The fabric strained, but held. He looked startled.

A handful of cameras and Dataphones lit up.

"Cut it out," Loup said irritably, ignoring the cameras. "Leave the kid be, okay?" She thumped him atop his head with her free hand and let him fall, slumping. She pressed her earpiece, already scanning for the next problem. "Security!"

The night was reckoned a disaster by management, a wash by security, and a success by the band.

"They loved us," Charlie crooned backstage, stroking his bass guitar. "It's a whole new audience, Rand. They loved the new shit. They wouldn't admit it, but they did."

"Uh-huh."

"So next album?"

"Yeah. Yeah."

"A whole new world."

"Yeah."

They were still talking about it on the way to the bus when a handful of men emerged from the shadows, led by the bald guy in the plaid shirt.

"Tighten up, team," Bill Jones murmured, taking the lead. The others moved closer to the band.

"Hey, Grampa." The bald guy swung a length of chain with casual menace. "Step out of the way. We just want a word with your precious little teen queens here."

"No, you don't, son," he said firmly. "You don't want that kind of trouble. Let's just all be sensible and go our separate ways, eh? No harm done."

"Fuck that!" The chain snaked through the air.

Loup darted forward and caught it.

"Hey!" He yanked in vain.

She yanked, jerking it out of his hand. He stumbled forward. She grabbed a handful of his shirt and held him upright. He stared at her with fear and hatred. Loup stared back at him without blinking and growled deep in her throat, the sound low and vicious, vibrating in a bloodcurdling, inhuman frequency.

"Jesus!" He backed away, putting up his hands. She let him go. "This is too bloody freaky. Forget it. We're out of here."

Loup watched them go with a smile.

Behind her, Pilar was laughing hard. "Jesus, baby!" she gasped. "I can't believe you did that!"

The others gaped.

"You're not..." Randall licked his lips. "You're not exactly *human*, are you?"

"Not exactly, no." Loup glanced at his pale face. "Oh, c'mon. That's it, that's as weird as it gets."

"You don't, like, change into—"

"No!"

"You do get a little crazy around the full moon," Pilar offered.

Loup gave her a look. "You're not helping."

"How can you laugh about it?" Donny asked Pilar, wondering. "All the hair on the back of my neck prickles."

"Oh, mine too," she assured him. "But did you see the look on the guy's face?"

"I was just trying to do what Clive taught us," Loup said mildly. "Control the situation. The guy wasn't going to listen to logic, so..." She shrugged.

"So you thought you'd growl in his face like a goddamn wild animal," Bill Jones finished. "Well." He ran a hand over his stubbly haircut. "Happens it worked. Let's be on our way, shall we? I think that's enough excitement for one night."

"Amen," the manager, Geordie, said fervently.

By the time the band played their second gig a few days later, their fan feeds were abuzz with rumors.

"Check it out." Pilar showed Loup a photo of herself crouching on the edge of the stage, the grinning man in his strained shirt dangling from her fist. The shot captured the look of irritation on Loup's face. "This one's all over the place, Mystery Girl."

"Am I still Mystery Girl?"

"So far."

"Any *news* news?"

"Nope." Pilar looked back at the screen. "Look at you, all cute and scowly. Do you know how many fans Kate has? There're gonna be one in a hundreds crawling out of the woodwork."

Loup yawned. "Great."

"I'll protect you, baby." Pilar gave her a mischievous smile. "Hey, I have to run out and pick up your new...what did Donny call them? Security togs. They want you to wear them tonight. Want to come?"

"Shopping? No, thanks. I was going to hit the fitness room." She rolled her shoulders. "Wonder if we could get a portable boxing bag for the tour? I could train backstage."

"I'll look into it. I'm going to a sporting goods store anyway."

"Thanks, Pilar."

She gave her a quick kiss. "You bet."

An hour and a half later, Pilar returned, eyes sparkling. She tracked down Loup in the fitness room.

"Hey." Loup abandoned the weight machine she was abusing. "Did it work out?"

"Hmm?"

"The bag?"

"Oh, yeah. It'll be delivered and ship with the rest of the heavy equipment. The roadies will be overjoyed." She rustled a shopping bag. "It's almost time to go. Don't you want to see your new togs?"

Loup eyed the bag suspiciously. "Isn't it just more T-shirts? Ones that fit better?"

"Not exactly."

Upstairs, she tried on one of the outfits—a black sports bra with

SECURITY in white letters across her chest and a pair of low-slung black track pants that barely clung to her hips, SECURITY emblazoned in white across her ass. It left a lot of bare skin in between.

"Oh, for God's sake."

"Mmm."

"You're smoldering at me."

"Can't help it." Pilar shivered. "You look all kinds of sexy. It kinda makes me want to act unruly just so you'd throw me up against a wall and—" She let out a squeak.

"Like this?" Loup breathed, pinning her hard.

"Uh-huh." She clutched Loup's shoulders and shuddered against her. "Oh, fuck!"

Several minutes later, the phone rang.

"Goddamnit!"

"I'm good," Pilar said languidly. "Sorry, baby. Really, *really* like the new gear."

Loup shook her head and answered the phone. "Hi. Yeah. Twenty minutes? Okay. We'll be there."

"Twenty minutes?" She brightened.

"Mm-hmm." Loup eased the phone back into its cradle.

"Plenty of time." Pilar slid her hand down Loup's stomach and into the waistband of her track pants.

"Not the pants!"

"You don't like this?"

"Yeah, but I don't want to stretch the elastic." She wriggled, torn between desire and pragmatism. "C'mon! They're barely staying up as it is."

"I have my hand down your pants and you're thinking about elastic?"

"No! Just let me take them off."

"I don't think so." Pilar slid her hand lower and bit Loup's earlobe. "For the next month, you're going to be running around wearing this in front of thousands of delirious Kate fans and one infatuated drummer," she whispered. "I kind of like the idea of knowing I've had you just like this."

Loup squirmed. "Pilar..."

"Hmm?" Her fingers teased.

"Never mind."

Hours later, they were enduring the mind-numbing tedium of waiting around backstage while the sound and lighting technicians made last-minute adjustments and the band got themselves into the zone. Charlie listened to music, his eyes closed. Randall was scribbling in a notebook. Donny looked longingly at Loup, who was leaning against a wall, arms folded.

"You're doing that just to torture me, aren't you?" he said.

"Doing what?"

He nodded at her taut belly. "You're flexing."

"I'm *breathing.*"

He sighed. "Doesn't it drive you crazy?" he asked Pilar, who was reading a magazine.

"Obviously, I have more self-control than you," she said calmly.

Loup laughed.

Donny gave her a suspicious look. "What do you have against guys, anyway?"

"I don't have anything against guys," she said honestly. "I just happen to think girls are sexier."

"Sexier." He mulled over the word. "So you don't *not* think men are sexy. But you don't date them?"

"I don't date anyone. I'm with Pilar."

"Yeah, but hypothetically. Say you weren't. Would you go out with me?" He pressed her when she didn't answer. "Ah, c'mon! Just say yes or no. Have you ever even been with a bloke? Because if you haven't, you might really like it. You might, you know. You don't know until you try it. And you shouldn't go through life without—"

"Yes, I have!" Loup said in exasperation. "He said it was kind of like having his dick stuck in a vise grip, okay?"

Pilar winced. "Mackie said that?"

"Yeah. It wasn't as mean as it sounds. He was just being honest."

"You know, I know that's supposed to turn me off, but it doesn't." Donny sighed. "Maybe he was just a lousy lay."

"He wasn't," Pilar said, returning to her magazine.

"You slept with the same bloke?"

"Small town, remember?"

"Right." A funny look crossed Donny's face. "Ah, fuck me! You're like that..." He gestured at Loup. "The way you are, you're like that everywhere?" She didn't answer. "I bet you do, like, crazy, sexy tricks with your tongue, huh? Do you? Do you?" He turned to Pilar. "Does she?"

"Yes," she said without looking up from her magazine.

"Ah, God!" He groaned and put his head in his hands. "Why'd you tell me that?"

"I thought it might shut you up." Pilar glanced at Loup, who flicked her tongue at her lightning quick. Pilar smiled.

"I hate this," Donny murmured.

"I'm sorry," Loup said, feeling contrite. "Look, do you want to release us from our contract? I'm sure Magnus would negotiate a settlement."

"Nah." He lifted his head. "That'd be a load of bollocks, wouldn't it? Anyway, Rand would have a fit. Now that you're here, he's decided you're his muses or something. And the fans are excited." He was quiet a moment. "I just couldn't stop thinking about the first time I saw you, eh? Walking across the stage with that kid over your shoulder like she didn't weigh a thing."

"She barely did," Loup said.

Donny smiled. "Yeah, well...it wasn't just that. It was the way you moved, the way you stood. Everything."

"You do have it bad," Pilar said with sympathy, closing her magazine.

"You know what it's like?"

"Yeah." She smiled ruefully at him. "Believe me, I know exactly what it's like."

He eyed her. "Any chance of a three-way?"

"No!" they said in unison.

Donny heaved another sigh. "Worth a try."

THIRTY

Their second official gig went better than the first. Afterward, the band autographed photos, T-shirts, and various body parts for a handful of lucky fans with backstage passes.

"Hey, now." Loup peeled a determined fan off of Randall, unwinding her clinging arms. "Let the nice singer go."

She squealed. "Ooh! Mystery Girl! Can I take a picture with you?"

"Nope. I'm working."

Cameras flashed anyway.

Randall tossed his bangs. "Welcome to show business."

"Yeah, great."

There was an after-party at a nearby club. The band demanded döner kebab on the way. Pilar consulted her Dataphone and directed the limo driver to a hole in the wall with the best late-night Middle Eastern takeaway in the city.

"Fuck me!" Charlie chewed blissfully. "How'd you know about this place?"

"Research. There was an article in one of my magazines that listed döner kebab as one of your top-ten favorite things. I'd never even heard of it before."

"Research, huh? I like it."

Pilar smiled. "Guess I kind of like it, too."

More cameras flashed at the after-party. The band and their entourage were hustled into a VIP room.

"Hey!" one of the paparazzi shouted as they passed. "Mystery Girl! Over here!"

Loup blinked at the flash. "Ow."

"Told you," Pilar murmured in her ear. "One way or another, you're gonna end up a star, baby."

"Yeah, but this is just bizarre."

"I'm beginning to realize that the world's a pretty bizarre place," Pilar said philosophically. "At least your pants didn't fall down."

"No thanks to you."

She hooked one finger inside Loup's low-slung waistband. "It just looks so fucking tempting."

Loup caught her wrist. "Pilar Ecchevarria, I swear to God, if there's a photo in the tabloids tomorrow of me with your hand in my pants, Sabine's head will explode and we will so get fired."

Pilar laughed.

"I'm serious!"

"I know, I know! It's okay, no one's watching. And they don't allow cameras back here." She sobered. "I like hearing you say my name. I kind of miss it, you know? Every time someone calls me Ms. Mendez, it feels wrong."

"Me too." Loup squeezed her hand, steering it clear of her pants. "But we'll get them back someday. We'll help fix things and make it right. Make the world a little less weird. We just have to figure out... Okay, quit looking at me like that."

"I can't help it! When you get all heroic, I just want to grab you and kiss you until you can't breathe."

"Yeah, and I'm two seconds from letting you." She nudged Pilar's hip. "Go take your smolder over there and scare away that girl Charlie's hitting on. She looks awfully young to be in here."

"Okay, fine."

The night ended with a very crowded limo ride back to the hotel, giggling girls—all at least eighteen years old—sitting on the band members' laps.

"So what *are* you?" one of them asked Loup curiously. "I mean really?"

Randall nuzzled her neck. "She's a werewolf."

She squealed. "Really?"

He nodded. "Growl for them, Loup."

"I thought I was the future face of humanity," she reminded him. "Fearless, wild, and free."

"Fearless, *noble*, and free," he corrected her. "But that was before I heard you growl. C'mon, please?"

"She's not a trained animal," Pilar commented.

Charlie giggled. "Dance, monkey, dance!"

"Shut up!" Donny punched him in the shoulder. "You're a bloody asshole when you're pissed."

"Please?" Randall repeated. "I really do want to hear you do it again. Please?"

Loup rolled her eyes and growled softly. It was a low warning sound without as much menace, but it was still inhuman enough to silence the limo.

"Ohmigod!" the girl said, wide-eyed. "I can't *wait* to post about this tomorrow!"

"I don't know if that's such a good idea," Donny said quickly. "Loup's...um, Lupe's situation is kinda complicated."

"No, it's okay." Loup gave him a thoughtful look. "Pilar and I talked about it before we took this job. People should know. I mean, part of the problem is that the U.S. government is denying that people like me even exist. No one else seems to want to tackle it head-on. Sabine says I can't be...what was the word? Extradited? So why not let Kate's fans spread the word? They're already doing it anyway. It's bound to come out."

"So Loup's going to become the poster child for werewolves," Pilar added.

"Pilar!"

She laughed. "Loup's not a werewolf," she assured the apprehensive-looking fans. "That's just a joke, okay? But she is the product of genetic engineering. Sort of."

"She's a geemo? For real?"

"For real," Loup agreed. "Except that I wasn't made in a lab. My father was. My mother was normal. I'm a genetic mutation."

One of the fans shivered. "That's trippy."

"Yeah." Randall tossed his bangs. "Real trippy. It's giving me some ideas for the new album. About what it means to be human and all. And the fear thing. You can't feel fear, right?" he asked Loup.

"Nope."

Randall's girl wriggled on his lap. "That's deep!"

"Yeah." He slid his hands under her shirt. "Real deep."

"It's not, really," Loup said pragmatically. "It's a kind of being stupid. There's a good reason people feel fear—"

"Baby." Pilar nudged her. "I think they quit listening."

"Huh." She watched the band members make out with their fans, kissing and groping. "So much for deep."

Pilar smiled. "It *is* deep, you know. More than you realize." She trailed her fingertips along Loup's bare forearm, tracing the subtle curves of muscle that shifted under her smooth skin. "What did Father Ramon say the night before the big fight? About how you weren't a leader, but you were something more rare?"

"Yeah, it was some word I didn't know."

"I had to look it up, too." She stroked Loup's palm. "Catalyst. Something that causes a change without being changed itself. That's you, baby. These boys don't know what they're in for."

"You think?"

"I know."

"Okay, you're doing it again. The look."

"Oh, for fuck's sake!" Pilar said. "They're not going to notice."

"Oy!" Donny surfaced for air, his expression wounded. "*I* am."

"Sorry!"

Back at the hotel, they saw the band and their chosen groupies safely ensconced in the suite, which was considerably cleaner and tidier than it had been.

"You can stay, you know." Randall waved a bottle of whiskey at them. "Stay and party. It's cool. Mission accomplished. You're off the clock."

Pilar looked sidelong at Loup. "Thanks, but no."

"It's late," Loup agreed. "I'm tired."

"That's a big fuckin' lie," Donny mumbled. "Look at her!" He waved drunkenly in Loup's direction. "Told you I was right about the togs. Looks hot. You're gonna go have sex with hot, crazy tongue tricks, aren't you?"

Charlie perked up. "Oh, yeah?"

"Donny, come here." Pilar kissed him sweetly on the cheek, ignoring his glaring groupie. "Quit thinking about it, okay?"

"I'll try," he mumbled.

"Try harder."

In the hotel room, Loup stripped off her security gear. "I'm gonna shower. It's really hot under those lights and I feel like I've had other people's hands all over me all night long."

"You kind of did, baby."

"Yeah." She made a face. "Stage rushers. It's crazy. If this keeps up, I'm gonna be causing more security problems than I'm solving."

Pilar kicked off her shoes and stretched out on the bed, folding her arms behind her head. "It's all about the PR. You're a novelty act and they're going to exploit you for all it's worth. Randall knew exactly what he was doing with that werewolf thing. He might have been drunk and horny, but he's not dumb." She paused. "Does it bother you?"

"Being treated like a trained monkey?"

"Well, yeah."

Loup shrugged. "Yeah, I kinda hate it. But if we can make it work for us, I'll live with it."

"Devious." Pilar smiled. "Hurry up and shower. I'm going to get in bed. It really *is* late."

A few minutes later, Loup reemerged, warm and damp and clean. She slid under the sheets to join Pilar, propping herself on one elbow. "So we're really gonna let this happen, huh? You're not gonna try and talk me out of it?"

"Nope."

"You think it's a good idea?"

Pilar blew out her breath. "I didn't say *that*. It's a pretty fucking ridiculous idea. But in case you hadn't noticed, ridiculous seems to work for us. And anyway, like you said, it's already happening." She touched Loup's cheek. "I want the same things you do, Santa Olivia. I want my name back. I want to be able to go home. I want the truth to get out. Okay, now you're doing it."

"Doing what?"

"That big, shiny-eyed thing."

Loup smiled. "Can't help it. You know, we *could* just go to the press and tell the truth. Tell the whole story."

Pilar shook her head. "I'm not willing to take *that* big a risk, baby. I mean, I believe Sabine because she'd rather die than get her facts wrong, but governments do lie about that kind of stuff. We oughta know. Or what if they decide they need to take you into protective custody like Miguel? You'd hate it."

"True," she admitted.

"And I'd hate it even more." Pilar kissed her, then gave her a long, serious look. "I told you, I never, ever want to lose you again, Loup. Ridiculous or not, being the mysterious poster child for geemo werewolves is a lot safer than being *you*, so let's just see what happens, okay?"

"Okay."

THIRTY-ONE

A week later they were in Australia.

The first gig of the tour was at a stadium in Perth. Loup was backstage pounding happily on the portable heavy bag when Bill Jones appeared, a wadded black T-shirt in one hand.

"C'mere." He beckoned to her. "You oughta see this."

She followed him to the dressing room where the band was prepping under their manager's supervision. Pilar was in the far corner, talking quietly to someone on the earpiece of her Dataphone.

Randall lifted his head from his notebook. "What's up?"

Jones tossed the wadded T-shirt at him. "Bootleg merchandise. Some punk's selling these in the parking lot. Very popular item."

He shook it out and held it up. KATE was emblazoned across the chest in grainy white letters. Underneath was an equally grainy print of Loup in her security attire, legs braced, head cocked.

"Whoa," Loup said, startled. "Where did that come from?"

"Fuck." Randall contemplated the shirt. "Geordie? We didn't license anything like this, did we?"

The manager winced. "No."

"Well, we'd fucking better, don't you think?"

He eyed Loup. "Umm..."

Pilar ended her call. "Not so fast, guys. I don't remember anything in our contract about using Loup's image for promotional purposes."

Randall gave Loup a yearning look. "You don't mind, do you?"

She glanced at Pilar.

Pilar smiled sweetly at Randall. "Are you offering a percentage or a flat fee?"

He blinked. "A flat fee?"

"Five percent," Geordie said quickly, intervening. "This fad is a flash in the pan. It won't last."

"Gross or net?"

"Net."

She shook her head. "No way."

He sighed. "Okay, okay. Five percent gross. We're not going to be able to get them into production until the end of the tour anyway."

Pilar was already dialing. "Oh, yes we are!"

The crowd in Perth was huge and wildly enthusiastic. It was still predominantly young, predominantly female—but there was a visible contingent of non-teenyboppers. They were a little older, a little edgier. One managed to clamber onstage while Kate played one of their works in progress. He thrust lanky, tattooed arms into the air, hips gyrating to the snaking bass line.

"Ohh-kay." Loup scooped him up and slung him crosswise over her shoulders, wearing him like a yoke. "Here we go." His arms flailed and his feet kicked. Donny faltered on the drums, but Randall kept singing and Charlie's bass line went lower, growling and feral. She turned a few times, then whipped the stage rusher upright and lowered him back into the throng, where eager arms received him.

The crowd screamed.

It was like that all night.

By the time the tour bus rolled into Melbourne, Pilar had arranged a photo shoot with a local photographer and coordinated with the promotions and merchandising people.

"C'mon," she said to Loup as soon as they checked into the hotel. "Put your sexy togs on. We've got a nine a.m. appointment."

Loup yawned. "Can't we reschedule for later? I hardly got any sleep on the bus."

"Nope. This was his only opening. We've got to act fast if we're gonna get the stuff into production."

"Okay, okay!" She splashed cold water on her face and changed her clothes.

The photographer, Lane Staggerford, was an older man with craggy features and a shock of unruly gray hair. He admitted them to his studio without ceremony and took Pilar's chin in his hand, tilting her head this way and that, studying her.

"Very pretty," he said impersonally. "Good skin, too. You can take strong lighting."

"Um...thanks. It's not me. I'm Pilar...uh, Mendez. We spoke on the phone?"

"Oh." Staggerford let her go and glanced at Loup. "You, eh?"

"Yes, sir."

He gave her a longer, hard look, then nodded slowly. "I see it. Cute kid, but that's all on the surface, innit? There's a lot of *there* there."

Pilar showed him the bootleg T-shirt. "This is the fake version. We want to produce something like it, only better."

"Ah." Staggerford examined the image. "You want iconic."

"Iconic?"

He smiled a little, furrows deepening around his mouth. "Powerful. Symbolic."

"Yeah, exactly!"

Staggerford nodded. "Take off your jacket and go stand over there," he said to Loup, nodding at a white backdrop. She obeyed. His smile deepened. "Oh, yes. I think we can do iconic."

For the better part of an hour, he photographed Loup. She struck pose after pose at his direction, patient and uncomplaining.

"Right," he said when they finished. "I'll print twenty of the best shots and a contact sheet and send them over this afternoon. You're staying at the Crown Towers?"

"Yeah, we are. Can't you just email them to me?" Pilar asked.

Staggerford gave her a look. "You're going to reproduce a printed image, you need to *see* a printed image. I'll send the files after you've seen the photos."

"Okay, thanks."

The photos arrived in the early afternoon. Pilar called Geordie. They woke up the band and assembled in their suite to review the photos, spreading the glossy black-and-white prints across the dining table.

"Nice," Randall mumbled. "Real nice."

Charlie cracked open a beer. "Uh-huh."

"Don't do that." Pilar took it away from him. "If you start drinking now, you won't stop and you'll be trashed by the concert."

"Will not!" he protested.

"Yeah, you will." Randall tossed his bangs out of his eyes. "Whaddya think?"

"This one." Donny pointed unerringly to a shot of Loup standing with her weight on her right hip, thumbs hooked in her low waistband, her gaze direct and challenging. He sighed. "Definitely this one."

"Yep," Pilar agreed.

"You sure?" Geordie shuffled through the photos. "Lots of good shots here."

They exchanged a glance. "We're sure," Pilar said.

"Let 'em pick," Randall said. "They know what's gonna appeal to the...whaddya call 'em? One in a hundreds?"

Donny sighed. "Yeah."

"And the others are gonna buy the shit anyway 'cause it's the trendy thing to do," he finished. "They don't care what it looks like."

"Okay." Pilar pulled out her Dataphone. "I'll get the file from Mr. Staggerford and send it on to promotion. We're just doing white on black, right? T-shirts and camis?"

"Hang on a tick." Geordie caught her arm. "I'll need to see the final design to approve it."

"Of course."

"And Kate...the band's name's going to be prominent, right? Big font? This *is* all about Kate, right?"

She gave him a look of wide-eyed innocence. "Yeah, of course!"

Geordie returned it dubiously. "You're disturbingly good at this."

Pilar smiled, dialing. "Turns out I'm good at all kinds of things."

"Ah, fuck me." Donny stared at the multiple images of Loup while Pilar talked on the phone. "Wish there *was* a way to make more of you."

"I'm sorry." Loup touched his shoulder lightly. "I really am. This is uncomfortable for me too."

He looked hopeful. "You don't—"

"No."

Donny sighed again and picked up the photo they'd chosen. "You think maybe I could keep this one?"

"I guess." Loup eyed him. "You're not gonna do anything gross with it, are you?"

"No!" He flushed violently.

Charlie giggled. "Are too, mate. You're gonna wank off all over it."

"Ew." She plucked the photo from Donny's hands. "Okay, I really am sorry, but we've got to work together, you know? I don't want to have to think about that."

"He does it anyway," Charlie informed her.

"Sod off!" Donny shoved him. They scuffled until Loup parted them forcibly, holding them apart at arm's length.

"No fighting," she said sternly. "No teasing, and no talking about wanking, okay?"

They agreed reluctantly.

"Good boys." Loup let them go.

"Hey, baby." Pilar ended her call. "What was that all about?"

She looked at Donny's flushed face and felt bad for him. "Nothing."

"Okay."

THIRTY-TWO

They played two sold-out gigs in Melbourne, then went on to a smaller venue in Hobart. There, the demographic skewed noticeably older than teenage girls and the merchandising caught up with them.

"Selling like hotcakes," Bill Jones reported backstage. Loup worked the heavy bag without comment. "You're a full-blown fad, girlie."

She slammed her fists into the bag, throwing in a couple of

roundhouse kicks for good measure, making the bag teeter on its base. "Good."

Jones shrugged. "Enjoy."

Kate played.

Fans rushed the stage.

Loup picked them up and put them back.

The fan boards buzzed with rumor and speculation. Randall continued to work on new songs. He played one of them on the bus to Sydney, singing and playing acoustic guitar.

"It's called 'Cages,'" he explained.

The song was about loss and despair, and the cages of fear, paranoia, and hatred that people build. And it was about courage and hope being the keys to unlock those prisons. The melody wed the upbeat pop harmonies that Kate was known for with the harder, driving sound the band was evolving, contrasting with the lyrics in unexpected ways.

It was a really good song.

"Wow," Pilar said softly when he finished. "Wow."

Randall smiled at her. "You like it?"

"Yeah, a lot."

"It'll sound real different when we're done. Charlie's working on a bass line that'll take it to the next level. But you get the idea."

"I think it's pretty amazing," Loup offered.

"Thanks." He turned his smile on her, and it was genuine and sincere without a trace of guile. "You inspired it, the both of you. I'm glad you like it."

"You've got some interesting stuff going on behind all that hair, Randall," Pilar said.

He laughed. "Yeah, well...you're a little surprising in your own right, eh? How many people figure out you're more than just a pretty face and a world-class set of tits?"

"Not many," she acknowledged. "But it took me a while to figure it out myself."

"I knew," Loup said.

Pilar nudged her. "You don't have to be all smug about it."

"I'm not!"

"Yeah, you are." Her voice softened. "But I forgive you."

"Oh, go on," Donny said morbidly. "Kiss her. You know you want to. Everyone on the bus can tell when you do. Everyone on the fuck-ing *planet* can tell."

"Hey!" Pilar said indignantly. "I work very hard at being profes-sional."

Charlie snickered.

"I do!"

"And you do a very good job," Randall said in a diplomatic tone. "But Donny's right. Anyway, we don't mind, do we?" he asked the bus at large.

A chorus of "No!" answered.

"Oh, fine." Pilar kissed Loup.

The bus applauded.

Donny sighed.

They played a sold-out gig at a major stadium in Sydney and had so many stage rushers that Bill Jones had to double up on onstage security.

"She's become a fucking liability!" he railed at Geordie afterward. "They're coming here just to try to get past her!"

Kate's manager folded his arms. "And do they?"

"Not yet, no. But this is ridiculous."

Geordie shrugged. "A draw's a draw. Right now, she's a big one."

In the hotel room, Loup rolled her shoulders and tipped her head from side to side, cracking her neck. "Fuck," she murmured. "I'm tired."

"Sorry, baby." Pilar knelt behind her, rubbing her shoulders. "Does that help?"

"Yeah. That's nice, thanks. It's not that hard lifting them, it's actu-ally lowering them. Puts a weird strain on my back and neck."

Pilar kissed the back of her neck. "Loup, you don't have to be out there every night."

"Yeah, I kind of do." She turned, her gaze searching Pilar's face. "I mean, we started this. We made it a thing. There hasn't been any news from the States. It's like nothing's happening. And you said that journalist wanted me there at the interview tomorrow? From *Rolling Stone*?"

"Uh-huh."

"Well, it's a start, isn't it?"

"Yeah." Pilar looked worried. "But it's not worth it if you burn yourself out, baby. I don't think you're getting enough to eat, and you're not meditating like Christophe showed you. You skipped the last two days."

"Did I really?"

"Yeah, you did."

"Okay, okay. I'll make up for it. I'll do it right now." Loup closed her eyes and sank deep into herself, thinking slow thoughts. Twenty minutes later, a knock at the door and the smell of charbroiled beef tugged her out of it. She sniffed the air. "Hamburgers? The really good, expensive kind?"

Pilar gave her a wicked smile. "You really are a little animal, aren't you?"

"I guess."

"Eat." Pilar shoved a burger at her.

Loup ate, ravenous.

"I thought so. Loup, we need to talk about what you're going to say at the interview tomorrow. How much you're going to tell them, you know?"

"Yeah, I was thinking about that." She took another bite, chewed, and swallowed. "Do you remember that article I used to have? The one my mother kept about the Lost Boys?"

"An army of ravening wolf-men poised at America's back door," Pilar said. "Yeah, I remember. But Jaime always said that was mostly bullshit."

"It was." Loup ate a few fries. "But there was like a kernel of truth in it. Maybe just enough, but not too much. For all anyone knows, some of the original kin could have escaped to Canada. Do you think you could get a copy?"

"Do you remember what paper it was in?"

"The *Weekly World News*."

"Sure." She flipped on her Dataphone. "It's in the archive. I just need to go to the business center to print a copy first thing in the morning."

"Thanks, Pilar."

"Sure."

"No, I mean for taking care of me." Loup smiled at her. "You were right; I really needed to slow down a little. And I needed food. I feel a lot better."

"Good." Pilar kissed her cheek. "It's all this travel and freaky hours. And I've been busy with this assistant shit. I'll try to pay better attention and make sure you don't get too burned out."

"Thanks."

She shook her head fondly. "You know, half the people in the world would expect it and the other half would get annoyed at me for fussing. You, you're just sweet."

"Yeah?"

"Very." Pilar pointed at the bathroom door. "Now go wash off the icky fan-sweat, then go to bed. And I mean to sleep."

Loup eyed her. "You sure? I'm really feeling a lot better."

"I'm being nurturing. Don't tempt me."

"Okay, okay!"

The following day, a sharp-witted young journalist named Kate Dunbar from *Rolling Stone* Australia interviewed the band in their suite.

"Kate on Kate," she said crisply. "That's what we're calling the feature."

Charlie gave her a friendly leer. "I like the sound of it."

"Right." She gave him a piercing look over the top of stylish reading glasses. "Let's get to it, shall we? Kate the band is known for radio-friendly bubblegum pop, but rumor has it you're trying out some more mature fare on this tour. Tell me about it."

They deferred to Randall, who rambled on at length and with occasional eloquence. Loup leaned against the wall in her security togs, arms folded.

Kate Dunbar scribbled efficiently. "Fans coming of age, hmm. You think they're ready to embrace the darker side of Kate?"

"It's not *darker*, exactly." Randall pushed his bangs back. "It's deeper."

She played a clip of concert footage on her Dataphone. "A harder sound, wouldn't you say?"

"Yeah, sure."

"Are you seeing a shift in your fan base?"

He glanced at Loup and smiled. "Yeah."

"Let's get some background." Kate Dunbar consulted her notes. "So you all grew up as friends together in a working-class neighborhood..."

For the next hour, she excavated colorful anecdotes about their boyhood and life on the road touring, the kind of material their traditional fan base adored. Then she changed the subject.

"So." Her sharp gaze pinned Loup. "You."

"Me?"

Kate Dunbar nodded. "According to my research, you're either a human GMO, a werewolf, a clever hoax, a publicity stunt, the actual Kate who inspired the band's name, or some combination of the above. Tell me."

"I can't."

The journalist looked taken aback. "What do you mean, can't?"

"It's complicated." Loup shrugged and pulled a folded copy of the Lost Boys article out of her waistband and handed it over. "All I can tell you is that one of these guys was my father."

She scanned the article. "This is ridiculous."

Loup smiled. "You think?"

"I do." Kate Dunbar whipped off her reading glasses and rose. "And I don't intend to play along—" She blinked, startled, as Loup crossed the room with inhuman speed, hands on her shoulders urging her gently and inexorably to retake her seat. "Oh!" The journalist stared. "You're..."

"Not a hoax," Loup said softly.

"No." She swallowed visibly. "There's a story here, isn't there?"

"Yeah," Randall answered, tossing his bangs. "But it's not one we're ready to tell yet, is it, lads?"

They shook their heads.

Kate Dunbar was still staring at Loup. "You *are* a GMO. There are fairly well-substantiated rumors in North America and actual documented cases in Mexico, although none from a source willing to go on record. I know, I looked into it."

"Tell her she oughta look into the other thing," Charlie suggested to Loup. "Those...whaddya call 'em? Outposts?"

Loup winced, and Pilar put her face in her hands.

"Charlie!" Randall threw an empty beer can at him. "Shut it!"

Kate Dunbar's gaze flicked back and forth between them. "Is that about those internment camps along the southern border of the U.S.? They were in the news a while ago."

"I can't say anything about that," Loup said.

"Can't or won't?"

"Won't."

"Can you give me a name? Date of birth? Hometown?" the journalist pressed her. Loup shook her head.

"Our Mystery Girl's gotta stay a mystery for a while. It's for her own good." Randall gave her his yearning look. "You're not gonna kill the story because of it, are you?"

"Hardly." The journalist summoned her resolve. "All right, this has been very interesting." She stood tentatively. Loup stepped back and let her. "I'd like..." She licked lips gone dry. "I suspect this may be a bigger story than I reckoned. If I'm right, we might be talking a cover story. The band's scheduled to do a photo shoot in the warehouse district this afternoon. I'd like you to be in it."

"If it's okay with the band."

Randall grinned. "Hell, yeah!"

The very collected Kate Dunbar left the suite in a daze. "I'll be in touch."

"Nice work." Geordie congratulated them all around. "Well played!"

"It's not a game, man," Donny objected.

"Even so."

"It's really not," Pilar murmured. "You guys do realize this could get political, don't you?"

"Geemo rights!" Charlie thrust his fist into the air. "Fight the power!"

"I'm serious! Charlie, you shouldn't have said anything about Outpost. You could put Loup in a lot of danger."

He looked sheepish. "Sorry."

"This is serious stuff, okay?" Pilar said. "It's not just about having a gimmick."

"We know." Randall tossed his bangs. "Like you say, I'm not stupid, eh? After hearing your story, I figured there's no way you and Loup would let us exploit her for PR if you weren't planning on exploiting us right back. It's cool. We're down with the fight."

"Excuse me?" Geordie Davies looked from one band member to the next. "Fight? What fight?"

"Freedom."

"Whose bloody freedom?"

"Theirs." He pointed at Loup and Pilar. "Geemos in America. All those poor sods stuck in... whaddya call 'em? Outposts?"

"Yeah," Loup said.

"Oh, no." Geordie was shaking his head. "Oh, no, no, no! I don't know what this is all about, lads, but it is *not* cool and we are *not* down with the fight."

"Yeah, we are," Donny said.

"You're a fucking drummer in a fucking pop band!"

"C'mon, Geordie, man." Randall's voice took on a coaxing tone. "We can be crusaders for social justice. How many times have we talked about how to take the next step? Used to be bands did this kind of thing all the time. This is it. This can be our thing. It's our cause. It makes us relevant."

Geordie glowered at him. "You want to be a big fucking hero, Rand? That it?"

He thought about it and smiled. "Yeah, maybe."

"Oh, fuck me!"

They argued for a while longer, but it was obvious that the band was adamant and this was an argument their manager was going to lose.

"It's official," Pilar whispered in Loup's ear. "The Loup Garron effect is in full force."

"I guess so."

THIRTY-THREE

After a final sold-out gig in Brisbane, the band flew to Osaka.

"Ever been to Japan?" Donny asked Loup on the airplane, leaning forward in his seat.

She laughed. "No."

"You'll like it," he assured her. "The fans are different. Way more polite. Bet we won't have any stage rushers."

"I wouldn't mind a break from it."

"This is so weird," Pilar murmured. "We're gonna be, like, all the way on the other side of the world, baby."

"We already are," Loup reminded her.

"Yeah, but it didn't seem like it. I mean, they speak English in Australia. This is gonna be way different."

She shrugged. "I don't think we're going to see much more than the hotel room and the concert venue."

"You will in Tokyo," Donny offered. "We've got back-to-back gigs at the Budokan and a whole day to recover before we fly back."

"A whole day." Pilar nudged Loup.

"I'll take it."

They had an uneventful flight followed by a long wait in the immigration line. All the agents wore surgical face masks. Loup watched them perform a strange procedure on the travelers in line ahead of them, inserting their index fingers into a small handheld device.

"What the hell?"

"Blood test," Pilar said. "Checking for flu virus. I read about it. Guess they did it everywhere for a while. They're still being extra careful in Japan. They were hit hard because the population's so dense."

"Huh." Loup smiled tiredly at her. "You're a wealth of information."

"I try."

Their Japanese liaison met them on the far side of customs and immigration and whisked them in short order to a waiting hotel.

"Right." Geordie Davies glanced at his sleepy-eyed flock and consulted his watch. "Sound check at six. Let's try to get a little shut-eye, shall we?"

In the hotel room, Loup flung herself on the bed. "Told you."

"We could go out," Pilar said. "Unless you'd rather sleep."

"Does it involve food?"

"Yep."

"Okay." She bounced up, suddenly more energetic. "I'm in."

Outside, they walked the teeming streets. Pilar consulted the GPS system on her Dataphone with dubious results, while Loup gazed all around at the colorful signage and unfamiliar characters, listening to a rush of language that was wholly unfamiliar. A smiling young woman in a T-shirt that said FRISK! addressed her.

"Sorry?"

"Please to try?" The young woman handed her a tiny can of soft drink labeled FRISK from a tray slung around her neck. "Frisk is frisky!"

"Sure, thanks." Loup tried it. "Not bad."

"Excuse me." Pilar showed the promoter her screen. "Do you know where this place is? The famous noodle place?"

She beamed and rattled off a string of heavily accented directions.

"Okay, thanks."

They found it after a considerable amount of trial and error and stood in line to order. The shop was packed and tiny, people hunched over bowls slurping happily. When Pilar ordered two bowls of udon noodles, the cook gave her an impatient glare.

"Which one?" he asked abruptly.

"Um...the famous kind?"

His voice rose. "Which one you want?"

"I can't remember!" She glanced behind her. "Help!"

A woman in business attire laughed and spoke to the man in Japanese. His glare eased. He handed over two steaming bowls and pairs of chopsticks.

"*Kitsune udon*," the woman said helpfully. "Very famous in Osaka. Do you know what is a *kitsune*?"

They shook their heads.

She pointed to the curls of tofu atop the noodles, fried to a russet hue. "*Kitsune* is fox. It is the same color, you see?"

"That's really interesting." Pilar smiled at her. "Thank you."

The woman smiled back. "You are very welcome."

They found seats at a crowded table and copied the other diners, holding the bowls close to their lips and shoveling in noodles.

"Good?" Pilar asked.

"Awesome." Loup swallowed an enormous mouthful. "They're super-slippery and fun to eat. So what makes this the best noodle place in the city?"

"Secret ingredient in the broth."

"What is it?"

"I don't know, baby." Pilar laughed. "It's a secret."

"Oh. Duh." She scooped up the last of her noodles and drank the broth. *"Kitsune udon, kitsune udon.* I'm gonna get another bowl; it looks like the line's pretty short. You want anything?"

"I'm good."

"You're great." Loup smiled. "Thanks for thinking of this."

"Sure." Pilar rested her chin on her hand. "Funny, when we first stayed in that place in Mexico City, I never thought I'd get sick of nice hotels and room service. But after a while, it all seems the same and none of it feels real. This does. Confusing, but real."

"I like it," she said wistfully. "I miss *real.*"

"Me too."

The venue in Osaka was a modest one, holding no more than fifteen hundred people, but it was sold out to a standing crowd. Donny was rights; the Japanese fans were more polite. They bobbed and danced to the music and were quiet in between songs. They recognized Loup in the wings immediately and there was a lot of pointing and photo taking, but for the better part of the night, no one rushed the stage. It wasn't until near the end of the concert that a gaggle of daring young teens boosted their smallest member onstage—a slip of a girl who couldn't have been more than thirteen, wearing a Kate camisole with Loup's image over a miniskirt and striped socks.

Once onstage, she froze, overcome by the lights and shyness.

"Hey, you." Loup caught the girl around the waist and tossed her high into the air, catching her and perching her narrow backside on one shoulder, holding her in place with one arm. The girl's friends convulsed with giggles. "You want to take a picture?" She mimed it with her free hand.

A dozen cameras flashed.

"Okay, down you go." She lowered her to the stage.

"Sank you!" the girl breathed. She gave Loup a quick, unexpected hug. "Tell Charlie I love him best!"

Loup laughed. "Okay, I will." She swung the girl back down to her waiting friends, who fell all over themselves to congratulate her.

It was the only incident of the night.

"That was sweet," Pilar said afterward in the hotel room.

"Yeah. She was cute." Loup wriggled on the bed and stretched luxuriantly, happy not to be tired and achy. "Probably bound for a bad end. She's got a crush on Charlie."

"Oh, she doesn't know any better. She's just a kid."

"I dunno, that bad-boy gene's pretty strong."

"Mmm." Pilar stroked Loup's bare stomach. "So how come I ended up with the good girl?"

She smiled. " 'Cause the one-in-a-hundred gene's stronger."

"I don't think it's genetic." Pilar slid closer, inhaling her scent. "I think it's pheromones or something. Did you know you smell good even when you're hot and sweaty?"

"I didn't work hard enough to get hot and sweaty tonight."

"Yeah, but when you do."

Loup twined one hand in Pilar's hair. "So I'm a good girl, huh?"

"A badass, but a good girl." She kissed her. "You never do anything mean and spiteful. You made that kid so happy tonight."

"I was just doing my job."

"You're good with kids." Pilar cocked her head. "You think we might want 'em someday?"

"Kids?"

"Yeah."

"I dunno." Loup blinked. "Do you?"

She considered. "Yeah, maybe. Not for a long, long time. But maybe after you get done saving the world or whatever." She gave Loup a little shake. "Because I *do* plan on being with you for a long, long time. Did you do your meditation today?"

"On the plane, yeah."

"Only on the plane?"

"For over an hour." She pulled Pilar effortlessly atop her. "And I'll do it again tomorrow morning when you're in the shower, because you take for fucking ever. But right now I don't want to talk about meditating or our imaginary kids or how long I'm going to live."

Pilar smiled. "No?"

"No." Loup tugged her head down and kissed her.

"Saving the world, maybe?" she asked, a little breathless.

"Pilar!"

"What? Am I being a tease?"

"Yes," Loup growled, rolling her over and pinning her to the bed. "It's late and I'm *not* tired. And you are so getting ravished."

She sighed happily. "Yay!"

THIRTY-FOUR

Tokyo was crazy.

It was hustle and bustle and relentless neon street scenes that beggared the imagination.

"Do you know there are sex clubs where you can get anything you want?" Charlie said dreamily aboard the tour bus. "*Anything.*"

Pilar eyed him. "Yeah, it's in your dossier."

"Hey, I thought you were down with the whole schoolgirl fantasy!" He sounded wounded.

Geordie Davies groaned.

"Well, maybe. But only with Loup, not some hooker."

"I dunno," Loup said. "I think I'd look pretty silly."

"You wouldn't," Donny muttered.

"You looked pretty silly as a cabin boy," Pilar reminded her. "In an adorable kind of way. Remember? Besides, you wearing nothing but that stocking cap—"

"Okay, okay!" Loup glanced at Donny's pained face. "Enough."

He sighed. "I don't mind."

"I do." She clamped her hand over Pilar's mouth. "So, hey! Last venue, huh?"

The band exchanged glances. "Yeah," Randall said softly. "Contract's up after this, eh? Turns into a question of what comes next, doesn't it?"

Pilar pulled Loup's hand away. "What are you thinking?"

"We're headed into the studio after the tour. But we don't want to lose you, do we?" He smiled wryly and nodded at Loup. "New face of Kate and all. I hear Ms. Dunbar called. We're gonna make the cover. It's a thing now, isn't it? We're in it for the long haul."

"It's a thing," Loup agreed.

"Call Magnus," Pilar suggested. "Mr. Lindberg. I'm sure he can arrange some kind of retainer deal."

"So you'd be ours? All ours?" Donny flushed.

"In a manner of speaking."

His flush deepened. "Well, I know *that*!"

Their gigs in Tokyo were at the Budokan, a famous and venerable venue that held ten thousand people. Both gigs were sold out, and it was obvious even before the first concert started that this crowd was different from the one in Osaka.

"A lot of hipsters out there tonight," Bill Jones confirmed backstage.

Charlie snickered. "Hipsters?"

"Posers, Goths, punks, whatever they're called these days. Lots of dyed spiky hair, black leather, and ripped jeans. Plus some that look like they came out of those cartoons they have here."

"Cool." Randall bobbed his head. "Very cool."

Still, the crowd stayed docile while Kate played the upbeat pop tunes from their hit album. It wasn't until they tried out some of the new music that the crowd began to roil, the older fans pushing their way through the ardent teenyboppers to mob the front of the stage.

"Heads up," Bill Jones' voice said in Loup's earpiece as the band launched into "Cages," playing it live for the first time.

She nodded.

There was a surge. Two young men were crowd surfing, being

passed hand by hand over the audience toward the stage. Loup picked the closest one and grabbed his ankles the minute his boots hit the stage. She dragged him backward, then whipped him around, hooking her arms under his and lowering him back into the pit before he had a chance to blink.

The second surfer was onstage, raising his arms. He shot a triumphant sideways glance at Loup through a shock of red-streaked hair and prepared to stage dive into the crowd.

"Oh, no you don't." She got there in time to catch him middive, staggering a little under the impact. He let out a woof as her shoulder drove into his midsection. She spun him once, then lowered him without fanfare.

More were coming. A lot more.

"Gonna need backup," Loup said into her headset.

Before it could arrive, the music stopped abruptly and the crowd quieted.

"Hey," Randall said, his mellow voice echoing over the amplifier. "Be cool, people. We know you all want a shot at the world's best bodyguard. And she's cool, she'll let you take it. But if you're all gonna rush the stage at once, we're gonna have to pull her and replace her with a bunch of big ugly guys who aren't as nice to look at. Don't you have some kind of samurai code here? One at a time, okay?"

There was a general murmur of assent, and a few catcalls for the samurai comment.

"Okay." He motioned to the band and they started playing again.

Loup watched the crowd. After several moments of nonverbal communication, they picked one spiky-haired hipster to hoist in the air and surf toward the stage. She touched her headset. "I'm good. Cancel backup."

Jones' voice crackled in her ear. "You sure?"

"Yep." She moved to intercept the spiky boy. "The fans really *are* more polite here, even when they're not."

After the usual backstage mayhem, the band put in a brief appearance at an after-party at a noisy club. Even in their private room, the music was loud and pounding. The band members surveyed the hopeful fans outside the door, preparing to pick and choose.

"Do they have food here?" Loup shouted to Pilar. "I'm starving!"

She shook her head. "Want an energy bar?"

Loup made a face. "I guess."

"I have a better idea." She put her lips close to Loup's ear. "Ask Bill if he can handle this without you for a few minutes."

"Okay."

With Bill Jones' blessing, Loup let Pilar lead her outside to a yakitori stand where a handful of club-goers were clustered on stools around a counter and others were milling around, eating charcoal-grilled barbecue chicken on skewers.

"Oh, wow." Loup sniffed the air. "That smells really good."

Pilar pointed and held up two fingers. "Two, please? Yakitori? Am I saying that right?" The vendor smiled and handed over a pair of skewers. She passed them to Loup. "Good?"

Loup took a bite. "Really good. Maybe two more?"

"You bet, baby."

The club-goers murmured among themselves. At length a pretty girl in a minidress and high platform boots was dispatched, tripping over to question them.

"Excuse me?" She nodded at Loup's security togs. "You are... Kate?"

"I'm with Kate, yeah."

The girl called something back to the others in Japanese. Out came the cameras and Dataphones. "Mystery Girl, yes! May we take photos with you?"

"Can I finish eating?" Loup asked helplessly.

"You don't want to get between her and food," Pilar warned the girl. "She'll bite your hand off."

Her eyes widened. "So sorry! You are Kate, also?"

"Sort of, sure. I'm with the band."

One of the club-goer boys swooped over to scoop up the girl in the minidress, slinging her over his shoulder. "Kate, yes!" he cried, twirling her. She yelled at him and pounded her fists on his back. He ignored it. "Now I am Mystery Girl!"

Pilar giggled.

"Okay, okay," Loup said, good-natured. She tossed her empty skewers in the receptacle on the counter. "I'm done. Everyone can take a picture if they like."

They were still posing and chatting with the fans, drawing an increasing crowd when the security team emerged from the club with the band and their chosen groupies.

"Oy!" Bill Jones said, disgruntled. "That was a helluva lot longer than a few minutes! You're on the job, eh?"

"Yes, sir! Sorry, sir!"

"It's cool." Randall had his arms draped over a pair of Japanese fans who might or might not have been sisters. "It's publicity, man. It's all good." He peered at Loup and Pilar through his bangs. "You're in the limo with us, right?"

Loup shrugged. "If you say so."

"I do."

"Oh, just get in." Jones opened the limo door and started shoving bodies inside. "Horny prats."

Back at the hotel, they saw the band safely ensconced in the suite with their groupies and declined the traditional invitation to stay and party with them.

"You feel okay, baby?" Pilar asked in their room. "Not too sore?"

"Yeah." Loup rolled her shoulders. "Think I might shower."

"Okay." She turned on the TV and flipped it to the international news channel. "I made an appointment for a massage for you at the hotel spa tomorrow. I think you might like it. It's supposed to be really good."

"Thanks, Pilar."

"Sure."

Loup took a quick shower, washing off the sweat of the night's exertion and the impression of strange hands grabbing at her. She emerged to find Pilar staring at the television, transfixed. Her pulse quickened instinctively. "News?"

"News," Pilar affirmed. She shook herself. "Holy fuck, yes. Some guys on the Oversight Committee have crossed over to join the Reform Caucus. Congress is gonna hold hearings on the Outposts."

"That's great!"

"Yeah, but." Pilar turned a stricken face her way. "There's a rumor that their star witness has disappeared."

"Miguel?"

"Miguel fucking Garza, yeah."

"Shit!" Loup swore and rummaged for her Dataphone. "Shit, I need to talk to that senator. I can't call him now, can I? It's the middle of the night."

"Not in the U.S."

"What time is it there?"

Pilar calculated. "Midafternoon yesterday. You're good."

"It's yesterday there? That's so weird." Loup rang the number. "Yeah, hi! Hello, Senator Ballantine. This is Loup Garron. What's going on? Is it true that Miguel's disappeared?" She listened. "Oh, c'mon, he's like family! It's a small town, you know? Please?" There was a long pause. "That's...wow. Oh, Mig! Okay. We have to figure out a way to get him out of this. About those hearings—" She caught a warning look from Pilar. "Let me call you back."

She ended the call.

Pilar shivered. "Baby?"

"Mig's being held hostage." Loup paced restlessly. "Fucking idiot. He finally managed to give them the slip two days before the announcement. Then the announcement comes out and they get a call from some skeevy hotel bigwig in Las Vegas. Says the casino caught Mig cheating at blackjack and they're keeping him in custody until his fine's paid."

"How much?"

"Ten million."

"That's ridiculous!" Pilar said indignantly. "That's just blackmail. Why don't they call the police?"

Loup shook her head. "Can't trust 'em. There's too much government pressure to make Miguel disappear. They're trying to keep it quiet while they negotiate, but the rumor's already out there. And without Miguel's testimony, there might not be any hearings."

"Fuck." She was quiet a moment. "Loup, can we please be smart about this? Why don't *I* go testify?"

Loup blinked. "You?"

"Why not? I was born and raised in Outpost. My testimony's as good as Miguel's. And the army's not after me, just you."

"You'd do that?" Loup's voice softened. "All alone? It's not like it would exactly be safe for you, either. Not with a fake passport."

Pilar swallowed. "No. I know. But maybe I can get them to promise me...whaddya call it? Amnesty? It's *my* town, too, baby. Those were *my* friends we left behind, the closest thing I had to family other than you. Father Ramon, Sister Martha, Mackie...do you think I wouldn't do anything I could to help them?"

"No, I know you would." Loup smiled, her heart aching a bit. "You're *muy macha* now, *sí*? But what about Miguel?"

"Fuck Miguel fucking Garza!" Pilar raked her hand through her hair in a quick, angry gesture. "He got himself into this, let him get himself out of it!"

"I pushed him," Loup said stubbornly.

"To cheat at blackjack? I don't think so, baby."

"No, okay. If that part's true, it was monumentally stupid. Maybe it is, maybe it isn't. Miguel's a lot smarter than he acts, but he's lazy and he likes taking shortcuts. But the hero thing." Loup shrugged. "You say I have this effect on people. Maybe that's true, too. But it's never on purpose. I never pushed anyone to take that kind of risk. Except Miguel. I *asked* him to do this. I owe him. I can't just leave him in trouble. I have to do something!"

"Loup..."

"I do!"

"Look." Pilar spread her hands. "Maybe Senator Ballantine can negotiate knowing he's got a sure witness. If he's got me, he doesn't need Miguel. Maybe he can persuade the skeevy hotel guy to let him go once he's not that valuable."

"Maybe," Loup said reluctantly.

"Can we at least try it?"

She hesitated, then nodded. "Okay."

"Give me the phone." Pilar put out her hand. "I'm calling him back." She rang. "Hi, Senator? No, this is Pilar. Okay, this is what I'm thinking." She told him, then listened for a moment. "Okay, thanks. Call us."

"Well?"

"He thinks it's worth trying. He'll let us know. And he thinks we'd—*you'd*—better not do anything stupid and dangerous."

"What if it doesn't work?" Loup asked.

Pilar didn't answer.

"Pilar, please? It's important to me."

She gave Loup a long, level look. "Baby, listen to me. You know I love your hero complex. But it's one thing to risk losing you over the fate of all of Santa Olivia and maybe thousands of other people. It's another to risk it for Miguel fucking Garza's dumb mistake. If I say I don't want you to have anything to do with this, will you go off on your own and try it anyway?"

Loup was silent, struggling. "No," she said at length. "I won't."

"You mean it?"

"Yes." She nodded. "I did it to you once. I won't do it again. I promise."

"Thank you." Pilar kissed her cheek. "Now stop looking like a small thundercloud and help me think. Did Senator Ballantine say where they're holding Miguel hostage?"

"Huh?" Loup gave her a dumbstruck glance.

"Did he say where they're holding him?" she repeated patiently, turning on her Dataphone and entering the password for Global's secure databases.

"At the casino, he thinks. Hellfire Club. They've got him under guard in one of the suites."

"Hellfire Club, Hellfire Club..." Pilar smiled. "Yeah, here it is. I figured. All the big casinos are in the database, even the American ones." She showed the screen to Loup. "Complete security specs. Do you remember anything from the chapter in Clive's bodyguard manual on hostage extraction?"

"Something about securing your avenue of retreat. Pilar, are you saying you'll *help* me? Even if it means we could get caught?"

"Of course. I don't think I could handle it by myself, and there's no way I'm going to let you go it alone if it comes to it."

"Then why did you...?"

"Because I really, really wanted to know what you'd choose," she said evenly. "And now I'm glad I do. Okay?"

"Okay," Loup said. "You're really gonna help?"

Pilar shrugged. "I figure we didn't become secret agent bodyguards for nothing."

THIRTY-FIVE

They broke the news to the band backstage while their manager was busy elsewhere.

"I'm really sorry," Loup said after they'd explained the situation. "Maybe it will all work out like Pilar hopes. But if it doesn't...I can't say for sure when I'll be back."

"Or me," Pilar added. "If we get caught and they *do* take you into custody, I'm sure as hell not going anywhere."

The band exchanged glances.

"Vegas, huh?" Randall tucked his bangs behind one ear. "We might be able to use some R & R in Vegas, eh, lads?"

"You can't do that," Loup said.

"Sure we can." Charlie grinned. "Viva Las Vegas!"

"I'm serious!"

"So am I." Randall smiled sweetly at her. "And it's not your choice." He rummaged under a tattered notebook and pulled out a mock-up of the cover of next month's *Rolling Stone* Australia. It bore a photo from the shoot in Sydney. The band was on a pedestal, framed by a battered tin warehouse cargo door—Randall in the center with his arms outstretched in a lazy Jesus pose, Charlie and Donny flanking him, slouching sideways. In front of them on the street Loup stood in her security togs with arms folded, looking enigmatic.

The headline read KATE'S CRUSADERS.

"It's a thing, right?" he said. "Our thing?"

"Yeah, but..."

"Shut up," Donny said brusquely. "It's *not* your choice. Just let us know, all right?"

Loup glanced at Pilar, who raised her eyebrows. "Okay, okay!"

"Good," Randall said mildly. "Now bugger off and go hit your punching bag or something, will you? It's the last concert of the tour and I want it to be a good one. Pilar, can we get some single malt back here?"

"Right away!"

The last concert was a good one. The band played well, old music and new alike. The audience was at once enthusiastic and respectful, obeying the rules laid down the night before. Loup caught them up and put them back, showing off every now and then to the delight of the crowd. She felt a nostalgia for something that might be ending, and a faint underlying hollowness where fear of what might come should have been.

The last after-party was wild.

It took place at a club called Mermaid with submerged swimming pools on opposite walls where topless women performed languid arabesques underwater. The entire place was suffused with an eerie subaquatic glow.

"This is *not* what I authorized!" Geordie Davies said, flushed with anger.

"Sure it is, man." Randall smiled lazily. "You just didn't look close enough at the fine print."

The band proceeded to get spectacularly drunk. Donny threw up and passed out in the bathroom and had to be carried to the limo. Randall and Charlie managed to stagger out on their feet, propped up by a bevy of female fans, at least one of whom appeared to be wearing a schoolgirl outfit.

"We need exshtra girls," Charlie slurred. "Case Donny wakes up."

"Gotta have at least one member of the security team in there," Bill Jones informed Loup with malevolent cheer. "You're the smallest."

"Great."

Pilar eyed the crammed limo. "I'll ride in one of the taxis. See you back at the hotel."

"After-after-party in our suite." Randall poked his head out of the sunroof. "C'mon! You've gotta come. You've gotta. Could be historic." He put on his best wheedling voice. "Please? Half an hour?"

"Five minutes."

"Ten?"

She rolled her eyes. "Okay, ten. Fine."

Ten minutes turned into two hours of babysitting drunk rock stars, consoling sobbing extras left unchosen and calling taxis for them, confiscating illegal drugs, and cleaning up room service refuse.

"Our would-be heroes," Pilar commented.

"They mean well." Loup fetched an extra blanket from the closet and spread it over Donny, who was unconscious on the couch.

"You really think they could help?"

"I have no idea."

"Loup, Loup." Donny's eyelids opened a crack. He plucked feebly at her low-slung track pants. "Promise we will. Can I have a kiss g'night? Puh-leeze?"

She kissed his forehead. "Go back to sleep, Donny."

He sighed and did.

Their day of rest found the band hungover and torpid. After checking in with Bill Jones, Loup and Pilar managed to get out and do a little sightseeing in the city, culminating at the famous Sensoji Temple in the heart of old Edo. They passed through a gate beneath a massive red lantern into a market thronged with people. Pilar browsed the stands while Loup gazed at the crowd. As they grew closer to the temple proper, fragrant smoke drifted. Loup stifled a cough, her eyes stinging and unable to water.

"It's supposed to be purifying," Pilar informed her. "You want to get a fortune?"

"Sure."

Inside the temple they paid two hundred yen to shake a metal canister until a numbered stick popped out. A group of friendly Japanese tourists helped them match it to a drawer with fortunes written on slips of paper, explaining that if it was a bad fortune, all they had to do was tie it to a tree to let the bad luck blow away.

"You pick, baby," Pilar said, apprehensive.

Loup pulled out a slip and read the English translation in fine print. "A million drops of water can wear down a mountain. A thousand tears can melt the hardest heart."

"Is that good or bad?"

"It is not bad." One of the tourists, a middle-aged woman with a warm smile, spoke up. "You face obstacles, yes?"

"That we do," Loup agreed.

Her smile broadened. "Then it is good. Difficult, but good."

"Oh," Pilar said with relief. "Thank you!" She attempted a polite Japanese bow. The tourists laughed and returned it.

"Do you want to pick one?" Loup asked. "We can get another stick."

She shook her head. "I like this one. Can we share it?"

"Sure." Loup searched her face. "This scares you, doesn't it?"

"To pieces." Pilar kissed her lightly. "But I am going to be *muy macha* and not let fear control me. C'mon, let's find you an interesting snack to try, then we have to head back to the hotel to pack."

"Okay." Loup folded their fortune and stowed it carefully in her wallet.

They had dinner that night with the hungover band and their concerned manager in one of the hotel's very excellent restaurants.

"So," Geordie said when they'd finished. "This geemo business. Ms. Dunbar sent me a preliminary draft of her article for approval. She's done some digging. She found correlations between unconfirmed accounts of a Chinese program in Haiti that was shut down by the Yanks, unconfirmed experiments in the U.S. Army, and confirmed accounts of rogue geemos in Mexico. That's supposed to be you, right?"

"Maybe," Loup said.

"And yet you hail from Canada." He smiled wryly. "At least that's the story Mr. Lindberg told me. Somehow I don't think that's the story the lads are covering up for you. And now there's this business about the States?"

She shrugged.

"Look, sweetheart." Geordie leaned forward. "If I'm guessing right, you *need* me. Mr. Lindberg was very clear that you had an exclusive contract with Global. I don't know why one or both of you has to go to the States or why the lads are hell-bent on going with you if you do, but if Kate doesn't keep you on retainer—"

"Geordie, man." Randall took off the sunglasses that had been obscuring his eyes throughout dinner. "You're fired."

"What?" He blinked.

"Yeah?" Randall glanced around at the other two. They nodded. "Fired."

"You're joking."

"No, man." He shook his head. "This is not cool. Not cool at all."

"You signed a contract, too, boyo—"

"Yeah." Randall gave his lazy smile. "One with an opt-out clause that kicked in, oh, about two weeks ago. You've really got to read that shit more closely. Look, man. We've done everything you said and you were right, everyone got rich. Now we're gonna do what we want to do, and you're either with us or against us." He glanced at Pilar. "You're good at arranging stuff. Think you could manage a band?"

"Sure," she said with false conviction. "How hard can it be?"

Geordie snorted. "You have *got* to be joking!"

"We're not," Donny said.

The manager looked at Charlie.

"Don't look at me." Charlie thrust his fist in the air. "Fight the power! Viva Las Vegas!"

"So that's the deal," Randall said. "Do you want the job or not, man?"

He gave Pilar a sour look. "I sure as hell don't want you to turn your career over to some inexperienced tart to screw up."

"Hey!" she said, indignant. "What have I ever screwed up?"

"My life, apparently." Geordie stared at the ceiling. "All right, all right. I want to hear the whole story, the true story." He raised his hand. "I won't tell a soul or interfere, I promise. My hand to God, swear on my mum's grave. But I want to know what load of codswallop these girls have been selling you before I make any decisions."

"That's fair," Randall agreed. "You cool with it?"

"You trust him?" Loup asked.

He nodded. "To keep his word? Yeah."

So they told him. By the time they got to the part about escaping through the smugglers' tunnel, Geordie's mouth was hanging open.

"Are you having me on?" he demanded.

"No," Pilar said. "Don't you ever watch the news? That's why we have to go back, or at least I do. The congressional hearings. You can call Senator Ballantine if you don't believe us. We have his private number."

"Have you sold the rights?" Geordie gestured impatiently at their blank looks. "To your life story! You haven't sold the rights, have you? Book? Film?"

"No," Loup said. "Nothing like that."

He leaned back in his chair. "You're a fucking gold mine, you are."

"Told you," Randall said mildly. "So you want the job?"

The manager gave him a sharp look. "The timing's tight, but I know a few people. What would Kate say to playing a free concert on the Mall in Washington D.C. to call attention to the hearings? Raise awareness for GMO rights and freedom for all Americans?"

He grinned. "I'd say you're hired."

THIRTY-SIX

At the band's insistence, once they returned to England, Loup and Pilar accompanied them to a rented estate in Surrey that had been owned by a famous musician of years gone by and had a professional recording studio.

There, they waited for news.

Geordie Davies made an offer to keep them on retainer for the next six months.

Magnus Lindberg and Sabine flew in to negotiate.

They started by taking Loup and Pilar out to dinner at an expensive restaurant with a private dining room. Before drinks had even been served, Magnus nodded to Sabine, who opened her briefcase and placed a copy of *Rolling Stone* Australia on the table.

"Kate's Crusaders," Magnus observed. "Seems you've made a connection with the client. Very good article. Very political."

"Thanks," Loup said.

"Sabine here has been following the news out of America. Something about hearings? A missing witness, rumors of a new mystery witness?"

Pilar winced. "Yeah, about that—"

"And this absurd business about a concert," Magnus continued. "You do realize, Ms. Mendez, that such an appearance on American soil would put Loup in considerable jeopardy? A prospect you seemed so anxious to avoid?"

"She knows," Loup said softly.

Pilar nodded. "It's complicated."

"I see." He steepled his fingers. "Too complicated for my tastes, I fear. Too…indiscreet. I'd be well advised to insist that Mr. Davies buy out your contract, wouldn't I? Wash my hands of the two of you?"

"Probably," she agreed. "You've been fair with us. You ought to get your money's worth. If everything works out, we'd be happy to work for you again. But if it doesn't…" She shrugged. "I'm sorry. At least Kate will probably make up their money in merchandising."

Magnus regarded her. "Or I could put an end to this with a single phone call. You risk exposing some of Global Security's more dubious machinations."

"The passport thing? I won't."

"She won't," Pilar agreed. "Me neither. If it comes up, we'll say we got 'em in Mexico from some guy who sells stolen and forged passports. There are guys like that out there, right?"

"There are."

"And you could probably get your Canadian connections to back us up, right?"

"It's possible."

"So will you let us go?" Loup asked. "Please?"

He glanced at Sabine, who returned his gaze impassively. After a long, long moment, he let out his breath in a sigh. "Yes, fine. I'll allow it." Magnus touched his steepled fingers to his lips. "Let us say that I am not entirely a cynic. I've witnessed many very unpleasant things in my lifetime. I've profited from the paranoia and greed of others. But I never completely abandoned hope, and I cannot help but admire the heroic impulse, no matter how absurd it may be."

"Loup," Pilar said softly.

"Loup?" His gaze slewed round at her. "No, my dear. Loup is Loup. She is exactly what I hired her to be. *You* are what surprised me."

"Me?"

"You."

Pilar flushed. "Thank you." She shot a suspicious look at Sabine. "Aren't you going to snort or roll your eyes or mutter something?"

"No."

"You sure?"

Her lips twitched. "Yes, you little twit!"

The following day they met with Geordie and the band and hammered out an agreement that was acceptable to all parties. Kate the band bought out the remainder of Loup and Pilar's contract for half a million euros. Geordie grimaced as he poised his pen over the contract.

"You know there's still a chance we could be pissing this money away?" he warned the band one last time. "This could get ugly."

Randall glanced at Pilar. "How many of the Loup T-shirts sold?"

"A little over twenty-three thousand."

"If it gets ugly, we'll sell a million," he predicted. "Two million, maybe. Sign away, man."

He signed. "Done."

Charlie cheered and popped open a bottle of champagne. They passed it around for everyone to have a swig.

"Ah, no. Thank you." Magnus declined the bottle politely, looking amused. Sabine merely looked horrified. "The deportment and etiquette lessons turned out to be rather a waste, eh?"

"I wouldn't say that," Pilar offered. "I have a feeling they're gonna come in handy in these hearings. Don't you think, baby?"

"Yeah. Um, yes. I do."

Magnus consulted his watch. "We should be off."

They accompanied them to the car. Sabine opened the door for her employer, then favored Loup and Pilar with a curt nod.

"Godspeed," she said briefly. "I hope you succeed."

"As do I." Magnus shook both their hands, then kissed them on both cheeks, European-style. "Take care."

"Hey, Magnus! C'mere." Pilar put one hand on the back of his neck, tugging his head down, and whispered something inaudible in his ear. He pulled back and gave her an incredulous look. She nodded encouragement. "I'm serious. Try it and see."

Something in his face softened. "I just might at that."

"Good." She smiled happily, ignoring the return of Sabine's scowl.

Loup watched the car pull away. "Pilar Ecchevarria, what in the world did you say to him?"

She looked smug. "I told him to open his eyes and ask Sabine out on a damn date."

"Seriously?" Loup laughed.

"Yep. Did you see his face? He didn't have the first clue."

"No, he did not." She took Pilar's arm affectionately. "I have a feeling Magnus knew a lot of things he wasn't telling us, but that was *not* one of them. C'mon, Cupid. Let's go see what our new bosses want."

Not much, as it transpired. For the better part of a week, the band rehearsed and recorded in the studio, honing and refining the new material. There was no news on the Miguel Garza front. Geordie Davies worked frantically to coordinate arrangements for Kate's concert on the mall, scheduled to take place the day before the hearings began. He assigned Pilar the task of sending a press release and the link to the *Rolling Stone* Australia cover story to every media contact he had in the United States.

Calls and emails came flooding in.

"They want to interview *you*," he complained to Loup.

"Keep it about the band for now," she said calmly. "I won't do any advance interviews. Stick to the plan. Don't give them my name, anything. Keep the mystery alive."

He nodded. "Right."

The band recorded a decent rough cut of "Cages" and leaked it.

It was very, very popular.

"Check it out." Pilar showed Loup a video mash-up on her Dataphone, the new recording interspersed with amateur concert footage from the tour. Half featured the band playing; the other half featured Loup onstage, hoisting and whirling delighted fans.

Christophe called. "Hey, *prima*!" he shouted into his phone over considerable background noise. "I am in this club in Monterrey. You are on the video screens!"

Loup smiled. "Yeah?"

"Yes! Hey, I watch the news. Are you the mystery witness in America?"

"No, Pilar. Unless, um, we get caught."

"Caught?"

"Yeah, um...you know that missing witness? He's a friend, and he's gotten himself in trouble. We might have to try to rescue him."

"I see." Christophe sounded disgruntled. "So much for all my hard work rescuing *you*, eh? Well, if you *do* get caught, they are going to ask how you got out. Both of you. Call John Johnson, okay? He took a big risk for you, he and his brother who covered for him, and many other soldiers, too. If you go public, there will be many, many questions. I gave him a what do you call it? Up head?"

"Heads-up."

"You have his number? I put it in your phone."

"Yeah." Loup winced. "I kind of forgot. Thanks, Christophe."

"Yes, all right. Anyway, nice work, *prima*!"

She hung up, brooding.

"What's up, baby?" Pilar asked, anxious.

"Johnson."

"The guy from the tunnel? The guy who killed Tommy?" She paused. "Yeah, he could get in pretty serious trouble for letting you out of prison, couldn't he?"

"Yeah." Loup frowned. "I wasn't thinking. If it's just you, explaining the tunnel's easy enough, but if anything happens to me, we're gonna have to come up with a good story about how I got out of that damn cell. Fuck! Everything we do puts someone else at risk. I'm gonna call him and see if he has any ideas." She dialed. "Hey, Johnson? Loup Garron. Yeah, they're talking about us. Sort of, anyway. Pilar for sure. It's a long story. But we can cover—" She listened. "Are you sure? I mean, *sure* sure?"

"He's sure," Pilar murmured. "He's like you."

"Okay. Okay, I will." Loup ended the call. "Fuck!"

"He wants us to tell the truth if we get caught, doesn't he?"

She nodded.

"Loup." Pilar put her arms around her neck. "Honey, this could get messy. You can't protect everyone, okay?"

"I hate that!"

"I know." Pilar kissed her tenderly. "I know, I know. I do. It's one of the many, many reasons that I love you. But you can't, okay? You have to let people make their choices. Like Randall and the band, like that Johnson guy. Even me. Okay?"

"Okay," Loup said softly.

Her Dataphone rang.

"Hi!" She snatched it up. "Senator, hello." She listened. "Seriously? Why?" She listened some more. "No...no. I can't promise that. But I *can* promise you that Pilar will be there to testify." She smiled. "The concert? Yeah, it's become kind of a thing, hasn't it?" Her expression turned serious. "Okay, thanks. I appreciate the warning. We'll be in touch."

She ended the call.

Pilar regarded her with trepidation. "Bad news?"

"Yeah." Loup flung herself onto a couch. "The skeevy hotel guy didn't go for it. He thinks they're bluffing."

"What else?"

She looked up reluctantly. "He knew about the concert. He doesn't think Kate's mystery bodyguard is on the government's radar yet, but it's not gonna be long. They'll be able to get our names from the flight records. And once it happens, I won't make it through immigration. I'll be detained the minute we land."

"I see," Pilar said slowly. "How long do we have?"

"A week, tops. Maybe less."

"And you're hell-bent on trying to rescue Miguel?"

Loup hesitated. "Not if you ask me not to," she said in a quiet tone. "I promised, and it's starting to look...bad. If you ask me not to go, I won't. But I get the feeling they've given up on Miguel, Pilar— especially now that you've promised to testify. And if the bad guys in the government figure it's not worth paying to have him disappeared, the skeevy hotel guy might just cut his losses and get rid of him anyway to cover his own ass. This might be our only chance to save him. No one else is gonna do it."

"Miguel fucking Garza."

Loup nodded.

"Okay." Pilar took a deep breath and let it out. "Guess I'd better start booking flights to Las Vegas. Let's go find the boys and see if they're serious about this."

THIRTY-SEVEN

The boys were serious.

"I give up," Geordie said. "I absolutely, positively surrender. Who is this person you're attempting to rescue and why?"

"Miguel Garza. My sparring partner. He was supposed to be the one testifying at the hearings."

"Oh, of course! It all makes perfect sense." He sat down and put his head in his hands. "Is any of what you're plotting remotely legal?"

"Well, it's not *illegal*." Loup patted his slumped shoulder reassuringly. "Look, we know he's being held at the Hellfire Club. All we have to do is find out which room and get him out. Simple."

"Simple," he echoed. "And why, I ask, is Kate involved?"

"They're not, really."

"The fuck we're not!" Randall smiled slyly. "You want to find out what room he's being held in? Give me five minutes with any hotel chambermaid."

"Hmm," Pilar said thoughtfully. "I was thinking give *me* five minutes with the room service delivery guy."

"Want to make it a contest?"

"Sure."

Geordie groaned.

"My money's on Pilar," Charlie offered. Randall gave him a

wounded look. "What? Look at her! If the chambermaid's not a Kate fan, you're just another skinny English bloke with silly hair, mate."

"Why are we doing this?" Geordie asked no one in particular.

"Because we are," Donny said firmly. "Loup, can I ask a favor?"

She looked curiously at him. "Sure."

His face was open and earnest. "Before we go, will you have dinner with me? Just you and me? Please? I just want to talk to you."

Loup glanced at Pilar, who shrugged, leaving the decision to her. "I guess. But it would just be dinner, Donny. Seriously."

"I know."

"Okay."

He glowed. "Thanks!"

By the end of the day, Pilar had reserved an expensive suite at the Hellfire Club for the band and regular rooms for the rest of them, and booked flights for two days after tomorrow.

"You and I get in earlier," she said. "If they're gonna start cross-checking flight records any day now, I figured it was best if we didn't travel with the band."

"Good thinking."

"Thanks." She hesitated. "Loup...this dinner with Donny."

"It's just dinner!"

"To you, maybe." Pilar took her hand. "And I would have said yes, too, because he looked that pathetic, and they're good guys in their own way, and we owe them for helping us, and it kind of reminds me of the way T.Y. used to look at you. All of that. But T.Y. wasn't a one in a hundred, as much as he wanted to be. Donny's gonna plead his case to you. He can't help himself. And whatever you decide—"

"Pilar!"

She shook her head. "Hear me out. We're doing this thing. And, Loup..." Tears filled her eyes. "It's beginning to sound like sooner or later, you *are* going to be taken back into custody." She rubbed her eyes and sniffled. "All I ask is that you save the last night we know we're safe together for me."

Loup raised her eyebrows. "Pilar, I know this is getting scary, but are you crazy? You think I'm going to sleep with Donny?"

"I don't think anything. I'm just saying what I'm saying. Promise?"

"Yes. Now will you quit being weird?"

"I'll try."

Pilar was right; the following night, Donny took Loup out to dinner and pleaded his case. He ordered brandies after they'd eaten and summoned his courage.

"Can I ask you something?"

"Sure."

He swirled the brandy in his snifter, nervous. "The bloke you mentioned. The, um, dick-in-the-vise fellow. Was he like me? Feeling the way I do about you?"

"No," Loup admitted.

Donny gulped his brandy and signaled for another. "So you've never been with a fellow who was?"

"No."

"Or anyone that was but Pilar?"

She sipped her brandy. "No."

"It's just..." He took another deep drink, then slammed down his snifter. "Fuck me, Loup! You're *young*. You're fucking, what? Eighteen years old? How can you say you know what you want? You're going to throw your whole life away on the first person to want you when there are so many options you haven't even tried?" Donny tugged his hair in frustration. "I don't mean any disrespect. Pilar's great. But for fuck's sake! You don't know until you've tried. Two days from now, you could vanish into the system. Don't you want to *know* you've lived?"

"You think I haven't?"

"No!" He sighed. "And yeah. I think you settled for the first thing to come along. And I know you owe her and all, giving up everything to be with you. But I don't think you're being fair to yourself. I don't."

Her heart ached for him. "Donny...love's not fair."

"Love." He pronounced the word glumly.

"Yeah, love." Loup smiled ruefully. "Maybe I haven't made it as obvious as I could have, because...well, I knew how you felt. I didn't want to throw it in your face, and God knows, Pilar's enough of an exhibitionist for both of us. But I really *do* love her, Donny. Not just a little. A lot. A whole lot."

"I know," he mumbled.

"No, you don't." She shook her head. "All she has to do is smile at me in this one way, and it feels like my heart's turning over in my chest. It was that way in the beginning, and it's that way now. I'm sorry, but it is."

"I know." Donny traced the rim of his snifter. "I've seen that smile."

"Yeah?"

"Yeah," he said sadly. "Makes you look all dopey and gooey-eyed, which of course I find ridiculously adorable and painful. I fuckin' hate that smile."

"I'm sorry," Loup repeated.

"Don't you wonder about what you're missing?"

"No."

"Never? Other girls, even?"

"No."

"Fuck! That's not natural. It's not healthy."

"Maybe not for you, but it is for me. For us." She made a face. "GMOs. Stupid term. But we are what we are. That Johnson guy, he said that when we fall in love, it tends to stick. It did with my father and all of his kin, the ones who found someone. It did with me. My cousin Alejandro, he's sixteen. He has this girlfriend, Amaya, and he looks at her like she's the only girl in the world. I know how he feels."

Donny smiled a little. "You're not *that* gooey."

"Yeah, I am."

"I just don't believe..." He sighed. "I just can't fucking believe that I can feel something this strong for you, and you could feel nothing at all."

Loup gazed at him with pity.

"Fuck me. You really don't, do you?" Donny drank the rest of his brandy. "You really, really don't."

"I *like* you."

He threw his snifter. It shattered on the floor. A hushed server hurried over with a dustpan. "*Like* sucks!"

"Yeah, well, so does petulant rock star." Loup folded her arms and gave him a stern look. "Donny, we can be friends or not. That's up to you. If this is all too much for you, I'm sure we can dissolve the contract. You'll probably lose some big deposit, but that will be the end of it."

"I don't want that." He rubbed his temples. "Besides, Rand would kill me."

"So?"

He gave her a hopeful look. "Can I guilt you into a pity fuck?"

"No."

"Oh, c'mon! Just once. So I don't have to die not knowing."

"You wouldn't like it," Loup said gently. "Believe me, I know. Because I *have* been with people who didn't want me that way, no matter how much they might have wanted to or cared about me. And it's not a good feeling. Not at all. Afterward, you'd just feel alone and empty."

"I'll risk it."

"I won't." She rose in one seamless motion and put out her hand. "C'mon. Dinner's over. Friends or not?"

He heaved one last sigh. "Friends."

She drove them back to the estate. On the doorstep, Donny caught her arm as she began to unlock the door. The electric lantern above the door cast shadows over his face.

"Thanks," he said. "Thanks for listening. You know I had to try?"

Loup nodded. "Yeah."

He stooped quickly and kissed her. She could have stopped him, but didn't.

"You have really soft lips," Donny said dreamily, moving closer. "Softer than I imagined—"

She put her hand on his chest and held him at bay.

"Ow." He winced. "Fuck, you're strong!"

"Uh-huh."

"Sexy little bitch." Donny smiled despite himself. "All right. I get it. I do. End of story, eh? It was nice, though, wasn't it? It was a nice kiss."

She smiled back at him. "Yeah, Donny. It was a nice kiss."

"Hey, Loup?" he said as she unlocked the door. "I have an idea. About Las Vegas and this guy you're trying to rescue. I think I know how we can get him out past hotel security."

"Yeah?" She followed him inside and locked the door behind them.

"Yeah. But we can talk about it in the morning."

"Okay."

In the room they shared, she found Pilar reading a magazine in bed, trying very hard to look casual and unconcerned. Loup leaned against the bedroom door, watching her.

"Hey, baby," Pilar said at length. "Nice date?"

"It wasn't a date."

"It was a date."

"Did you think I was afraid I was missing out on something?" Loup asked curiously.

"Well, not *afraid*, no." Pilar closed her magazine. "Jesus, I know you better than that. But what if you are, Loup? Missing out? Charlie said something to me. He said I was being selfish—"

She laughed.

"He did!"

"No doubt," Loup said in a low voice. "I'm sure Charlie has nothing but my best interests at heart." She crossed the room, shedding clothes. "I'm sure he'd never play on your sense of guilt and fairness in the hope that I'd sleep with his infatuated boyhood friend..."

"I know! But—"

She pounced on the bed, straddling Pilar. "But what?"

Pilar wriggled beneath the covers. "What if you *are*? I know the difference between you and not-you. You don't. Between me and—"

"Don't want to know." Loup kissed her. "Don't care."

"You can't be—"

"Sure?" She tugged off Pilar's camisole. "Sure, I can. *Sure* sure." She sat back on her heels and regarded her, cocking her head. "Do you not want me to feel the way I do, O sexiest sidekick in the universe?"

"Are you kidding?"

"A little."

Pilar caught her around the waist. "Oh, for fuck's sake. Okay, it was stupid. Get your cute little butt under the covers and make love to me, Supergirl. Okay?"

Loup smiled happily. "Okay!"

They made love for a long time. Sex hadn't changed since the beginning, either; only deepened. For Loup, the sheer joy of physical intimacy was a revelation every time. She delighted in all of it; the give and take, the slow languor and the rising urgency. She liked it when Pilar was indolent and lazy, her body writhing with luxurious waves of pleasure. And she liked it when Pilar was ardent and aggressive, rolling her over to devour her hungrily.

She liked it all.

A lot.

"Is it supposed to change?" Loup asked afterward.

"Hmm?" Pilar came back from a faraway, satiated place.

"Sex."

"God, I hope not." She smiled. "I mean, yeah, that white-hot, gotta-have-you feeling usually does fade after a while. At least with everyone else. But I don't know, baby. I've never known anything as intense as being with you. Maybe it won't ever change." She turned on her side. "You really don't ever wonder what it would be like with someone else?"

"Do you?"

"No, but I told you, I already know. You're *not* like anyone else in the world, Loup."

"There are my cousins."

"True." Pilar glided her hand along the firm curve of Loup's waist. "But it's not the same thing. I *like* you being a girl."

"Don't I seem to remember you turning a dozen shades of red and telling me you weren't queer when I told you I wished Mack was you?"

"Oh, hush." Pilar kissed her. "Queerer than I thought, okay?"

"You think?"

She gave Loup's hair a yank. "You never answered my question."

"No," Loup said honestly. "I mean, I'm not oblivious. I can recognize when someone's attractive and appreciate it. But I don't wonder. I love you. And maybe we found each other because we were meant to be together, you know? Maybe it just works that way sometimes. You make me happy like no one else in the world does. Including poor Donny, okay?"

"Was it okay with him tonight? Your date?"

"It wasn't a date!"

"Did he try to kiss you good night?"

Loup hesitated.

"Did you let him?" Pilar raised her eyebrows. "Ohmigod, you totally did."

"There was no touching and no tongue, okay? Very chaste. Like a goodbye kiss." She gave her a serious look. "And don't go teasing him about it. I think we really did need to have the talk we did. It was good. I think he understands now. Really and truly."

"Hmm."

"Oh, please! You are *not* going to get jealous after I just finished explaining for the second time tonight that you're the only person in the world I want."

Pilar relented and leaned over to kiss her. "Okay, okay!"

"I mean, ten minutes ago you were all worked up about trying to be selfless!"

"Yeah, more like two hours ago. And you did a pretty thorough job of convincing me not to." She sighed. "I'm sorry, baby. It's not about Donny. I think it's sweet that you let him kiss you good night instead of knocking his head off, I do. I'm just scared. About what we're doing, whether we're doing the right thing. And most of all, I'm scared of losing you again, maybe forever this time, because I love you so fucking much it hurts."

"You won't."

"You can't know that, Loup."

She slid her arms around Pilar. "I won't let it happen. *You* won't let it happen. We have to believe, remember?"

"*Sí*, Santa Olivia." Pilar gave her a teary smile. "And I do, you know I do. You're my miracle. I just can't help being scared."

"That's okay." Loup kissed her cheek. "You be scared for both of us. Someone has to."

"Thanks, baby."

"You bet."

THIRTY-EIGHT

In the morning, Donny revealed his idea.

"Mob the place with Kate fans," he suggested. "We'll smuggle your bloke in the middle of them, sneak him out with the entourage, yeah? Have a couple of limos waiting and Bob's your uncle."

"Can we do that?" Loup asked.

"Sure." Pilar waved her Dataphone. "All we have to do is leak it to the fan feeds. Tell them Kate's gonna be there signing autographs and giving away T-shirts to raise awareness for their new civil rights cause."

"The timing's tight."

"Well, we can give them a heads-up about the Hellfire Club. Once we know where Miguel is, we can figure out the timing."

Geordie cleared his throat. "Exactly how do you plan to get into the room where this Miguel is being held?"

"I dunno." Loup shrugged. "Break down the door?"

He winced.

"Aw, c'mon!" Donny said. "Don't you watch the movies? You steal a cart and pretend you're there to deliver room service. If they say they didn't order anything, you just say, 'Compliments of the house, sir.'"

"You ever notice how in the movies, they skip over the part where they actually steal the delivery cart?" Pilar said, skeptical. "They don't just leave those things sitting around unattended. And there's a *lot* of security at this place. Cameras, guards. I'm pretty sure they'd be on us right away."

"Chambermaid uniform," Charlie suggested.

"They don't leave those lying around, either," she pointed out. "And I'm not real crazy about mugging a maid and stealing her clothes. What are we gonna do, tie her up and lock her in the bathroom?"

Geordie groaned.

"Nah." Charlie grinned. "These casinos cater to their VIP guests, right? Call the concierge and tell him one of the members of Kate fancies some authentic Hellfire Club chambermaid togs for a bit of role-playing."

Pilar gave him a startled look. "You know, that's a pretty good idea."

"Takes a pervert."

They planted the rumor on the fan feeds and watched it spread.

"Think Kate has enough fans in Las Vegas to make a mob?" Loup asked. "I mean, it's not a place where a lot of real people live, is it?"

"Sure it is," Pilar said. "All those casinos, people work there. Dealers and housekeeping and waiters and stuff. Working their butts off so a handful of people like Mr. Skeevy can get rich." She made a wry face. "Kinda like the way everyone in Outpost worked their butts off so a handful of people like Miguel Garza could get rich."

"True."

"I can't believe we're doing this for him."

"You don't have to," Loup said earnestly. "You could fly directly into D.C. and we could meet you there."

"Oh, no." Pilar shot her a glance. "I'm not letting you out of my sight, fearless wonder. Loup, I'm not so sure flying's gonna be a good idea after the casino. If we really do get Miguel out of there, we're definitely not gonna be off the radar anymore."

"Tour bus?"

"Pretty easy to spot." She hesitated. "Much as I hate to say it, I think it would probably be for the best if you and Miguel and I made the drive alone."

"What about Kate?"

"They can fly, they'll be okay. After all, I don't think Mr. Skeevy's gonna go to the police and say I think a rock band helped steal my hostage. They'll be there legally; they're too famous to get conveniently disappeared, and I'm pretty sure none of them are fugitives from a military prison." She sighed. "I don't know, baby. Maybe I'm just being paranoid. But this guy, Harwell—"

"Who's Harwell?"

"Mr. Skeevy. That's his name, Terrence Harwell. We'll be caught on camera; there's no way to avoid it. Maybe he hasn't sold Miguel to the bad guys yet, or maybe the bad guys don't want him anymore, but I'm pretty sure he's skeevy enough to sell them the intel if we pull this off. And I'm pretty sure they'll want it."

Loup nodded. "Okay. I trust you."

"Believe me, I'd never suggest it if I didn't think it was important. A long cross-country drive with Miguel fucking Garza is *not* my idea of a good time."

"Mine either."

They broke the news to the band over dinner.

"Bummer." Randall tossed his bangs. "So we'll meet up in D.C. after the Vegas caper, yeah?"

"That's the plan," Loup agreed.

"Cool."

Loup and Pilar flew out early the following morning, the band and the rest of their entourage to follow later in the day. Pilar was anxious at check-in, but the agent only gave their passports a cursory glance before returning them. Throughout the takeoff, Pilar held Loup's hand in a tight grip, releasing it with a shudder once they were well in the air.

"*Muy macha*," Loup whispered softly in her ear.

"I'm trying."

At the end of a long, boring flight they landed in Las Vegas.

"Holy shit!" Loup gazed out the window during the approach, amazed by the sight of the hulking casinos dwarfing their surroundings on the flat desert floor. "There's a pyramid, and a castle, and a roller coaster, and an I-don't-know-what. They're crazy huge. It's totally...what's the word?"

Pilar took a firm grip of Loup's arm and snuck a peek. "Surreal?"

"Yeah." She gave her a wide-eyed look. "America, huh?"

A hard swallow. "Uh-huh."

It felt strange to enter a country that should have been home and legally wasn't. A hard-eyed immigration agent studied their Canadian passports and questioned them at length about their travel, their backgrounds, and their plans for the duration of the visit. Pilar, visibly nervous, launched into a long, babbling explanation of the purpose of their visit, inventing a fantasy about being a Las Vegas showgirl.

"Enjoy the show and go home," the agent said curtly. He stamped her passport. "We don't hire illegals here."

"Okay. Thanks, I will."

He stamped Loup's passport. "Next!"

"Jesus!" Once they got through customs, Pilar wilted. "What an asshole!"

"Welcome home," Loup said philosophically. "At least we know for sure that Guadalupe Herrera and Pilar Mendez aren't on the radar yet. You okay?"

"Yeah." She gathered herself. "Let's get out of here."

Outside, a dry heat assailed them. Waiting in the line at the taxi stand, Loup breathed deeply, smelling the acrid desert smell beneath the gas fumes. "It does remind me of home, though. The way it smells."

"Santa Olivia."

"Yep."

"Father Ramon, Sister Martha," Pilar murmured under her breath. "Anna, Mack, Jaime and Jane, C.C., Kotch, T.Y., Diego, and Maria... okay. I can do this. Miguel fucking Garza. I can do this."

"Of course you can."

"Shut up."

The taxi took them to the Hellfire Club, tall and gleaming. A pair of artificial rivers flanked the impressive entrance, black water cascading into an apparent abyss. Mildly sulfurous fumes floated above the water. A doorman with horns and a forked tail poking out beneath his scarlet brocade livery coat winked at them as he ushered them through the vast automatic doors. "Good afternoon, girls. Welcome to Hell."

They entered the casino.

"Whoa," Loup said.

"Whoa," Pilar agreed. Acres of tenebrous casino stretched before them. More Stygian water trickled from the rocky walls, wafting fumes. The flickering lighting mimicked oil lamps. The dealers wore scarlet vests and devil horns. "Why couldn't Miguel get himself taken hostage at that nice place with the gondolas?"

Loup eyed a pert waitress dressed as a scantily clad scarlet imp. "I'm guessing he liked the decor."

"Figures."

They found the reception Grotto of Doom where a behorned and bespectacled desk clerk greeted them with nonsinister cheer. She offered to change their reservation from a single king-sized bed to a pair of doubles.

"No thanks," Pilar said absently, signing the registration form.

"It's no trouble."

She gave the clerk a look edged with low-grade smolder.

"Sorry!" The clerk slid two laminated tickets across the counter. "Let me give you a couple of complimentary passes to Hades with my apologies." She smiled brightly. "It's our underground club. They cater to all kinds of tastes there. I'm sure you'll find it very interesting."

Loup glanced at the image of a bound, writhing soul in torment on the ticket. "No doubt."

"Charlie's gonna love it here," Pilar murmured. "The little pervert."

"Charlie, Charlie..." The clerk frowned and typed something into her computer. "Ohmigod! I should have seen the note. You're Kate's liaison!" She looked Loup up and down, her eyes widening. "That means you're—"

"Shhh." Loup put her finger to her lips. "A secret."

"I know!" The desk clerk lowered her voice to a hushed whisper. "You're Mystery Girl, aren't you?"

"Don't tell a soul about her," Pilar warned her. "Not even management."

"I won't." Her eyes were bright. "Is it true Kate's going to be signing autographs and giving away T-shirts later?"

"Yep." Pilar scooped up their room keys. "Watch the feeds and tell all your friends."

"I will!"

Their hotel room was a chamber of crimson murkitude. Pilar threw herself on the bed and nearly slid right off the scarlet satin cover. "Holy shit, this thing's slippery!"

Loup laughed.

"It's not funny!" Pilar smiled. "Okay, it's funny. But I'm not so sure about Devil Girl downstairs. We're here five minutes and you're already on someone's radar."

"Yeah, well, we can't have it both ways," she said pragmatically. "You want to go check the place out?"

"Sure."

They wandered through the labyrinth of eternal night that was the Hellfire Club casino, trying not to giggle at the horn-sprouting dealers who tried to entice them into games of blackjack, craps, or roulette. There was a distant soundtrack of atonal music that was meant to be spooky, but even though the casino was sparsely populated, the mood was offset by the constant ringing and dinging of slot machines.

"You wanna try it?" Pilar offered.

Loup eyed a slot machine. "I guess." She fished out a quarter and fed it into the machine, then pulled the lever. Two leering devil heads and a grinning skull lined up. Nothing else happened. "Huh."

Pilar tried it and got a skull and two hooded hangmen. " 'Kay. I'm over it."

They worked their way to the center of the casino. It was built on an open plan around an immense escalator that rose in stages into the loaming gloom. A bored-looking guy wearing a white loincloth and angel's wings stood at the base of the escalator.

"Stairway to Heaven!" he called, catching Pilar's eye. "C'mere, sweetheart."

"Heaven, huh?"

He pointed upward. "All the way to the top, and only accessible by the moving stairs."

"Bet that seemed like a good idea at the time," Loup observed.

"Yeah." The angel grinned ruefully and handed them a pair of tickets. "The club opens at seven. They like me to comp the pretty ones. The action's not as hot as Hades, but I can guarantee you won't have to pay for a drink all night."

"Thanks." Pilar kissed his cheek.

He blinked. "You're quite welcome!"

"That was for luck." She smiled at him. "I never met an angel before."

The angel regarded her with distinctly secular approval. "Sweetheart, trust me. You don't need luck."

"Oh, you'd be surprised." Her Dataphone rang. She moved away to answer it. Loup followed, waving a cheerful goodbye to the amused angel. "Yeah, okay. We're here. Call us when you get here."

"The boys?"

Pilar nodded. "They just landed at the airport. Operation Free Miguel is about to get underway."

THIRTY-NINE

Pilar scored first in her contest with Randall. She ordered room service while the band was still napping after their flight.

Exiled from their room, Loup was sitting at a roulette table alternately winning and losing money and trying to figure out the intricacies of the game when her Dataphone rang. "Yeah?"

"C'mon up, baby!" Pilar sounded happy and excited. "I got it!"

"Seriously?"

"Yes, seriously."

"I'll be right there." She hopped off the stool at full speed without thinking. The dealer gave her a startled look. Loup swore softly and reminded herself to be careful and slow down now that she was back in the United States. "Thanks," she said, tipping the dealer a chip the way she'd seen other players do. "Gotta go."

She found Pilar looking smug, wearing the clinging, low-cut floral dress she'd worn to Fiorella Picco's wedding, dangling a high fuck-me heel from one foot.

"So?"

"Suite fifteen-thirty."

Loup smiled. "He's sure?"

"Pretty much." Her smug look faded. "He's never actually *seen* Miguel, just heard the rumors. And I had to be kind of tactful in a flirty sort of way. But if a casino works the same way a small-town bar does, there's no keeping secrets from the staff."

"I'm sure it does." Loup sniffed the air. "Filet mignon?"

"Uh-huh." Pilar nudged the tray toward her. "Go ahead, you little carnivore. I ordered it for you. I'm not hungry."

"Thanks!"

By the time Loup had finished, the band was awake and had checked in with them. Their suite was on the sixteenth floor. Donny came up to deliver a room key to them.

"Otherwise the elevator won't stop," he explained. "Fifteenth and sixteenth floors are reserved access. Luxury suites and all."

Their luxury suite was decked out in the same scarlet Hellfire trimmings. The main parlor featured a large fireplace and was centered around an immense sunken black marble hot tub in which Charlie was lolling naked, a drink in his hand.

"Christ in a wheelbarrow!" He eyed Pilar. "Nice dress. Are you trying to give me a heart attack?"

"No. Just the room service delivery guy."

"Fuck me." Randall wandered into the room, a towel around his waist, his hair damp. "That's no fair. I haven't even started."

"I got a room number, that's all."

"What else do you need?"

"Confirmation," Loup said matter-of-factly. "Pilar's guy hadn't actually seen Miguel. And it would be good to know stuff like how many guards there are and whether or not they're armed."

"Give me." He beckoned. "I can use it for leverage, eh? Like I already know. Ooh, love, tell me about the bloke in…?"

"Fifteen-thirty," Pilar supplied.

He nodded energetically. "There you go."

"Um…mate?" Charlie gestured around with his drink. "House-keeping's done here for the day. You're gonna have to wait."

Randall snatched the drink out of his hand and dropped it, letting it shatter on the marble tiles around the hot tub. "Oops. Housekeeping!"

"Goddamnit!" Charlie hollered, standing upright and dripping. "That was my whiskey!"

Donny winced. "Go put some clothes on, you bloody tosser. No one wants to see your dangly bits. Let's get out of here and let Rand work his magic, right?"

"Fine." Charlie began clambering out of the tub.

"Mind you don't cut your feet, you idjit!"

"Ah, shut it."

They left Randall in the suite and descended on the casino, accompanied by Loup and Pilar and several of Bill Jones' more trusted security guards. The band members played endless hands of blackjack, drank copious amounts, and flirted with the waitress imps.

"Hey." Randall slouched down to join them. "You really gonna wear one of those maid uniforms?" he asked Loup.

"Why? What do they look like?"

He nodded at one of the scarlet imps. "Kinda like that only with a frilly apron."

Loup made a face. "Guess so." She took him by the arm and hauled him out of earshot. "So? Any luck?"

"Yeah." Randall gave her a slow, lazy grin. "She wasn't a Kate fan, but I plied her with liquor and charm. Pilar's right, they've got him in fifteen-thirty. Two armed guards. She never saw any guns, but she says everyone knows Harwell's guards carry. Sounds like he's a pretty dicey character."

"Thanks, Rand." She gave him an impulsive hug. "That's awesome."

"Oof!"

"Sorry." Loup let him go.

"It's cool." He looked around. "So no paparazzi, huh?"

"No, it's been quiet. I, um, don't think this place is exactly a hotbed of hipsters. And let's face it, a lot of Kate fans are in bed on a school night."

"Oh, well." He shrugged. "At least we get to party in peace."

Party they did. After losing a fair bit of money at the blackjack tables, the band decided it was time to explore Hades. They descended to the underground level in the special theme elevator that had massive grated metal doors operated by a burly man in a hangman's hood. It opened onto another vast, cavernous space lit by strobing scarlet lights. Tortured music wailed around a throbbing dance beat. Hades, at least, was hip enough that the dance floor writhed with bodies. All around the perimeter of the cavern various scenes were being played out in shadowy grottoes.

"Holy crap!" Pilar watched a woman in devil's horns and

thigh-high boots lift a narrow cane over a chained figure. "Is she doing what I think she's doing?"

The whistle of the cane was inaudible over the music, but the chained man jerked visibly when it landed.

"Yep," Loup said.

"Did you know this was Mig's scene?"

"No," she said thoughtfully. "I have to say I'm a little surprised."

It took almost two hours for the band to tire of it and round up a trio of Goth-looking newly converted groupies. After that they wanted to play more blackjack before hauling their prizes back to the suite. The scarlet waitress imps couldn't bring the drinks fast enough to suit them.

"Sorry, sir." One of the imps hustled over with a bottle of single malt and three glasses on a tray. "Courtesy of Mr. Harwell."

"Who's he?" Charlie asked belligerently.

"Your host." She nodded at a heavyset man in an expensive suit strolling through the casino. He had a gorgeous blonde on his arm and a pair of guards flanking them.

"Mr. Skeevy," Pilar murmured. "Who's the babe?"

The waitress smiled. "Trophy wife number three."

"Figures."

At last they got the band and their booty back to the suite. In short order the hot tub was filled with naked, splashing bodies and lots of streaked eyeliner.

"Champagne!" Randall called. "Pilar, we need champagne!"

"Yes, master." She rang room service and ordered several bottles of champagne, adding the request for a Hellfire maid's uniform. "Can you do that?" she said into the phone. "Wonderful! Thanks ever so much."

"Bet they've seen worse," Loup observed.

"Uh-huh."

The room service delivery guy handed it over without so much as blinking, studiously avoiding looking at the naked people cavorting in the hot tub. Pilar signed the tab and added a generous tip.

Loup glanced at the neatly folded bundle of scarlet and white material. "Looks pretty small."

"Mmm. It does, doesn't it?" Pilar handed her a bottle of

champagne. "Open that up to get the boys started; then we can go back to our room and you can try it on. I'm afraid if we leave it here Charlie will do something disgusting with it."

They left over the boys' protests.

"It's early!" Donny said with his wounded look. "Why don't you stay for a while and join us?" He paddled his hands in the water. "It's nice in here."

"You think you're too good for us?" one of the Goth girls asked suspiciously, eyeing Pilar. "You in your girlie-girl dress? You afraid you might catch something?"

Pilar wrinkled her nose. "Ew!"

"We're clean," one of the others assured Charlie.

"No, it's just that we work for these guys and we have a lot of planning to do," Loup said diplomatically. She caught Randall's eye. "For the special promotional event?"

"Right, right." He nodded, wet hair flopping. "Go ahead, we'll talk in the morning. Or, um, afternoon, maybe. Could be a late night. You're not trying to think of pulling off the event tomorrow?"

"No, the day after."

"That's a Saturday?"

"Yes," Pilar said. "So all the wee Kate fans will be out of school. Is it okay if I leak the details to the fan feeds?"

"Yeah, sure," Randall agreed.

"Thanks." She grabbed Loup's hand. "C'mon, baby. We've got work to do."

In their room, Loup unfolded the maid's uniform and regarded it with disbelief. It consisted of a scarlet bodysuit with capped sleeves and a very short flouncy skirt attached to it, a headband with a pair of satin devil horns, a frilly white apron, and a pair of red ballet flats. "They actually make people clean rooms wearing this? No wonder we haven't seen any of the housekeeping staff. They're all in hiding."

"Try it on."

"Oh, for fuck's sake!"

"Hey, you've got to make sure it fits, right?" Pilar pointed. "Try it on in the bathroom. I want to get the full effect all at once."

Loup went, grumbling.

It fit, sleek and tight. The skirt barely covered her buttocks. The apron was ridiculously nonfunctional.

Pilar giggled. "That's so wrong it's almost right."

"Oh, please!"

"Thought you didn't get embarrassed, baby."

"Yeah, well, that doesn't mean I can't recognize an absurdly cheesy fantasy when I'm wearing it." She gave Pilar a suspicious look. "Tell me you don't think this is sexy."

"On you?" Pilar reclined on her elbows. "Well, let's just say if you came in here wearing that right this minute, maybe I'd say I was oh, so tired after a night of dancing and gambling. And maybe I'd ask you ever so innocently to help me take off these strappy high heels…" She lifted one leg suggestively, pointing and rotating her foot, then let out a startled squeak as Loup grabbed her by both ankles and yanked her forward, sliding her effortlessly over the slippery satin comforter.

"And what if I said I wanted you to keep the strappy high heels on?" Loup asked in a low voice. "Hmm?"

"Who's got a fetish now?" Pilar asked, breathless. "I didn't expect the chambermaid to be so assertive."

"Complaining?" She slid her hands upward, pushing the fabric of Pilar's dress toward her hips.

"God, no!"

FORTY

First thing in the morning, Pilar posted the update on Kate's promotional appearance to their fan feeds, then called Geordie Davies to coordinate. She listened to him with a pained expression. "Yeah. Yeah, I'll handle the limo arrangements, and I'll book your flights to D.C. and the hotel. But after that—" She held the phone away from her ear. "Sorry!"

"He's pissed that we're bailing?" Loup asked when she was done.

"Uh-huh."

"But he's gonna go through with it?"

"Yep." Pilar rubbed her ear. "I think he knows this could be big."

They ordered breakfast from room service and pored over the hotel's security specs, putting a plan together.

"Wish the guards weren't armed," Pilar murmured.

"Yeah, me too." Loup caught her look. "What? I'm thinking. I can think."

She kissed her. "Yes, you can. And frankly, I don't want to think about the part with the armed guards anymore or I'll get all freaked out. Baby, can I give you a few errands to run? We need a few things and I need to do some research for our cross-country adventure with Miguel fucking Garza."

"Sure."

Loup ran errands.

Pilar made arrangements.

The band woke up, hungover.

"What?" Pilar said irritably into the phone. "Charlie, you're just dehydrated. It's too soon to be anything else. Drink more water. If it still burns at the end of the day, we'll call a doctor. And for fuck's sake, stay out of that hot tub! It's a breeding dish for germs." She hung up.

"Our heroes," Loup commented.

"God love 'em," Pilar agreed.

That night there were paparazzi—not many, but a few. They photographed the members of Kate in the casino. One in particular identified Loup.

"Hey! Aren't you their cult bodyguard? Over here!"

She turned her head away from the camera.

"Get her out of here," Donny muttered to Pilar. "It's too soon for her to be getting this kind of exposure here, eh? We'll be okay without you."

"Yeah?"

"Yeah." He shoved her. "Hurry."

They went to Heaven.

Heaven was lame.

"Tell me again what you do?" a businessman in a pin-striped suit asked, sidling close to Pilar on an overstuffed white satin settee. He pushed a drink in her direction and peered at her cleavage. "I'm very interested."

"Secret agent bodyguard."

He blinked. "Secret what?"

She ignored him and stood, holding out her hand to Loup. "Fuck this. You want to call it a night and go to bed?"

"Definitely," Loup said.

The next morning they went over their plan a final time and packed all their things in a single duffel bag. Loup was calm; Pilar was anxious and jittery.

"I feel like I'm gonna throw up," she complained. "How can you be so fucking calm? Oh, don't answer that! I know, I know."

"Did you call the boys?"

"Yeah, they're conscious and upright." She looked at the clock and sighed. "I just hate waiting."

"Why don't you go scope out the casino for Kate fans?" Loup suggested. "See if it looks like we'll have enough to make a mob?"

"You're just trying to distract me, aren't you?"

"Well, yeah."

Pilar sighed again. "Fine." She went and came back looking marginally calmer. "Yeah, it looks good. I counted at least forty or fifty wearing Kate T-shirts. If we can double it, that's enough to disappear into."

At one o'clock when the band was scheduled to begin signing, the number had swelled to hundreds.

"Okay." Pilar took Loup's face in her hands and kissed her. "I'm gonna go help get this show started. Go ahead and put on your uniform. I'll be back in a little while."

"Don't wait long enough for the crowd to thin out," Loup warned her. "A lot of them might leave as soon as they get their autograph and free shirt."

"No, no. Randall's gonna ask them to stick around. He's got a speech about the new album and civil rights. He'll start five minutes after I take off."

"Okay. I'll be ready." As soon as she left, Loup put on the ridiculous maid uniform and stretched out on the bed. She watched TV for half an hour or so, feeling her calm give way to a sense of anticipation and collected excitement. She looked up with a smile when Pilar burst into the room. "Go time?"

"Uh-huh." Pilar whipped her hair into a ponytail and flung an oversized Hawaiian shirt over the Kate camisole she was wearing, then hoisted the duffel bag with an effort. "You don't have to look so happy about it."

Loup grabbed a stack of folded towels from the bathroom. "Sorry!"

They hurried to the elevator. Donny's keycard got them access to the restricted fifteenth floor. No one got on the elevator. In the hallway, they passed a nicely dressed couple who ignored them.

"Fifteen-thirty," Pilar whispered outside the door to the suite, her face pale.

Loup motioned her back out of sight. She knocked on the door, holding up the pile of folded towels. "Housekeeping!"

There was a pause, then the sound of a lock being thrown. A tall, well-built guard in a suit opened the door to admit her. Somewhere beyond him a TV was playing what sounded like a war movie at a high volume. "I didn't call for—"

She dropped the towels and punched him out.

It was so fast he never even saw it coming. He dropped like a stone. Loup caught him and eased him to the floor, determining with one quick glance that they were out of the line of sight of anyone in the suite beyond the foyer. She reached into his shoulder holster and plucked out his pistol, then opened the door soundlessly and beckoned.

Pilar entered, lugging the duffel bag. She set it down quietly and took the pistol Loup handed her. She closed her eyes briefly, then opened them and nodded.

They sidled into the suite.

It didn't have a hot tub, but it had an enormous wide-screen TV. Miguel Garza and another guy in a suit were sitting side by side on a big black leather couch playing a video game, wireless consoles in their hands. They both looked up.

"What the fuck?" The guard put down his console and stood.

"Freeze!" Pilar took a shooter's stance, the pistol braced.

Miguel stared past her, thunderstruck. *"Loup?"*

The guard reached for his holster.

"I mean it." Pilar levered the safety, her hands and voice steady. "Don't move."

"She means it," Loup agreed. "Hi, Mig. It's good to see you." She approached the guard, who eyed her with stunned perplexity. "Sorry about this," she said to him. "It's nothing personal."

"What—"

She took him out with a judicious punch. "Whoops!" She caught him on the descent, wrestling him sideways. "Don't want you to hit your head on the coffee table. You're gonna feel bad enough as it is."

"Loup?" Miguel repeated, still staring. "Am I fucking hallucinating?"

"No." She went back to retrieve the duffel. "C'mon, we've got to hurry."

"Jesus, Ecchevarria!" He shifted his dumbstruck gaze to Pilar. "A gun? A fucking gun? Do you even have the faintest idea how to use that thing?"

"Yep." Pilar checked the chamber, then ejected the cartridge and handed it to Loup, who was rummaging in the duffel bag. She unbuttoned the Hawaiian shirt and shrugged out of it. "Grab me that other guy's gun, will you?"

Miguel fished it out gingerly. "Why are you wearing a shirt with Loup's picture on it? And why does it say *Kate*?"

"We've got one for you, too, big boy." Pilar ejected the second cartridge. "Got everything, baby?"

"Yeah. Here." Loup handed Miguel a Kate T-shirt and baseball cap. "Put those on." She glanced at his khaki pants. "Do you have any jeans? You'd blend in better."

"Um...yeah. In the bedroom."

She shoved him. "Go, go! Hurry!"

He went, stumbling with shock.

Loup stripped off the maid's uniform and yanked on jeans and a Kate T-shirt, shoving her feet into sneakers. Pilar took the elastic ponytail holder from her hair and handed it to Loup, who put her hair back. They crammed everything else into the duffel bag. At least at a casual glance, they weren't readily identifiable as the same two who'd entered the suite.

"The fuck?" Miguel emerged in T-shirt, jeans, and cap. "What are you fucking *doing* here? I thought the two of you were off on some nauseatingly cute lovebirds' honeymoon tour of Western Europe!"

"Rescuing you," Loup said simply. "And testifying to Congress, maybe."

"Goddamnit!" He grabbed her shoulders and shook her. "Goddamnit, you fucking little freak! You were safe where you were! Why didn't you stay there and let Jane fucking Bond here testify!"

She batted his hands away. "Are you done yelling at me? Because we really have to go."

"I need to pack!" Miguel protested.

Loup shook her head. "No time. C'mon, let's move."

"Radio, baby," Pilar reminded her.

She touched her earpiece. "It's on."

"No, theirs." Pilar checked guard number two. "Got it. I'll monitor it."

"Okay." Loup slung the duffel bag over her shoulder and put on a pair of oversized dark sunglasses. "Let's go!"

They made for the fire stairs, dragging a bewildered Miguel behind them.

"Hey, Bill," Loup said into her earpiece. "We're on the move. Okay. I'll let you know when we're about to hit the main floor." She glanced behind her. "C'mon, Mig! Hurry!"

He huffed and puffed. "Why not take the elevator?"

"Security cameras," Pilar said. "They'll get us anyway, but we're trying to make them work for it. Plus, according to the specs, security teams check in verbally every fifteen minutes. Standard procedure. If they cop to us—" She touched her earpiece and winced. "And they have. They've just figured out your guards aren't responding. They're on alert."

"Are they moving to block the exits?" Loup asked.

Pilar listened as they clattered down another flight of stairs. "Not yet. They're sending another team to the suite."

Miguel wheezed. "I'm fucking dying here!"

"Jesus, Mig!" Loup slowed. "Why'd you let yourself get so out of shape?"

"Because I've been a goddamned hostage!" he growled.

"Only for a few weeks."

"You think being in protective custody was any different?"

"I'm just saying."

"Okay, code red!" Pilar interjected. "They're not waiting for confirmation. They're sending guards to cover all the elevator banks and fire exits on the ground floor."

"Plan B." Loup keyed her earpiece. "Bill? We're coming down the escalator. Got a good crowd around it? Great."

"You're kidding me," Miguel said. "You're fucking kidding me. You want to ride down the escalator in plain sight?"

"That's exactly right." Loup hit a landing and yanked the door open. "As of this moment, you're no longer an escaping hostage. You're escorting your little sister and her best friend to get autographs from their favorite band, because you're just that kind of guy. In fact, you're such a nice guy, you're even wearing Kate gear to humor them."

He snorted.

"Move it!" Pilar snapped.

They hurried down the maze of hallways and reached the giant escalator. They had two stages to ride before the final descent to the main floor. Loup peered over the railing into the immense stairwell, trying to gauge the size of the crowd below. "Looks good." She straightened, pushing up the sunglasses that had begun to slide down her nose. "Oops."

Miguel regarded her. "Why the hell are you wearing sunglasses in here? It's like the fucking City of Night in this place."

"Thought you liked it here."

"Are you kidding?"

"Loup's, um, kind of semifamous with Kate fans," Pilar explained. "It's a thing. She's trying not to be recognized."

They stepped onto the last stage of the escalator.

Below, the band was clustered. Randall was holding forth at length, rambling. Donny and Charlie were still signing autographs. A small sea of Kate fans, teenyboppers peppered with a number of laconic hipsters, surrounded them. Beyond them, they could see security guards in neat suits circulating.

None of them gave the escalator more than a cursory look.

"Right behind you, Bill," Loup said into her earpiece as they descended.

Kate's head of security gave her a curt nod. His team directed fans to shift subtly, making room for their arrival. Randall began wrapping up his speech.

They hit the bottom of the escalator and melted into the crowd— more or less.

Loup thumped Miguel on the shoulder. "Try not to look so hulking."

"Fuck you! I'm a big guy."

"All righty-right!" Geordie Davies said brightly, taking over from Randall. "Everyone had a nice time? Got yourselves some nice swag and all? Well, we've got to be off. Let's give the boys from Kate a big round of applause and see them out to the limo, shall we?"

The crowd shrieked.

"Goddamn!" Miguel complained. "My ears!"

"Shut up." Pilar pushed him. "Follow the band."

Kate's security team closed around them. There were guards posted at the main entrance to the casino, but they stood back to let the entourage pass, scanning beyond them. They exited in a swirl of fans.

Two limos were waiting. Loup steered Miguel toward the farthest, while the band took the nearest. She glanced over her shoulder as Miguel squeezed himself through the car door and saw a guard talking into his earpiece with a suspicious look.

"Uh-oh." She clambered into the limo after Pilar. "Airport, please. We're in a hurry."

"Hold on, miss," the driver said, listening to his transmitter. "I'm getting an order from casino security to wait."

"Shit!" Loup glanced at Pilar, who looked stricken. It wasn't a contingency they'd considered. "Route to the airport?"

Pilar fumbled for her Dataphone. "I'll find it. Go!"

Loup whipped out of the limo and around to the driver's door, moving in a blur. The crowd of Kate fans clamored in sudden recognition. She jerked open the door and grabbed the surprised driver by the collar, hauling him out. "Catch!" she shouted to the fans, taking hold of the driver's belt with her other hand and sending him sailing. Half a dozen fans tumbled down under his weight. Loup scrambled into the driver's seat and locked the doors.

"Are you out of your mind?" Miguel demanded.

"No!" She felt for the clutch, struck by the realization that the steering wheel was on the opposite side of the cars she'd learned to drive on. "Pilar, everything's backward and I can't find the clutch!"

"Don't think it has one, baby." Pilar was frantically programming addresses into her GPS.

"Oh, yeah. That kind." Loup put it in drive and hit the gas.

The limo lurched forward. Kate fans scattered.

"Got it!" Pilar said triumphantly. "Take a right onto the Strip!"

"Okay!"

The limo shot out into traffic, narrowly missing getting sideswiped by a tour bus. Miguel pitched sideways and swore.

"Put on your seat belt," Pilar advised him. "Loup's a good driver, but her reflexes can make the ride...interesting."

"Plus everything's backward!" Loup added.

Miguel buckled his seat belt. "Where the fuck did you learn to drive, you fucking maniac? Bizarro World?"

"No, Scotland." She gunned it through a yellow light and switched lanes. "What's going on behind us, Pilar?"

Pilar craned her head around. "There's no pursuit. We're fading out of radio range, so I can't tell anything else. Can you still get Bill?"

Loup tried him on her earpiece. "Nope."

"Okay. We'll check in with them later and make sure everything's okay. For now, we're on our own. Take a left at the next light. And slow down, we don't want to get pulled over. On top of everything else, I guess we're, um, kinda driving a stolen car."

"Some rescue." Miguel slumped in his seat. "You two are fucking insane."

Loup pushed her sunglasses up onto her head and met his gaze in the rearview mirror. "Yeah, and you're welcome, by the way."

A faint smile tugged at the corners of his wide mouth. He shook his head and looked away, trying to hide it, then glanced back at her, smiling more broadly. "It's good to see you too, you little freak."

"Now that's exactly the touching reunion I imagined," Pilar commented.

"Give me a break! I'm in shock."

"Hey, I was being serious."

FORTY-ONE

They made it to the airport without incident and found the car rental agency. Loup and Miguel waited in the air-conditioned limo while Pilar went in to complete the paperwork.

"Why'd you do it?" he asked her. "Seriously, this is just dumb, Loup. It was a stupid risk. You were out, you were free."

"Yeah, but you weren't. And speaking of dumb...getting caught trying to cheat a big casino? Hello?"

He scowled. "I didn't fucking cheat! I banged the guy's wife. I was just there to meet her for a fucking drink. He framed me."

Loup laughed. "You banged Mr. Skeevy's trophy wife?"

Miguel's scowl deepened. "I didn't know who she was! She came on to me at the Palms. They set me up."

She laughed harder.

"It's not funny!"

"Yeah, it kind of is, Mig." She sobered. "Sorry. Are you okay? It looked like they were treating you okay. I mean, I didn't exactly expect to find you playing video games with the bad guys when we busted in to rescue you."

He shrugged. "Yeah, I'm fine. The guards were all right; they were just doing their jobs. And it's just as boring being a guard as a hostage. Guess things aren't really all that different here than back home, huh? There's always a big man and everyone else works a bullshit job for him."

"Yep. Only here it's not you."

Pilar came out. "Loup, they need to scan your driver's license. You guys catching up?"

"Yeah." She grinned from ear to ear. "Mig didn't cheat at cards. He banged Mr. Skeevy's wife and they set him up."

Pilar giggled. "You're kidding!"

"Enough!" Miguel pointed a thick finger at her. "I don't need to hear it from you, sweetheart. And speaking of catching up, the two of you have a lot of talking to do. I'm still trying to wrap my head around the sight of you with that gun, Ecchevarria, and I have no fuckin' idea what that business with the rock band was all about."

"It's a long story," Loup said, getting out of the limo.

"Fortunately, we have about..." Pilar consulted her Dataphone. "Three days' worth of driving ahead of us."

Miguel groaned.

"Hey, if you hadn't sexed up the trophy wife, we wouldn't be here," Loup reminded him. "Hope she was worth it."

He gave her a dour look. "She wasn't."

As soon as the paperwork was finished, they moved the limo to the airport's short-term parking lot to make it look as though they'd flown out of town, then set out on the road in the rental car. Loup took the first shift driving with Miguel crammed into the front seat beside her and Pilar navigating from the backseat. Once they hit a long stretch of highway, Pilar began making calls.

"Hi, hello. This is Pilar Mendez. About your limousine..."

"*Mendez?*" Miguel asked Loup. Behind them Pilar explained the situation with profuse apologies.

"Um, yeah. We kind of have these illegal Canadian passports."

"This just gets better and better, doesn't it?" He studied her. "So what's your nom de guerre?"

"Nom de guerre?"

"What does it say on your passport, Loup?"

She checked the speedometer and slowed down. "Guadalupe Herrera."

"It's not gonna be enough to protect you, you know. The casino, this car..." Miguel gestured. "Your name's on the invoice. They can track you down. It's not like Outpost. They've got systems. Computer networks. Databanks."

Pilar ended her call. "Yeah, we know all about it. That's why we're staying in out-of-the-way places and paying in cash."

"Ooh, my, my. Aren't you the crafty one?" he observed.

She smiled smugly. "I am, in fact."

"She is," Loup agreed.

On her next call, Pilar checked in with Geordie Davies and confirmed that all was well with Kate. "They got detained and interrogated by security," she informed Loup. "But they played dumb and claimed we used them. There really wasn't anything Mr. Skeevy could do. He couldn't exactly admit they were holding Miguel hostage and we stole him."

"So they're okay?"

"They're fine."

She checked in with Senator Ballantine and informed him that they had Miguel Garza with them and expected to arrive in a couple of days.

"Well?" Loup asked.

Pilar winced. "He says we're idiots. But he gave me the address of a safe house in Virginia."

"You *are* idiots," Miguel commented.

"Hey." She gave him a sharp look. "Look who's talking! Forget the trophy wife. If you'd stayed put, you'd be testifying to Congress in a week's time, and we'd still be enjoying our European honeymoon."

"Or at least babysitting the band," Pilar added.

"Yeah, about that." Miguel plucked at his T-shirt, glancing down at the image of Loup striking an iconic pose in her security togs. "You wanna tell me what the fuck's going on?"

They made it to Pilar's first destination by nightfall, crossing the border of New Mexico and turning off the highway to find a small roadside motel. By that time, Miguel had heard the entire story of their careers as secret agent bodyguards and their liaison with Kate. He was silent for a while, digesting it.

"You okay, Mig?" Loup asked after they checked in.

"Yeah." He shook himself. "I'm in the middle of nowhere at the mercy of a pair of teenage lunatics who seem to think they're living in a spy novel and I don't even have a fucking toothbrush, but I'm okay."

"C'mon, big guy." Pilar took his arm. "We'll go buy you a toothbrush and whatever else you need, and find someplace to eat. I have a feeling if I try to feed Loup another energy bar, she's gonna throw it at me."

There was a store on the outskirts of town that sold everything—a massive warehouse of a store with harsh fluorescent lighting and a lone stock boy wandering the aisles. They bought Miguel toiletries, clean clothes, and a cheap suitcase. He grumbled about the quality of everything.

"God, you big baby!" Pilar said while Loup paid the bill. "Just be glad this place is open. Doesn't look like they have a lot of customers."

"We're one of the lucky ones, honey." The tired-looking salesclerk smiled at her. "We're still here."

"The pandemic?" Loup asked.

The clerk nodded. "Rural areas like this, two out of three stores closed ages ago." She handed her her change. "You travel safe now."

They had dinner at a roadhouse down the street from their hotel. Loup polished off an enormous burrito platter and a side of nachos. Miguel drank three beers with his dinner and began eyeing the female clientele in the bar.

"Oh, no!" Pilar noticed his wandering gaze. "I don't think so. That's what got you into trouble in the first place."

"I'm just looking!"

"Keep it in your pants for a few days, Mig," Loup said in a practical tone. "C'mon! You'll live."

He raised an eyebrow at her. "Yeah, well, if that's your advice, the next time you rescue me, you might wanna consider a less provocative outfit. I gotta live with the image of you dressed up as Satan's

French maid seared into my brain. And I'm trying to be a good guy and work the big brother angle, but it's a little disturbing, you know?"

Pilar smiled. "Mmm. It certainly is."

Miguel glowered at her. "Don't even start. I don't need to know what the hell goes on between you two."

"Oh, poor you."

"Yeah, poor me!"

Back at the hotel, they retired to their adjacent rooms. In the hallway, Loup looked sharply at Miguel. "Promise you'll behave? You won't sneak out and try to get laid?"

"Yeah." He gave her a wry look. "I promise."

"Thanks."

"You're thanking me?" Miguel shook his head. "You really are a little freak."

"Love you too."

He chuckled and went into his room.

In their room after they'd washed up for the night, Pilar sighed and slid her arms around Loup's neck. "Jesus, baby," she murmured. "What a day, huh? What a long, fucking, scary day."

"Was it really scary?"

"Yes." Pilar kissed her, maneuvering her backward. "It was."

"I'm sorry." They fell onto the bed, Loup on top.

"I know," Pilar whispered, wrapping her legs around her waist. "I do. I'm just really glad we're both here and alive right now."

"Me too."

The cheap bedsprings squeaked fiercely in protest. And through the thin dividing wall between the rooms, the sound of Miguel's TV was audible.

"Goddamnit!" Pilar clutched Loup's ass, fingers digging into her flesh. "Hold still. You think he can hear?"

"Do you care?"

"No! Yes!"

"Really?" Loup rocked her hips.

Pilar caught her breath. "No!" The bedsprings squeaked and there was a disgruntled thump on the wall. "Yeah, okay, I do," she admitted hastily. "Let's play a game, huh? Who can make the other get off moving the least." She tangled one hand in Loup's hair, tugging it. "And you have to stay where you are. No doing that hummingbird thing with your tongue. That's just not fair."

Loup smiled, one hand gliding between them. "I'll win anyway."

"Cocky, cocky!"

"Nuh-uh." She shook her head. "'Cause you've got that spot…"

"What about your ears?" Pilar blew softly into Loup's left ear, licking her earlobe. "So cute and round, and oh, so sensitive…"

Loup squirmed, but managed to achieve her goal. After that, it was all about her considerable manual dexterity.

"Oh, *that* spot!" Pilar's back arched, drawing another squeal of protest from the bedsprings. "*Jesus!* Okay, okay, you win!"

There was a loud pounding that made the dividing wall shudder. Through it came the sound of Miguel's muffled, irritated voice. "Cut it out, you goddamn fuck-bunnies!"

"Don't you dare stop now!" Pilar warned Loup.

She smiled again. "Believe me, I wasn't planning on it."

FORTY-TWO

It was a long, long road trip.

On the second day they got a call from Geordie Davies informing them that the band had been detained on arrival at the airport in Washington and questioned by federal authorities regarding the whereabouts of Pilar Mendez and Guadalupe Herrera.

"So that's it, then," Pilar murmured. "We're officially fugitives. And they're threatening to yank the permit for the concert."

Loup concentrated on the road. "Does he think they're gonna?"

"No." She shook her head. "It's gotten too much publicity. He thinks they're afraid it will create more if they're banned from playing." She was quiet a moment. "Loup, Geordie wants to know if you're willing to do interviews now. He's got all kinds of inquiries. But if you go public…" Her voice trailed off.

Loup stole a quick glance at her. "I know."

Pilar looked away. "No one knows where we are. You could still go into hiding. We'd just need to come up with a new identity for you, figure out a way to get you out of the country. Magnus helped us once; maybe he'd do it again if we agreed to come back to work for him after Miguel and I testify."

Her heart constricted painfully in her chest. "Pilar...I think it's too late. You and Miguel, Geordie, the boys, the senator...there are too many people involved, and you could all get in a lot of trouble if you try to hide me." She shook her head. "We've gone too far to turn back now."

Pilar sighed. "I figured. I kinda knew it all along. But I had to say it."

"If you don't want me to—"

"Of course I don't! But I know you, Loup." Pilar looked back at her with quiet sorrow in her gaze. "And I'm not gonna make the same mistake twice, okay? If I ask you not to do this, I'd be asking you not to be *you*. It's like Rand's song, you know? I'd just be putting you in a different kind of cage."

Loup swallowed, her throat tight. "Thanks."

"I'll tell Geordie to coordinate with Senator Ballantine's office." Pilar picked up her Dataphone. "Might as well go big."

"I don't get it," Miguel grumbled. "Loup, you don't have to do this! Pilar and I can testify."

"About Outpost, yeah. But you can't testify on behalf of GMOs."

"What makes you think they're gonna let you?"

Loup shrugged. "I have to try."

"Goddamn hero complex." He scowled at Pilar. "I can't believe you're letting her do this."

"Oh, says the guy who helped her train for the fucking boxing match that got her taken into custody in the first place," she retorted.

"That was different!"

"Why? Because you got a ticket north out of it?"

"Don't get on your high horse with me, sweetheart!" Miguel growled. "And don't try to tell me you always had her best interests in mind. I was there when you broke Loup's heart, remember? I was the one who stuck around to pick up the pieces."

"Actually, you got me falling-down drunk and hit on me, Mig," Loup said mildly. "Then you bailed on me after I said no."

"Yeah, but I came back."

"Yeah, you did. Eventually." She rubbed the faint scar on her eyebrow. "Miguel, Pilar's right. And I might have beat Johnson that day in the ring, but I didn't really win the fight, you know?"

He gave her a dour look. "You got out. You beat the system. You were *free*, Loup!"

"Not really." She shook her head. "Not knowing everyone I cared about was still there, and I could never go home. Not knowing there are people like me who can never have lives of their own because they're considered government fucking *property*." Loup sighed. "Look, I'm here. It's right, okay? It's the right thing to do."

"I still think you're a goddamn idiot."

Miguel continued to grumble all the way across the country. He grumbled across New Mexico and northern Texas, across Oklahoma and Arkansas and into Tennessee. When he wasn't grumbling about Loup's intentions, he grumbled about the distance and the boredom, the discomfort of the rental car, the cheap hotels, the greasy diners.

"He's driving me crazy!" Pilar complained when they were alone. "How can you stand it?"

"I just let it wash over me," Loup said absently, reading the news feeds. "I've had a lot of practice. It's only because he's worried. Hey, these hearings are starting to get a lot of press."

"*I'm* worried, too, you know."

"I know." She looked up in surprise. "Pilar, hey! Don't cry."

"I'm not!" Pilar dashed impatiently at her tears and sat down on the bed beside her. "I'm just...I'm trying to be strong, okay? And I think I'm doing a pretty damn good job this time. But just so you know, I'm absolutely terrified inside."

Loup put her arms around her. "I know."

Pilar sniffled. "Stupid goddamn hero complex. I can't believe I'm agreeing with Miguel fucking Garza."

"Are you?"

"No," she said after a long moment. "No, I get it, I do. And I think deep down, Mig does, too. He cares a lot about you. I think knowing you'd escaped gave him strength to do the right thing himself. And now he's pissed that you're gonna get caught after all. And pissed at himself that it's sort of his fault."

"That sounds about right," Loup said.

Pilar kissed her cheek. "Okay, baby. I'll try to keep it together. And I'll try not to let Mig drive me nuts. Let's go find someplace to eat that won't offend his allegedly refined palate."

"Okay. I love you, you know. More than anything. If you want me to—"

"I know." Pilar kissed her again. "Now shut up."

Four days before the hearings were scheduled to begin and three days before Kate's concert, they pulled into the safe house in northern Virginia, a pleasant country estate an hour or so from Washington D.C. An attractive woman in a nicely tailored business suit met them in the driveway.

"Mr. Garza," she said in a neutral tone as Miguel climbed out of the rental car.

He grinned at her. "Ms. Westfield."

"And you must be Loup Garron and Pilar Ecchevarria." Her expression softened. "My Lord! You poor things must be exhausted. What an ordeal!"

"We're okay," Loup said.

"Stiff, mostly." Pilar, who'd driven the last stretch, rolled her neck.

"Oh, don't let those sweet, innocent faces fool you, Janine," Miguel said laconically. "They're tougher than they look. Loup can drop a man twice her size with a single punch and that sex kitten beside her is entirely too comfortable with a gun. But I've gotta say, they got me out of Vegas while your boss's Reform Caucus was twiddling its thumbs and dithering about blackmail."

The woman eyed him. "I'd forgotten how very charming you could be, Mr. Garza." She turned back to Loup and Pilar. "I'm Janine Westfield, one of Senator Ballantine's aides. Come inside and I'll bring you up to date."

Inside, she summed up the situation. Military arrest warrants had been issued for all three of them.

"Jesus!" Pilar turned pale.

"Don't panic," Janine Westfield assured her. "In light of the pending congressional hearings, Senator Ballantine procured an emergency hearing with the District Court judge. He played the testimony he recorded in Mexico and the uncut interview with Miguel for the judge. Two of the three warrants have been declared invalid."

"Not mine," Loup said quietly.

"No." The aide gave her a sympathetic look. "Not yours. Mr. Garza and Ms. Ecchevarria were charged with conspiring to endanger national security. Based on their recorded testimony, the judge determined quite the opposite. But you're charged in addition with assaulting an enlisted soldier, destruction of military property, flight, and theft of classified materials."

Loup blinked. *"What?* I never stole anything like that."

"Your DNA." Janine Westfield folded her hands atop the table. "To the best of our knowledge, the genetic experimentation program based on the captured Sino-Haitian operatives was suspended years ago. However, the details of the program remain classified. They're claiming that by fleeing the country, you absconded with classified material."

"That's absurd," Miguel said flatly.

"Yes, it is," she agreed.

He raised his voice. "I've known Loup all her damn life! She's just a kid, not a top-secret military science experiment. A freaky-ass kid, but a kid. A pretty good one. Her mother was a waitress, for fuck's sake!"

"Are you finished?" Janine asked.

Miguel glowered. "Doubt it."

The senator's aide sighed. "In point of fact, I'm quite in agreement with you, Mr. Garza. However, the law as written does not acknowledge Ms. Garron as a human being entitled to any of the rights and privileges thereof."

"Stupid law," Pilar muttered, a tremor in her voice.

"It's okay." Loup gave her a quick hug. "We knew something like this was gonna happen."

Janine Westfield cleared her throat. "If you wish to attempt to flee—"

"I'm not fleeing."

"All right." She studied Loup. "Understand that we cannot protect you. Senator Ballantine has been issued a subpoena to divulge your whereabouts. And that he can't refuse without being held in contempt and jeopardizing the hearings. We're quite sure his office is under surveillance and have taken measures to circumvent it. Technically speaking, he doesn't know you're here yet. We have a very small window of opportunity to exploit the situation."

"Publicity," Pilar said. "You want to stage a PR blitz."

"Yes." The aide permitted herself a tight smile. "This business with Kate's Crusaders and the concert is attracting a good deal of media attention. It's put the issue of GMO rights on the national radar, right alongside this Outpost business."

"Interview time?" Loup asked.

"Yes."

"Let's do it."

Over the course of the next forty-eight hours, a string of journalists arrived and departed at the safe house. They interviewed all three of the Outpost escapees, working different stories with different angles. For the first time, Loup told the whole truth, holding back none of the details.

The best of the lot was an aggressive young journalist named Brian McAfee from *Rolling Stone* USA, who came with a skilled filmmaking crew. "So are you really going to show at the concert?" he asked when the interview was largely concluded. "We're going live with this tomorrow, and that's what all the fans want to know." He ordered the cameras turned off and lowered his voice. "This is off the record, but according to my sources in intel, they plan to make a move if you do."

Loup glanced at Pilar. Pilar shivered and wrapped her arms around herself, but held her gaze and gave her a tiny nod. An empty chasm yawned in Loup's heart. "Yeah," she said softly. "We figured." For Pilar's benefit, she managed a faint smile. "But you've gotta give the fans what they want, right? And what's a concert for GMO rights without a GMO?"

"I doubt they'll let you get that far," McAfee said pragmatically. "You'll be picked up backstage before it begins."

Pilar paled. "So no one would even know what happened?"

Loup eyed the cameras thoughtfully. "Unless someone recorded it."

Brian McAfee grinned. "Funny you should say that." He held up a slim, expensive Dataphone. "Miz Garron, I don't want to encourage you to endanger yourself. But if you *do* plan on showing, we'll have a real ostentatious film crew backstage. And they'll get shut down. Meanwhile, I'll get the footage Kate needs on the sly. They can air it on the big backdrop screen, yeah? Mix it up with the footage that's already out there and what we've got? We can edit it together lickety-split, send it out live to all the feeds."

"Yeah?" Loup inquired, intrigued.

His grin widened. "Hell, yeah!"

"Pilar..."

She sighed, dialing. "Calling Geordie, baby! He'll be thrilled."

"Are you okay?"

"No." Pilar swallowed hard. "But I'm trying."

FORTY-THREE

An unmarked black sedan carried Loup to the concert on the Mall. "You understand—" Janine Westfield began, worried.

"Yeah, yeah. No protection. I know."

Miguel planted a rough kiss on her temple. "Stupid fucking girl! Why do you have to be such a goddamn martyr?" He held her at arms' length, surveying her security togs, his expression racked with regret. "Nice getup. You look hot."

"Thanks, Mig."

Pilar...

They'd stayed up late into the night saying their goodbyes. Now it didn't seem like enough. Loup wrapped her arms around her, holding her tight. She felt Pilar tremble. "Shh," she whispered, burying her face against her neck. She breathed deep, inhaling her scent, never wanting to let her go. "It's okay. It is."

"I could still go with you," Pilar whispered in tears. "It's not too late."

"No." Loup let her go with an effort. "For all the reasons we talked about. You're gonna make a great witness. We can't risk it."

"Okay."

It was a soft, broken word. Loup looked away, unable to bear the pain in Pilar's face.

"Are you ready to go, miss?" the driver asked sympathetically.

"Yes." She looked back at Pilar, her heart aching. "It won't be forever. I promise. I'll come back to you, just like before."

Pilar nodded and took a deep, shaking breath. "Tell the boys I'm sorry I couldn't be there. Tell them I'm proud of them."

"I will."

"I love you, Loup."

"I love you too."

In the sedan, Loup pressed the heels of her hands against her burning eyes, wishing that she could shed tears like normal people. When she lowered her hands, the driver was gazing at her in the rear-view mirror.

"You all right, miss?" he asked.

"Yeah. Just sad. Thank you."

"You're the band's GMO bodyguard." It was a statement, not a question. She nodded. There was wonder in his gaze. "The stories, the rumors you hear...I didn't know you could feel the same way we do. Humans."

Through her pain, Loup summoned a rueful smile. "Love?"

"Love." He watched her in the mirror. "Loss."

She turned her head and looked out the window. "We hurt and bleed the same as you."

He was silent for the rest of the drive.

A huge stage had been erected on the Mall. It was hours before the concert was scheduled to begin, but there was video footage playing on the big backdrop screen and a large crowd had already assembled despite the cool weather. Loup gazed at the scene—the throng of people on the green lawn, the soaring obelisk of the Washington Monument at one end, the white dome of the Capitol Building at the other.

"Quite a sight, isn't it?" the driver said.

"Yeah." She closed her eyes briefly. "I hope it all stands for something."

They slipped past the outskirts of the throng, Loup shrouded in the driver's overcoat, and passed through security into the tents backstage.

"So you're really doing it," Bill Jones said by way of greeting.

"Yep." She shrugged out of the overcoat. "Any trouble?"

"Not yet."

Loup gave the driver back his coat. "Thanks."

"You're welcome, miss." He shook her hand. "Good luck to you."

Brian McAfee was there with the ostentatious film crew he'd promised, doing follow-up interviews with the band. Donny leaped up the moment he spotted her and hurried over, tripping over cables in the process.

"You made it!" he said, breathless.

"Yeah." She smiled sadly. "Pilar said to tell you she's sorry she couldn't be here today. And that she's really proud of you guys."

Donny flushed. "Is she okay?"

"Not really."

"I'm sorry." He touched her hand. "What you're doing, what all of you are doing...it's really amazing. And I just want you to know that we're all honored to be a part of it." He smiled a little. "Loads of press, too. Geordie's beside himself."

"I'm glad. You deserve it."

The film crew took a break and Loup greeted the rest of the band. Randall surprised her by folding her in a gentle hug, pressing her carefully to his lanky body.

"Just wanted to be sure I got a chance," he explained.

"Me too!" Charlie followed suit, copping a quick feel in the process. "Huh. Different."

Loup plucked his hand away. "This is not hand-on-the-ass time, Charlie."

He grinned at her. "Says you."

She smiled despite herself. Donny leaned over to give her a chaste kiss on the cheek. "I'm not gonna hug you," he said. "Because I'll fucking well lie awake thinking about it for days if I do. But just know I really, really want to."

"You're a good guy, Donny."

"Yeah." He sighed. "How the fuck did that happen?"

The crowd outside grew. The band settled into performing their preconcert rituals. Geordie Davies came over to shake Loup's hand.

"It's been an interesting journey," he said formally. "All I can say is that I hope this isn't the end of it."

"Thanks, Geordie," she said. "So do I."

Brian McAfee asked to get some footage of Loup working the portable heavy bag that had been set up backstage for her. She agreed gladly, grateful for the distraction. She fell back into the old familiar rhythm, eschewing the kicks and elbow strikes that Clive had taught her in favor of the pure boxing technique she'd learned from Coach Roberts and practiced for hours and hours in the church's garage. It was comforting.

It made her think of home.

It helped dull the vast sorrow she felt every time she thought of the pain on Pilar's face.

It blotted out the sound of the National Guard arriving.

The silence settling into the background alerted her. Loup stopped and turned around. A dozen men in uniform moved through the tent, issuing orders, shutting down the film crew.

"Freedom of speech!" one of the cameramen protested.

"National security," was the curt reply.

Brian McAfee held his Dataphone cupped in his palm at waist level in an unobtrusive manner, aimed at Loup. He gave her a wink.

The officer in charge strode toward her. "Loup Garron? aka Guadalupe Herrera?"

She folded her arms. "Yeah."

"I have a warrant to take you into military custody."

Loup didn't move. "You know what you're doing totally sucks, right?"

The National Guard officer blinked. "I don't make the rules, miss. Just come along peacefully, all right? No one wants trouble." He caught her arm and attempted to turn her around.

She shook him off and took two steps backward, lightning quick. "Sure you do. Make the rules, I mean. This is a democracy, right? You vote, don't you? It must be nice. I've never had the chance."

He beckoned for backup. "Take it up with the courts. Right now, you're resisting arrest."

"No," Loup said thoughtfully. "If I were *resisting*, you'd know it. I'm just asking you to think about what you're doing."

The officer drew a stun gun. "You going to make this hard?"

Loup cocked her head. "I just want a chance to—"

He fired.

"Goddamnit!" Donny yelled. "She's just a girl!"

The electrode darts made contact with the bare skin of her abdomen. Loup doubled over, her muscles seizing. She straightened, wincing. "Is that all you've got?"

The officer's jaw dropped. "Holy fuck!"

Another guard stunned her from behind, and then another.

She doubled over again and braced her hands on her knees, riding out the agonizing muscular convulsions.

"Loup!" Charlie's voice, genuinely alarmed. "Cut it out!"

"America *sucks*!" Randall added fervently. "This is bullshit!"

"It's okay!" Loup hauled herself upright, breathing hard. Out of the corner of her eye, she saw Brian McAfee giving her an enthusiastic thumbs-up. "It's okay," she repeated, exhaling hard. "I've kind of done this before." She put her hands together in front of her. "Jesus, guys! I said I wasn't resisting!"

The National Guard descended on her. They spun her around and handcuffed her hands behind her. Real metal cuffs, no plastic strips this time.

Loup let them.

"Hey, Donny!" She stumbled past him, shoved from behind. "Tell Pilar I'm okay, will you? This doesn't mean anything. It's just for show."

"You're hurt!" he protested. "They hurt you!"

"Not bad. Just tell her, will you?"

He nodded, eyes damp. "I'll tell her."

"Thanks." Loup craned her head around for a last look. "Good luck. Play good, guys. Have a good concert. Sorry I couldn't be there for it."

"You fucking bet we will," Randall said softly.

They did.

They played very, very well.

FORTY-FOUR

N iiice." The guard drew the word out.

"Yep," Loup agreed. She watched the concert footage on the Dataphone the guard held thoughtfully for her. A montage of clips featuring her played on the big screen behind the band while Randall addressed the crowd.

"This all started out as a lark," he shouted. *"People said it was a gimmick when we hired the world's only GMO bodyguard, and it was. But it's bigger than that now. And an hour ago, it stopped being a lark!"*

On the big screen, the footage of Loup being shot with the stun gun played.

The guard winced.

The crowd yelled in protest.

"This one's for Loup!" Randall called as the band launched into "Cages," an ongoing montage playing in the background all the while.

"Thanks," Loup said when the video clip ended. "I appreciate it."

The guard shrugged and pocketed the device. "Thought you'd like to know. It's all over the news." His voice softened. "I got a kid sister your age, and you don't seem all that different from her. What they're doing to you, I don't think it's right."

"Is there any news about the Outpost hearings?" she asked. "They're supposed to start today."

He hesitated. "Maybe. I'll see what I can do, okay?"

"Thanks."

The guard left, taking her breakfast tray and locking the door of her cell behind him. Loup lay down on the cot and folded her arms behind her head, staring at the ceiling.

At least it was a lot better than the last time. She wasn't sure where she was being held, but she had a cot with a pillow and a blanket. The cell had a toilet and a sink. The temperature was tolerable. She had a clean orange jumpsuit to wear instead of sweat-soaked boxing gear. She hadn't been interrogated or hosed. So far, she'd been served meals at regular intervals even if it was MREs, and they'd turned the lights off overnight.

It was still prison, and the empty feeling told her she should be scared that this time there would be no escape.

It was boring and it was lonely, horribly lonely. She missed Pilar; and that was worse than before. They'd been separated for long months before the boxing match, only reuniting the day before the event. It was harder being alone now. And it was doubly frustrating not to know what was going on in the outside world. The first time, Loup had been resigned to an unknown fate. Now she was desperately curious to *know*.

Hours later, the same guard returned to serve her lunch, sporting a grin. "You're in luck. The duty officer's a soft touch."

"Yeah?" Loup opened the warm pouch. Diced turkey and gravy steamed unappetizingly. "What does that mean?"

"Eat up. I'll be back."

He came back a while later, opening a small sliding window in her cell door. "Stick your hands out." Loup complied. He put on handcuffs. "You do that like you've had practice."

"Unfortunately, yeah. Hey, what's your name?"

The guard hesitated. "Bradford. Bradford Prince." He unlocked the cell door. "Come on. Duty officer says you can be allowed a couple hours of rec time as long as I'm willing to supervise."

"Okay." At his direction, she preceded him down an empty, brightly lit industrial hallway to a sizable carpeted room. There were books and magazines on the shelves, a few board games, and a single television. "What is this place anyway?"

"Recreation room." Bradford Prince turned on the television and began flipping channels.

"No, I mean where am I?" She glanced around. "And how come there's no one else here?"

He hesitated again. "You're, um...let's just say it's a detention center that hasn't gotten much use in the past few years. We're running a skeleton staff recruited on short notice."

"All for me?" Loup asked wryly.

"For now. But if you're tempted to get any ideas, don't. Security's tight and you've got nowhere to go."

"If I was going to run, I wouldn't have gone to the fucking concert," Loup observed. "I'm not stupid."

"Glad to hear it, because that's exactly what I told the duty officer." He found the channel he was looking for. "Okay, they're carrying the hearings live on C-SPAN. As long as you behave yourself and don't give me any trouble, you can watch a couple hours every day."

"No strings attached?"

He shook his head. "No strings."

She glowed. "Thanks, Bradford!"

He smiled back at her. "You're welcome."

The hearings were already in progress. It was a dry, tedious process that should have been boring, but Loup sat glued to the TV, watching Senator Ballantine construct a painstaking history of border security and the creation of the Outposts, laying out how many decades ago a raid by Mexican forces desperate for medication on a hospital in Laredo had spawned the legend of Santa Anna El Segundo that had created the basis for the entire policy.

"So there really was an El Segundo," Loup murmured. "Sort of."

"*...creating a climate of paranoia that led to these extreme measures!*" Senator Ballantine thundered. "*Measures that led to an edifice of deception intended to justify their ongoing existence!*"

There was testimony from Esteban Sandoval from the Department of Foreign Relations in Mexico, who produced documents establishing that the rebel general, Marcos de la Jolla, on whom the El Segundo legend was based, had been tried and convicted for his crimes by a Mexican military tribunal.

There was countering testimony from American military brass

who produced evidence to the contrary, documenting the continued alleged activities of El Segundo.

"That's bullshit!" Loup said indignantly to the TV. "After a certain point, it was all us, wasn't it? We faked it."

Bradford Prince glanced at his watch and turned off the television. "My shift's ending. Time to go."

She sighed. "Okay. Hey, Bradford? Did you ever serve on one of the Outposts?" He didn't answer. "Did you?"

"I'm not at liberty to discuss it."

"You did. You so did!" Loup rose effortlessly, extending her handcuffed wrists in a pleading gesture. "Look, I know they made it illegal for military personnel to tell the truth. But there are thousands of guys like you, good guys who were just doing their jobs. If you all stuck together, it could make a difference. And if the good guys don't tell the truth, who will? What if Miguel and Pilar aren't enough? They're only two people."

He steered her down the hall. "I stay out of politics."

"Why?"

"Because it's the smart thing to do." He maneuvered her into her cell and locked the door. "Give me your hands."

Loup stuck her hands through the window. "Doesn't mean it's the *right* thing."

Bradford Prince unlocked her cuffs. "You've never been in the military, have you? I'll see you tomorrow."

Several tomorrows later, the situation was largely unchanged. The hearings continued to move at a glacial pace, rehashing the details of the past. Neither Miguel nor Pilar had been called to testify yet.

But Loup was appointed a lawyer.

His name was Tom Abernathy and he was a military attorney serving at the behest of the Office of the General Counsel of the United States Department of Defense, and the first thing he informed her of was that under the current rule of law she had absolutely no rights.

"None," he said primly. "None at all."

"So what do we do?"

Tom Abernathy's pale eyes gleamed. "Change the law."

"How do we do that?" she asked.

"We try to get the Human Rights Amendment repealed." He glanced at her startled expression. "It's a deceptive title. It's meant to sound like legislation designed to protect individual rights. It's not. In essence, it decrees that only individuals with one hundred percent human DNA are entitled to rights and protection under the law. And as long as it's in effect, you can be held indefinitely without any right to a trial."

"So how come I have a lawyer?"

He gave her an unexpectedly boyish grin. "Because the DOD's taking a lot of heat over your detention. That video was a piece of genius. Whose idea was it?"

Loup didn't answer.

"That's okay, it doesn't matter." Abernathy opened a laptop. "Look, I don't expect you to trust me. But I'm not just here to provide cover. I want to help."

"I've heard that one before," she said. "First I just have to make a good-faith gesture, right? Admit I had help in the Santa Olivia conspiracy? Tell you how I escaped? Or maybe now I'm supposed to confess that I was involved in a plot to smuggle my precious DNA out of the country in the service of pop music?"

He pursed his lips. "No. But the situation's complicated. The Santa Olivia business..." He shook his head. "Ms. Garron, none of your recorded history can even be formally acknowledged outside a military tribunal at this point."

Realization dawned. "Because it all took place on an Outpost. Which supposedly doesn't exist."

"Right." Abernathy nodded. "So pending the results of the hearings, our hands are tied. If that dam breaks, we can tackle the next one."

"And that's the Human Rights Amendment."

"Right."

Loup sighed. "What are our chances?"

"It's a long shot," he admitted. "But it's not entirely outside the realm of possibility. I think we might see a significant shift in the next few weeks. And if that happens, things will begin to move. They won't move quickly. But they will move, slowly and inexorably." He glanced at his laptop. "Now, if you don't mind, I'd like to verify your history and confirm your testimony regarding those crimes to which you *have* confessed."

"I thought you said it was irrelevant."

"At this point, yes. I'm anticipating that that will change."

"Okay." She answered his questions while he took notes. When she got to the part about dressing up as Santa Olivia in a blue dress and a white kerchief and throwing a small boulder through the windshield of a Jeep, he interrupted her.

"Why did you do it?"

"Doesn't it say?"

Abernathy consulted his notes. "No. The rape charges against the soldier you assaulted earlier are on file. No motive given for the destruction of property."

"Jesus!" Loup said. "So you guys keep a record of this stuff? That a girl who supposedly doesn't exist was raped?"

"The private was acquitted."

"Yeah, because his buddies lied for him!" she said in frustration. "That's why I did what I did. Anyway, that's not the point!"

"Yes," he said after a moment. "Throughout history, people have documented all sorts of atrocities they denied committing. We're no better."

Loup shook her head in disgust. "*You* could be the one to break the dam, couldn't you? You know all this stuff; you've got documentation. You're only admitting it to me because I can't do a fucking thing about it."

He had the decency to flush. "I angled for this post, Ms. Garron, because I do believe the Human Rights Amendment is an abomination. If I went public with classified information, I'd be cashiered and pulled from your case in a heartbeat. Most likely, I'd be replaced with someone far less sympathetic to your plight. The public is fickle and they have a short attention span. There's already speculation that the Kate video is a hoax. You could easily vanish into a black hole here. Is that what you want?"

She thought about the anguish in Pilar's face and murmured, "No."

"All right. Why did you throw a rock at the Jeep?"

"Because the soldiers driving it ran over an old man's dog for fun, okay?" Loup said. "He left a petition for Santa Olivia at the church praying that one day they might repent of having destroyed his last happiness. We checked it out—"

"We?"

Loup fell silent, cursing inwardly.

"It's all right," Abernathy said in a quiet tone. "General Argyle was more than a little paranoid there at the end. No one has any interest in digging deeper into the affair. I think matters have progressed far beyond that point. I just want to know what sort of person I'm dealing with here." He studied her. "One with a rather keenly developed sense of justice, I'd say. You might make a good lawyer."

She smiled reluctantly. "Nah. Too much research."

Tom Abernathy returned her smile and closed down his laptop. "That's enough for today. I'll be in touch as matters progress."

"Hey, can you get a message to Pilar for me?" Loup asked. "Can you tell her I'm okay and that it's not like last time? That they're not starving me or anything? I know she's gonna be worried sick about it. I can give you her number or you can reach her through Senator Ballantine's office."

He hesitated. "I'm not permitted to communicate directly with the family or friends of the detained. But I'll be issuing a press release confirming that I've met with you and you're receiving excellent care."

"She won't believe it," Loup said glumly.

"I'm sorry. It's the best I can do."

FORTY-FIVE

The Outpost hearings wore on.

"So who's on the docket for today?" Bradford Prince asked cheerfully. He'd gotten engaged in the proceedings.

"Science geeks."

They watched two hours of testimony from experts analyzing satellite photos. None of it offered conclusive proof of a civilian population, only a certain amount of undemolished infrastructure. Senator Ballantine railed about the existence of a no-fly zone over the cordon. Military brass defended it.

"Boring," Bradford said.

"Yeah." Loup sighed. "Why don't they just call the damn witnesses?"

"They're saving the big guns for the last. That's how it's done." He checked his watch. "Cell time."

She went obediently. "Thanks, Bradford."

Days passed.

The testimony grew warmer.

Senator Ballantine unearthed a parade of refugees who had fled the Outposts when the military gave them the opportunity. An endless stream of middle-aged to elderly men and women recounted tales of friends and neighbors left behind, too sick or impoverished to flee.

"My mom was there when it happened," Loup mused. "She didn't understand what it meant when they said that by agreeing to stay, she wasn't an American citizen anymore. She was only thirteen. Her and her cousin Inez. My aunt and uncle were already sick. She said what she remembered most was the generators and the lights, and how healthy the soldiers looked. She always liked soldiers, you know?"

Bradford Prince was quiet.

Military experts debunked the refugees' testimony, pointing out that they had no way of knowing what measures had been taken to evacuate the remaining civilian personnel.

"None," Loup muttered. "Not a fucking one."

"You don't know that," he said. "You weren't even born."

She eyed him. "Well, all those civilians were still there when I was. And they were still there when I left. I'm pretty sure they're still there now."

After two weeks of testimony, they called in the big guns.

Loup took a sharp breath when the name Pilar Ecchevarria was announced. She scooted as close as she could to the television, sitting cross-legged before it.

"You'll wreck your eyes," Bradford warned her.

She ignored him.

Her heart hitched painfully as Pilar entered the chamber. She was wearing the navy-blue polka-dotted dress that Vincenzo Picco had complimented and she looked worn and worried and utterly lovely. Loup stroked her hair on the television screen with her manacled hands, her eyes burning.

"That's your girl?"

"Yeah," she said softly.

"She's pretty."

"I know." Loup sat glued to the television as Pilar was sworn in and testified, relating in a steady, unfaltering voice her life story as a child born in forgotten Santa Olivia and orphaned there.

They asked her how she'd gotten out and why.

She told them.

"Wow." Bradford had moved to sit beside Loup, transfixed by the testimony. "She really loves you a lot, huh?"

"Yeah." She pressed the heels of her hands against her eyelids. "A lot."

He gave her an awkward one-armed hug. "I'm sorry."

"Thanks." Loup dropped her hands, watching the screen hungrily as Pilar was escorted from the chamber. "Aw, fuck! Just a little more? Please?"

There wasn't.

Loup sighed and rested her forehead against her knees, encircled by her manacled hands. "I'm sorry," she murmured. "It was just nice, you know? Nice to see her. I miss her so much, that's all." She gathered herself. "Cell time?"

"Yeah." Bradford Prince helped her unnecessarily to her feet. "You got a book to read?"

"I almost finished one. Why?"

"I might not be here tomorrow and I don't know if the guy taking my place will be willing to supervise your rec time."

"Why? I thought your rotation lasted three weeks."

"Don't ask questions." He didn't meet her eyes. "You want to take another book to read or not?"

"Pick something out for me."

He plucked a dog-eared copy of *Great Expectations* from the nearest shelf.

"You like Dickens?" Loup asked. "My friend T.Y. read all of *Tale of Two Cities* to me while I trained on the treadmill. He thought it was boring, but I liked it."

Bradford shrugged. "I dunno. Thought the title suited you."

The next day he was gone. The guard who took his place was professional and impersonal. When Loup asked about watching the hearings, he informed her that her rec time had been curtailed due to staffing issues.

She missed Miguel Garza's testimony.

And she missed the dam breaking.

The influx of new prisoners was the first sign of it. Two days after Bradford Prince vanished, Loup heard the doors onto the empty cell block opening, sensors beeping. And footsteps, lots and lots of footsteps. She pressed her face to the cell door's high little window, standing on tiptoe.

The prisoners were GMOs.

All of them—every one of them. They were all men at least five to ten years older than her. They varied in height and size and coloring, though all bore some stamp of mixed racial heritage. They had close-cropped military haircuts.

All shared an intensity of physical presence, dense muscled and sleek, moving with a precise fluidity, even in handcuffs.

Like her; like her cousins.

Loup stared, awed. One caught her eye and flashed her a fierce grin. He turned his head and said something she couldn't hear to the prisoner behind him, the cell door muffling his words. After that, every prisoner that passed acknowledged her.

Somewhere toward the end was John Johnson.

His was a face she would never forget. He'd killed her brother by accident. She'd beaten him in the boxing ring. And his was the one face she wasn't surprised to see, because his fate had been sealed from the minute Pilar told the truth about their escape from Outpost. He stopped outside her cell door, cool green eyes meeting hers in a fearless gaze. The guard escorting him prodded him to no avail.

"What did you do?" Loup whispered, her breath clouding the security glass. *"All* of you?"

Unable to hear her words, he gave her a hard smile and moved onward.

Doors slammed, door after door.

Days passed.

Different guards came and went, harried and overworked. They delivered MREs to cell after cell. After being rebuffed a few dozen times, Loup gave up on asking for rec time or news and lay on her cot, reading *Great Expectations*.

At last, Tom Abernathy came for her.

"What the fuck's going on?" Loup asked, sitting across the table from him in the official interview room, her hands manacled before her. "Those guys! There's like a hundred of them. All GMOs."

"This." He played a video clip for her on his laptop.

It was from the hearings. A man in an army dress uniform was sworn in before the congressional committee.

"I know that guy." Loup squinted at the small screen.

"Staff Sergeant Michael Buckland," Abernathy murmured.

"Yeah! He took me to the hospital the night Tommy died." She glanced up. "He was dating Kotch when I left. Katya. One of the Santitos."

"Yes."

She watched him testify to having served in an Outpost with a civilian population. Watched him beckon to someone offscreen. Congressional aides began pouring into the chamber, steering wheelbarrows full of sealed envelopes. One by one, they dumped their loads on the floor and withdrew. A pile of paper grew and grew.

"What—"

"They're affidavits, Loup." Abernathy gave her a weary, victorious smile. "From tens of thousands of military personnel. All affirming more or less the same thing. The Outposts exist. They have civilian populations."

Her eyes burned. "That's what Bradford meant. So the dam—"

"The dam has broken." He nodded. "Yesterday, under considerable pressure, the president signed an executive order. There will be a bipartisan investigation into activities in the cordon. The no-fly zone has been revoked."

"We won?"

"We won this round." Tom Abernathy sighed. "Now comes the next. They can't punish thirty thousand men at once, but they can pick their targets—especially the ones that scare them. Every single GMO serving in the military signed an affidavit. One hundred and twenty-seven, to be exact. And every single one has been rounded up and detained here. But you, you were the first. And you're the only one not subject to military regulations. You're ground zero. It starts with you."

Loup gazed at him with shining eyes. "You knew all along, didn't you?"

"I hoped." He closed his laptop. "I wasn't sure."

"Thanks." She slithered across the table with her manacled hands to kiss his cheek. "I'm sorry I doubted you."

Abernathy flushed to the roots of his neatly parted blond hair. "We're not out of the woods. A little propriety?"

She smiled. "Are you a one in a hundred?"

He blinked at her. "Huh?'

"Never mind."

FORTY-SIX

D ays dragged into weeks.
  Loup finished reading *Great Expectations* and started it over again.

Outside, the world was in an uproar. Tom Abernathy visited to give her periodic updates. The investigation had confirmed the existence of the Outposts and their civilian population. The news media was filled with outraged editorials. Decades' worth of foreign and domestic policy was under review.

"What about us?" Loup asked.

He sighed. "There's good news and bad. I filed a petition on your behalf for a writ of habeas corpus. The right to a hearing in court," he explained, noting her puzzled expression. "The judge dismissed it."

"Because of the Human Rights Amendment?"

"Exactly." Abernathy nodded. "The good news is that your story's still very much on the radar, and it's been validated by the Outpost findings. The government's under a lot of pressure to review the amendment." He smiled. "Seems there've been a record number of irate young people contacting their congressional representatives and writing to the president."

"Kate fans."

"It seems to be spreading." He showed her the cover of *Newsweek* magazine. It had a photo of Loup onstage at the concert in Osaka, the young Japanese fan in the striped socks perched on her shoulder. Loup was laughing, while the girl on her shoulder beamed with sheer delight, her arms spread wide. The headline read REDEFINING HUMAN? "You've captured the public's imagination."

"I remember that night." Loup smiled. "Wonder where they got the photo."

"They're all over the place. I imagine they bought the rights to one." Abernathy gave her a curious look. "What in the world gave you the idea? How much of this was orchestrated?"

She shrugged. "It was a fluke at first. Then it turned into a gimmick. I thought maybe I could use it to make people aware. Once the band decided they wanted to make it their thing, it just kind of took off. Can I keep the magazine? Ever since Bradford left I can't get anything new to read."

"No, sorry," he said apologetically. "I'm not allowed to give you any materials."

Loup sighed. "Okay. So what about the others?"

"Others?"

She gestured in the direction of the cell block. "The other detainees."

"Ah." Abernathy frowned. "Because they're subject to military regulations, their cases are different."

"Have any of the normal soldiers who wrote affidavits been detained?"

"No. They've been suspended from duty for the moment, but we don't have the facilities to detain them."

"Goddamnit!" Loup scowled. "Why only the GMOs? What the fuck are they afraid of?"

"I'm not sure," he said hesitantly. "Except that throughout history, there are innumerable tales of man's creations turning against their creator. I suspect it's a deeply ingrained fear."

"That's stupid."

"You're not angry at how you've been treated?" Abernathy asked.

"Angry? Yeah, sure. This sucks." She shrugged again. "I'm bored and lonely and pretty sure I'd be scared if I could be. There's that empty feeling. But I don't want to get back at anyone for it. I just want things to be fixed. Fair."

"Do you think the others feel the same way?"

"I don't know why they wouldn't."

"Interesting." He rose. "I'll be in touch."

More waiting.

To keep from losing her wits, Loup kept active in her cell. She shadow-boxed and did push-ups and crunches, adhering to the discipline honed by endless hours of training. She made sure to meditate every day. She finished rereading *Great Expectations* and started it over for a third time. She daydreamed about running freely along the coast at Huatulco like she'd been able to do the first time she visited her family there, the sun at her back and the water splashing under her feet.

And about Pilar.

She daydreamed a lot about Pilar.

There were so many good memories now. Some of her favorites were the funny ones. It made her smile every time to think of Pilar flung over Raimundo's shoulder, swearing indignantly; or Pilar provoking Sabine with disingenuous innocence. Then there were the nice ones, like Pilar giving her the necklace on the train, or Pilar looking happy and pleased with herself for finding the best places to eat, knowing how much Loup would enjoy it.

A thousand good memories.

All of them were better than remembering her broken look when they said goodbye.

A solid month after the Outpost hearings concluded, Tom Abernathy came to see her with a bounce in his step, a gleam in his eye, and a military doctor in tow.

"News?" Loup brightened.

"*Very* good news," Abernathy confirmed. "The president has appointed an independent commission to study the Human Rights Amendment." He grinned at her. "You're the genie they couldn't put back in the bottle, Loup! They can hide a lot under the guise of national security, including your fellow detainees, but too many people saw that footage of you, and there are too many people who had actual contact with you willing to testify it's not a hoax."

"That's great!"

"Dr. Morgan is here to take a sample of your DNA."

She opened her mouth obediently and let him swab the inside of her cheek. "Do I get to see the results?"

"Do you want to?" the doctor asked.

"Maybe." She thought about what Christophe had said about preferring not to know. "I'm not sure."

The doctor gave her a sympathetic look. "They'll be available if you want them."

"Thanks."

He left, having gotten what he needed.

"So what happens now?"

"It depends," Abernathy said. "The GMO Commission will issue subpoenas for all the materials relating to the Sino-Haitian program and subsequent experiments. The Department of Defense will refuse in the interest of national security. My guess is that while that gets settled in the courts, they'll proceed by considering your particular case."

"Whether or not I'm fit to be considered human."

"Yes."

"Do you think I am?"

He flushed. "Of course I do!"

"People don't know," Loup said thoughtfully. "All they know is rumors and stuff. The driver who took me to the Kate concert, he was surprised that I was so upset about leaving Pilar. Like he thought I didn't feel."

"It's obvious that you do."

"To you."

Abernathy sighed and rumpled his tidy hair. "I won't hold any influence over the commission, Loup. I can't control what they ask or don't ask. Can you cry on cue? Because that would be helpful."

"No," she said. "I can't cry."

"No?"

Loup shook her head. "Not like you. My eyes hurt, but they don't make tears."

He was quiet a moment. "You understand theater, though, don't you? That footage with the stun gun...you provoked them on purpose, didn't you? You knew there was a camera on you."

"Maybe."

"Maybe," Abernathy echoed. He summoned a smile. "Well, maybe I have an idea or two of my own. And maybe a word or two dropped in certain unofficial channels might produce results."

"Yeah?"

"Yes. Don't ask."

"Why?"

"Because whatever happens, I want your reaction to be honest," he said earnestly. "I want the commission to *see* it. I want them to see what I see in you. Are you willing to trust me, Loup?"

She searched his eyes. "Yeah. Yeah, I am."

He sighed. "Good."

FORTY-SEVEN

The GMO Commission began its investigation.

Their opening moves played out as Tom Abernathy had predicted, and when the issue of classified documents moved to the courts, the commission's attention turned to Loup.

First came a battery of physical examinations. She submitted to them without complaint, letting a team of doctors poke and prod her in the medical facility of the detention center. In the center's unused gym, they hooked her up to a heart-rate monitor and had her run on a treadmill. She increased her speed gradually, moving slowly from a normal human pace to a full flat-out run until the belt moved in a whining blur and the motor began to smell hot.

"Jesus Christ," one of the doctors murmured.

Loup laughed and slowed down. "Nah. I can't walk on water." He gave her a startled look. "It's a joke, okay? Yes, I have a sense of humor."

That made him smile. "I'll pass that on to the psychology team."

The psychological tests came next. At least it was a change from the lonely tedium of her cell and *Great Expectations*. They hooked her up to more monitors and had her watch a multitude of video clips, analyzing her responses and interviewing her about them.

"What's all this supposed to prove?" Loup asked Dr. Sheridan, the head of the psych team.

"We're measuring the range of your emotional responses." She consulted a monitor. "How did the last clip make you feel?"

"Bored."

The doctor raised her eyebrows. "You didn't feel any empathy for the woman being stalked?"

"It's just a movie. I know it's not real."

"What if I told you it was actual video footage from a security camera and the woman was in fact killed?" Dr. Sheridan inquired.

Loup's pulse increased. "Then it would make me mad." With an effort, she kept her voice level. "And if it's true, I'd say that's a pretty sick thing to show me."

"Mad," the doctor mused. "Do a lot of things make you angry?"

"No."

"What does?"

She thought about it. "People getting hurt."

"And yet you've hurt a number of people. You have a history of violent assault. Were you angry at the time?"

"Sometimes." Loup sighed. "Look, I get angry when *innocent* people are hurt, okay? I was mad at the soldier who raped Katya and the dog killers. I was mad at the terrorist guy in Switzerland who wanted to shoot that kid. Wouldn't you be?"

Dr. Sheridan didn't answer. "Do you always act on your anger?"

"If there's something I can do, I guess."

"Do you think violence solves problems?"

"Not always, no. Of course not."

"Sometimes? Most of the time?"

Loup eyed her. "Well, I'm starting to get pretty fucking irritated right about now, but I don't think getting violent would solve anything."

"But you're having violent urges."

"No! Jesus, lady, I was being ironic. You're trying to make me out like I'm some kind of psychopath."

"That's interesting you would say that," the doctor observed. "Do you think you're a psychopath?"

"No!"

"You trained as a boxer. Do you like fighting?"

"Yeah, I do." Loup sighed again. "I enjoy the sport, okay? But no, I don't get off on hurting people."

"How *does* it make you feel?"

"Depends." She searched for a way to answer. "Bad, sometimes. Like those guards in Vegas, they were just doing their job. In the boxing ring, at least in the only real fight I ever had, it was just about winning or losing. I felt good about winning, but I was glad to know Johnson was okay afterward. I guess the only time I really felt good about hurting someone was the guy in Switzerland. And believe me, if you had someone try to shoot you, you'd feel pretty good about punching them out, too."

"Do you—"

"Want to know the worst I ever felt about hurting someone?" Loup interrupted her. "I said something that hurt my brother Tommy's feelings the day he died, and I never got to tell him I was sorry for it. He died hurt and mad at me. I felt awful about it. I still do. Want to know the next worst? Leaving Pilar. There are all kinds of ways of hurting people and most of them suck."

Dr. Sheridan cleared her throat and consulted her notes. "Let's talk about your brother, shall we? He was a boxer, too. Did you admire him?"

"Yeah, I did. He was a great guy."

The psychological interview continued for several hours and Loup didn't feel good about it. The empty feeling where fear should be grew bigger. The feeling was confirmed when Tom Abernathy reported on the psych team's report to the GMO Commission.

"They're pushing the violence angle," he said glumly. "Expressing concern that your history of violence coupled with the inability to experience fear and your extraordinary physical skills makes you highly dangerous."

"Yeah, it kinda felt like Dr. Sheridan was out to get me. What gives?"

He raked a hand through his hair. "They're supposed to be neutral, but I suspect the brass have been leaning on them. If they can convince the commission that a perfectly adorable teenage girl is a menace to society, it lays the groundwork for convincing them that scores of grown men with extensive military training are all the more so. It plants seeds of doubt. They'll recommend against repealing the Human Rights Amendment out of sheer caution."

Loup smiled involuntarily. "Adorable?"

Abernathy turned bright red. "We have a real problem here, Loup."

"I know, I know! So what do we do?"

"At this point? Pray."

Two days later, the GMO Commission summoned Loup. She was escorted by Tom Abernathy and a pair of armed guards to appear before them in her orange jumpsuit and handcuffs.

"Look harmless," Abernathy advised her.

"Doing my best."

There were five members on the commission, chaired by Marian Gallagher, a former Secretary of the Department of Health and Human Services whose grandmotherly appearance was belied by her sharp gaze.

The chairwoman peered over a pair of reading glasses as Loup was sworn in. "We've heard a lot about you, Ms. Garron."

"So I understand, ma'am," Loup said politely. "And not much of it good."

It won her a faint smile. "We're eager to hear *from* you."

For three hours, the commission quizzed her on her life story, focusing heavily on incidents of violence. Loup struggled to tell the truth while painting a picture in the least incriminating tones possible.

At noon they broke for lunch.

"Well?" she asked Tom Abernathy.

He shrugged. "We'll see."

The commission resumed its hearings an hour later. Instead of recalling Loup to the stand, they summoned a character witness.

She caught her breath and shot to her feet when Pilar was escorted into the chamber.

Tom Abernathy grabbed her arm. "Steady!"

"Hey," Loup said softly, her eyes stinging. "Hey!" Across the room, Pilar gave her a dazzling, tremulous smile that made her heart ache. Her entire body quivered with yearning. The members of the commission glanced back and forth between them, curious at the sudden tension. "Can't I just—"

"No!" Abernathy tugged at her. "Sit down, Loup!"

She sat reluctantly.

Pilar was sworn in.

"You wish to address the commission?" Marian Gallagher inquired.

"Yes. Thank you, ma'am." Pilar took a deep breath. "I guess...I guess you know I testified at the Outpost hearings. And it's kind of ironic that I'm here at all, because I would have stayed in Outpost all my life if I hadn't fallen in love with Loup." She snuck a sideways glance at her, eyes bright with tears. "I never had a lot of ambition."

Loup wriggled in her seat.

"But then everything changed." Pilar gazed at the ceiling a moment. "And this policy you guys are debating...it says that the person I fell in love with isn't a *person*. I just want you to know that she is." She collected herself, her voice growing stronger. "I know there are ways that she's different. Believe me, I know it better than any of you ever will—and I love those differences. But Loup's still a person just like you and me. Just like anyone. She gets cranky if you wake her out of a sound sleep. She has bad hair days, especially when it's humid. She likes pancakes, and she knows all the lyrics to every song in *The Sound of Music*." She gave a choked laugh. "Maybe that one doesn't count. All of us Santitos do. It was one of the last videos that still worked."

The chamber was quiet.

One of the members coughed. "Ms. Ecchevarria, have you ever had cause to fear Ms. Garron's temper?"

She gave him a blank look. "*Loup's?* Are you joking?"

He looked taken aback. "No."

"God, no!"

"Do you deny witnessing violent incidents?"

"No, but—"

"Given her history, isn't it fair to describe Loup Garron as having violent tendencies?"

"No!" Pilar flushed angrily. "Have you even bothered to get to know her? Yes, Loup's willing to fight for what she thinks is right. And yes, she can get worked up about something that's unfair while the rest of us are just trying to get by. Or worse, trying to sweep it under the carpet like you've done here."

"I don't think that's—"

"Oh, please!" She gave him a scathing look. "You don't *want* to see her as a person. You want to see her as a science experiment or a—a tricky political issue because it makes it easier for you to do the wrong thing. And you think because she doesn't share the same fears you do, it's okay. Is that what makes us human? Fear?" Pilar shook her head. "I can tell you, she shares the same hopes and dreams you do. And I can tell you that she hurts the same. I watched her grieve for her brother when he died. And I hurt her once, badly." She stole another glance at Loup, tears spilling over her cheeks. "I'd rather cut off my right hand than do it again. And if she's missing me half as much as I miss her, she's hurting pretty badly right now."

There was another silence in the chamber. Loup closed her eyes, listening to the thud of her aching heart.

"Are you finished, dear?" Marian Gallagher asked sympathetically.

"I'm sorry." Pilar tried in vain to dash away her tears. "It's just...if any of you are tempted to think of Loup as less than a person, please remember that to me, she's much, much more." She smiled across the room through her tears. "She's my life."

They thanked her for her testimony. An aide stepped forward to escort her from the chamber.

Loup rose, helpless. "Abernathy, please! Can't I just see her for one minute? For one *second*?"

"No." He restrained her. "I'm sorry, Loup."

She watched Pilar go. Pilar went slowly, glancing over her shoulder, her face streaked with tears. The commission watched them both. When Pilar was gone, Loup sank into her seat, burying her face in her manacled hands.

"Mr. Garza," the chairwoman announced.

"Mig?" Loup raised her head.

Miguel Garza sauntered into the chamber with a lazy grin on his face. "Hey, kid!" he called to Loup. "You okay?"

"Please don't address the subject," one of the members said sternly.

His lip curled. "Is that what you're calling her?" After being sworn in he took his seat. "Look, I'm not gonna waste time doing the gravitas thing. I can sum up Loup in one sentence for you. She's a good kid with some freaky gifts, a hero complex, and a big heart. What the hell else do you need to know?"

"You and Ms. Ecchevarria paint a portrait very much at odds with what our psych team concluded," Marian Gallagher said shrewdly.

Miguel snorted. "Yeah, I overheard some of the questions you were asking. Is that where all this bullshit about violence is coming from? Maybe because we actually *know* Loup. And maybe because we're not in the Defense Department's hip pocket." He leaned forward. "Look, I know from violence. Me, I'm a violent guy. When I don't get my way, it's what I resort to. I've been known to pick fights in bars. I can be a belligerent drunk." He jabbed a finger at Loup. "She's not like that."

"Her history—"

"Of what?" He raised his heavy brows. "Crusading do-gooderism? Avenging wrongs? Rescuing her friends? Let me tell you, Loup wouldn't be here if I hadn't gotten myself in trouble in Vegas. She could have stayed safely out of the country with her cushy body-guard gig and her sweetheart. Speaking of whom, if you don't think *those* two dingbats aren't ridiculously in love, you're fucking blind. All the way out there in the hallway, I could practically hear the violins playing."

Several members smiled.

"And the thing is," Miguel continued. "That hero complex? It starts to work on you after a while. Because Loup looks at things so fucking fearlessly, you start to, too. Once you confront your fears, you start thinking maybe you're big enough to do the right thing after all. You think that crazy British pop band started out thinking they were gonna dedicate themselves to GMO rights?" He nodded at Tom Abernathy. "Bet you know what I mean, don't you?"

Abernathy colored. "I...uh, yes."

A murmur ran around the room.

"Look at the little freak," Miguel said with rough affection. "Two minutes ago she was a wreck. Now she's sitting there giving me that goddamn shiny I-believe-in-you look. That goddamn look made me a better man. Menace to society? Please."

"Are you also...enamored...of Ms. Garron?" a retired general asked delicately.

"Nah." He smiled, leaning back in his chair. The chair creaked under his bulk. "She's just a really good kid, that's all. And a little too fearless for her own damn good. I care about her, okay?"

"Do you have anything else to add, Mr. Garza?" the chairwoman inquired.

Miguel considered. "Nope."

"Thank you for your time."

The commission ordered a brief recess before continuing. Tom Abernathy brought Loup hot tea with milk.

"Are you all right?" he asked anxiously.

"Yeah, I'm okay." She glanced at him. "That was your big plan to make me seem more human? Bring in Pilar and yank my heart out of my chest?"

"Ah...yes."

She sighed. "Good plan."

He was quiet a moment. "What Mr. Garza said. It's true. If the Outpost hearings hadn't gone as they did, I'd have gone public with my knowledge."

"You're a good guy, Abernathy."

He smiled wryly. "Not really. I've known about it for a long time."

"Yeah, really." Loup sipped her tea, manacled hands clasped around the cup. "Sometimes things happen for a reason, you know?"

"God, I hope so."

The GMO Commission reconvened and put Loup back on the stand. Marian Gallagher peered over her reading glasses with a curious gaze. "Ms. Garron, we have highly conflicting descriptions of your nature. How do you account for this?"

"Honestly?"

"Preferably, yes," she said dryly.

"I think Miguel's right," Loup said. "Dr. Sheridan diagnosed me before we ever met. Everything she ever asked me was about violence and anger and hurting people. Did it say in the report that I'm a psychopath because I think scary movies are boring?"

The chairwoman hesitated. "Your lack of affect raised concern."

"Hello?" Loup gestured at herself, the chain between her wrists rattling. "Can't feel fear? It means I get bored watching scary movies, that's all. I know the difference between fiction and reality. If you ask me, I think it's weirder that normal people get off on being scared and watching imaginary characters get killed and tortured. Don't you?"

She blinked. "Umm..."

"Look, I can't help what I am. But it's not this psychotic trait you're trying to make it out to be. It's more like a learning disability. We GMOs—" She made a face at the hated term. "We have to be taught how to recognize danger and avoid it. That's it. That's the main way we're different from you. Why does it scare you so much?"

"Ms. Garron..." Marian Gallagher paused. "Because it's unnatural."

"Marian," one of the other members began.

She raised her hand. "Let's at least be honest here. I want her to respond."

"I get it," Loup said slowly. "But nature evolves, doesn't it?

Sometimes on its own and sometimes because we mess with it. That's it, isn't it? The thing Abernathy said to me about creators and created. You're afraid if you let us live our lives, one day we'll turn on you."

The retired general scoffed. "All one hundred and twenty-eight of you?"

"I didn't say it made sense. A lot of fear doesn't. Maybe that's easier to see from the outside."

The chamber was quiet, digesting the comment. Tom Abernathy nodded to Loup.

"Look..." She struggled for words. "I don't know what I can say to change your minds. If you believe the psychologists and decide to play it safe...I guess I'll get sent back to that stupid cell to reread *Great Expectations* until I've memorized every line. Maybe you'll find better doctors with better tests. Maybe the courts will decide in your favor and you'll get all those documents you want. I bet when you review the service records of those hundred and twenty-seven guys, you'll find out that they're no more violent—"

Marian Gallagher's eyes widened. "General Tansey," she said, interrupting Loup. "The enlisted men's service records. Are those actually classified?"

He shook his head. "No. Only their medical records. But the service records were requested as part and parcel of the classified materials documenting the GMO program, so it's still tied up in court."

"But we could file a separate request?"

"We could."

"Interesting," she mused. "If the records don't show a disproportionate history of violence, that would certainly bear out Ms. Garron's testimony." She turned back to Loup. "Tell me, what would you do if the Human Rights Amendment was overturned and you were released from custody?"

Her eyes shone. "Seriously?"

The chairwoman smiled. "Seriously."

"Are you kidding?" Loup laughed, giddy at the first ray of hope she'd felt in days. "God, I don't even know! I can't think past seeing Pilar." She shivered with pleasure at the thought. "I *hate* seeing her so miserable, you know?"

"I do." The chairwoman eyed her. "And I think I begin to understand that disconcertingly shiny look your friend Mr. Garza mentioned." She glanced around the chamber. "Any further questions?"

Heads shook.

"Thank you for your cooperation, Ms. Garron. Mr. Abernathy will keep you informed."

FORTY-EIGHT

It took two more weeks for the second dam to break.

Giddy hope gave way to resignation. Tom Abernathy came twice with nothing to report. Loup finished rereading *Great Expectations* for the third time. There was a change of rotation and the new guard on the day shift took pity on her and brought her a copy of Steinbeck's *Of Mice and Men* to exchange for her well-worn Dickens. She thanked him so profusely he blushed.

On Abernathy's third visit, he was grinning from ear to ear.

"The commission's report's out." He showed her a thick spiral-bound document. "They're recommending repealing the Human Rights Amendment!"

"No!" She stared at him. "Seriously? You're not kidding?"

He shook his head. "I wouldn't."

"So what happens now?"

"Senator Ballantine's introducing legislature today. They expect to vote on it within the week."

"Will it pass?"

"I think so." His grin was undiminished. "And the president has indicated he'll sign it."

Loup let out a whoop. "Then I get to go?"

Abernathy raised a cautionary finger. "There's still the issue of the charges against you, three of which are valid. I'm pretty sure I can get the theft charge dismissed, but we'll have to negotiate on the others. And that can't happen until the amendment is repealed."

"Shit."

"Don't worry," he said. "I'm good at what I do."

"What's gonna happen to all the GMO soldiers when it happens?" she asked. "Will they be let go?"

"Some of them." He hesitated. "My guess is that there's going to be a general amnesty for all the enlisted personnel who submitted affidavits on the Outposts. There are just too many to prosecute and it's a thorny issue. But those involved in helping you escape face more serious charges."

"Is there anything you can do about it?"

"Maybe." Abernathy smiled. "You want me to try?"

"Yeah, please!"

Another week passed.

The Human Rights Amendment was repealed by a wide margin.

Tom Abernathy showed up at the detention center with another wide grin, a box of chocolates, a copy of the *Washington Post*, and three paperback novels.

"I thought you weren't allowed to give me anything," Loup said, bewildered.

He pointed to the *Post*'s headline, which read THEY'RE PEOPLE LIKE US. "As of today, you have civil rights, Loup."

"Can I talk to Pilar?"

Abernathy winced. "Not yet, I'm afraid. Military custody has its own rules."

"Oh."

"It won't be long. I promise." He opened his laptop. "I want to review the details of your original detention in Outpost. You were subjected to sleep deprivation and withholding of food?"

"Yeah. And hosing."

"Walk me through it."

She did.

It was another week before Abernathy returned. Loup read the *Washington Post* from cover to cover, marveling at the changes that had taken place while she'd been detained. She lingered over an article in the Entertainment section that quoted Kate's manager as saying the band was poised to return to the States to celebrate their bodyguard's freedom.

She allowed herself one chocolate a day, savoring the luxury.

The taste reminded her of eating *pain au chocolat* in Paris, and the wonder and delight on Pilar's face.

The memory made her happy.

She finished *Of Mice and Men* and began reading one of the paperbacks Abernathy had brought her. She kept up her daily meditation, thinking about how Pilar would be proud of her. She shadowboxed and did push-ups and crunches until she was bored and wished she had a jump rope just to mix things up.

Abernathy came back, looking somber.

Her heart sank. "Well?"

"How do you feel about paying a fine?"

"A fine?" Loup asked. "For what?"

He began to smile. "Destruction of property. The Jeep's windshield. Three thousand dollars and time served under extreme duress and dubious circumstances the government doesn't wish made public, what with the harsh coercive techniques and all. How does that sound?"

She gaped. "Three thousand bucks?"

"Is it too much?" he asked. "It's a lot for a windshield, I know. But from their perspective, it's the point of the thing. There has to be a substantial fine."

"No!" Loup leaped to her feet. "No, no, no! That's all? It's okay, it's fine. I don't care. We have money left from our signing bonuses and the deal with Kate and stuff. It's just...that's all? I can pay three thousand bucks and get out of here?"

"Yes."

"No strings?"

Abernathy shook his head. "No strings."

"I can go?" Loup bounced on the balls of her feet, filled with irrepressible energy. The manacles on her wrists jangled. "Really go? I can see Pilar?"

He smiled sadly. "I'll miss you."

"I'm sorry." She caught his hands. "I will, too. Thank you. Thank you so much."

"It was my honor. Truly."

It took two more days to arrange the transfer of funds from Loup's bank account in Switzerland, and then another day to sort out the paperwork, but after what seemed like an eternity of waiting, the day of her release arrived. When the new day guard came to fetch her, he grinned and shook his head when she thrust her hands through the sliding window of her cell door.

"No more handcuffs," he reminded her. "You're free, sweetheart."

"Oh! Right!"

He led her to a small dressing room where her civilian clothing and personal items were waiting for her in a plastic bag. Loup changed into her security togs and fastened Pilar's necklace around her neck.

Tom Abernathy flushed at the sight of her. "*That's* what you were wearing?"

"Yeah." She glanced down at herself. "I was at the concert when they took me, remember? Working."

"Yes, of course." His flush deepened. "I've seen the footage. It's just, um...more striking in the flesh. And there's a press conference scheduled on the Capitol steps."

"Is it a problem?"

He thought a moment and shook his head. "No. You know what? It's not. You're a bit of an icon. Why not give the people what they want?"

"Okay."

Outside it was cool and gray and overcast, drizzling a little. Loup stood a moment, breathing deeply, reveling in the freedom. She spread her arms wide, feeling the dampness against her bare skin.

"Here." Abernathy began to remove his coat.

"No thanks." She shook her head. "I like how it feels. And I'm kind of warm." She smiled. "Excited, you know?"

"All right, then."

They drove past the checkpoints and left the detention center. Loup craned her head around, watching it diminish in the distance.

"Thinking about the others?" he asked her.

"Yeah."

"Don't worry. They'll be all right."

A security detail met them outside the Capitol building and escorted them up the steps past the throng of reporters. The journalists turned, cameras flashing. Loup gazed past them, feeling dizzy and weightless with anticipation, her heart expanding inside her like a helium balloon. Senator Ballantine was there with a considerable crowd of politicians and civilians surrounding him. She scanned the crowd impatiently, familiar and unfamiliar faces half registering, looking for one in particular.

Pilar.

Their eyes met.

The day didn't need sunshine, only Pilar's smile. Loup froze for a moment, unable to breathe, transfixed with happiness. The senator strode forward, beaming, his hand extended. His lips shaped words she couldn't fathom. He stopped and followed her gaze, then gave her a courtly little bow and stepped aside, gesturing toward Pilar.

Loup found her breath and moved.

Fast—as fast as she could.

She caught Pilar around the waist and spun her in a circle, delirious with joy. Pilar laughed and cried at the same time, cupping Loup's face and showering her with kisses. The press corps went wild with the cameras.

"I've missed you *so much*!" Pilar whispered against her lips.

"Me too." Loup kissed away her tears. "It's okay, you can stop crying now."

She laughed through her tears. "I can't! I'm too happy. Loup, promise me we'll never, ever have to go through this again."

Loup held her tight. "I promise."

"Jesus," a familiar voice rumbled. "It was only a few months! You'd think it was half a lifetime."

She released Pilar reluctantly. "Hey, Mig!"

Miguel folded her in a gruff hug, pressing her head to his broad chest. "Good to have you back, kid."

And then there were others pressing around. Loup shook Senator

Ballantine's hand, thanked him and all his aides. She thanked dozens of other politicians, their names passing in a blur.

Kate; Kate was there. All the boys. They posed for the photographers, Randall clasping Loup's hand and raising her arm in a victory salute.

"You guys gonna come back to work for us?" he asked, giving her a sly smile from behind his bangs. "You're still under contract and we've sold a *lot* of T-shirts."

She laughed. "We'll talk."

At last the furor died and Senator Ballantine took the podium. He gave a speech about civil rights and the triumph of the human spirit, about truth, justice, and the American way, about reclaiming the nation's dignity. Loup barely listened to it, letting his sonorous voice wash over her, content to have Pilar's fingers entwined with hers.

"You okay, baby?" Pilar whispered. "Did they feed you enough?"

"More or less." She squeezed her hand. "It wasn't like last time, honest."

"I worry! Did you do your meditation?"

"Yep. Every day."

"Good girl." Pilar gave her a long, lingering kiss. The cameras flashed.

"—a few words from Ms. Garron," the senator said in conclusion. "After which I'm sure she'll be happy to take your questions."

Loup glanced up. "Huh?"

He beckoned her to the podium.

"Okay." She stepped up to lower the microphone. "Umm...Hi. I wasn't expecting this part. And I'm not really good at making speeches. That's not a GMO thing," she added hastily. "It's just a me thing. I'm really happy to be here. Thanks so much to everyone who made it possible, and especially to all the soldiers who came forward. I wish I could thank everyone in person, but I don't know all your names."

"What do you plan to do next?" a reporter shouted.

"Like, right away?" Loup looked at Pilar and smiled. "Duh."

A wave of laughter rippled through the crowd.

"Ah...afterward," the reporter clarified. "Obviously."

"I don't know," she said thoughtfully. "We kind of have an obligation to these guys." She nodded at the members of Kate. "And I guess it's sort of lucrative. But I'd really like to go home, too—at least to visit. To Santa Olivia. Outpost. I guess we'll figure it out." Inspiration struck her. "Hey, Pilar! Maybe we could set up, like, a scholarship fund?"

"For the Santitos?"

"Yeah!"

Pilar's eyes shone. "That's an awesome idea, baby!"

There were questions and more questions. Loup struggled to answer them gamely until Senator Ballantine stepped up and took the microphone back.

"Thank you all so much for coming," he said cordially. "This is a great day in our nation's history."

The press dispersed, grumbling.

The senator presented Loup with an American passport. "Welcome to citizenship, Ms. Garron."

She opened it to find her photo and her real name inside. "I get my name back? No more Guadalupe Herrera?" She glanced at Pilar. "Did you?"

"Yep." Pilar showed her. "See? No more Mendez."

Loup hugged her. "Hey! We're us again!"

"Mm-hmm." Pilar's hands caressed her back. "Jesus! You have no idea how good you feel."

Senator Ballantine cleared his throat and beckoned to his aides. "I believe your hotel reservations are in order. We'll leave you to the *obviously*, shall we?"

"Okay!"

FORTY-NINE

I s this okay?" Pilar asked anxiously.

Loup surveyed the lowered lights, the lit candles, and the covered dish domes. Soft music was playing and a bottle of champagne chilled in a stand. "Are you kidding?" She lifted a dome and sniffed. "Lobster *and* steak?"

"I wasn't sure. I wanted everything to be perfect."

"It is."

"Are you sure?"

"Pilar!" Loup pulled her close. It felt good, so unspeakably good, to have Pilar's body pressed against hers, warm, lush curves melting into her embrace. She nuzzled her hair and breathed her in. "Yes. It's perfect."

Pilar pushed her away with an effort. "Eat first. I worry!"

"Okay. I am kinda hungry."

She ate. It was luxury on luxury, the succulent lobster melting in her mouth, the filet tender and juicy. Pilar, watching. Eating, too, but mostly watching.

"Tell me everything I missed," Loup said between bites.

"Oh God!" Pilar ran a hand through her hair. "It's been crazy, baby." She described the months of endless tension and suspense, the constant agony of uncertainty. "I just wished I could *see* you and know you were all right. That footage from backstage at the concert." She shivered. "Did you know those stun gun things can actually kill people?"

"Uh...no."

"Loup!"

"I'm fine, I'm fine." She smiled. "I did see you, you know. On TV, testifying at the Outpost hearings. You were great."

Pilar shrugged. "I just told the truth."

"No." Loup shook her head. "You made them feel what it was like to grow up in Outpost, made them believe. And when you addressed the GMO Commission..." She put down her fork. "Pilar, I'm pretty sure they wouldn't have recommended to repeal the amendment if it wasn't for you. Miguel, too—but especially you."

She turned pale. "Don't say that!"

"Why not? It's true. Everything you said was true. They didn't want to see me as a person." Loup reached out to stroke her cheek. "You *made* them."

Pilar drew a shuddering breath. "If I'd known there was that much riding on it, I would have been too nervous to get the words out."

"But you weren't and you did." Her eyes widened. "Ohmigod! It was our fortune coming true. From that temple in Tokyo. Do you remember how it went?"

"Not exactly."

Loup scrambled out of the chair and rummaged through the new suitcase Pilar had brought to find her billfold. Inside was the scroll of paper, neatly folded. "A million drops of water can wear down a mountain," she read aloud. "A thousand tears can melt the hardest heart." She looked up, eyes shining. "All the soldiers, all the affidavits...that was the million drops of water. And you! It was your tears that melted their hearts."

"Wow." Pilar looked a little stunned. "That's pretty weird."

"Yeah." She folded the paper and put it back.

"Loup..." Pilar gave her hair a gentle tug. "You think maybe we can get by without any great and terrible destinies for a little while?"

She nodded. "Definitely."

"Good." Her tone changed. "Are you done eating?"

"Mm-hmm."

"Are you sure?" Pilar teased her. "There might be a shred of lobster still clinging there."

Loup eyed her. "Oh, I'm sure! You're starting to get your smolder on, which means I'm *definitely* done eating. Let me take a quick shower, okay? I want to wash the jail cell–ickiness off me."

"Make it *real* quick."

She did.

She emerged to find Pilar lounging on the hotel bed wearing nothing but an apricot-colored bra and panties, looking so impossibly sexy it almost made her heart skip a beat. She stood for a long moment just looking at her.

"You look amazing," she said at last.

Pilar smiled and crooked her finger. "Drop that bathrobe and get over here."

Loup obeyed.

And this was perfect, too; the most perfect part of all. The candles burned lower and the soft music played. Pilar kissed her tenderly for a long, long time, caressing Loup's body with a delicate touch, assuring herself that she was really there and unharmed.

It felt like coming home.

"I'm really proud of you, baby," she whispered. "Just so you know."

"Yeah?" Loup traced the scalloped lace along the edge of Pilar's bra, the palm of her hand brushing the fullness of her breast.

"Yeah."

"Me too." She kissed her. "And I thought about you all the time while I was in there."

"Did you think about this?" Pilar's hand glided over her taut belly and lower.

Loup caught her breath. "Uh-huh."

"And *this*?"

"Yep! That, too."

"Mmm." Pilar gave her a long smoldering look, then kissed her with rising passion, hard and fierce and deep. "I'm about to give you so many, many more things to think about."

Loup shivered with pleasure. "Yeah, but—"

She nudged Loup's thighs apart with one knee. "But what?"

"You're not gonna be fair about this, are you?"

Pilar laughed softly. "Baby, you don't get a turn tonight if that's what you mean by fair." She laid a flurry of kisses on her face. "It's you. All you. Believe me, I've been thinking about this for a long, long time. I've missed you so fucking much. And by the time I'm done with you, you won't complain. Okay?"

"Okay, okay!"

Hours later, Loup watched Pilar climb out of bed to blow out the guttering candles. She wriggled under the bedsheets and turned them down. Pilar slid in beside her, her body naked and warm and delightful.

"Good?" she whispered.

"So good," Loup whispered in reply. "Perfect, even."

Pilar sighed happily. "I'm glad."

"Did you—"

"Yeah." She settled her head on Loup's shoulder, her voice dreamy. "I always get off making love to you. It's kind of weird."

"Bad weird?"

"No." Pilar glanced up at her. "Are you kidding? Good weird. Like everything about you. Just hold me for a while, will you? It feels really nice."

Loup tightened her arms around her. "Like, forever? Because I will."

"Yeah." She smiled. "Forever's a good start."

FIFTY

The next day, they managed to leave the hotel room in time to catch the tail end of the elaborate brunch buffet. Miguel was there, reading the newspaper.

"Well, well." He folded the paper. "America's sweethearts emerge."

"Huh?"

He showed them the cover. The lead photo was a close-up shot of their reunion, Pilar's hands cupping Loup's face.

"Aww!" Pilar smiled. "That's so cute!"

"Are you kidding?" Miguel snorted. "If it was any more sickeningly sweet, I'd be in a diabetic coma. Go get yourselves something to eat. We should talk."

They returned from the buffet, Loup with two laden plates.

Miguel sipped his coffee. "Worked up quite an appetite, huh, kid?"

"Don't be pervy, Mig."

He laughed. "Since when do you care? So, hey, what did you think of the big news?"

Loup looked bewildered. "Which news?"

"You didn't tell her?" He glanced at Pilar.

"Um, no," she admitted. "I figured it would kind of overshadow everything else, and I just wanted us to have some quiet time alone first."

"Quiet time?" Miguel snorted again. "Is that what the kids are calling it these days?"

"Shut up, Mig," Loup said absently. "Pilar, what news?"

She flushed. "Remember when Geordie said you were sitting on a gold mine? Well, there are a couple of studios in Hollywood that are interested in buying the rights to your life story. For a *lot* of money."

"How much money?"

"A lot." Pilar took a deep breath. "Geordie thinks as much as three million."

Loup stared at her. "Dollars?"

"No, strings of wampum, you little idiot." Miguel raised his brows at her blank look. "Beads? The Indians used to trade them? Never mind."

"That's a lot of scholarships," Loup said softly. "Jane could go to medical school like she always wanted. And what was it Jaime wanted to study?"

"Biological engineering," Pilar said. "He was interested in it because of you."

"Right."

"Fuckin' do-gooder," Miguel commented. "I'd take the money and run."

Loup smiled at him. "No, you wouldn't."

"Yeah, I might. Don't overestimate me, kid. That hero effect of yours only goes so far." He pushed his chair back from the table. "That's one of the things I wanted to talk to you about. I'm gonna take off tomorrow."

"For where?"

He shrugged. "Thought I might go back to Vegas for a week or two. Take in a fight, do some gambling. Meet a hot babe who isn't some jerk's wife. After that, I don't know. California, maybe. I just want a chance to see the world and do all the shit I left Outpost to do in the first place." He drummed his fingers on the table. "I gotta find a way to score a driver's license."

"Vegas?" Her voice rose. "And you call *me* an idiot?"

"What, because of Mr. Big at the Hellfire Club?" Miguel waved a dismissive hand. "He's not gonna bother with me. I'm a citizen now. I could file charges against him. Anyway, I'm not going anywhere near that place."

Loup sighed. "If you're wrong, we're *so* not coming to rescue you this time."

"Don't worry, I'll be fine. Look…" He paused. "I'm not cut out to be a hero, Loup. I'll feel better knowing you're safe. And it's good to know that the two of you can take care of yourselves. But you've got all kinds of big plans and dreams that don't fit me. I'm not ready to go back to Outpost. I'm not the guy I was when I was there. I'm not sure exactly who I am these days. I need some time to figure it out, okay?"

"Okay. You'll stay in touch?"

"Yes, you little freak!" Miguel tousled her hair. "Always."

"Another touching moment," Pilar observed.

"Oh, you hush." He pointed a finger at her. "I just babysat your miserable, languishing ass for the past few months. And believe me, it was no picnic. Do you realize it's impossible to get any action when you're stuck with a teenage sexpot threatening to burst into tears at a moment's notice?"

She smiled at him. "You were great. I'll miss you."

Miguel eyed her cleavage. "Yeah, me too."

They agreed to meet for breakfast the following day to say their final goodbyes. Afterward in the hotel room, Pilar told Loup more about the possibility of a movie deal.

"Geordie says we'll want to meet with the studio executives in person," she explained. "That it's not always about money. There's the vision thing. Like, you want to go with someone who sees things the way you do and wants to tell the same story you do. After all, it's your life."

"Do we have to do it right away?"

She shook her head. "No. We can do whatever we want. You want to go home first?"

Loup wrapped her arms around her knees. "Yeah."

"I could maybe arrange for media coverage," Pilar speculated. "It's a pretty good angle, the hometown hero returning. While you were in jail, there was a film crew that got permission to cover—"

"No media," Loup interrupted her. "I don't want a big scene. I just want to see everyone, you know?"

"Yeah, I do. Sorry, I kind of got used to thinking about how to do everything possible to keep your story out there while you were detained. No media."

"Thanks. Pilar...there's something I need to try to do before we leave here."

"You want to talk to that Johnson guy." She smiled at Loup's surprised expression. "I figured you would."

"You know me pretty well, huh?"

"Yep." Pilar kissed her. "You think there's a chance? After all, no one was allowed to see you."

"Abernathy thinks so. Something to do with extraordinary circumstances, the image of the military, and the fact that I've already been inside the detention center...I dunno. He said he'd call within a day or two."

"Okay. You want to meet with Geordie to talk about the movie deal?"

"Sure." Loup nodded. "Guess we need to talk about our contract with Kate, too."

"True," Pilar agreed. "They're being cool about it, but I know they'd love to have us tour with them in North America this fall."

"It *is* kind of fun. And we owe them."

"Oh, they came out of it okay, believe me." Pilar's Dataphone rang. "Hello?" She beamed. "Magnus, hi! Yeah, thank you. Oh, believe me, we're delighted. Yeah, she's right here." She passed the phone to Loup.

"Hi, Magnus! Thanks, thanks so much." She listened, smiling. "Yeah, we've got some things to take care of, but we'll keep it in mind. Thanks, I appreciate it. Say hi to Sabine, will you?" She listened some more, eyes growing wide. "No kidding! Wow, well, congratulations. That's wonderful. I'm sure we'd love to come. You don't think Sabine's head would explode?"

"No!" Pilar breathed. "They're getting *married*?"

Loup nodded vigorously. "Okay, well, thanks again for everything. Take care." She ended the call.

"Seriously?"

"Yep." She grinned. "And Magnus wants to invite us to the wedding."

"Ohmigod! Sabine will have a fit."

Loup shook her head. "He said he thinks she's come to bear a—a certain grudging respect and perhaps a soupçon of affection for us."

"Soup's on?" Pilar said, bemused. "What does that mean?"

"I think it's French for 'I no longer consider you a guttersnipe' or something." She flopped back on the bed. "God, this is all so bizarre! We went from being stuck in Outpost and having no futures at all to having all the possibilities in the world open to us."

"You deserve it." Pilar sat cross-legged, settling Loup's head in her lap and stroking her hair.

"You too." She gazed at the ceiling. "And so many people to thank, you know? Senator Ballantine and all of his people in their Reform Caucus, that Mr. Sandoval, Abernathy, Magnus and Sabine...Jesus, Clive and Addie!"

"Ms. Coxcombe."

"Yeah." Loup smiled. "You were right, those deportment and elo-cution lessons did come in handy. That's why you were so good on the stand."

"Mm-hmm." Pilar kissed her forehead. "And then there's Randall and the boys..."

"All the Kate fans..."

"All the soldiers..."

"Christophe," Loup said wistfully. "Tía Marcela, and all my aunts and cousins." She craned her head around. "Jesus, I should call them! Hey, Pilar? Do you still think you might like to live there? Huatulco, I mean."

"In a cute little house near the ocean?" She kissed her again. "You bet, baby."

"It wouldn't be full time," Loup mused. "Not for a while. But it would be nice to have someplace to call home. And as excited as I am about going back to Santa Olivia, I don't think that's gonna be it."

"No." Pilar's hands went still.

"In a way, it always will be. I mean, that's where we're from, right? It's a part of us; it's who we are. But I don't think it's where we're meant to stay."

"I couldn't live there." Pilar shook her head. "Not in the shadow of that military base, remembering what they did to you."

"Yeah, but they're still our people there."

Her hands resumed their idle stroking. "And some will stay and some will leave. Some might even want to come to Huatulco."

Loup's eyes brightened. "You think?"

"Maybe." Pilar twined a length of Loup's hair around her fingers. "Maybe we could get funding for a nice little church dedicated to Santa Olivia."

"For Father Ramon?"

"Sure." She smiled. "And Sister Martha, and Anna...I mean, I don't know how all that works or if it's even possible. And, um, there's the fact that he doesn't exactly believe in God and was never actually ordained."

"Or celibate."

"That, too," Pilar allowed. "But they're awfully good people who worked harder than humanly possible to keep the world together when it fell apart. Who knows?" She shrugged. "I'm just thinking out loud."

Loup smiled wryly. "They'll never leave Outpost while there's work to be done there."

"So we help them do the work." She leaned over to plant a lingering, upside-down kiss on Loup's lips. "Right?"

"Right."

FIFTY-ONE

L oup hugged Miguel fiercely. "Just try to stay out of trouble, will you?"

He huffed, the air leaving his lungs. "Jesus! Lighten up, freakshow!"

"Oh, for fuck's sake! I'm serious."

"Yeah, whatever." He squeezed her briefly, then pushed her away. "Ecchevarria...take care of her, will you?"

Pilar nodded. "You bet I will."

"That's my girl." Miguel kissed her cheek. "Hey, have you still got that sexy little Hellfire maid costume Loup wore for the big rescue mission?"

"Um...yeah. Why?"

He grinned. "No reason. I just like to think about it from time to time."

They watched him saunter away, suitcase in hand. Pilar shook her head. "Miguel fucking Garza, huh?"

"Yep."

"I get it, though. Now." She glanced at Loup. "He was really good to me while you were gone. In that totally grouchy, pervy, big-brother way. Whenever I was really down, he'd find a way to bully me out of it."

"That's Mig." Loup's Dataphone rang. "Whoops! It's Abernathy. I've got to take this." She answered. "Hi, it's Loup. What's the news?" She listened. "That's great. Sure, I can be ready by two. I'll be waiting at the entrance."

"They're gonna let you see Johnson?" Pilar said when Loup ended the call.

"Yeah, this afternoon."

She shivered. "I understand, baby, I do, but the idea of you going back to that place gives me the creeps."

"It'll be okay." Loup hugged her. "I promise."

"I believe you." Pilar sighed. "I just don't much feel like letting you out of my sight. But that's okay, I'll start working on our travel arrangements. Once this is over, we want to get to Santa Olivia as soon as possible, right?"

"Don't you?"

"Yeah. But we can't just *go* yet. We have to apply for a cordon visa." She smiled ruefully. "They're still monitoring access in the interest of national security. Senator Ballantine's office thinks they can expedite the process for us."

"Thanks, Pilar."

"You bet, baby."

Tom Abernathy pulled up at two o'clock sharp and drove Loup to the detention center. She pestered him for news about the GMO detainees.

"It's good," he assured her. "We're in the process of working out the terms of the general amnesty I mentioned. As soon as that's finalized, most of them will be released."

"What about Johnson?"

He shook his head. "He'll do time and so will his brother, even though he's not a GMO. They've confessed to aiding in your escape. There's no getting around it. But since you weren't classified as an enemy combatant, I'm pretty sure I can swing a minimum sentence for them."

"How long?"

"Two years."

Loup was silent.

"It could be a lot worse." Abernathy glanced at her. "And now that the Human Rights Amendment has been repealed, once this is sorted out, I ought to be able to get him transferred to a much better facility. No more solitary confinement and MREs. Gym and library privileges, rec time." He smiled. "I hear there are a couple of facilities where you can get a good basketball game going. That would be something to see, hmm?"

She smiled reluctantly. "Yeah."

Inside the detention center, she was issued a security pass. Abernathy escorted her to the familiar interview room. It felt strange to sit on the opposite side of the table. A few minutes later, a guard brought in John Johnson. He was clad in an orange jumpsuit, his hands manacled in front of him.

Loup rose. "Hi."

"Loup Garron." Johnson met her eyes and smiled. "Can I shake her hand?" he asked his guard.

The guard shrugged. "Go ahead."

They shook awkwardly, the chain jingling between them.

"So." He sat with a precise economy of movement. "You did it."

"Not alone."

"No," he agreed. "Not alone."

She pointed at the handcuffs. "I'm sorry about this."

"Don't be." His green eyes were unblinking. "When I agreed to trade places with Ron, I knew what I was doing. When I stepped into that ring to face your brother, I knew the risks. I thought I could control the situation. I was wrong. Your brother was a good fighter—better than I expected."

"Tommy spent his whole life training to be a good boxer."

"I know," Johnson acknowledged. "And I underestimated him badly. If he'd been a GMO, he'd have taken me out in the first round. As a result, I was careless. I hit him too hard." He was silent a moment. "We talked about this before we fought, you and I. I know you understand that it was a terrible accident. I never meant for it to happen."

"Yeah, I know," Loup said softly. "I do."

He shook his head. "And yet...I knew the risks." He shifted his hands, the chain rattling. "Ron and I, we consider ourselves guilty of manslaughter. It doesn't matter that the sentence we serve is for a different crime. The punishment fits."

"You freed me," Loup reminded him. "And Pilar."

"Yeah." John Johnson smiled crookedly. "I thought that might be enough to grant me absolution in my own heart. It wasn't."

She gestured at his manacles. "Will this?"

He considered it. "In sofar as anything can, I believe so. That's why I asked you to tell the truth. And that's why I'm asking you to let it go, Loup. You don't bear any guilt in this matter. It was my choice."

"Okay." Loup cocked her head. "The affidavits...that started with the GMOs, didn't it?"

Johnson grinned. "Yeah. Pretty good, huh?"

"Why now?"

He shrugged. "Why not sooner, you mean? It wouldn't have been effective. And we had our own interests to look out for. Things had to reach a critical mass, a tipping point, before a majority of enlisted men grew brave enough to join us." He pointed at her. "Which you provided."

"Me?"

His laughter rumbled deep in his throat. It was a sound that made his guard reach reflexively for the butt of his gun, though it didn't bother Loup in the slightest. "You gave us a good face to present to the world." He flexed his hands in their steel cuffs. Corded muscle and sinew in his forearms bunched and shifted. "We *look* dangerous. You don't."

She smiled. "You know better, though."

Johnson's eyes gleamed. "At least I lasted eleven rounds. Maybe I'll have a chance to train while I'm in the brig. We could have a rematch."

Loup shook her head, not without regret. "If you'd trained half as hard as I had for that match, I'm pretty sure I wouldn't have stood a chance. And I'm *very* sure that Pilar would lock me in a cellar before she'd let me try it again."

"It would be fun, though."

"Yeah." She grinned. "It would."

"So." He cleared his throat. "Have I set your mind at ease? Can you walk out of here and enjoy your freedom without any hint of reservation? Because I'd like that. Trust me, the time will pass a lot quicker knowing it was all worthwhile."

"I'll try," Loup said honestly. She laid her hands over his. "Thank you."

John Johnson squeezed her hands. "You take care."

It was the same thing he'd said before.

Her eyes burned. "You too."

She was quiet and thoughtful as Abernathy escorted her to the car. He drove back toward the hotel, glancing at her periodically.

"How can you bear him so little resentment?" he asked at length.

"Huh?"

"For your brother's death."

Loup rested her head against the window of the car door. "You heard him. He feels awful about it. I could tell that from the beginning. How would resenting him help? It wouldn't bring Tommy back."

"It's human, that's all," he said.

She gave him a look. "Yeah, well..."

"I know, I know!" Abernathy drove. "I wonder...being unable to fear, does it make it easier to forgive, do you suppose?"

"I don't know."

"I suspect we have a lot to learn about ourselves from your kind," he mused. "The big differences, they're not the obvious ones, are they?"

"I guess not."

He gave her a fleeting smile. "You definitely make life more interesting."

At the hotel, Pilar was waiting by the front entrance, worried and pale. Her face lit up when she saw the car pull into the entry. Loup felt her heart grow lighter at the sight of her.

"Hey, baby!" Pilar greeted her with a hug and an exuberant kiss. "Sorry, I got nervous waiting. Everything okay?"

"Yeah. Yeah, it is." Loup turned. "You remember Tom Abernathy? You met him at the press conference."

"Hi." She gave him one of her dazzling smiles and shook his hand. "Thanks again so much for everything."

"It was my pleasure." He turned to Loup. "Loup? Now that everything's finished, I don't know when we'll see each other again."

She kissed his cheek. "You're one of the good guys, Abernathy. Don't ever think you aren't."

There was a shadow of sorrow in his smile. "Thanks."

They watched him drive away.

"You didn't tell me your lawyer was a one in a hundred," Pilar commented.

"Looks that way, huh?"

"Definitely." Pilar gave her another quick kiss. "So how do you feel about going home in two days?"

"Two days? Seriously?"

"Yep."

Loup took a deep breath. "Good. Really good."

FIFTY-TWO

Two days later, they flew into San Antonio, which had the closest functioning airport to the cordon.

"Are we picking up the rental car here?" Loup asked, glancing at the signage.

"Nope." Pilar looked smug. "And it's not a car."

"Huh?"

"I rented us a cargo van." She flashed her credit card. "We're gonna pick it up tomorrow morning and fill it with all kinds of excellent presents. I was thinking TVs and computers and stuff since everything there is like forty years old. We may not be millionaires yet, but you sold a *lot* of T-shirts, baby. Even five percent adds up."

Loup smiled happily. "That's an awesome idea!"

"It is, isn't it?"

They spent the night at an elegant hotel overlooking the placid San Antonio river. Their room even had a balcony where they could sit and sip champagne, watching people stroll along the Riverwalk.

"How far of a drive is it?" Loup asked.

"About three hours."

"It's so weird, isn't it?" She gestured at the people below. "To be so close and in a totally different world."

"Yeah, it is." Pilar shrugged. "Out of sight, out of mind, I guess. Who are you looking forward to seeing the most?"

"Mack," Loup said promptly. "But don't tell T.Y. I said that. You?"

"I can't decide." She made a face. "I know who I'm looking forward to seeing the least."

"Rory Salamanca?"

"Yeah." Pilar contemplated the bubbles in her champagne flute. "I kind of have to, though. I owe him that much."

"Yes, you do."

Pilar tossed a grape from the complimentary fruit basket at her. "You don't have to be so goddamn fair-minded, Supergirl."

Loup plucked the grape out of midair. "Can't help it."

"Do you know what you're going to wear yet?"

She blinked. "I hadn't thought about it. Why?"

"Oh, c'mon! On the one hand, we want to look good, right? I mean, this is our big homecoming." Pilar ticked off the reason on one finger, then ticked another. "On the other, we don't want to look *too* sophisticated and make them think we've gotten all snooty. Like you said, they're our people, right?"

Loup tossed the grape back at her. "You're such a girlie girl."

"True." Pilar caught the grape deftly. "And yet I am also *muy macha, sí?*"

"*Sí,*" Loup agreed.

"So can I pick out your clothes?"

"*Sí.*"

In the morning, Pilar fussed over their luggage, finally settling on a yellow sundress with matching stacked wedge-heeled espadrilles for her, and jeans and a white camisole with eyelet-lace trim for Loup.

Loup eyed Pilar's sandals. "Those are new. Looks like I'm driving, huh?"

"I can drive in these! Um...maybe." She examined her reflection in the full-length mirror. "You like them, don't you?"

"Mm-hmm." Loup brushed Pilar's hair away and kissed the nape of her neck. "Very sexy. It's okay, I'll drive."

She smiled. "Thanks, baby."

After checking out of the hotel, they took a cab to the rental facility and picked up the cargo van. The clerk was friendly and cheerful.

"You gals moving?" he asked. "Doing all the work yourself, well, that's mighty ambitious of you!"

"Not exactly," Pilar said absently, filling out paperwork. "We're visiting one of the Outposts and bringing them a bunch of stuff."

"Oh, honey!" he said in a sympathetic tone. "Haven't you heard? You can't just go, you need a permit. There's a waiting list."

"We have permits," Loup said.

The clerk glanced at her, then did a double take. "You're the one from the TV! The GMO!"

"Yep."

He beamed at her. "Well, God bless you, sweetheart, of course you've got a permit!" He lowered his voice to a conspiratorial level. "What do you say I throw in insurance for free?"

"Thanks! That's really nice of you."

"Not a problem at all."

They got the same reception at a big electronics store on the outskirts of the city, where salesclerks fell all over themselves to load up the cargo van with televisions, stereos, computers, Dataphones, video game players, and anything else they could think of.

"Surge protectors," advised a skinny young clerk who turned bright red every time Pilar spoke to him. "Lots and lots of surge protectors."

"Perfect."

The bill came to over forty thousand dollars. Loup whistled softly. "*How* many T-shirts?"

"Trust me, a lot."

At last the van was full. They stopped at a convenience store to pick up sandwiches for the road and hit the highway.

"Hey, Pilar? How are we gonna decide who gets all this stuff?"

She shrugged. "We'll let Father Ramon figure it out. He'll know who really needs it, like the clinic and the school. Maybe they can hold a drawing for some of it, give everyone a ticket."

"That's a good idea."

"Thanks." Pilar smiled wryly. "I guess this isn't exactly the most practical thing in the world. I mean, they won't even be able to use the phones or get the computers online until the civilian wireless tower is installed, which could take months, and no one really *needs* video games, but...I dunno. Supposedly, they're getting stuff they *really* need, like medical supplies, from the relief agencies. I just wanted to do something special."

"They're gonna love it," Loup said sincerely. "Who wouldn't?"

"Good point."

The closer they got to the cordon, the more desolate and deserted the landscape appeared. There was almost no traffic, only the occasional military vehicle. After a solid two hours of driving, they saw the gray concrete wall that marked the northern boundary of the cordon.

"There it is," Pilar said unnecessarily.

"Yeah." Loup eyed it with distaste. "Think they'll take it down someday?"

"I hope so."

At the checkpoint, a fresh-faced young soldier examined their permits. "Holy shit!" He looked up, startled. "Excuse me, ma'am. It's just…"

Loup smiled. "Yeah, I know."

He grinned. "Hometown heroes, huh? Very cool."

"Thanks. Are we okay to go?"

"Ahh…I have to inspect the contents of the van." The checkpoint soldier went around to the rear of the van and opened the doors. He came back looking apologetic. "We're gonna have to search the packages."

"Seriously? All of them?"

"'Fraid so." He pointed. "Pull over there. You can wait in the gate-house," he added. "It's air-conditioned."

"They're just presents for everyone back home." Pilar gave him a sweet, pleading look. "We bought everything this morning. I can show you the receipts!"

"Sorry, ma'am." The soldier shook his head, smiling. "I can't bend the rules, even for a pretty girl like you."

She sighed. "It was worth a try."

They waited in the gatehouse while a team of guards unloaded the entire van and began opening package after package, inspecting the contents. Their checkpoint soldier, who introduced himself as Dave, brought them cold Coca-Colas and kept them company.

"So what's it like?" he asked Loup.

"What's what like?"

"Being you?"

"I don't know," she said. "I've never been anyone else."

Dave planted his elbow on the counter and thrust out one hand. "Arm wrestle me?"

"Why?"

"I just want to see what it's like!"

"Will you let us go if she does?" Pilar inquired.

He shook his head again. "Can't do that, ma'am. But..." He rummaged under the counter and came up with a roll of packing tape. "I can ask the boys to make sure your presents are boxed up good as new!"

"Good enough." Loup put her elbow on the counter.

Dave hesitated. "You want a box to stand on or something? You don't have a lot of leverage."

"No."

"Okay." He clasped her hand and nodded at Pilar. "Will you give us the count, ma'am?"

"One, two, three, *go*. And quit calling me 'ma'am.'"

"Just a courtesy, ma'am!" Dave grunted, straining with all his might, the veins at his temples popping.

Loup eyed him mildly. "Satisfied?"

"Yes, ma'am!"

"Okay, then." She forced his arm gently and inexorably down to the counter. "There you go. That's what it's like."

"Wow!" Dave shook out his hand, grinning. He pushed up one sleeve. "Will you sign my arm?"

"Are you serious?"

"Yeah!"

"Sure, fine." She handed him the packing tape. "Can you ask them to work quick? We're pretty excited about going home."

An hour later, they were back on the road.

"Sorry, baby," Pilar apologized. "I should have thought of that. I read the regulations, but I got carried away and forgot."

"That's okay." Loup concentrated on the endless, barren road. "Anyway, they were nice about it."

"Yeah." Pilar was quiet a moment. "Does it still bother you? Everyone wanting a demonstration? Because it's gonna keep happening more than ever now."

"I know." She slowed and pointed to a utilities truck parked beside a distant power line pylon. "Hey, look!"

"Yeah." Pilar nodded. "They promised to bring all the Outposts back on the grid by the end of the year."

"No more generators?"

"Nope." She shook her head. "No more generators, no more paying the Salamancas' blackmail prices for kerosene."

Loup drove for a while. "I'm okay with it."

"Electricity?"

"No!" She gave Pilar an affectionate look. "The demonstrations. I mean, speaking of prices, that's a pretty small price to pay, don't you think? For everything good that's happened?"

"Yep." Pilar leaned over to plant a resounding kiss on her cheek. "I do."

"Me too."

Less than an hour later, they pulled into Outpost No. 12.

Santa Olivia.

"It looks so *small*!" Pilar whispered as they drove past the reservoir and the golf course where no civilian had ever played in their lifetimes.

"Yeah." Loup paused at an intersection of dusty streets. "Left here, right? Or is it the next block?"

"I don't know. I never saw it from a car. Everything looks different somehow." Pilar reached for her Dataphone. "Let me check the GPS...oh, that's not gonna work, is it?"

"No."

"I think it's the next block."

After two wrong turns, it all came back to them.

"Ohhh! There it is!"

"Yeah." Loup swallowed at the sight of the Spanish mission–style church, the adobe walls and arched windows, the wrought-iron gates. "Wow."

They parked the van in the street and walked up to the church.

There was a car in the driveway, an ancient maroon Mercedes that had belonged to Father Gabriel, who had been Santa Olivia's last ordained priest and committed suicide before either of them was born. The hood was propped open and a lanky figure in jeans and a faded black T-shirt was bent over the engine.

"Hey, Mack," Loup said softly.

"Hey, *loup-garou*," came the absent reply. Mack froze, then straightened abruptly, banging his head on the raised hood. "*Loup?*"

Her eyes burned at the sight of his familiar face, the faint white scar creasing one cheek. "Hi."

He rubbed his head. *"Pilar?"*

She smiled. "Hi, Mackie. Aren't you gonna give us hugs?"

"Hell, yes!" Mack hugged them both, careful not to touch them with his grease-stained hands. "We saw the news. Everyone was hoping you'd come."

"You saw the *news*? Here?"

"Yeah." He grinned, gray eyes bright. "There was a film crew here a few weeks ago. Jaime got to talking with one of their tech guys. The guy hooked him up with a working satellite dish and a set of coordinates."

"No shit," Loup marveled.

"Yeah." Mack nodded. "We set it up in the old legion hall so anyone can go watch anytime they want. Rosa Salamanca's pissed as hell that she can't find a way to make a profit off it."

"I bet," Pilar said. "Wait till you see what we brought."

They dragged him over to the cargo van and threw open the doors. Mack stared in awe. "Jesus! What'd you do, rob a bank?"

"Nope," Loup said. "Got sort of famous and sold a lot of T-shirts."

"That thing about the band? No one could quite figure out what that was all about."

"It's kind of a weird story," she agreed.

Mack pulled a rag out of his back pocket and wiped the grease from his hands. "Can't wait to hear it. Come on inside—"

"Umm, hang on." Pilar took a deep breath. "There's something I have to do. And I kinda want to get it over with first. Otherwise I'm just gonna be dreading it."

"Rory?" Mack guessed.

"Uh-huh."

"He's probably at the Gin Blossom." He tucked the rag back in his pocket. "Why don't you give me the keys to your van? I'll pull it in the drive where it will be safer, then start spreading the good news." He grinned again. "All the Santitos are gonna make money on this. The fucking Salamancas have been taking odds on whether or not you'd make it here for Santa Olivia's Feast Day. We all bet you would."

Loup blinked. "Santa Olivia's Day?"

"Your birthday? The anniversary of the big fight?" Mack regarded her. "It's Friday. You forgot?"

She laughed. "Yeah, I did."

"Jesus, Loup!"

"I've had a lot going on, okay?"

"Yeah." His voice softened. He touched her cheek. "It's good to see you."

"You too."

Mack nodded at Pilar. "Go do your penance and hurry back. Everyone's gonna be dying to see you."

"Okay."

FIFTY-THREE

Outside the rustic Gin Blossom where she'd worked as a bartender, Pilar hesitated, clutching the bottle of very expensive tequila she'd brought.

"You okay?" Loup asked.

"Feeling guilty, that's all."

"Are you sure you want me here for this?"

"Yeah." She nodded emphatically. "I'm ashamed of the way I used Rory. I'm *not* ashamed of being with you. I want that clear."

"Okay, then." Loup opened the door and ushered her in. "Let's get it over with."

The place was mostly empty and it took only a few seconds for their presence to register. Behind the bar, Joe, the manager and bartender, let out a loud whoop. He vaulted over the counter and crossed the room to grab Pilar in an embrace, lifting her off her feet.

"Hi, Joey," she said, a little breathless. "You remember Loup?"

"Fucking hell I do!" He grabbed her hand and shook it hard, grinning. "The goddamn vanishing boxing champion of Santa Olivia!"

A handful of regulars began to converge, then halted. From the back of the room, Rory Salamanca walked forward, a pool cue in his hand.

"So," he said in a neutral tone.

The bar got very, very quiet.

"Hi, Rory," Pilar said awkwardly. "I'm back in town visiting for a little while. I didn't want you to hear it from anyone else." She held out the bottle of tequila. "Look, you know how bad I feel. I brought a peace offering. It's your mom's favorite, the kind you can't even get in the States."

He regarded the tequila. "How'd you swing it?"

"This Mexican diplomat, Mr. Sandoval, gave it to Senator Ballantine, and I begged him...oh, just take the fucking bottle, will you?"

Rory took the bottle.

"Thanks." Pilar relaxed a little. "You, um...remember Loup?" She flushed when he gave her an incredulous look. "Okay, stupid question."

"No shit." He glanced at Loup. "Hi."

"Hi," Loup said, eyeing the pool cue in his hand.

He dropped it with a clatter. "I was worried sick when you disappeared, you know," he said to Pilar. "I might have been pissed as hell, but I *did* care about you."

She winced. "I'm sorry. I had to."

"Yeah, I know." Rory sighed and ran a hand through his dark hair. "I was stupid not to have seen it all along."

"No, you weren't."

"Yeah, I was." He smiled ruefully. "You had this...sparkle...that went out after we were together. And sometimes I acted like a jealous asshole because deep down, I knew that sparkle had never been for me. I just couldn't bring myself to believe it was for Tom Garron's kid sister. And how the fuck was I supposed to know she was some kind of secret superhero? So." He shrugged and hoisted the bottle. "Welcome home."

Pilar smiled with gratitude. "Thanks, Rory."

"Ah, fuck it." He raised his voice. "Drinks on the house!"

The bar resounded with cheers.

They only stayed for one drink, anxious to return to the church, but by the time they left the atmosphere was happy and convivial.

"Thanks again for being decent about this," Pilar said to Rory, kissing his cheek. "I really *am* sorry about everything."

"Yeah." He gave her a wry look. "You might want to avoid my mother. She thinks you're a filthy whoring abomination. And believe me, a bottle of tequila isn't gonna change her mind."

"You can't win 'em all," Loup said philosophically. "After the miraculous conversion of Sabine, Rosa Salamanca's a lot to ask for."

Pilar stifled a giggle.

It drew another reluctant smile from Rory. "Go on, get out of here. I know you've got people waiting for you."

They headed for the door.

"Hey, Pilar!" he called after her. "Thanks. You didn't have to do this. And, um...you look really good." This time, his smile was genuine. "Sparkly."

Once they were outside the bar, Pilar breathed a profound sigh of relief. "Thanks, baby." She squeezed Loup's hand. "I know that wasn't the first thing either of us wanted to do here, but I just didn't want it hanging over my head, you know?"

"I know." Loup returned her squeeze. "Feeling better?"

"Tons."

"Let's go see our people."

By the time they reached the church, there were four familiar figures playing a short-handed game of stickball in the street outside the gates.

"Hey!" Dondi shouted, pointing.

"Loup?" T.Y. swung wildly at a pitch, letting go of the broom handle as he spun around, looking for her.

She laughed. "You guys are playing *stickball*?"

"We were going crazy waiting!" He raced over and gave her an impetuous hug with only the slightest hint of flinch. "Jesus, it's good to see you!"

Loup hugged him back carefully and ruffled his brown curls. "I've missed you."

"Hey, baby doll," C.C. said to Pilar, grinning. "Couldn't stay away from me, huh?"

She smiled fondly at him. "You wish, loverboy."

"Holy crap!" Dondi eyed Pilar's stacked wedge heels. "Could those *be* any higher?"

"They're in style, okay?" She tugged him down to plant a kiss on his cheek. "When did you get so tall, little man?"

"Umm...way before you left, remember?"

In the background, Mack was gathering up stray tennis balls and the discarded broomstick. Loup caught his eye and smiled. He smiled back at her. "So where's everyone else?" she asked T.Y.

"Oh, hell!" He grinned. "It's like old times. Kotch and Jane are helping Anna in the kitchen, bitching about how the women always get stuck with the nurturing roles—"

"I *offered* to help cook!" Dondi said, aggrieved.

"He did," C.C. confirmed.

"—and Jaime couldn't wait. We unloaded the van and he's already got his hands on one of those fancy computers you brought," T.Y. finished.

"Diego and Maria? Are they okay?"

"Yeah, yeah!" He nodded vigorously. "Trying to find a babysitter, I think."

It was like old times, and it wasn't. All the Santitos were a year older, their lives following divergent paths within the narrow confines that Outpost allowed. They trouped through the wrought-iron gates, chattering, young adults returning to their childhood.

Inside the church, Loup halted.

"Whoa." She reached unthinking for Pilar's hand.

"Whoa," Pilar agreed.

The effigy of Santa Olivia sat in her niche; the child-saint in the pretty blue dress and white kerchief with her dark, unblinking gaze, her basket over one arm. Her basket overflowed with the handwritten petitions that had once been proscribed. Hundreds of votive candles flickered around her, and a sea of handmade paper flowers spilled over her feet. In her own niche, Our Lady of the Sorrows looked on with gentle approval.

"Did you guys do this?" Loup asked, bewildered.

"No, Loup." Mack's hands rested on her shoulders. "*You* did."

"I didn't—"

"Yeah, you did, baby." Pilar kissed her softly on the lips. "I told you, you have no idea what it was like here after the fight."

She felt dazed. "Guess not."

T.Y. tugged her arm. "C'mon!"

And almost everyone was there; Father Ramon in his cassock, his handsome face lined with age and his hair more silver than black; Sister Martha with her intent gaze and generous heart; Anna, still lovely and kind; tall, blond Katya, her imperious youth given way to a warmer maturity; sharp-tongued, quick-witted Jane; clever Jaime, tearing himself away from the new computer. Everyone hugged and wept and exclaimed all at once, and Diego and Maria arrived in the midst, baby in tow, to start the process all over again.

At last they sat down to eat, crowded around the long table. The food was simple, chicken in adobo sauce, rice and beans, but there was plenty of it. After the platters had been passed around, Sister Martha cleared her throat.

"All right," she said. "What in God's fucking name have the two of you been up to?" She gestured broadly, looking at a rare loss for words. "What did you *do* out there to turn the whole fucking world upside down?"

Loup and Pilar exchanged grins.

"You eat," Pilar said, pointing at Loup's heaped plate. "I'll talk. So it started with this guy, Magnus Lindberg, who wanted to hire Loup to be the world's only GMO bodyguard..."

She began telling the story, charting its unlikely twists and turns from Huatulco to Aberdeen, London and Sicily and Switzerland, training, the first Kate concert, Vincenzo Picco, the wedding, the birthday party, the fire and the pirate terrorist.

"You shot a guy?" T.Y. interrupted in disbelief. "You? With a gun?" He pointed his finger. "Bang, bang?"

"Why does everyone have so much trouble with that part?" Pilar asked with some asperity.

"Because the Pilar Ecchevarria we knew would have shrieked and hidden behind the nearest available male," Jane said calmly. "Preferably an attractive, wealthy one." Jaime elbowed her discreetly in the ribs, and she raised her eyebrows at him. "What? She would have."

"Maybe we didn't know her as well as we thought," Mack murmured.

"No, I guess it's pretty true," Pilar admitted. "But people do change, you know. Anyway, we went back to Huatulco to spend time with Loup's family…"

She continued the story—touring with Kate through Australia and Japan, the stage rushing, the rising Mystery Girl phenomenon. The hearings, the disappearance and abduction of Miguel Garza and the decision to rescue him.

"*That's* why you came back, Loup?" Jaime asked. "To rescue Miguel fucking Garza?"

"Pretty much," she agreed. "Then other stuff happened."

"Jesus! He's a cretinous thug who ran roughshod over this town for years!"

"He's really not that bad once you get to know him," Pilar offered. "I mean, he's crude and he's a bully, but he's sort of decent underneath it all. Smarter than you'd think, too. Well, except for getting himself in trouble in Vegas. That was dumb."

"I take it you succeeded in rescuing him?" Father Ramon interjected. "We've seen footage of his testimony, but there was nothing about an abduction."

"Oh, yeah!" She smiled and described the Vegas caper.

"Excuse me," Anna inquired delicately. "Are you…are you having fun with us?"

Loup blinked, a forkful of rice and beans in hand. "No, of course not."

"It's just—"

"Look, I know it sounds pretty crazy, especially when you string it all together. But we're not making any of this up, honest." She ate her forkful of food. "Pilar, you haven't even eaten. Go ahead and I'll tell my part."

"Okay."

Loup finished her end of the story—the cross-country drive, her detention. The Outpost hearings and the happy result. "After that, I guess you know what happened. They overturned the Human Rights Amendment and I was released."

"Yeah," C.C. said in awe. "We saw it on the *news*. We saw *you* on the *news*. Real live news!"

Sister Martha dabbed her lips with a napkin. "Which is a true goddamn miracle." She glanced around the table. "I'm not joking, children. As much as I've railed against God in my lifetime, I can recognize a goddamn fucking miracle when I see one."

"Amen," Maria whispered with heartfelt fervor, and blushed.

Father Ramon smiled. "Amen, indeed."

FIFTY-FOUR

They spent the night in the church's empty girls' dormitory room. Pilar watched Loup push a pair of cots together, making them up with threadbare sheets Anna had given them.

"Jesus, this is weird," she said. "Do you remember—?"

Loup sat on the improvised double bed. "That first night we were alone here?"

"Uh-huh." Pilar straddled her lap.

"Mm-hmm." She slid her arms around Pilar's waist. "It was the first time we got to spend the whole night together."

Pilar kissed her at length, exploring her mouth in a delicious, leisurely fashion. "We stayed up all night fooling around."

"Until dawn," Loup whispered. "That's when you told me you loved me for the first time, and I told you I loved you too."

"Want to relive history?"

She laughed. "Are you kidding?"

When the pale gray dawn broke through the narrow, arched windows, they were tired and languorous, replete with pleasure and happiness. Loup ran a lock of Pilar's hair through her fingers, watching the early sunlight pick out the glinting blond streaks in its brown, silken fineness.

"I love you," she said softly. "I wanted to say it first this time. I love you an awful, awful lot."

Pilar sighed. "Oh, God! Me too."

Later in the morning, they met with Father Ramon and Sister Martha to talk seriously about topics overlooked in the joy of the previous day's reunion—the disposition of the gifts they'd brought, Santa Olivia's most pressing needs, and their desire to set up a scholarship fund for the Santitos and other deserving Outposters.

It was the latter that engaged them the most.

"Are you quite serious?" Father Ramon asked, dumbstruck.

"Well, yeah," Loup said. "Why?"

"It's just..." He looked apologetic. "You never struck me as much of a scholar, Loup. Neither of you did."

"No, I know." She smiled sidelong at Pilar. "Although it turns out Pilar's really good at research and all kinds of stuff."

Pilar smiled happily. "Thanks, baby!"

"Well, you are. And people should be able to do what they're good at, right?" Loup shrugged. "In Huatulco, I got to run outside for the first time in my life, as far and as fast as I wanted. It felt so good, like setting a part of me free. I used to think about it a lot in my jail cell. I think for someone like Jaime or Jane not being able to use their minds, not being able to study and learn, must be like a kind of prison."

"And it might make Jane less crabby," Pilar added. "Which would be a good thing, right?"

Sister Martha shook her head. "Children, you are a wonderment."

They learned it would be a while before they could implement the plan. The Red Cross had set up a temporary medical clinic, relieving Sister Martha of some of her burden, but for now she was busy coordinating with the government to provide a census and establish birth records for everyone born in Outpost after the occupation in order to complete the paperwork that would render them American citizens.

"Guess they cut a few corners for us, huh?" Loup said.

"Sweetheart, I don't think anyone's going to begrudge you," Sister Martha said wryly.

Father Ramon made his recommendations for the disposition of their gifts—the majority of the computers for the school, a few items for the church, phones for the Santitos, a big flat-screen television for the improvised theater of the legion hall—and agreed that a free raffle for the rest was a fine idea.

"Everyone gets a ticket," he said in approval. "It will be the most democratic thing to happen here in decades."

"Plus, it will drive Rosa Salamanca crazy to see stuff given away for free with no way for her to make a profit on it," Pilar said with a certain glee. "The greedy old witch."

He smiled. "It will at that. When—?"

"Santa Olivia's Feast Day," Sister Martha interrupted him. "When else? We'll set up a table in the square where everyone can claim a ticket and use the census list to keep track."

"Perfect."

With two days yet to go before Santa Olivia's Day, with the help of the Santitos, they made flyers announcing the free raffle and posted them around town, finding in the process that the town had changed. There were barely half as many soldiers around, and the boxing ring in the center of the town square was gone.

"Wow." Loup stared. "When did that happen?"

"A while ago," T.Y. said. "General Argyle was replaced about a month after you disappeared. As soon as the new guy took over, they tore down the ring."

"No more fights?"

"Nah." He shook his head. "Yours was the last." He brightened. "Hey, you know what they *are* gonna have this year? Fireworks! The ban's been repealed."

"Really?"

"Yeah." T.Y. made a face. "Though I suppose that's no big deal to you, huh? You and Pilar probably saw fireworks tons of times, traveling all over the world and everything."

"Nope." Loup smiled at him. "Not a one."

"Only in the movies," Pilar agreed. She nudged Loup with her hip. "Though I can think of something that's a lot *like* fireworks."

"Mm-hmm."

T.Y. covered his ears. "I don't need to hear this!"

They went past the gym where Loup had spent so many hours sparring in secret with Miguel Garza. The UNIQUE FITNESS sign had faded further and dusty blinds covered the windows, untouched for almost a year. Loup touched the windows lightly with her fingertips.

"Thinking about your coach?" Pilar asked sympathetically.

"Yeah."

"We'll look him up one day. Florida, right?"

"Yeah." She gave her a grateful look. "Thanks, Pilar."

It made them pensive. On the eve of Santa Olivia's Day, they visited the extensive, rambling graveyard behind the church filled with largely unmarked graves. Even knowing what they were looking for, it was hard to find. Mack, who tended the grounds, consulted the charts and showed Pilar the plots where her parents were buried, and Loup the plot where her mother rested.

"We bought her a comb for her hair not long before she died," she murmured, remembering. "Tommy and I. The first time he won money betting on a fight because I told him what would happen. I wanted her to have something pretty. She was buried wearing it."

Mack touched her shoulder. "Want me to show you Tommy's?"

"No." Loup shook her head. "That one, I can find."

A pair of cracked and faded boxing gloves still dangled from the makeshift cross. Loup sat cross-legged on the hard earth, remembering the big brother who'd always taken care of her and taught her to be careful. Tommy, with his sunny disposition and his ready smile; tall, strapping, blond Tommy, looking nothing like her, but her brother nonetheless. Tommy, who was meant to be Outpost's hero.

"Hey, baby."

"Hey." She looked up at Pilar, seeing the marks of tears on her cheeks. "You okay?"

"Yeah." Pilar sank down beside her. "You?"

"Mostly."

They sat side by side.

"He'd have been so goddamn proud of you he'd burst," Pilar said after a while.

"You think?"

"I know." She stood and held out her hand. "C'mon, Santa Olivia. We've given the dead their due. Time to celebrate the living."

"Okay."

Santa Olivia's Feast Day dawned hard and bright and clear. In the empty girls' dormitory on their makeshift bed, Pilar smiled at Loup, her head pillowed, her face still soft and sweet and lovely with sleep.

"Happy birthday, baby. No shadows today?"

"No shadows," Loup promised.

The Santitos assembled, yawning, to help carry the effigy of Santa Olivia to the town square, where she was enshrined on a pedestal. There was already a handful of people around to cheer, waiting to garland the effigy with fresh strands of bright paper flowers. Many of them smiled and touched Loup's hands, thanking her. It made her feel warm inside.

Banners of paper lacework adorned the square, and there were strings of colored lights that would be turned on when the sun went down. As the sun rose higher in the sky, the first band of the day began to set up onstage. More and more Outposters trickled into the square, staking out picnic spots before lining up at the table where Sister Martha sat with numbered tickets they'd printed, checking names off her census roll.

It was a good day.

An expectant buzz hung over the festivities. There was music, and dancing in the space where the boxing ring had once stood. People picnicked and gossiped and compared ticket numbers, speculating on the nature of the prizes. Children laughed and shrieked and raced around the square like crazy, pelting one another with hollow eggs filled with confetti.

It wasn't freedom—not quite. No one from Outpost but Loup and Pilar had been issued a passport, and there were still MPs patrolling the event. But the taste of freedom was in the air, and even the MPs were smiling.

By two o'clock, the last raffle ticket had been given away.

At three o'clock, the Santitos went to fetch the reloaded van and bring the prizes to the square. The most recent band vacated the stage. The Santitos unloaded the van, stacking valuable prizes on the stage. An awed murmur ran through the crowd.

"You're fucking crazy," T.Y. grunted, hauling a heavy box. "Remind me why'd you do this again?"

"I dunno." Pilar smiled. "Because we could?"

He set down his box. "Some lousy excuse for a gold digger you turned out to be."

She laughed.

"No kidding." Jane, rearranging the prizes into a more aesthetically pleasing pile, glanced up with a tentative expression. "Are you guys serious about this scholarship thing?"

"Yeah, of course." Loup set down a boxed television. "You and Jaime are first in line. Why?"

Jane scowled. "I don't know if you noticed, but I haven't exactly been *nice* to you."

"Yeah, but you're still our people," Loup said. "And you worked really hard at the dispensary with Sister Martha. You'd have taken over from her one day if all this hadn't happened, wouldn't you? Taken care of people?"

She nodded reluctantly. "Someone has to."

"That's nice enough for me." Loup headed back toward the cargo van for another load.

"Does that ever get on your nerves?" Jane asked Pilar in an acerbic tone. "That too-good-to-be-true shtick?"

Pilar smiled dreamily, watching Loup wrestle a stereo box out of the van. "No."

"God, you really *do* have it bad!"

"Hmm?"

Jane shook her head. "Never mind. And, um...thanks."

At four o'clock, they held the raffle. Father Ramon took the stage, waiting for the crowd to fall quiet. He beckoned for Loup and Pilar to join him. Once the crowd was still and listening, he spoke.

"Providence," he said in his deep, resonant voice. "Grace. These are words I feared I might never speak in earnest in my lifetime. I speak them here today." He gestured at the pile of prizes. "These gifts, these things, these material items...they are merely symbols. But what they symbolize is a gift of providence and grace."

"He's good," Pilar whispered in Loup's ear. "Ms. Coxcombe would approve."

She nodded, shivering at her warm breath. "Yep."

Father Ramon gave them a stern look. "The bearers of these gifts are, I grant, unlikely messengers. But they are messengers nonetheless, and the message they bear is one of hope." He spread his arms, settling them on Loup and Pilar's shoulders. "Let us rejoice that they are with us today! Let the raffle begin!"

Everyone cheered.

C.C. came onstage, holding up a fishbowl filled with ticket stubs. Loup grabbed an item at random. Pilar thrust her hand into the glass bowl and pulled out a stub.

"Three hundred ninety-two!" she called.

A young woman stumbled forward, waving her ticket, propelled by the people with her. "I think it's me!"

Pilar checked her ticket. "Yep, sure enough."

Loup handed her a portable stereo. "It might be a couple months before you're able to get music for this, but trust me, it's pretty cool."

The raffle went on for almost an hour, the pile of prizes dwindling. People laughed and exclaimed in delight or envy, examining their prizes, making trades and generous promises to share. Under the influence of Father Ramon's speech, the lucky winners were gracious and the unlucky folks who would go home empty-handed bore their loss good-naturedly.

The only thing close to a sour note came when Rosa Salamanca's ticket was drawn. She stood glowering, torn between greed and disgust, while her grown sons pleaded with her to claim the prize. At last greed won out and she stalked across the square to present her ticket.

Pilar gave her one of her sweetest smiles. "Congratulations, Ms. Salamanca."

"I'm sure you'll enjoy this." Loup handed her a video game player with a straight face. Rosa bit her tongue with a visible effort and contented herself with giving them both the evil eye before stalking back to her delighted sons.

And then the last prize was given. There was a disorganized, heartfelt cheer, followed by a lull as people began ferrying their bounty home.

"Now *that* was fun," Pilar commented.

Loup smiled. "Yeah. Totally worth it."

They merged back into the thinning crowd, mingling with the Santitos. Loup spied an opening at the torta vendor and went to buy a couple of sandwiches, having gotten hungry during the course of the raffle.

"My treat," Mack said, intercepting her. "Pulled pork?"

"Yeah, but you don't have to—"

He gave her a hard look. "Let a guy keep his dignity, okay?"

"Okay. Thanks, Mack."

They found an opening on one of the low walls surrounding the square and sat eating pulled-pork tortas and drinking cold beer. Some yards away, Pilar was flirting with Joe the bartender, with whom she'd had a brief relationship and an amicable breakup. She glanced around in search of Loup, and spotting her, smiled and blew her a kiss. Loup smiled back at her and blew her a kiss in return.

"You and Pilar," Mack mused. "Who ever thought that would last?"

"I did."

"You're happy." It wasn't a question.

Loup nodded.

"I'm glad."

"I know," she said softly. "You were the only one who didn't laugh or make fun when we were first together."

"Yeah." Mack smiled wryly, rubbing the knee of his faded jeans. "I wish things had been different between us. I do. And I could have wrung her neck for breaking your heart. But the way she lights up whenever she looks at you..." He shook his head. "Like a little kid who's just heard she can have cake *and* ice cream. You deserve it."

Loup didn't reply.

"And you..." He clinked his beer bottle against hers. "I didn't realize I'd never seen you truly happy before you hooked up with Pilar. How can I not be happy for you?"

She clinked him back. "Thanks."

"Yeah." Mack regarded her. "You're not staying, are you?"

"No." Loup shook her head. "I'm not sure where we'll go. Things might be a little crazy for a while. There's the band, and this movie deal thing. But, um, we talked about buying a place in Huatulco, where my cousins live. You could come. There are jobs. Construction?"

"Nah." Mack surveyed the crowd. "I belong here. Thanks, though."

"Sure."

"What are they like?" he asked, curious. "Your cousins?"

"Kind of wild." Loup smiled. "Rambunctious, you know? Isn't that what Sister Martha called C.C. when he got out of control?"

"Uh-huh."

"But in a good way," she added. "They like to have fun, like to make the tourists point and stare. They're the only ones of us to grow up free, truly free. And my aunts, they're all so sweet and nice. Tía Marcela, especially. You'd like them."

Mack slung an arm over her shoulders and gave her a hug. "I'm sure I would."

"Come visit?"

"Someday, maybe."

Day turned to dusk over Outpost; Santa Olivia, Santa Olvidada, forgotten and remembered. Blue dusk settled. People came back to the square, prizes stowed, the youngest babies bedded for the night. The generators hummed and the colored lights came to life. A new band took to the stage. Dusk gave way to velvety darkness.

Loup found Pilar.

"Hey, baby!" Pilar fished in her purse and pulled out a slim case. "Give me your necklace."

She touched it. "Why?"

"Because I had a replacement made while you were in jail." Pilar unfastened it deftly and settled a new gold chain around Loup's throat. "I know, I know. That one was special. But this one is, too. And this time, the diamonds are real. Happy birthday, okay?"

Her throat tightened. "Pilar—"

"Oh, hush." Pilar kissed her.

Fireworks went off.

The army had a team of demolitions experts supervising the process. There was a *whoomph* of sound, and then a bone-rattling *boom*. A chrysanthemum of sparkling golden fire blossomed in the sky above them.

"Whoa!" Loup whispered, awed.

"Yeah, whoa." Pilar hugged her, gazing at the night sky. "It's beautiful. Like you."

"Like *you*."

There was more, so much more. Silvery rocket trails that whistled and fizzled into nothingness, starbursts of emerald green and startling violet, glittering periwinkle anemones that turned to pale stardust, graceful cascades of golden sparkles. The smell of cordite hung in the air, a reminder of long-ago childhood festivals for those old enough to remember. On and on, the fireworks burst and crackled and sparkled above the town. All of waking Santa Olivia stood beneath the desert sky and marveled at the sight, silent with wonder. The dead would always be mourned, the long injustice a source of sorrow and regret. But the day had been a day of providence and grace, and the night was filled with magic.

Loup held Pilar's hand, stealing glances at her rapt face.

When you were full of too much happiness for one heart to contain, fireworks were a very good thing.